The girl entwined her fingers in her skirt and tugged the fabric tight. "Your hair is the same color as my cat, and she's the best cat in the world." In a heartbeat, she fled and buried her face in the man's lap.

"My goodness. What a compliment. Thank you." She fumbled with the clasp of her wallet, discovering only then she smooshed her thumb deep into the whoopie pie.

The elfin child giggled and bounced on bare toes.

Standing, the man swept her into his arms and smiled down at Tessa. "Rebecca has not seen many women with ginger hair."

Ginger hair. For years, she was tormented by boneheaded boys shouting, "Carrot Top" and "Flame." No one ever called her mane ginger. Beneath his candid gaze, her curls heated like embers, warming her from top to toe. Who was this man?

The girl wriggled, knocking askew his straw hat.

He tossed her under one arm like a sack of flour and righted it, loosening a tawny curl that escaped the wide brim and fell over one brow. His gaze passed over Tessa's face.

Her unruly hair and short shorts tweaked at her consciousness. What did the Amish call outsiders? English? She was definitely dressed like an English woman. And not one from a Jane Austen novel.

He deposited the giggling girl right-side up on the floor and approached the table. "I've rarely seen hair that color myself. Like a copper penny."

She stared at the mangled whoopie pie and blushed even deeper. For a brief moment, she felt his gaze trail down her body like a caress. Or did she?

D1600117

Hometown

by

Wendy Rich Stetson

Hometown

Cover Art by *Diana Carlile*

The Wild Rose Press, Inc.
PO Box 708
Adams Basin, NY 14410-0708
Visit us at www.thewildrosepress.com

Publishing History
First Edition, 2021
Trade Paperback ISBN 978-1-5092-3564-3
Digital ISBN 978-1-5092-3646-6

Published in the United States of America

Dedication

For my carpenter and my fairy.
You are my home.

Acknowledgments

My most sincere thanks to the many wonderful people who supported me in my writing journey. HOMETOWN wouldn't exist without you.

To my editor, Leanne Morgena, thank you for meticulous reading and thoughtful guidance. I am so grateful to everyone at The Wild Rose Press for believing in my book and welcoming me with open arms.

Where would I be without the brilliant friends who read early drafts, listened to my story over coffee, and nudged me in the right direction: Gabra Zackman, Liz Wise, Rebecca Asher, Rebecca Lowman, Sarah Cusick, and Rebecca Harris. Big thanks to Gretchen Holly who is as wonderful an editor as she is a friend. My life is so much richer for having you all in it.

Thanks to my mom and dad for years of adventures in the pop-top and for always encouraging me to do what I love to the best of my ability.

For my husband Pete, who is both doctor and carpenter, and my daughter Cate, who fills every day with magic, I have nothing but bottomless gratitude and endless love.

Chapter 1

Green Ridge Farmers' Market
Wednesdays 7 a.m. - 7 p.m.

Look out, whoopie pies—I'm back in town!
Tessa Meadows yanked the wheel of her father's 1979 camper van and pulled a hard right into the parking lot of the Farmers' Market. Gravel sprayed from beneath balding tires. What she wouldn't give for power steering. Narrowly dodging a gaping pothole filled with fresh rainwater, she muscled the van into what passed for a space, flattening a patch of weeds at the tail end of a long row of cars. She tromped on the brake pedal and huffed a sigh. Had the market always been this crowded?

Wrenching the gearshift into Park, she peered at thick, dark clouds scudding over the line of Amish buggies nearby. With any luck that gusty west wind would banish the humidity with the afternoon storm. She caught a glimpse of crazy red curls in the rearview mirror, stuck out her bottom lip, and blew the hair from her eyes. Ugh. She was a giant fuzzball.

Grabbing her trusty shopping bag, she slid from the van and landed ankle-deep in a puddle. Water seeped under her arches, and she wiggled her toes. The pothole was hardly a swimming pool, but this stifling June afternoon, she'd take any refreshment she could get.

Three cheers for waterproof shoes! The inventor of women's sport sandals deserved a humanitarian award.

Shaking her feet, she scanned the parking lot for familiar faces. She so wasn't up for getting ambushed by her high school math teacher. Or her parents' coworkers. Or anyone really. Maybe she'd get lucky, and no one would recognize her. Get in. Get whoopie pies. Get out. Oh, and maybe french fries. She slipped on her chic, new sunglasses.

A little too hip for central Pennsylvania...but perfect for New York City.

She had visions of donning sleek shades as a strapping young man helped her into a horse-drawn carriage.

"How you doin'?" he'd say like Joey on *Friends*.

Iced coffee in hand, she'd settle into a romantic ride through Central Park, catching the eyes of handsome joggers galore. Granted, she hadn't set foot in New York in over ten years. But soon...very soon.

Squaring her shoulders, she threw open the door to the Farmers' Market. The odor of fried onions bowled into her with suffocating sweetness. She chuckled. The sprawling indoor market smelled exactly the same as when she was a little girl. Sacrificing anonymity for clear vision, she slid the sunglasses into her hair and blinked into the dimly lit hall. Heck, it even looked exactly the same.

The town butcher and the stinky cheese man hadn't aged a day. Maybe sausage and Gorgonzola held the secrets to eternal youth. She peered through swarms of shoppers and breathed a sigh of relief. Her mother's favorite plant vendor, an ancient little Amish lady, was still hawking tomatoes. Of course, when Tessa was young, her mother insisted on arriving at seven a.m. to get the cream of the crop. Not today. She was flying solo and so not a morning person. Then again, maybe her afternoon arrival was why she had to park in the pucker brush by the creek. And why the place was an absolute madhouse. She dodged a double jogging stroller. What were the odds she could avoid running into someone she knew?

"Why bless my heart, it's Tessa Meadows!"

Zero, apparently. The piercing voice emanated from behind. She searched for an escape route. None presented itself.

"Over here, Tessa dear."

Never mind the red hair, why did she have to be five feet ten? Sunglasses or no, she didn't have a prayer of blending in. She braced herself, plastered on a smile, and turned. With no warning, the short, squat woman moved in like a heat-seeking missile, enveloping her around the midsection. "Mrs. Diefenderfer. How are you?"

The woman plumped her voluminous hairdo. "Oh, getting by. I never imagined I'd see you this summer. Aren't your folks away?"

"They're in Tucson. Dad's on sabbatical."

"You don't say. Your mother is working on another cookbook, I suppose?"

"Mexican."

Mrs. Diefenderfer tugged her purse to her belly. "You Meadows, traipsing all over the country."

Her mom was a minor celebrity in the cookbook world, and despite Mrs. Diefenderfer's disapproval, she basked in the reflected glow. "You know us. A bunch of traipsers."

"Well, we sure miss your mother on the hospital auxiliary board, and we've never had a sweeter candy striper than you, dear. Can I get you to come back for a few shifts?"

She flashed a grin, the feel of that crisp, red-and-white-striped pinafore still clear in her memory. "I'm afraid I've outgrown the uniform."

Mrs. Diefenderfer surveyed her from head to toe. "I don't believe it for a second. You're as much of a string bean as you were in high school."

Feeling like a prize-winning pig at the county fair, she dipped her chin. Mrs. Diefenderfer leaned in, and cloying perfume momentarily overwhelmed the odor of fried onions.

"How is our college professor? Your dad must be so proud. Will you be home for a while, or are you teaching summer school?"

So, the news hadn't spread. She sighed. Better she put the actual story on the gossip line than have someone like Mrs. Diefenderfer concoct her own version of events once the rumors started. "To be honest, I left my teaching job last week. The university closed three branch campuses." She gave a resigned shrug. "Mine was one of them."

Mrs. Diefenderfer brought a dimpled hand to her bosom. "Oh, for Heaven's sake. I heard they were having money troubles up at State, but I didn't know it was that bad."

"Yeah..." Getting blindsided by her school closing just weeks before summer break pretty much stank. Luckily, her father's position at Green Ridge College was secure. She had somewhere to live, anyway.

Mrs. Diefenderfer narrowed her eyes. "Well, since

you're here, we could certainly use a gal with your qualifications on our Special Events Committee up at the hospital."

How exactly a master's degree in English qualified her for inclusion on the Special Events Committee, she did not know. Perhaps her genetic tie to Margaret Meadows, master chef and event coordinator extraordinaire, was sufficient. She curled her lips into a remorseful smile. "I'm only in town until I find a house sitter for my parents. As soon as I can, I'm moving to New York City."

Mrs. Diefenderfer's blue-lidded eyes went wide. "New York City? Why on earth would you move somewhere you don't know a single soul?"

Apparently, Mrs. Diefenderfer never once longed for anonymity. "Oh, I'm not going alone. I'll be living with my college roommate, Jennifer."

"New York City…" Mrs. Diefenderfer unzipped her purse and rifled through it. "Mr. Diefenderfer's cousin Harold lived there in the seventies. He moved back to Scranton in 1984. No place for decent people; that's what he said."

Welcome back to Life in Your Hometown. *In this episode, Tessa's Sunday School teacher ambushes her in the Farmers' Market and tramples her dreams.*

She snugged her backpack tight to her shoulders. "New York has changed a lot from what I hear."

With a grunt, Mrs. Diefenderfer extracted a pencil and notepad from her bag. "Well, in case you change your mind, or if you have some time before you go, here's the number of the volunteer office at the hospital. You give us a call, and we'll get you on that committee before you can say Statue of Liberty." She guffawed and dabbed the corners of her eyes with her pinky fingers. "The Sixth Annual Celebrity Auction is in two weeks. We're expecting an autographed copy of *Chicken Soup for the Soul,* and if it doesn't get here on time, I'll just spit."

She crossed her fingers and prayed a silent prayer Mrs. Diefenderfer wouldn't be reduced to spitting.

"Well, it sure is nice to have you back home where you belong." Mrs. Diefenderfer came up on tiptoes and scanned the crowd. "Now, where is Mr. Diefenderfer? If he's eating another sausage sandwich, I don't know what I'll do for supper. If you see him, send him my way."

"I will. And thanks for the invitation."

"New York City?" Mrs. Diefenderfer clucked her tongue. "We'll see about that."

Tessa pushed down the frisson of anxiety the good woman's tirade triggered in her belly. She'd heard horror stories, too, and she struggled to separate urban fact from urban legend. City life was nearly unimaginable. Where did you get groceries in New York? How did you hail a cab? Did people really ride the subway after dark?

She grabbed her sunglasses, swiped back her hair, and shoved the shades onto her head. Mrs. Diefenderfer couldn't scare her. Maybe losing her job at State was just the shot in the arm she needed to make a change. After all, Jennifer had been living in Manhattan almost seven years and was already hunting for a cozy, two-bedroom apartment. They would browse museums, go to the theater, and order takeout every night. Jenn gushed nonstop about the smart, successful guys who worked in the law firm with her boyfriend, Adam. With

Jennifer at her side, moving to New York would be the ultimate adventure. No, Mrs. Diefenderfer couldn't rain on her Macy's Thanksgiving Day Parade.

A vinegar-scented breeze jarred her back to present surroundings. She wasn't strolling down Fifth Avenue; she was shuffling through the Green Ridge Farmers' Market. Her stomach grumbled. So much for flying under the radar. Might as well take her time and indulge.

Already tasting the exquisite combination of salt and vinegar, she zipped into line at Troutman's Famous French Fries stand. New York might be a culinary epicenter, but it would have to work to one-up Troutman's fries. Mouth watering, she surveyed nearby booths for her second course. Strawberries…hot pretzels…baby spinach…aha! A whole stand overflowing with Amish baked goods. A whoopie pie would complement the french fries beautifully. She licked her lips and made a note to pick up fresh vegetables for tonight. A big salad would cancel the calories from the fries and pies, right?

Scanning the room once more, she let out a wistful laugh. Who needed a time machine when she had the Farmers' Market? Just standing there, she was thirteen again. The new guy selling kombucha notwithstanding, the whole place existed in a bubble, impervious to progress. Even the clothing styles hadn't changed. Mrs. Diefenderfer looked the same, and of course, the Amish hadn't updated their dress.

Tessa never exchanged more than a few words with the Amish vendors. They were private folk. But their whoopie pies…with whoopie pies, she was intimately acquainted: two rounds of rich chocolate

cake sandwiching a dense layer of sweet white cream—
a little slice of heaven wrapped in cellophane.

Popping a steaming fry, she beelined for baked
goods at Rishels' Farm Stand. The Rishels took their
whoopie pie selection up a notch, branching out from
traditional chocolate with white icing to pumpkin,
peanut butter, chocolate chip, and strawberry. So many
options, how would she choose? Then again, who said
she had to? She just got fired. Bring on the carbs.

A girl, seven or eight years old, peeped between
wide plastic trays heaped with treats. Garbed in a teal
dress, the child tucked a bare foot behind the other
ankle and scrunched her nose in a smile.

Evidently, some Amish children were permitted
respite from the heat, even if it constituted a modest
exposure of the flesh.

A handwritten sign dangled from a crate: "*Whoopie
pies, seventy-five cents.*" Had they cost a quarter back
in the day? Still, seventy-five cents seemed a darned
good price for a taste of paradise. But which to choose?
She nibbled her bottom lip. Forget these new-fangled
flavors—she was going old school with classic
chocolate and vanilla. Surveying with scientific
precision, she set down her fries and selected the
biggest pie from the tray. As she pulled off her
backpack and fished out her wallet, she caught the girl
staring with an unabashed openness she'd never seen
from the Plain people. She smiled and looped her hair
behind one ear.

The child scampered to an Amish man sitting on an
upturned milk crate against the wall. She cupped her
fingers over her lips and whispered in the man's ear.

He inclined his head toward the girl and glancing

up, met Tessa's gaze.

In that instant, every fiber of every muscle in her legs turned to barely congealed gelatin. To say his eyes were blue wasn't sufficient. They were cobalt and cerulean, blue sky on glacial water, infinite, bottomless blue. His expression was as open as the child's. Not a trace of cynicism darkened the creases at the corners of his eyes. By sheer force of will, she didn't collapse onto the table of baked goods.

Blood rushed to her cheeks so quickly they burned. She hadn't believed she could feel any hotter that steamy summer day. She was wrong.

He lifted one corner of his mouth in a half smile. "You may tell her yourself, Rebecca."

Though the words weren't intended for her, his voice washed over her like a warm wave, leaving her bobbing in the undertow.

The girl shook her head, waggling a blonde bun coiled like a cinnamon roll beneath a gauzy head covering.

"Go on, if you like," he said.

With small, skipping steps, the girl approached and peeked from beneath pale lashes.

Tessa gazed into bright eyes nearly as blue as the man's. "Hello."

The girl entwined her fingers in her skirt and tugged the fabric tight. "Your hair is the same color as my cat, and she's the best cat in the world." In a heartbeat, she fled and buried her face in the man's lap.

"My goodness. What a compliment. Thank you." She fumbled with the clasp of her wallet, discovering only then she smooshed her thumb deep into the whoopie pie.

The elfin child giggled and bounced on bare toes.

Standing, the man swept her into his arms and smiled down at Tessa. "Rebecca has not seen many women with ginger hair."

Ginger hair. For years, she was tormented by boneheaded boys shouting, "Carrot Top" and "Flame." No one ever called her mane ginger. Beneath his candid gaze, her curls heated like embers, warming her from top to toe. Who was this man?

The girl wriggled, knocking askew his straw hat.

He tossed her under one arm like a sack of flour and righted it, loosening a tawny curl that escaped the wide brim and fell over one brow. His gaze passed over Tessa's face.

Her unruly hair and short shorts tweaked at her consciousness. What did the Amish call outsiders? English? She was definitely dressed like an English woman. And not one from a Jane Austen novel.

He deposited the giggling girl right-side up on the floor and approached the table. "I've rarely seen hair that color myself. Like a copper penny."

She stared at the mangled whoopie pie and blushed even deeper. For a brief moment, she felt his gaze trail down her body like a caress. Or did she?

"Jonas!"

She started and whipped up her head.

An angular Amish woman stood silhouetted in the doorway at the rear of the stand.

"*Mamm*!" The little girl whirled and bounded toward her.

The woman thrust out a hand. "Slow down, Rebecca." She swiveled to the man. "Jonas, see to the horse. The storm—"

"In a moment." He turned to Tessa. "Seventy-five cents, please."

"I'm sorry?" She winced at the tremor in her voice.

"For the pie. Seventy-five cents."

"Right. Of course." She dug in her wallet and handed him three quarters.

"Thank you." The change clanged into a metal box, and he smiled. "Have a nice day."

He sauntered out the door with the easy confidence of a man who earned his right to exist by simple hard work. No apologies. No pretensions.

"Will that be all?"

The wiry woman assumed his place at the table. Her light brown hair was combed so tightly under a white prayer cap that she had a quarter of an inch part down the middle of her forehead. She drummed two fingers on the box and glared.

Tessa felt the woman's modest dress and the firm line of her mouth like a silent rebuke. "Yes, thank you. Good afternoon."

The woman sniffed and scowled.

Behind her, the little girl touched her hair and wiggled her fingers in a secret goodbye.

She veered from the booth, and the market swam in a dreamy haze of color and sound. Jonas. His name was Jonas…and he thought her hair looked like a copper penny. As she retreated into the throngs, a rumbling for more french fries vied with the butterflies in her stomach. She pulled up short. All she held was a single, squished whoopie pie. Sneaking a glance over one shoulder, she blew out a breath. Her fries stood forsaken and alone on the Rishels' table.

Rebecca was there, too, flitting about and rearranging pies.

She blinked, but the child persisted. Part of her believed the girl was a fairy who would disappear the moment she turned away. Those iridescent blue eyes just one shade on the paint chip lighter than the man's... Of course. Her heart sank. The little girl was his own. Obviously, Rebecca was his daughter, and that sour woman was his wife. They probably had three or four other children back home on the farm.

Behind Rebecca, the woman perched ramrod straight on the milk crate, almost daring Tessa to return. She surrendered the notion of retrieving her fries. And marrying the Amish dude. *Easy come, easy go.*

Laughing off a sigh, she set a course for veggies. What was she thinking? He was Amish. Even if he were single, she couldn't just ask him out. But as she picked out the salad she promised herself for supper, she couldn't chase away the memory of that real or imagined gaze over her body.

Her shopping bag bursting with produce, and her arms full of flower seedlings she intended to plant before leaving for New York, she pushed open the door and stepped into fresh air. Sunlight sliced through distant clouds, igniting raindrops on the buggy roofs and transforming them into bejeweled, horse-drawn carriages.

Suddenly, he appeared—striding around a buggy, bucket in hand.

Weak-kneed, she gawked. A man who could look that beautiful in a parking lot? He was too handsome to walk among mortals. He should be bronzed.

Glancing across parked cars, he met her gaze. One side of his mouth lifted into a half smile.

She flushed and smiled back. Through the glare from a dozen windshields, she studied his face, feeling tiny hairs rise on the back of her neck. Was he laughing at her? She squinted and caught a flash of derision in his look. Steeling her knees, she yanked down her sunglasses and pivoted toward the van. Sure, she'd been a bit awkward at his booth, but he had no right to laugh. A genuinely sincere guy unburdened with attitude, huh? Wishful thinking.

In a few quick paces, she reached the van. His gaze was steady on her. She could feel it through her shoulders like a heat lamp. Shifting the packages, she grabbed hold of the sliding door handle.

Just load your stuff and drive away like a normal person.

But she couldn't resist. She darted another look.

Grinning even wider, he set down the bucket and crossed his arms in front of his chest.

Not for nothing, in a manner that made his biceps bulge heart-stoppingly through damp shirt sleeves. She cast aside that swoony thought and mustered her outrage, jerking open the side door and dumping in her purchases.

Wait a second. She'd seen that look before and more than once. Maybe he wasn't laughing at her. Or rather, not only her. Dollars to doughnuts, he was laughing at her van—this two-toned monster of a vehicle, this green-and-tan cereal box on wheels, she was about to mount like a Clydesdale and drive away. She'd lost count of the men who thought she couldn't handle this car. Was Jonas the Amish guy one of them?

With as much dignity as she could summon, she climbed into the driver's seat and turned the key. The van coughed and sputtered a percussive *chug-chug-chug*. Threading the needle between rows of cars, she drew near the line of buggies. Did she have enough room to squeeze through? The last thing she wanted was to spook the horses and start a stampede. She massaged the brake and crawled within inches of him, expertly negotiating the limited space.

He offered the hint of a nod. Maybe he couldn't drive, but she sure as heck could. She lifted her chin in response.

Still smiling, he touched the brim of his hat, shook his head, and turned to the buggy.

What did that nod mean? And then why did he shake his head? Was he mocking her or not? The guy's expression was like Ancient Greek. Utterly inscrutable.

Driving home, she barely noticed the tree-lined streets and quaint Victorian houses of her hometown. Why were the Amish so compelling? Their allure ran deeper than jewel-toned shirts, straw hats, and suspenders. They seemed to possess some secret knowledge—as if they'd inherited the key to living happily without constantly scrambling to get ahead.

Or was it just that they could handle horses? Horsemanship was sexy as all get out.

She'd seen movies about the Amish and had, of course, been surrounded by a fairly large community for most of her childhood. But what did she truly know about their lives?

When outsiders asked, she could attest that yes, the Amish really rode around in buggies, and yes, they lived without electricity, and no, she had absolutely no idea what was up with those beards. Jonas, she noted, didn't sport that characteristic full beard and no mustache look. Interesting. Her listener's curiosity piqued, she'd typically wrap up her Amish symposium with a story one of her father's colleagues relayed.

The elderly professor returned home one afternoon to find her Amish housekeeper sitting at the kitchen table, head in her hands. When asked what troubled her, the girl blanched. "I turned a knob on that box over there." She pointed to the radio with a trembling finger. "I know my action was a sin, but please, can you tell me…what sort of instrument is a symphony?"

She loved that story, but she'd never really thought about its implications. Imagine not knowing what a symphony was. Although she'd grown up near the "simple folk," she recognized now she had no idea what their lives were truly like. They were real people, not costumed characters at a tourist attraction. Probably, their existence wasn't simple at all. Life would be tough without modern conveniences.

Who needs them? Chest thrumming with back-to-basics purism, she rolled down the window. Give me the simple life. Lots of time to slow down and get in touch with what's really important.

She pictured acres of fields to be plowed without tractors. Piles of dishes to wash by hand—probably without hot running water. Lots of physical labor to fill that time. She caught her bottom lip between her teeth. Jonas sure didn't get those guns working out at a gym.

With a sharp turn off the main road, she entered the woodsy landscape of her childhood. Pulling up to her house, she cataloged all she'd miss were she Amish. No automatic garage door openers. No trusty camper van. She hopped out and unloaded her Farmers' Market booty, already tasting that whoopie pie. Such a bummer she forgot her fries. Still, no way would she go back with Rebecca's mother staring daggers across the market.

Inside, the kitchen blasted an air-conditioned welcome. No AC on an Amish farm, but plenty of good food, she wagered. She grabbed a carton of milk and the whoopie pie. Pulling out her phone, she smiled at the voicemail alert. No cell phones for the Amish. Add that gadget to the list. "Two messages." Her voice rang in the empty kitchen. She plopped on a chair and kicked off her sandals. "Somebody loves me."

A slightly squished whoopie pie is still a delicious whoopie pie. She balled the sticky plastic wrap and savored her first bite. With a sigh of delight, she tapped the message button.

"Tessa, sweetie, it's Mom. This morning, we moved to the rental house. You should see the cactus garden—it's spectacular. Dad's already best friends with the town librarian, and I discovered the most wonderful recipe for salsa verde. It's just beautiful out here. Maybe you can visit for our anniversary in August? Oh, don't forget to water my asparagus. Call me."

A glob of cream lodged on her soft palate, and she spluttered. How could she have forgotten? This year marked her parents' thirtieth wedding anniversary. What in the world would she get them?

Usually, she relished the special feeling of being an only child, but not when the time came to dream up a perfect gift for a couple of great parents. For such an occasion, a sibling sure would be handy. She gulped skim milk—no skim milk in Amish kitchens, probably—and licked chocolate residue from her thumb. Maybe she could ship her parents a ten-layer cake made of whoopie pies.

On to her second message. "Hey, it's Jenn. I've got some good news and some bad news. Well, it's all kind of the same news, actually—"

Something in her roommate's voice brought her out of her confectionary reverie.

"Tessa, Adam asked me to move in with him."

The whoopie pie turned to sawdust in her mouth.

"And I said yes!"

The phone slipped from her fingers and fell in her lap. No New York City.

Chapter 2

Minutes later, Tessa held her breath and listened to the sound of her well-made plans being dashed to smithereens on the rocks of Jennifer Sweet's love life. Ensconced in her bedroom, she shifted the phone from her lower lip and clenched her belly. No use. Her breath fluttered high and trembly in her chest. "I'm so happy for you."

"I couldn't believe it. He took me out to this fabulous Indian restaurant in the East Village and asked me. He was so nervous—he might have cried a little. His eyes got all teary. Then again, he had a lot of curry."

"When do you move in?"

"Next week!" Jennifer uttered a squeal, which turned into a laugh, which turned into a full-bodied snort.

She slumped against her closet door. She missed that snort—that infectious, totally unexpected, often utterly inappropriate snort. Usually, it made her laugh, too. Today, she just wanted to weep.

"I never thought he'd make this kind of commitment. You know Adam. He's such a guy."

She did know Adam. She knew the whole string of guys who came in and out of Jennifer's life over the course of their friendship. This one seemed different, though. This one seemed likely to stick around.

"Totally. This is a big deal for him. For both of you."

"So, you don't hate me?"

Jenn's voice crept up an octave. The fact that she wasn't completely cavalier about ruining their plans helped. Somewhat.

"You aren't furious?"

"No, no." Tessa picked at a loose thread in her sock. The sound of a televised baseball game cut through the silence. Jenn was with Adam that very moment. She had already lost her.

"You can still come over every night for popcorn."

"Long drive for a bowl of popcorn." She tugged the thread, and her big toe emerged through a new hole. "Not that your popcorn isn't worth a couple of hours in the car—"

"A couple of hours? I choose to ignore the implication you aren't still moving here. Try a five-minute walk. We'll find you the perfect place near us. One of Adam's buddies is a realtor, and I'm sure he can get you a great deal."

She stripped off her socks, balled them, and tossed them at the trashcan. She missed.

"Or," Jenn continued, "we have another friend whose roommate just got a job in Boston. She's super sweet, and I think you two would really get along."

"Another roommate? Besides you?"

"Her name is Lizzy. She's a paralegal, and she lives just a few blocks north of our new place."

Well, why not? Lizzy was probably nice. Why cancel her entire plan just because she wouldn't be living with Jennifer?

"You're still moving here, aren't you?"

She grabbed the closet doorknob, heaved to her

feet, and immediately collapsed onto her bed. Nice or not, Lizzy wasn't Jenn. "I guess I just need a little time to figure out everything."

"How much time? I want you here now. Yesterday. Hey, why don't you visit for a weekend? We can look at apartments and see the sights. Then you make up your mind."

She stared at the ceiling. "Maybe…"

"Look, Meadows, you're coming to Manhattan if I have to drag your skinny, redheaded butt tied to the roof of my car."

"Wow. That's quite a visual."

"You might be a foot taller than I am but don't think I can't do it. I'm a New Yorker now. I know people."

Jenn attempted a New York gangster voice.

She laughed again and snorted. "I suck at accents."

"I know." Tessa couldn't help but chuckle, her belly unclenching a smidge.

"How do you get from Green Ridge to New York anyway?" Jenn asked. "By train?"

She propped herself on one elbow and peeped through the window at the angled sliver of sky. "No idea. I'm not sure anyone from Green Ridge has ever been to New York."

"Bus, train, or dirigible—I'll find a way. Or there's always the felony kidnapping route." Jenn giggled.

"I'm confident you will." She laughed, too, and let the sound fade into a silence that wasn't quite easy but wasn't strained either. A ball player in New York hit a home run, and the televised crowd cheered so loudly she could hear it all the way in Green Ridge.

"You can't stay in Smallville forever," Jenn finally

said.

"I know. Bye, Jenn." She tossed her phone onto the bed and wandered down to the kitchen. Who wanted to eat salad now? She should have gotten a dozen whoopie pies at the market.

Padding down the hall, she passed through the door to the garage. Eight boxes stood stacked in the corner, ready to move to New York. She scanned the clutter for furniture. Everything in her charmless faculty digs remained when she left. Just how did she plan to fill this mythical New York apartment? She had nothing of her own to speak of. Twenty-eight years old, she still ate ramen noodles from the same plastic cereal bowl she used in middle school.

Cheap, dollar store tape bunched around her fingers. She balled it and tore open a box labeled, "Brontë, popcorn popper, thrift store juice glasses, *The Eagle*." Several copies of their school newspaper nested at the top of the carton. Jenn parlayed their shared undergrad journalism experience into a promising position at a major news site. She was ticking off the boxes of her dreams one by one. Tessa shoved the papers deep into the carton and went back inside, clutching the popcorn popper like a beloved stuffed animal.

Within minutes, steaming, air-popped kernels poured into her hands. She flinched and dropped them in a bowl. How had ancient people discovered popcorn anyway? Who looked at those hard, brown seeds and thought, "Hey, let's torch these things and see if they explode into food." If it happened accidentally, how flabbergasted were the first to witness it? And then what made them think, "Hmm. Better eat that."

She hunched over the kitchen table and rolled an unpopped kernel between her thumb and fingers. Unlike Jenn, she came to college with no plan for the future. After grad school, she stumbled into teaching like it was a giant pothole. She had a newly minted master's, and State was hiring an adjunct English professor. The transition couldn't have been easier. Now, she'd been effectively fired from a position she never really wanted, and the heat was on. She tossed the kernel into the sink and chuckled. If one of her students wrote the metaphor, she'd say it was too on the nose. Still, the analogy was apt.

What will I be when I finally pop?

She smothered the popcorn in butter, but it didn't taste as good as Jennifer's. Nothing was as good when she wasn't around.

Why not move to New York? Just go and work out the details later. So she wouldn't be sharing a place with Jenn. What difference did it make?

She bit down on a kernel and grimaced. Not living with Jenn made all the difference in the world. Her friend would have far less time for her now, and Tessa would find herself alone in Manhattan. The romantic comedy she envisioned for her life risked turning into a sad and lonely drama. Running her tongue over her aching tooth, she plunged a hand back into the bowl, risking pebbly kernels and perfectly popped corn alike.

She had no idea how to function on her own in the city. Somehow, she had to muster the courage to try.

****

The next morning, Tessa slid a rainbow sheet over one shoulder, nestling deeper into her single bed. Another morning alone in her parents' house. Another breakfast for one. Maybe she should get a cat. She cracked a sticky eye and squinted into the sun. A strip of faded, floral wallpaper buckled away from the window. Her brain buckled in sleepy solidarity.

She flexed and pointed her feet beneath the covers. Her body was refreshed from a good night's sleep. But still, pajama-clad and lying in the same bed she slept in her entire childhood, she felt the weight of aimlessness descend like a storm cloud. Not a sudden and ferocious squall, like the wild thunderstorms out West. Hers was a Pennsylvania storm—steady, dark, and absolutely inevitable.

Leaves rustled outside the open window, and she sprang upright. She did have a mission. Six flats of flowers waited on the back patio, roots withering in the sun. She couldn't stay in bed all day. Tiny living things needed her.

Without bothering to dress, she dashed outside and snatched the seedlings. Carefully balancing the wobbling stack, she grabbed a trowel and the watering can from her mother's potting bench and made off for her flower gardens.

Kneeling beside her favorite bed, she brushed matted leaves from perennials she planted years ago. Wet grass tickled her bare feet. Without Tessa's care, the flower beds had gone wild and brambly, but with a little work, she could restore order. After all, wasn't she the kindergartener who grew a record-breaking marigold in a paper cup?

Between a blossoming bleeding heart and a still-small cluster of bee balm lay a promising spot for coralbells. With their heart-shaped leaves, they'd look so pretty amongst more slender, spiky plants. Aware her summers in Green Ridge were dwindling, she focused her teenage gardening on flowers that returned season after season. Maybe she should have filled the beds with short-lived annuals. At this rate, she'd be gardening in Green Ridge forever.

She troweled a clump of earth. Why not plant sunflowers this summer? Sunflowers existed solely to spread joy. Not a bad life's work. Tapping the bottom of a pot with the trowel's butt end, she eased out a tender seedling. She should plant a whole cutting bed of annuals just like Nana Shiffer had. With a delicate touch, she separated the roots and filled the hole with a scoop of compost and a splash of water, mixing them with soil to form a welcoming mud bath, just as her grandmother taught. She re-ensconced two squirmy earthworms and settled the baby plant into its new home.

As she worked, grass staining her pajamas at the knees and dirt caking her hands, her early morning ennui seeped into the earth. Her mind cleared. She wouldn't make any decisions about New York until she talked the whole matter over with Jennifer in person. In the meantime, she'd just have to stay busy. She sat back on her heels. Two-and-a-half acres of lawn and gardens were already in serious need of tending. No call for a house sitter now. Of course, she'd have no choice but to return to the Farmers' Market for more plants. Maybe staying in Green Ridge all summer was worth it, if only to get an eyeful of Jonas the Amish dreamboat every Wednesday.

Pajama top plastered to her back, she blinked away sweat and settled in the last of the flowers. Shower time. She unfolded her legs and staggered to her feet, her right knee cracking in protest. The lilacs beckoned, and she made a quick detour on her way inside. Late this year, lilac season was one of her favorite times of the year. She had just buried her nose in a fat, fragrant flower, when inside the house, the landline rang.

She twirled and dashed across the yard. Maybe Jenn was calling to say she'd come to her senses and wouldn't dream of breaking their sacred roomie bond for some boy.

Chest heaving, she snatched the phone just as the answering machine whirred to life. "Hello?"

"Tessa Meadows, are you all right?"

She drooped against the kitchen counter. "Yes, Mrs. Diefenderfer, thank you. I just dashed in from the garden."

"Well listen, sweetie, I'm up a creek. Phyllis Kiefer—you remember Phyllis, don't you? Curtis and Judy's mom?"

She had a vague recollection of a surly football player named Curt who sat across from her in homeroom.

"Well, wouldn't you know, Phyllis' grandson fell off his bike and broke his arm. So, Phyllis can't take care of the dessert table at the celebrity auction, after all. Now, I don't know when you're leaving for New York, but could you work some of that Meadows' magic and help out in the treats department? It's for a good cause."

She wrapped the phone cord around her fingers. Little did Mrs. Diefenderfer know, she was not possessed of a single secret to the Meadows' magic. Her diet in the past three years consisted entirely of organic frozen food, and despite her mother's encouragement, she never learned to bake. Gazing out the window, she tightened the cord. Then again, she only had so many flower gardens to tend. "Actually, my move is temporarily on hold. I'd be happy to help."

"Oh, thank heavens. I don't know what we'd do without you Meadows gals. Now the auction is a week from Saturday under the tent at the college. When you get there, just ask for the wonderful Claire MacMillan. She'll tell you what to do."

She replaced the phone in its wall-mounted cradle and trudged upstairs, glimpsing herself in the front hall mirror. Masses of hair flew in every direction, and green eyes sparkled beneath a dirt-smudged brow. Who was that young woman? Would she run for office some day? Write a best-selling novel? Or live in an attic with forty-nine cats? Would any man want to cover that face with kisses? Maybe a man with insanely blue eyes and biceps for days.

Well…probably not *that* man. He was married, after all. Did he have a brother? Statistically, the odds were good. She'd just have to find out.

This Wednesday. When she returned to Rishels' Farm Stand and ordered a zillion delectable treats for the St. Luke's Hospital Annual Celebrity Auction.

Chapter 3

Tessa downed a final marshmallowy bite and licked her lips. Yet another joy of adulthood: eating sugary cereal on the living room couch while binge-watching home and gardening shows. Buckle up, folks. Mrs. Diefenderfer had no idea what she did when she unleashed this sweet tooth upon the citizens of Green Ridge.

How many desserts would she need, anyway? Mrs. Diefenderfer omitted a few critical details in her call yesterday. She dumped blue-tinged milk into the sink and grabbed a hat. Not only had she changed out of pajamas, she even had the presence of mind to protect her fair skin from the sun. She couldn't magically erase her freckles, but with a modicum of precaution, she could prevent them from multiplying.

Grabbing her supplies, she zipped to the new cutting garden to plant sunflower seeds she found on her mother's potting bench. In a few short months, she'd have glorious, giant blossoms. This afternoon, she would call the hospital volunteer office and relay her plan to purchase enough homemade goodies from Rishels' Farm Stand to overflow the auction table. Who could argue with supporting local business? Who didn't like pie? Her plan was solid.

She never for a second considered baking the treats. She knew her limitations, and catering for a crowd was one of them. Catching a whiff of lilac, she resolved to arrange festive bouquets and leave the baking to the experts. At the end of the day, being Amish was far more marketable than being an English major. With any luck, Jonas Rishel would be at the market this Wednesday to take her order personally. Just because he was married didn't mean she couldn't admire him. From an appropriate distance, of course— like a painting or Michelangelo's *David*.

She dropped a seed into the dirt and covered it. *Wait a minute. This Wednesday at market?*

The event was next Saturday—exactly one week away. Ordering on Wednesday gave the Rishels only two days to prepare the pies. How fast did they bake, anyway? Would two days be sufficient? Besides, she wasn't sure the Rishels would fill a bulk order. She needed to leave time to come up with a backup plan in the event her Amish pie scheme fell through.

Well, if the Amish couldn't wait, she supposed her sunflowers could. She stuck a twig in the row to mark her progress and gathered her tools. She had to contact the Rishels immediately. But how? They probably didn't have a website or even a phone listing. Amish farms stretched for miles across the countryside. Who would know how to find them? Standing, she shook clumps of soil from her knees. The local Amish community couldn't be that big, could it? Didn't they all know one another like the people in *Little House on the Prairie*?

She grimaced at her own small-mindedness. Of course, they didn't. But emboldened by the desire not to disappoint Mrs. Diefenderfer, she would try anything. She scooted back to the house. In between the weekly

Farmers' Market, her mother often stopped at an Amish farm stand a few miles out Route 45. What were the odds they'd know the Rishels? Peeling off her gloves, she snatched the van keys. Whatever the odds, she'd take them.

A hand-painted sign on the red tin roof read simply, *"Fresh Produce."* Inside, an ocean of strawberries welcomed her. The humidity inflated her hair to twice its normal size, but a breeze wafted the scent of berries through the open-air building, cooling the back of her neck. Her mother always said you knew strawberries were fully ripe when they actually smelled like strawberries. These were good and ripe.

A birdlike Amish woman stood alone behind the counter. Tessa wandered among tables and studied her from the corner of her eye. Her face was spiderwebbed with wrinkles, but beneath a white prayer cap, merry eyes shone with spirit. Plain as they were, Amish folk wore clothing of such brilliant colors. They dressed in jewel tones—garnets, sapphires, and emeralds—shades far brighter than she ever dared to wear.

A couple dressed head to toe in black approached the counter and asked directions to a local quilt shop.

The old woman's face lit up.

Who knew what secret dreams and unspoken joys dwelled in her heart? Perhaps, this matron lived a life just as vibrant as her amethyst dress. Tessa kind of believed so.

But could she guide Tessa on her quest? What's more, how should she even broach the topic? *Hey, so…do you happen to know Jonas Rishel and his sorta-mean wife and their super-beautiful kid?*

The elderly lady leaned over the counter and

pointed down the road.

Though her joints were swollen, and her skin was thickly veined, her hand was as graceful as a ballerina's.

"Four miles west of here, out Mifflintown way, turn right onto Old Cowan Road—you can't miss it— then Stoltzfus' farm is third on the left. A wee sign that says "*Sarah's*" sits in a pot of pink geraniums. You'ns go on down their lane and knock on the door. Now, not the front door. The side door. Sarah makes the prettiest quilts in the county."

The Amish woman spoke with the same lilting accent as Jonas. The sound was comforting, even familiar. But why?

The woman slipped the couple's jam into a paper bag and bid them farewell.

Of course. Nana Shiffer had spoken with just the same melody. No wonder Tessa was drawn to these people.

Seemingly up for an adventure in cow country, the couple exchanged excited glances. Although Green Ridge didn't lure the vast numbers of city people who flocked to Lancaster County, a few more adventurous quilt-seekers made it to the Amish communities of central Pennsylvania and were well rewarded.

Again, she scanned the tables. If she wanted information, she should definitely buy something. She selected a pint of berries. Perhaps she'd try her hand at her mother's strawberry shortcake recipe. How hard could it be? Wouldn't a shortcake, by definition, be easier than a tall cake?

Steps from the counter, she spotted the label of a flaky-looking pie: "Rishels' Baked Goods." Bingo!

This woman could certainly help. She plunked her strawberries on the counter.

As she rang up the purchase, the woman smiled. "Two fifty for the strawberries. Picked fresh this morning, don't you know."

Stalling, she slipped off her backpack and groped for her wallet. "They smell heavenly. I'd love to make shortcake. My mother has a wonderful recipe."

"They'll do for shortcake. Real good in fry pies, too. They're a might sweet, though. Go gentle on the sugar." The woman slid the carton into a brown paper bag and creased the top in one smooth swipe.

She really didn't want to break some ancient Amish code of privacy, but the time was now or never. She drew in a breath. "I wonder if you could help me with something."

"Oh?" The woman perched on a stool and folded her hands in her lap.

She beamed her most sincere smile. "Do you happen to know the Rishels? I need to find their farm."

"Nora and Jonas or Elam and Lovina?"

Nora. So that was Mrs. Rishel's name. "Nora and Jonas."

The woman tilted her head. "Are you a friend?"

Like a copper penny.

Giddiness flickered in her belly. "I don't know them personally, but I need to ask them a favor. Well, not exactly a favor—I need to buy a bunch of pies."

"Pies? Well, Nora's the one for pies. I never knew a woman could bake a shoofly pie like Nora, but she'll take that recipe to her grave, mark my words." The woman fluttered a hand toward well-laden tables of food. "We have some here. You needn't go out to the farm."

Maybe the code of privacy was real. The woman didn't seem angry, but she also didn't seem ready to fork over GPS coordinates. Still, Tessa couldn't give up now. "I need a lot of pies—several dozen. I'd like to place a special order with the Rishels, if they do that sort of thing."

"That many? Well, I imagine Nora would be grateful for the work. You tell her Esther King sent you."

Back in the van, she popped a sugar-sweet berry in celebration. Her bit of sleuthing had been remarkably easy. Had she overlooked a career as a private investigator: the solo Charlie's Angel of Green Ridge, PA? Why go to New York? She'd have all the excitement a person could dream of locating missing persons among the mountains of Pennsylvania.

Repeating the directions in her head, she veered onto Route 45. The Rishels' farm was also located out Old Cowan Road, but it lay several miles beyond Sarah Stoltzfus' quilt shop.

Watch for the new Mennonite church on your left and the round barn on your right, then cross the metal bridge over Buffalo Creek. Rishels' lane is just beyond a mess of honeysuckle—don't blink or you'll miss it.

She navigated west into deep farm country, where newly tilled fields stretched to forested ridges. When she moved to the city, she'd miss this landscape. Speckled with quaint churches and farmhouses and crisscrossed by meandering brooks, the land had a quiet, rolling beauty—a small and peaceful splendor.

Wheels of countless buggies rutted Old Cowan Road like the thoroughfares of the Oregon Trail. She passed in turn Sarah Stoltzfus' pink geraniums and the "new Mennonite church," which honestly looked pretty darned old. Despite being jounced until her teeth rattled, she spotted the round barn on her right and ticked another landmark off the list. She was close now.

"*Raise Plows*" declared a sign on a low, metal bridge. The van slalomed over the grooved surface, and she gripped the wheel to keep on course. A wide creek, still swollen from spring rains, rushed below. Sure enough, on the far side of the bridge, nearly obscured by a tangled mass of honeysuckle, opened a narrow lane.

She made the turn, following the winding dirt lane until a pristine farmhouse came into view. So, this was where he lived. Correction: where they lived. A gray-topped buggy stood in the shadow of a deep, red barn, and dark fields, recently plowed, extended on either side of the home. She steeled herself. Could she really crash an Amish farm?

Shifting into Neutral, she hesitated, fluttering her fingers over the gearshift. What if she had the wrong place? She checked her exit route in the rearview mirror. Even if she wanted to bail, she couldn't leave without swinging around in the open space in front of the barn. Backing down that lane would be impossible. The idling engine chugged like a motorboat. How long before someone came to investigate?

No way can I knock on that door like a Girl Scout selling cookies. She tromped on the clutch. Mission aborted. Grocery store pies would suffice.

Just then, a lithe, little form darted around the house, teal skirts flying. The shape vanished behind a tree and reappeared on the other side. She'd found the

Rishels all right.

Rebecca crept around the trunk, hugging it close, and peered with a funny half-smile. Tessa leaned into the passenger seat, cranked down the window, and waved.

The girl shot behind the tree and popped out on the other side.

Lured by the wee imp, she shifted into gear and inched forward. At a safe distance, she cut the motor and swung her legs out of the van. The expanse of bare flesh blinded her with pasty whiteness, and she groaned inwardly. Tugging at the hem of her shorts, she ventured into the yard. "Hello. Do you remember me?"

"Of course." Releasing one arm, Rebecca swung around the tree and reappeared on the opposite side.

"I remember you, too."

"How did you find me?" Rebecca sprang up and caught hold of a branch.

Fingers latched tight, she dangled like a monkey. Tessa lifted her cheeks in a smile. "I asked directions."

Rebecca dropped to the ground and giggled. "Your car looks like a mallard duck."

She laughed. "It's actually my father's. It's pretty old. Older than I am."

Rebecca's eyes widened. "That's old. What's your name?"

"Tessa. I don't need to ask yours because I already know you're Rebecca."

The child scrunched her nose into a smile just as a shrill voice rang from the house. The words echoed across the yard, but they sounded like gibberish.

"The ginger lady from market!" Rebecca called back.

The unseen woman spoke again.

Though still not understandable, the sounds were familiar. Tessa recognized the language as Pennsylvania German. The women at the market sometimes spoke it to each other.

"That's my mother," Rebecca whispered. Then she dashed up the steps to the porch.

An angular figure in a black apron, dark blue dress, and prayer cap appeared in the doorway. She held open the door with one hand and grabbed for Rebecca with the other.

The child slipped through her fingers and scampered to the far side of the wide front porch. With a nimble leap, she perched atop the railing.

The woman she now knew to be Nora frowned.

"Can I help you?"

Her belly fluttered, but she inched forward. "I'm Tessa Meadows. I'm sorry to bother you at home. I hope I'm not intruding."

Nora stared stone-faced.

Clearly, she was intruding. Why hadn't she thought to put on a skirt? She took a deep breath. "I need some pies."

"We sell pies Wednesday at market. You can buy them there." Nora shook her apron with a snap and spun.

"But I need lots of pies. A whole bunch."

In the doorway, Nora pivoted. "How many are you needing?"

Darn it! She forgot to call Mrs. Diefenderfer. Thrusting a hand in her pocket, she twitched for her phone. Nora was barely tolerating her presence as it was. She didn't seem likely to bide a call. Besides,

Tessa probably wouldn't have service way out in the country. Releasing the device, she squared her shoulders. "Three dozen," she answered with a certainty she almost believed she possessed.

"Three dozen?" Nora raised her brows to the bottom edge of her head covering. "And when will you be needing them?"

"Saturday. Next Saturday."

Nora frowned again. "Not much time."

"I know, I'm sorry. I don't even know if you do this sort of thing, but I just love your baked goods at the Farmers' Market, so I was hoping you might help me out, even though it's fairly short notice. It's for a good cause—a charity event at the hospital." Her voice trailed away. Babbling was probably not a trait valued by the Amish.

"What kind of pies?"

Another essential element she hadn't considered. "Any kind?" The words came out more of a squeak than she would have preferred.

"Any kind," Nora repeated through tight lips.

"All kinds. An assortment." She threw her hands wide, as though a panoply of pies dangled from the trees. "I love strawberry. And the woman at the produce stand recommended your shoofly."

"Esther sent you here?"

"Yes, Esther King. She told me to tell you so." Nora scrunched her nose in an expression uncannily similar to her daughter's, but the result was a scowl not a smile. Tessa hoped she hadn't risked Esther King's life by coming to the Rishels' farm and pestering them for three dozen pies.

Clutching a post, Rebecca hopped to her feet. "You

can do it, *Mamm*. You baked lots more for Marcus Dersham's wedding last November."

Nora shuffled forward and swatted at the railing. "Get down before you break your neck."

Tessa stared. Nora's gait was awkward and halting. Her left leg hung rigidly, like a weight she had to drag along beside her. How had she not noticed the woman's limp at market? She must have been…distracted.

With a huff, Rebecca plopped onto her backside and kicked her heels against the rail.

"Three dozen strawberry and shoofly for next Saturday?" Nora swept both hands over her apron in a single sharp stroke. "I suppose. You can pick them up Saturday morning, eight o'clock."

She sealed her lips to check the goofy grin welling inside. "Thank you so much."

"Three hundred and six dollars."

"That'll be fine—wonderful!"

"Rebecca, fetch my notebook."

The girl vaulted, catlike, and sprinted into the house.

With a flourish, Tessa signed her name and formalized the order. She had done it. And escaped with her life, no less. Flush with success, she bounded into the front seat, reached for her keys, and froze.

Jonas, his emerald-green shirtsleeves rolled to the elbows, emerged from the barn. Spotting her van, he, too, drew up short. His lips curled into a lopsided smile.

Somehow, he managed to nod and shake his head at the same time, honey hair glinting in the afternoon sun. She risked a wave. He was laughing at her again— though definitely not with malice but with something else. Something she still couldn't identify. Regardless, his smile at seeing her melted her insides. Beneath a gaze that bordered on admiring, she executed a flawless, three-point turn and caught him in the rearview mirror.

He leaned against the barn, twirling his hat in his hands and watching her go.

"Dude, you're married," she said with a giggle. "Okay, then. See you in a week."

****

When Tessa returned to the Rishels's farm, she wore a skirt. Despite relentless humidity and thanks to a healthy dose of leave-in conditioner, her curls were under control, and she left them loose around her shoulders. Though the calendar hadn't made it to July, she was already sick of ponytails and messy buns. Besides, her hair looked so much prettier down. The question was, just whom was she trying to impress: the ladies on the volunteer committee or one Jonas Rishel?

Bracing herself for another encounter with Nora, she slammed the van door and twisted her skirt aright. At least she didn't have to worry about bumping into the woman at the supermarket or the gas station. Although, those places were neutral territory, at least. Showing up at the farm was like covering herself in chum and jumping into a shark tank. She crossed the front yard, mounted the porch, and paused at the door. Did they have a doorbell?

"Hello!"

She recognized that voice. *Like a copper penny.* Whirling, she spotted Jonas striding from the barn.

He broke into a broad smile.

Her quads reverted to a gelatinous state. "Hello." She slid a hand to the porch railing for support. "I'm looking for your wife."

He stopped short. "Who?"

The warmth seeped from his smile. She swallowed. "Ah…your wife? I'm here to pick up some pies."

"Three dozen pies, if I'm not mistaken." He mounted the steps in a single leap, tossed his hat onto a spindled bench, and turned. "And she's not my wife."

Her face flamed. "I'm sorry, I thought—"

"She's my sister."

"And Rebecca?" She caught herself. "Sorry. It's none of my—"

"My niece." He ran a tanned hand through his hair. Tiny beads of sweat dotted his upper lip, and his indigo shirt clung to his shoulders. No doubt he'd worked hours already.

"Nora told me someone was coming. I figured it was you."

He skimmed past and tromped down the porch steps, leaving the sweet scent of hay in his wake.

"Come on around," he called over one shoulder. "The pies are in the pantry."

Certain the color would never fade from her cheeks, she followed him around the house to where a neat kitchen garden lay, surrounded by fruit trees. She lingered at the gate, an intricate, arched, wooden trellis around which morning glories twined. Within the fence, raised beds teemed with herbs and vegetables. Ducking under a low-hanging bough, she hustled to catch up with him. "Your garden is lovely."

He gestured her toward the back door. "Nora keeps it up. I don't do much."

"She should be proud." She paused at the doorstep and pivoted. "I'm Tessa, by the way. Tessa Meadows."

Lifting her chin, she thrust out a hand.

With a tilt of the head, he regarded her, and his eyes crinkled at the corners.

She willed down the blood that throbbed toward her still-burning cheeks but seemed to be making a pit stop at her neck.

"Jonas Rishel."

He enveloped her hand in a firm handshake. Her racing blood made a detour to her collarbone and set it on fire.

"Pleased to meet you," he said.

A rough patch at the base of one finger chafed tender skin on her palm. Even her scalp tingled at his touch.

He nodded once and released her hand.

The back door opened to a sizeable pantry. "Your home is beautiful."

His face darkened. "It's too quiet."

The simple white curtains hung still. A rainbow of jams, jellies, and preserved vegetables didn't make a peep. Nine crates of pie sat soundlessly on the wide, wooden counter. But somehow, she didn't think that's what he meant.

She leaned over the crates, inhaling the buttery scent. "They're gorgeous."

He stacked the trays and turned. "How did you find us last week?"

"I came looking."

One tawny brow rose.

Great. Now she was a stalker. "Well, that sounded crazy—I just mean—I came looking for your farm. Esther King gave me directions."

"So, we have Esther to thank."

"Or to blame." She shrugged. Maybe she should stop talking.

He settled back against the counter. "You've got yourself a lot of pies."

"They're for a celebrity auction."

"Ah, you fatten them before you sell them. Very clever."

"Oh no! We don't sell the celebrities." She swallowed a giggle, unsure if he was teasing. He smiled that half smile again, cheek creasing in a delicious wrinkle just to the side of his raised lip. "We sell things that were autographed or owned by famous people—you know—to raise money for the hospital."

"No, I didn't know entirely." The other side of his mouth completed the smile. "But it sounds interesting."

"Well, I've never been to one so...I guess." She grabbed a stack of crates. It was heavier than she expected and teetered in her arms. Stumbling backward, she sucked a hissing breath.

In an instant, he reached from behind and steadied the pile.

His inhalation was a warm whisper just above her ear, and his chest grazed her shoulder blades. She straightened. "Thank you, I can manage."

"I don't doubt that."

Just as quickly, he was gone. Unmoving, she clutched the stack. Hard plastic dug into her palms as the phantom touch of his pecs tingled on her back.

"You coming?"

She blinked.

He was outside, propping the door with one arm and hefting a towering pile of pie in the other.

"Yeah."

Balancing the crates on one knee, she trundled open the van's side door and lowered the pies to the floor. After one more trip, the van was full.

Jonas stepped inside and wedged the crates in place. Pies secure, he sat on the back seat, propped his elbows on his knees, and surveyed the interior.

Ergonomically designed with cabinets and drawers tucked into every nook and cranny, the vintage van was something of a design masterpiece. At least she thought so. "Neat, huh?"

He nodded. "Very neat."

An invitation to pop the top and offer the grand tour quivered on the tip of her tongue. However, for the first time that morning, she thought before speaking. The tour could wait. She unzipped her backpack and retrieved her checkbook. "Who should I make the check out to? Nora…?"

"Beiler," Jonas said.

"Beiler. Right."

He looped his thumbs through his suspenders.

She snuck a glance at his left ring finger. No ring. Then again, did Amish men wear wedding rings? How old was he, anyway? Didn't these guys marry at, like, nineteen? His face was deeply tanned, and he had those heart-stopping laugh lines around his eyes. The mark of years working in the sun, she supposed, as much as years on the planet. He didn't wear a beard, but he had to be in his late twenties, at least. Maybe older. She peeked again. Something else lay hidden in his face. A heaviness. Something dark in the lines around his mouth. Something sad in the creases on his forehead. What caused those lines? She handed him the check. "When should I return the crates?"

"You can bring them by Monday. Around sundown."

Sundown it was. Jonas Rishel managed his day not by a calendar app but by the rising and setting of the sun. Refreshing…and darned attractive. "Thank you. And thank you for your help."

"You're welcome, Tessa Meadows. Enjoy your three dozen pies." Whistling, he turned and loped back toward the barn.

She slid behind the steering wheel and paused with her key in the ignition. Beyonce's "All the Single Ladies"? She chuckled.

Nah. It couldn't be.

****

"Jenn, I think I want to be Amish."

"You're kidding."

Tessa tucked the phone under her chin and yanked open the fridge. Just thinking about the pies in the pop-top made her mouth water. As did the guy who put them there. "Why?"

"You'll never have sex, for one thing. They only do it like twice, to have kids—"

She guffawed, and the phone slipped an inch or two. "Twice?"

"Well, eight or nine times, I guess."

She giggled again and shoved aside a jar of sweet pickles. "Might be worth it."

"Tess, *Witness* was just a movie. Harrison Ford won't dance with you in the barn."

The chorus of "Wonderful World" echoed in her thoughts. Dancing with Jonas by lamplight? She could imagine worse ways to spend an evening. "Technically, Harrison Ford wasn't the Amish guy."

"You'd never see another movie. Never binge-watch TV. You'd waste away."

"I don't know. I mean, you'd be living off the land." She gathered Esther King's strawberries, a tub of plain yogurt, and a pitcher of iced coffee. "This week at the Farmers' Market, I saw this…Amish man." She kicked closed the fridge door with one foot.

"Don't even tell me. You're hot for an Amish guy!"

The pitcher was icy, but her palms flamed at the memory of simply shaking his hand. Hot didn't begin to cover it. "No…"

"Oh, sweetie. You've got to move to New York. I'll introduce you to guys. We'll go to clubs."

She poured a healthy dose of coffee into a mason jar. "Seriously, he's the most gorgeous man I have ever met."

"Wait a minute, you actually met him?"

"Well, this morning at his farm—"

Jenn let out a shriek. "You went to his farm?"

She stirred in a tablespoon of raw sugar and a glug of half and half. Granules swirled in a mini whirlpool. "Pies, Jenn. I was buying pies for this thing at the hospital—it doesn't matter. It's just—this guy. We sort of sparked."

"Do you even hear yourself?"

"An upper lip like Batman. And muscles for days."

"Have you forgotten Stephen and James and even that jock from high school? Amish Batman is another unattainable guy."

"I know. I'm not serious." She took a swig and crunched down on undissolved sugar. Jenn didn't need to rehash her mediocre track record with men. She certainly hadn't forgotten it.

"So, when are you coming to visit?"

"Soon, okay? Soon." Conversation finished, she tossed her phone onto the counter and rinsed the berries. As usual, Jenn was right. Her love life was an endless litany of hopeless infatuations, starting with Brent, the star sprinter for the high school track team who never even knew her name. Brent was followed by Stephen, undergrad environmentalist who smiled from the cover of *The Eagle* as he summited a mountain of recycling. During grad school, she joined the Hemmingway Seminar. Dr. Harris insisted the students call him James. During his lectures, she closed her eyes and swore he was Jimmy Stewart reincarnated in tweed. Unfortunately, his wife looked like Grace Kelly.

Now, Jonas the Amish guy. Add him to the list.

She spooned strawberries and yogurt and glanced at her phone. Just enough time to eat before the auction. Sticky juice ran down her chin, and she licked her lips.

What was so wrong with high standards, anyway?

She could hear Jenn's response. "Table for one?"

I'm not crazy. He's as curious about me as I am about him.

Maybe Monday night at sundown, she'd get some answers.

Chapter 4

Thirty-six pies and two armloads of lilacs smelled like…? Tessa sank into the driver's seat and closed her eyes.

Like Martha Stewart's sock drawer.

Who would have guessed butter and lilac produced such intoxicating perfume? Maybe she'd just pop the top and nap in the camper all afternoon. She had, after all, set her alarm for an obscene hour that morning so she'd have time to make flower arrangements before the pie pick up.

Just after dawn, she cut a big bundle of the fragrant flowers and arranged them in a tumbling cascade in an old ironstone pitcher. The remaining blossoms she'd bunched in antique milk jars of varying sizes. Cracking open one eye, she surveyed the containers clustered on the passenger's side floor. The bouquets were casual and country but still elegant. She guessed "the wonderful Claire MacMillan" had fully decorated the venue, but fresh flowers were never out of place. Besides, as far as she knew, the dessert table was entirely her responsibility.

Her vision partly obscured by lilacs, she tottered toward the open-air, party tent. It rose as pearly and inviting as she remembered from her youth. After graduation and reunion weekends, Green Ridge College donated the tent to local organizations before returning it to storage. She peeped through blossoms. Bunches of red and blue helium balloons bobbed in the breeze. Despite overcast skies, the atmosphere under the canvas was a festive summertime picnic.

Once inside, she dodged an army of volunteers hustling among the tables. Which one was Claire? She scanned the crowd. Next to an elevated riser on the far end of the tent, a dark-haired woman in a cherry-red shirtdress huddled with the members of a Dixieland band.

Glancing up from her clipboard, the woman spotted her and beckoned with a wave.

"I'm Claire." She grinned, and dimples puckered apple-round cheeks. "You must be Tessa. Marion Diefenderfer wasn't kidding when she said you have hair like Lucille Ball—though I would have said Jessica Chastain. Yours is natural, isn't it? So jealous. It's nice to finally meet you."

She returned Claire's grin, and the tension in her shoulders eased. "You, too."

Tossing a sleek bob, Claire nodded to a gaggle of older women. "I hope Marion didn't overwhelm you. She's just highly excitable."

"I've known Mrs. Diefenderfer since she was my first grade Sunday School teacher. She doesn't scare me."

Claire leaned in close. "I like the 'tude! We can use some new energy around here."

"I'm glad I could help." She shifted the flower arrangements and cringed. "I do have a confession. I bought pies for the dessert table. I'm completely useless in the kitchen."

Claire widened her eyes. Then she smiled and

swatted the air between them. "Please. Baking is for schmucks who don't know how good grocery store cupcakes really are." She gave a throaty laugh, glanced at her phone, and groaned. "Oh jeez, I'm late picking up the kids at swimming. Why Tyler can't get out of rounds to retrieve his children just this once, I will never know. Somehow, I show houses and parent at the same time—go figure. I'll be back." She threw a chic, floral bag over one shoulder and narrowed her eyes. "Look for Dr. Richard Bruce. Unlike my husband, he escaped the hospital. He's around here somewhere in a ridiculous chef's hat. He'll help you carry your store-bought pies."

"Actually, they're Amish pies," she said.

"Even better." Claire squeezed her hand. "I'm so glad you're here."

She whirled on perfectly coordinated, designer sneakers and took off toward the parking lot. Clutching the lilacs, Tessa joined the pre-auction madness. Keeping watch for a guy in a funny hat, she wandered among tables overflowing with items. Many donations were of a literary nature: autographed books, magazines, and—saints be praised—the much-anticipated copy of *Chicken Soup for the Soul*. Mrs. Diefenderfer could die a happy woman. She saw playbills, movie posters, memorabilia, and photos. The Volunteer Committee outdid itself.

Partway down one aisle, another auction piece veritably leapt off the table and stopped her in her tracks. The book appeared to be a first edition. A tree branch covered most of the dust jacket, its mass of emerald leaves vibrant against a brown background. She set the flowers on the table and picked up the copy of Harper Lee's *To Kill a Mockingbird* like it was the Gutenberg Bible. With trembling fingers, she cracked the cover. Actor Gregory Peck's signature scrawled across the title page. She studied the angular printing. Atticus Finch himself autographed that book.

" 'Remember, it's a sin to kill a mockingbird.' "

The voice over her shoulder came with a whiff of citrus and spice. She swung around and encountered a pair of dark-lashed hazel eyes and a brilliant white smile. Her heart whammed in her chest. Good thing she was surrounded by doctors. Since when was her hometown crawling with hot guys?

"Man, I love that movie," he said.

"Have you read the book?"

He stuck the non-business end of a spatula under a chef's hat and scratched his head. "Not since ninth grade."

"No kidding. I read it in ninth grade, too."

"I figured."

She replaced the precious item on the table. "I guess it's par for the course in freshman English."

"Well, it is at Green Ridge High School."

Wow. She took a step back. Was it that obvious she was a local girl?

The guy grinned. "Richard Bruce. Green Ridge High School alum and veteran of Mrs. Nuttall's ninth-grade English class." He extended a hand.

She took it, releasing her jaw into a smile. "Tessa Meadows."

"I figured. Claire sent me to find you. 'The stunning redhead who's about a million feet tall,' she said. That would definitely be you. What she didn't tell me, though, was that you'd smell so damn good."

49

She thought she'd met her daily quota for blushing. She was wrong. "It's the lilacs." A cog turned in her memory. "Hold on, I remember you." She flashed back to the cement block walls of her high school gym. The vision was less traumatizing than she might have imagined. But yes, Richard Bruce. His name was emblazoned on championship banners, and his photo graced the athletic and academic trophy cases. She took in his dark, wavy hair and trim, athletic figure. He looked pretty much the same as he had smiling from the halls of her school. "You played basketball. Your picture was always in the paper when I was in middle school."

"Shortest point guard ever to win a state championship. At your service." He flourished the spatula.

Dropping a quick curtsy, she let out a giggle. "The pleasure's all mine."

"May I escort you to your post?" He eased several jars from her hands.

She followed him to a table draped with a pretty, blue-checked cloth and deposited the arrangements. "So…my car is full of pies."

"Pies? Music to my ears."

"If you have a second, I could use help carrying them. I bought three dozen."

"Many pies. Even better."

"I hope you still feel that way when you find out how much they weigh. I had no idea pie was so heavy."

Nearing the van, Richard barked a laugh. "Don't tell me it's you I've spotted in this groovy love wagon."

Would her car ever cease to amuse the male inhabitants of Green Ridge? "Hey, don't knock it. It's

50

my father's pride and joy. I have it on loan, and it's served me very well."

He raised thick, groomed brows. "It has, huh?"

"Not that kind of well," she shot back. Okay, time to get a ski mask. This blushing was out of control.

"Love the plaid interior. I wouldn't have pegged you as a flower child."

She stacked the front-most crates. "Actually, I'm not. My parents are totally straitlaced. My dad just likes camping, and my mom hates sleeping on wet ground."

"You know, I read online this manufacturer is producing a new camper. It's only available in Europe now, but they're making headway back into the market." He picked up a stack and started toward the tent.

"Yeah…my dad's gonna drive this thing until the wheels fall off."

Hefting her own pile of pie, she followed him past a shiny, black SUV sporting a Yale decal. She knew without asking it was his ride.

Twenty minutes later, her table was ready. She tucked empty crates and extra pie under the tablecloth and wiped her fingers on a napkin.

The band struck up a toe-tapping tune, and right on time, prospective bidders streamed into the tent.

To her credit, Nora put together a lovely assortment of strawberry, strawberry rhubarb, and her famous shoofly pie. Satisfied with the display, Tessa stepped back and rolled achy shoulders. She twisted her hair into a messy bun and pulled on her shades.

Richard sidled up to the table, tying a blue apron over crisp khakis and plaid shirt. "Hoping to stay incognito, huh?" He grabbed two lemonades from the adjacent beverage table and offered one.

"Thanks. Sometimes I'd kill for a shred of anonymity." She took a sip and wrinkled her nose. Too sour.

He chuckled. "Tell me about it. Everyone in town knows old Doc Bruce's boy."

She laughed, but he spoke truth. She knew the elder Dr. Bruce, as well. He took care of her father when he had pneumonia some years ago.

"So, back in 'the Ridge,' huh?" Richard stirred his lemonade with a paper straw and took a long pull.

His comment went down as bitterly as the drink. She groaned. "Don't remind me."

An elderly couple approached and sauntered off with two pieces of shoofly. Each.

Doffing the shades, she cut four slices and filled the empty spots. "I hoped to be in New York City by now. My college roommate's been living there for a couple years."

"And?" He took a cell phone from his pocket and swiped the screen.

"Our plans have fallen through." A sigh slipped from her lips. "For now."

"So, here you are in the thriving metropolis of Green Ridge serving pie to senior citizens at"—he checked the device—"eleven fifteen in the a.m."

"You and me both. Don't they need doctors in other parts of the country?"

Shifting his weight, he pocketed the phone and looked away. "My father got sick during my fourth year of medical school. I moved back home for residency."

"I see." Sensing she touched a nerve, she offered a slice of strawberry pie.

With a nod, he took the plate. "Dad passed away last summer. Almost a year ago, actually."

His voice was tinged with pain. Did one ever get over the loss of a parent? She pictured her mother and father happy and healthy on their Southwest adventure. She didn't think so. "I'm sorry."

He met her gaze, and his lips rose in a sad smile. "Thanks." With a shrug, he forked a healthy bite. "So, I've got some pretty big shoes to fill."

"Flipping burgers at the hospital fundraiser is a good start. Hey, at this point, I'd consider doing it for a living."

Two metal stools were stacked by a tent post. He fetched them, dropping onto one and resting a foot on the crossbar. "That bad, huh?"

She took in a breath and scented coming rain. "So, the tale of my misfortune hasn't made the rounds?"

"Honor compels me to confess I heard via Claire, via the charming Marion Diefenderfer, that you are temporarily unemployed."

The guy was a consummate gentleman. She dipped her chin. "Kind of you to say 'temporarily.' "

Leaning back, he clasped his hands over one knee. "So, tell me, Miss Meadows, what's your plan now?"

A surprise guest on *The Dr. Richard Bruce Show*, she almost expected to be handed a mic. "Is it too late to become a professional tennis player?"

"Never, my darling."

She slid onto the stool next to his. "Well, then that. Or maybe a private investigator. Both excellent career choices for an English major."

He crossed his arms over his chest. "There's always snake wrangling."

She mimicked his pose. "Celebrity chef?"

"Race car driver?"

"Professional sports mascot?"

"With legs like yours? What a waste." He inclined his head toward the length of thigh, knee, and shin her casual perch revealed.

Leaping to her feet, she tugged down her skirt. Having no clever retort, she snatched a piece of shoofly pie and dug in. Good lord, Esther King was right. This was a recipe to guard with one's life.

Cheeks aglow, Claire bounced to the dessert table. "Looks like you two are having fun."

"I was just encouraging Tessa to run for governor," Richard said.

"She has my vote." Claire selected the smallest piece of pie on the table.

Richard handed her a fork. "She agreed on the condition I would be her running mate."

"Naturally." Claire beamed.

Tessa hid behind her pie.

"And now, if you ladies will excuse me, I have burgers to flip." Giving his hat a hearty poof, he kissed Claire on the cheek, winked at Tessa, and sauntered toward the grill.

Claire plopped onto his stool and heaved a sigh. "Isn't he a doll?"

"He certainly is charming." She licked crumbs from the side of her fork.

"That's an understatement. The guy radiates charisma like a neon light. He's the heir apparent of St. Luke's Hospital. Drop-dead gorgeous and desired by all." Catching her heels on the bottom rung, Claire slipped off her sneakers and wiggled brightly pedicured toes. "I've been here since six a.m. My feet are killing me."

"You must be exhausted."

Claire massaged her arches. "You have no idea." She righted herself and slid back into her shoes. "Richard and my husband Tyler are collaborating on research. Very high-tech, cutting-edge stuff. Honestly, Richard could have had his choice of positions. It's sad really."

With careful fingers, Tessa picked up the last bit of delicate pie crust and slid it onto her tongue. "He told me about his father."

Claire gazed toward the grill. "St. Luke's isn't the same without old Dr. Bruce. He was a mentor to Tyler, and now, Tyler works with Richard. Funny how those things happen. All I know is Tyler's doing everything he can to keep Richard right here in Green Ridge. Aren't you, honey?"

A slender man with sandy hair and glasses slung an arm around Claire's shoulders. "Aren't I what?"

"Keeping Richard here."

"That's the plan, Stan." He nodded to Tessa. "Do we have you to thank for these fabulous pies?"

"Sort of. I didn't make them."

"But you were clever enough to bring them, and for that we are grateful. Tyler MacMillan."

She took his offered hand. "Tessa Meadows."

"Good to meet you. Our kids, Caitlyn and Sam, are somewhere around here. I swear I saw them a second ago." He peered out under the tent. "Ah, there they are."

Tessa followed his gaze and spied two, impeccably dressed children somersaulting across the lawn.

The kids waved and made funny faces.

Claire rolled her eyes with a grin. "Couple of goofballs."

"Dr. Bruce."

"Dr. MacMillan."

Richard and Tyler greeted each other with the exaggerated formality of doctors on a dramatic television show and broke into smiles.

"I trust you have coverage on the wards today," Richard said.

"God bless the residents." Tyler gestured to Tessa. "You've met the lovely Tessa Meadows, bearer of pies?"

Claire beamed. "He has, and he'll get to know her better when he takes her out to thank her for jumping on board this crazy event."

Richard thrust his hands in his pockets and rocked back on his heels. "Fine by me. Name the time, Ms. Meadows, and I'll be there."

She looked from one beaming face to the next. "How can I refuse?"

Light rain pitter-pattered on the canvas roof. Sam and Caitlyn squealed and cartwheeled in the drizzle. A sliver of sunlight broke through the clouds, and she stepped into glowy mist. Over the far eastern ridge, a rainbow shimmered into being.

She shook her head and chuckled. Without even realizing it was happening, she'd just been set up on a date with Dr. Richard Bruce.

****

A molten slice of sun hovered over the ridge, and the sky above it was on fire. Tessa jumped out of the van, landing with a soft thud on a clump of dandelions and crabgrass. Closing the front door quietly, she peered through the side window at the empty crates she promised to return Monday at sundown. She was right on time.

Rebecca flew around the farmhouse and scampered across the yard. "I want to show you something."

In the gloaming, the girl was fully a creature of fairy realms. Tessa hesitated, scanning the yard.

"Come on."

Beckoning with a sylphlike arm, Rebecca spun, her narrow skirt ballooning, and skipped back the way she came. Tessa had no choice. When the little folk summoned, only the foolish stayed behind. Trailing Rebecca, she ducked under the fruit trees, skirted the garden, and followed a dirt lane bisecting the fields behind the house. Beyond the nearest field, she came to a low-sided, wooden bridge, just wide enough for a piece of farm equipment to pass. Below, Buffalo Creek gurgled in the windless twilight—the sound somehow cheerful and haunting all at once.

Rebecca kicked stones between slats, and they landed with hollow, watery plops below. Becoming one with the creatures of dusk, she flitted across the bridge and plunged into the forest.

The final fingernail of sun slipped behind the ridge, leaving a violet afterglow. Tessa scurried, stumbling over dried, muddy ruts as she strained to keep Rebecca in sight. Crunching over pebbles, she turned onto an almost-hidden footpath. Deep in the woods, the slivered sky flashed purple through thick branches. Were it not for the girl's flaxen crown, Tessa would have lost her. Her dark dress disappeared among the trees.

The path was short, though, and in minutes, she

emerged, joining Rebecca on the other side.

The girl inclined her face toward the treetops. "Look up."

In that instant, Tessa left her world behind and stepped into a fairy kingdom luminous with fireflies. The woods edging the field were alive with them, flickering like a million tiny Christmas lights. She felt her lungs expand and her heart crack open. "Oh."

Rebecca took her hand and led her from the tree line. The field hadn't been tilled, and the stubble of last year's corn crumpled beneath her feet. The air tasted of honeysuckle and meadow grass, and the sky glowed deep amethyst.

In the center of the field, Rebecca paused and turned slowly in place.

Surrounded by glowing sparks that brightened and dimmed as if fanned by miniature bellows, Tessa spun in tandem. She lifted her gaze to the evening star, believing for a moment she could see all three hundred sixty degrees at once. Perhaps, this girl really was magic.

"There you are."

She shivered, and her focus sharpened. She hadn't even heard him approach.

"I've been hunting for you, Rebecca," Jonas said. "I thought you'd stolen away our guest."

Rebecca gestured to the trees with open arms. "We're saying goodnight to the lightning bugs."

Tessa glanced over one shoulder. "Hi." The single syllable vibrated low in her chest, more a caress than a word. The sound was so intimate she might have been embarrassed, but her face stayed cool. Such was the sorcery of Rebecca's firefly field.

"Hi."

His gaze through the dark was like a warm hand on her cheek. An urge to lean into his chest tugged at her insides. His head, a silhouette in dim lamplight, tilted skyward, and she turned back to the trees. Minutes passed, and the only sounds were the mingled songs of the crickets and the creek.

"Is *Mamm* home?" Rebecca asked.

"Come along, and we'll see." Held high, the lantern lit a path through the field.

Rebecca danced into the light. "If she isn't, can I have a cookie before bed?"

"If you hurry." He gestured the way.

With one final glance to the treetops, Tessa turned and followed Rebecca across the field.

He drew up beside her, lowering the lamp to light the uneven terrain.

Rebecca leapt over a fallen stalk. "Can I have two cookies?"

"Just this once."

"You say that every time."

He chuckled. "You're too clever, Rebecca Beiler."

Rebecca twirled again, sure-footed in the night. "I know."

Tessa stepped carefully over the stalk. "I'd like to thank Mrs. Beiler for the pies. They were delicious."

Pausing at the edge of the woods, Rebecca caught a firefly in cupped hands. "Monday is her quilting night. She goes to Mrs. Stoltzfus' every Monday after supper, and Jonas and I can draw pictures and do whatever we like."

So, Jonas had known Nora wouldn't be home when he asked her to return that night at sundown. *Go figure*.

"I'll give her your thanks." Once beyond the forest, he led the way over the bridge and into the backyard.

The lamplight through the garden trellis cast spidery, shifting shadows.

Rebecca darted in and out of darkness. "Do you like our garden gate, Tessa?"

"It's beautiful."

"Jonas made it."

She paused at the garden entrance. "He did?"

"He builds things for lots of people. He's a carpenter like our Lord."

Tracing her fingers over the gracefully arched wood, she sighed. She could only dream of having such a gate in her garden.

Jonas took his niece by the hand. "I believe it's time for bed."

"No-o-o."

Rebecca whined her protest, and Tessa's heart went out to her. The transition to the mortal world was rough.

Settling the lantern atop a stump, he tickled the girl, urging her toward the door. "If you want cookies, go. Your mother will be home soon."

Rebecca wiggled free and plucked a leaf from a nearby tree. "Tessa, did you know that if you crumple up a peach tree leaf it smells like grass?"

"Go." With a nudge, he shooed her up the stairs.

"Goodnight." The girl dashed into the pantry. The screen door creaked and thwacked behind her.

"Goodnight." Standing at Jonas's side, she watched the slight form disappear. "She's a wonder."

"She is headstrong."

She gave him a sidelong glance. "You say that like

it's a bad thing."

He kicked at the grass with one leather boot. "So her mother thinks. I'm afraid I just encourage her."

Creases cut deep shadows over his toes. Her giant feet looked almost petite in comparison. "She's lucky to have you."

"Maybe. I just hope I'm enough."

Enough for what? His gaze met hers, and her belly heated as warm as the lamplight playing over his face.

He scrubbed a hand across his chin and took off around the house with long strides.

Free of pies, the crates were easy to wrangle, and after one trip, the van was empty. She stacked hers beside his on the counter and followed him into the night.

"Was your celebrity auction successful?" he asked.

She cast her mind back to the event—the lively tent bursting with music—the tables laden with so many things this Amish man would never in a million years want to have in his home. At least, she didn't think so. "It was."

"I'm glad."

She ran her fingertip over the rough edge of the key. "Please tell your sister how grateful I am. Everyone loved the pies. I wouldn't be surprised if she got a bunch more orders."

"I will."

The night softened into an impressionist landscape: cicada song…the evening breeze cool against the backs of her legs…a whiff of hay as he lifted the lamp and illuminated the van door.

"Thank you." She climbed in and rolled down the window. "And thanks for your help." She inserted the key but paused before turning it, loathe to shatter the stillness with that raucous, old motor—afraid if she left she might never come back.

"It was my pleasure."

He took in a breath as though he had something more to say. The shadows on his face deepened. She waited…hoping for what? An acknowledgement? A revelation? An invitation to return next Monday night? His expression cleared, and he smiled.

"I'm glad to see you again. Goodnight."

He thumped an open palm on the driver's side door, almost as if her van was a horse. She tightened her grip on the key. "Goodnight."

Then he turned and loped into the darkness.

As she swung around, she took a long last look at the house. She came seeking answers only to leave with more questions. A slender, ghost-like figure waved from an upstairs window, haloed in lamplight.

Come back soon, the wave seemed to say.

I'm not sure how…or why. But I will.

****

Thunder bellows, and lightning splits the clouds. Carrying an empty bucket, I cross the bridge behind Jonas Rishel's farm. Far below, the creek rages.

I am alone, but I suspect I am meant to meet someone. I think it is my grandmother. The sky is dark, and I slip on wet wooden slats. My yellow rain slicker sticks to my skin. The clouds detonate, and I wince. I am afraid the lightning will strike me. I run my tongue over braces on my teeth.

I emerge from a path at the edge of a vast field. A gazebo stands in the middle. I stumble across crumpled cornstalks, and my sneakers squelch. I shield the bucket with my body as best I can.

A man stands in the gazebo. His back is to me. I call, but he does not turn. I want to join him, but the gazebo is surrounded by a moat. I circle the gazebo, but no matter where I go, I can't see the man's face. The rain stings now. It pelts my cheeks like slivery shards of hail.

"I'm here," I call again. "I need to stay the night."

Neon blue lightning splinters the sky, and the man is now a deer. He leaps over the moat and runs off into the woods.

Tessa opened her eyes so quickly they made a sound like a doorknob turning or a book opening to a middle page.

A gazebo?

Thunder rumbled over distant ridges. The upholstered foam mattress was hard against her shoulder. Wind rushed through the half-moon screen, cooling sweat from her neck and cheeks. Her dream faded fast.

What else? She had a bucket, and there was a deer, maybe?

The canvas sides of the pop-top's upper story puckered with the change in pressure.

A gazebo.

She flipped onto her back and stared at the velveteen ceiling. A gazebo.

And she knew just the carpenter to build it.

****

"Will you build me a gazebo?" A round of applause for that beautiful bit of awkwardness. No "Hello." No "Hey, good to see you again. Thanks for the firefly show the other night." Nope. The following

Wednesday, Tessa strode up to Rishels' Farm Stand, looked Jonas in the eye, and lobbed her request like a cherry bomb into the whoopie pies.

So eloquent.

But the cherry bomb wasn't the only metaphorical firework that afternoon. The backs of her hands tingled like she held a sparkler in each one. Lingering behind his house in the lamplight, she found talking to Jonas almost easy. Now, beneath harsh fluorescents, simply forming a sentence proved nearly impossible.

Nora hovered around the whoopie pies.

"What's that now?" He crossed his arms and cocked his head.

Hello again, biceps. She sucked in a breath. "A gazebo. For my backyard. I figured since you do carpentry and all…" This encounter had gone much more smoothly in her head.

Beneath his wide brim, he slid Nora a glance.

Nora spun and, despite the catch in her step, stalked to the milk crate by the door.

Folding her hands in a manner that could only be described as prayerful, she lowered herself and radiated disapproval.

He ran a thick hand over the back of his neck and stared at the ceiling. "Well, most of the building I do is for…"

For the first time in her presence, he faltered.

"Well, for the family and for…other farmers."

She tugged the suddenly too-tight waistband of her skirt. Of course. Jonas Rishel limited his carpentry to the Amish. "I see."

"Now, you can buy a gazebo out Route 45 at King's Farm. Lucas King sells all manner of garden things. He does fine work."

She shook her head. "My gazebo has to be unique. It's a gift for my parents for their thirtieth wedding anniversary. I want it to be special."

Widening his eyes, he stepped closer. "Custom?"

A flicker of hope lit in her chest. She scooted to meet him, bumping her thighs against the stand and jiggling the pies. "Yes, custom."

"In what way?"

She looped her thumbs through her backpack straps and tugged it tight to her shoulders. Closing her eyes, she tried to summon the gazebo from her dream, but she couldn't. "I haven't quite figured it out, but it needs to be one of a kind."

"Doesn't Lucas King sell gazebos to tourists?" Nora called from her roost.

She shot the woman a glare. "I was born here."

Jonas's eyes crinkled at the corners. "I don't know that King fills custom orders."

The tingling in her hands surged up her arms and spread across her collarbones. "I just love your garden gate, and if you could build a gazebo like that—natural and whimsical—it would be the most perfect present ever."

Nora hauled to her feet with an unintelligible grunt.

A smile tugged at one side of his mouth. "You liked that, did you?"

"I liked it a lot." Turns out swooning wasn't limited to Victorian ladies whose corsets were too tight. The traveling sparks completed their journey to her head, and her brain buzzed like she took a sip of champagne. The hubbub of the market morphed into the adult voices in *Charlie Brown* specials. Placing one hand on the table, she steadied herself and found the courage to meet his gaze. "Would you maybe just consider building me a gazebo?"

"Bring me a sketch of what you want it to look like," he said, "and I'll see what I can do."

Nora gaped. "Jonas!"

He didn't flinch. "I could use the work. Thank you for thinking of me."

Tessa had no beef with Nora Beiler. She didn't even know the woman. Still, Jonas's assent felt like a mini victory. A flush of satisfaction bloomed in her cheeks, and she dropped her gaze. Gloating was unbecoming. "A sketch. I can do that. Thank you."

She hadn't made it two steps from the table when Nora launched into a tirade in Pennsylvania Dutch. Her tone left no doubt as to her meaning. Translation? This gazebo was so not happening.

"Enough, Nora," Jonas said.

His voice was heavy as wet cement. Glancing over her shoulder, she caught a glimpse of sky-blue shirt as he disappeared through the door. She whipped around and lit off for the refuge of Troutman's Famous Fries.

Something about that family just didn't sit right. Why was Nora angry all the time? How did Jonas endure her? Why did the three of them live alone in that big, old farmhouse? They were a mystery. She popped a fry and shivered at the tangy explosion of vinegar and salt.

A mystery she was determined to solve.

Chapter 5

When Tessa agreed to give Jonas a sketch of her gazebo, she was so giddy she conveniently forgot one key fact. She didn't draw.

So, on a balmy Saturday afternoon, hot on the heels of propositioning an Amish carpenter, she hoofed to the Green Ridge College library to lose herself among the stacks. Hours brainstorming gazebos while she weeded and an equally time-consuming Internet search yielded nothing. Try as she might, she just couldn't reconstruct the compelling structure from her dream. Short of hypnosis, she was flummoxed. Time to get on her old-school research.

She plopped at a computer terminal, slung her bag onto her lap, and unzipped the front pouch. What happened to all her good pens? Nothing was so satisfying as a really good pen. Extracting a lesser utensil and a sketchbook, she snorted. No pen on earth could magically transform her into a gazebo designer.

Maybe if she napped on a pile of garden books, she could summon the bizarre dream. Hazy snippets danced through her conscious mind. She huffed a quiet chuckle. The notion of literally dreaming up a present for her folks was laughable. Still, they loved their yard and gardens. Who cared how the idea arose? A gazebo was the perfect gift.

She twisted her ponytail into a tight bun and let it

fall over her shoulders. Navigating to the online catalog, she typed the keyword: gazebo. Dozens of titles flashed on the screen, and she scrolled the listings. Most were works of fiction with names like *Darkness Falls on the Gazebo* and *Gazebo Tryst*. Intriguing but wrong. Apparently, no one had penned *How to Design the Perfect Gazebo for Your Parents' Big Wedding Anniversary*.

Unwilling to abandon her quest so quickly, she returned to the search screen and entered: *garden architecture*. A different dizzying array appeared. Grabbing the inferior pen, she jotted the most promising titles.

"*Treatise on the Theory and Practice of Landscape Gardening*. A little light summer reading?"

The whispered words heated her cheek. With a yelp, she whirled.

The whisperer hovered inches away in a polo shirt and khaki shorts.

She drew in a quick breath. Her plan for a long research day didn't include an ambush by Dr. Suave. Resting an elbow on the desk behind her, she crossed her legs, hoping to communicate an unruffled composure she most definitely did not feel. Could he hear her pulse pounding? "What are you doing here?"

Richard's lips rose in a smirk. "Surprised doctors actually read?"

She shot him a wry smile. "So, you didn't learn everything you know from television?"

"Almost. But not quite." He chuckled. "Actually, Claire and Tyler wanted a morning off, so I offered to take the kids to their coding class—"

She blinked. "I'm sorry, their coding class? How

old are they again?"

"Eight and five."

"Five." She dropped the other elbow onto the desk and gave him a look. "Ambitious."

He thrust his hands in his pockets. "Sam is almost six."

"Oh, well, in that case. Claire's idea?"

"Of course. Actually, it's pretty great. After seeing what they're doing, I'd be tempted to send my kids to a class like this."

"I've no doubt it's a fabulous little program," she teased.

"These are the times, my dear. When our kids come along, I bet programming will be taught in preschool, if it isn't already." He leaned in close and studied the screen.

His cheek gave off a clean, citrusy scent with a touch of sunscreen. Her stomach executed an itty-bitty cartwheel. Not only was she surprised to see him—but she was surprised how happy she was to be surprised to see him.

Taking the mouse, he scrolled the list of books. "So, you're a student of garden architecture?"

"Not really." She swiveled and reviewed the titles.

"Horticulture then?"

"Kind of. I love plants, and my parents left me their house and gardens to tend while my dad's on sabbatical. I've given up on my mother's vegetables. The Farmers' Market will do. Instead, I'm planting a flower garden inspired by one my grandmother had." Her domestic endeavors sounded so lame compared to the lifesaving work he did every day. She flopped closed the cover of the sketchbook. "Exciting, huh?"

He pivoted and sat on the computer desk. "Very lovely, actually."

Beneath his gaze, she felt like something of a flower herself. Her cheeks heated. "Anyway, I want to give my parents a gazebo for their thirtieth wedding anniversary, and—"

"Have you looked online?"

Looping a curl over one ear, she nodded. "Didn't find anything. I want it to be really special, so I'm designing one myself. At least I'm trying. I'm looking for inspiration but not having much luck." She tapped her fingers on the sketchbook cover.

He jiggled her stool with one foot. "Why don't you blow this taco stand and come with us to Softee Freeze?"

She quieted her fingers mid-tap. Was he asking her out? A thrill shivered up her spine.

With a broad grin, he stuck his hands in his pockets and jingled his keys.

Nah. He probably just wanted babysitting backup. "Thanks, but I just got here—"

"You closed your notebook. I saw you. Come on, will you really read this stuff? *Landscape Design and Modern Thought*?"

In spite of herself, she giggled. "Hey, I might."

"*A Brief History of Garden Art*?"

"That one sounds like a page-turner."

He hooked his foot over the rung of the stool and pulled her closer. "I promise soft serve."

She pursed her lips and challenged him with a stare. "Do you always get what you want, Richard Bruce?"

"Not always…" He leaned in again. "But usually."

If she could bottle his confidence, she'd make a fortune.

"Besides, I need you," he library-whispered. "Sam and Caitlin are a handful, even when ice cream isn't part of the equation."

His face was inches from hers. She ran her gaze over the cleft in his chin where a hint of dark stubble was just emerging. "You only want me for my child-wrangling skills?"

"Among other things."

A high-pitched giggle rang out behind her.

"Please," he mouthed.

Her stomach did a full-fledged, back handspring. She tucked away her notebook. "Softee Freeze sounds great."

"You're an angel." Without asking, he took her backpack and flung it over one shoulder.

She reached to snatch it back but stopped—no harm in him carrying her bag. Just this once.

Sam careened around a desk with Caitlin on his heels.

Richard thrust out his hands. "Slow down, buddy."

"Are we going home now?" Sam dragged the back of his wrist across his nose and sniffed.

"Use your indoor voice." Caitlin huffed a volume-appropriate sigh. "We're going to Softee Freeze. Don't you remember anything for more than five seconds?"

With her unicorn book bag and matching leggings, Caitlin mimicked her mother's…well…everything. The uncanny miracle of genetics.

"Hello," Sam said.

His light brown eyes were fringed like a giraffe's with impossibly long lashes. "Hi, Sam. Hi, Caitlin."

"Is she coming with us?" Caitlin asked.

Her tone betrayed a decisively negative opinion on the matter.

Richard doffed an imaginary cap and made a courtly bow. "If you agree, my lady."

Breaking into a smile, Caitlin accepted Richard's hand. "Okay."

"I love Softee Freeze!" Arms flailing, Sam rocketed for the door.

Caitlin rolled her eyes. "Boys."

The black SUV with the Yale decal was, in fact, Richard's ride. Casting a glance over buttery upholstery, she resolved they would eat their cones on the outdoor benches. Ice cream and leather definitely did not mix. Joining Richard and the kids in line, she pulled out her wallet.

"No way. My treat."

Richard's tone brooked no argument. Would this guy ever allow a woman to take the check? She rezipped her backpack and shrugged her shirt from her shoulders. At some point—say, after the temperature dropped below ninety-five degrees—she might wage that battle.

Sam insisted on a chocolate-dipped, soft-serve cone, and she grabbed a hefty stack of napkins before settling him on the bench next to her. She alternated between sipping her coffee shake and dabbing the inevitable stream of vanilla ice cream leaking under the cracked, chocolate crust. Swinging his feet and humming to himself, the little guy attacked his treat with gusto, oblivious to the growing, sticky mess.

Sitting on an adjacent bench with Richard, Caitlin spooned cookies and cream from a sensible cup and bemoaned how boring computer class was when they did the same activities as the week before.

Intelligent eyes, so like Claire's, flashed as she spoke. Tessa swirled her shake like a fine wine and tried to imagine her own eyes looking outward from a child's face—a face that mingled her features with those of someone else. How would she feel?

Richard caught her gaze over Caitlin's head and winked.

She raised her milkshake in a wordless toast. As she mopped goo from between Sam's fingers, and Caitlin chattered on, the vision of a life blossomed. Alone in her faculty apartment, she hardly dared imagine having a husband and kids. Just then, it seemed close enough to touch. In her heart, the delicate bud of a dream unfurled a petal or two.

"Are you Richard's girlfriend?" Sam dragged a finger through a glob of chocolate on his shorts.

"What? No! Oh gosh, no." She clamped down on her straw. Could Richard hear them? The sitting area was packed with noisy families. She lowered her voice. "We're friends. We're just getting to know each other, actually."

He sucked his pinky with a loud slurp and rubbed it on his shirt. "Kind of like you and me."

"Yes, just like that."

"Because Mommy says Richard really needs a girlfriend."

The napkins slid from her knee and splayed at her feet. In a flurry, she gathered them and dumped them in Sam's lap. "Is that right?"

"She says it to Dad all the time." He crammed the last bit of cone in his mouth, smashed the napkins into a soggy ball, and thrust it at her. "What should I do with this?"

On the opposite side of the seating area, a garbage can overflowed. She pointed. "Run and throw it away."

Sam crouched in a runner's stance and took off.

She slid a glance at Richard. He leaned toward Caitlin, his fingers interlaced behind his head and his legs stretched long, seemingly absorbed in conversation. With any luck, he missed Sam's ruminations on his love life.

Caitlin dropped the spoon in her empty cup and stood. "I'm hot and tired and ready to go home."

"As you wish, my lady." Richard nested her cup in his. "Your chariot awaits."

Tessa checked on Sam's progress.

The boy hovered beside the trashcan, clutching the gooey mass.

"Time to go, Sammo!" She extended a hand toward Richard. "I'll take your trash."

He relinquished the cups with a smile. Returning to talk of ones and zeros, he and Caitlin headed for the air-conditioned car.

"Tessa!" Sam called.

His voice was high and pinched. She glanced over.

Still clinging to the wadded napkins, he stood frozen in place.

What in the world was he doing? "Come on, Sam. Throw it away, and let's go." A flicker of annoyance starting in her belly, she dragged sticky fingers over condensation on the outside of her cup and brushed them together. Time to get this kid home and into the tub. Maybe she had an old wet wipe she could use to mop him up. Juggling the trash, she zipped and unzipped the compartments of her backpack. The last thing she wanted was to return Claire a gummy mess of a child. Not to mention the damage he would do to Richard's upholstery. Failing to locate anything, she threw her backpack over one shoulder with a grunt.

Sam called her name again.

Clocking a tremor in his voice, she paused. Why was the air around him dark? It almost appeared to be moving. She squinted through a curtain of heat rippling from the asphalt and gasped.

A cloud of insects whizzed in circles around him.

Bees!

In a convulsive spasm, Sam swatted his head and shoulders. "Ow, ow, ow!"

She recoiled, slamming her calves into the bench. "Stand still, Sam!" Her body lurched toward the boy, but her feet stayed rooted—as if the soles of her shoes melted into the tar. She couldn't move.

She forced in a shuddering breath. She wasn't equipped to handle a swarm of bees. Somebody else needed to step up—some responsible adult like Richard. Swallowing hard, she swung around. He was already in the SUV, out of earshot.

Cursing under her breath, she crushed the milkshake cup in one hand. Sam was too young to go to the trashcan alone. Only an idiot would send him. Knees wobbling, she groped for the back of the bench. Her fingers adhered to gunk-coated slats. Where her Softee Freeze hero to save the day?

"Tessa! Help!"

Sam's terror cut through her rising panic. She fastened her gaze on the child, and the edges of his small form sharpened. Every detail came into stark relief. She saw the glob of ice cream on his right eyebrow. The smudge of chocolate across the tyrannosaurus rex on his tee. The wings of a bee traversing the cuff of his shorts. The ice cream stand blurred, and Sam alone stood out in high definition at the end of a tunnel.

She was the grown-up on call. This emergency was on her. Hurling the trash, she dashed across the lot. "I'm coming!"

With every step, the angry cloud loomed larger. Sam's sugar-soaked clothing lured them like honey. How could she get him to safety?

His face was white. His balled fists trembled by his thighs. "Make them go away," he whimpered.

She slowed to a creep. At close range, the swarm resolved more clearly. No ordinary honeybees, these were yellow jackets. She gritted her teeth. Yellow jackets were mean to the core.

In her periphery, fuzzy outlines of children pointed and stared.

Adults seized them by the shoulders and fled.

A car door slammed.

"What's going on?"

Richard's shout was a million miles away. "It's all right, Sam." She soothed him like a frightened animal. "Just drop those napkins on the ground, okay?"

Globs of matted paper plopped next to Sam's sneakers.

"Bees only get angry when people hit them and make quick movements that scare them. Don't move." The humming grew louder with every step. Her mind whirred at the speed of tiny wings. She wanted to grab him and run, but if she did, she risked crushing countless hornets against his skin.

"Please go away, bees," he said through tears.

"Tessa?" Richard called again.

She drew a long, slow breath and sharpened her focus once more. Sam stood like a miniature soldier, arms stiff at his sides, clothing alive with insects. Where could she grab him without both of them getting stung?

Wait. Yes! He was protected in one place. "Sam, when I say 'go,' lift your arms just a bit—just a little, teensy bit, okay?"

"Okay."

His voice was strangled. His face was red and swollen. How many times had he been stung already? "Ready? Go." As soon as his shoulders twitched, she lunged. Grabbing him under the arms, she swung him into the air.

He shrieked and stiffened.

She tightened her grip and ran.

Riled, the swarm redirected its fury.

With a wicked hum, they shot past her face and thumped into her limbs like buzzing hailstones.

Richard sprinted across the lot. "What happened?"

"Yellow jackets. I think he was stung, but I don't know how many times."

Sam's foot bumped her right thigh, and a white-hot needle seared into her leg. Another pierced tender flesh beneath her upper arm. She gasped. The initial sting was vicious, but as venom seeped under her skin, pain coursed in waves. With an adrenaline-powered surge, she hurtled toward the SUV. Yanking open the rear door, she rolled the sobbing boy inside.

"Keep the bees out of the car." Richard opened the

passenger's side front door and pulled a red-and-black first aid kit from under the seat. "Caitlin, has Sam ever been stung?"

Wide-eyed, Caitlin clambered into the front. "I don't think so."

Fresh panic gripped Tessa around the throat as she shooed away stragglers. "I should have been watching more closely, I—"

"Not now." Richard flung wide the opposite rear door. "I need you."

Abs quaking, she slowed her breathing. "What can I do?"

Wasting no time, he removed a cold pack, a tube of cream, and a blister pack of pills from the kit. "Help me strip his clothes and locate the welts."

As if they had been dressing and undressing wriggling children all their lives, she and Richard removed the boy's shirt and shorts in seconds. She counted stings as they worked. One on his back between his shoulder blades. One on the back of his thigh. Two on his hairline beside his left ear. Another on the meaty part of his hand under his thumb.

Howling, Sam thrashed between them.

Richard cracked the ice pack and handed it to her. "How many do you see?"

"Five so far." Pressing the pack between Sam's shoulders, she lifted his arms and scanned the delicate flesh.

"It's all right, buddy." Richard peeled off Sam's sticky shoes and socks. "You're doing great. We'll give you medicine, so they won't sting so much. Just hold on."

Sam only cried harder, gasping for breath between

sobs. His chest heaved in wheezing wails.

Caitlin peered over the front seat. "He sounds funny."

Tessa lifted the ice pack and pressed an ear to his back. "He does sound funny."

"Take deep breaths, Sam. Like this." Richard demonstrated, lifting his chest in an exaggerated motion. "Try to get quiet inside. I just have to check for stingers."

"Stingers!" Sam shrieked and flailed.

She recoiled just in time to dodge an elbow to the nose.

Richard caught Sam's hand and examined the sting on his palm. "I don't see any so far."

"They were yellow jackets." She ran her hands down Sam's body, stroking his arms and shoulders.

"I don't think they leave stingers," Richard said. "Do you see more welts?"

Turning the boy toward her, she took in Sam's tear-streaked face. His cries became odder—he sounded almost like a seal barking. And he looked odd. At first, she thought he was just red from crying. But no. Darker splotches mottled his forehead and cheeks, and his bottom lip was swollen. "No stings, but Richard—"

"I'll check his scalp." He handed her the tube. "Apply antihistamine cream to the welts."

Eyes bulging and lips convulsing, Sam looked like a fish in a net. A strangled wheeze tore from his throat. Her lungs tightened in response. "Richard, something's not right."

He parted Sam's matted hair. "What?"

"He can't breathe."

"Sam!" Caitlin lunged between the seats.

Tessa shot a restraining hand to the girl's shoulder. "Stay right there, Caitlin."

Richard wrenched the boy to face him, and his eyes widened. "Hand me the first aid kit. Now."

Caitlin snatched the kit from the dashboard where Richard tossed it aside.

"Good girl." Tessa passed the kit to Richard and squeezed Caitlin's hand.

"Should we call my daddy?" Caitlin whispered.

"In a minute," she said.

Richard thrust the sticky clothes at Tessa. "Get these out of here."

Almost before he spoke, she grabbed them and jogged away. A few lingering wasps dive-bombed her face. She swatted them with the bundle, tossed it, and ran. Returning, she discovered Sam curled up on the floor.

He gripped his upper arms with white fingers. "But I don't want a shot," he choked between sobs.

Caitlin peeked through the opening beneath the headrest. "Sam is uncommonly scared of shots."

Richard held a clear, plastic cylinder, about half the length of a paper towel roll. He popped a blue cap and drew out a smaller tube. "He's having an allergic reaction. I need to give him epinephrine before he goes into anaphylactic shock. Get him onto the seat."

His assessment was calmly clinical, but a lump of burning fear rose in her throat. She swallowed it and sprang inside, hauling the boy onto her lap.

"It'll only hurt for a second, Sam." Richard reached across them, gathering the meaty, outer flesh of Sam's left leg in his free hand. Gripping the syringe in his other, he lowered his forearm onto the child's thighs, securing them in place. "I know it's hard, buddy, but stay still." Richard met her gaze and lifted a brow.

Tightening her grip, she nodded her readiness.

He pressed the bright orange end of the epi-pen into Sam's leg, and it clicked.

With his throat too tight to scream, Sam wheezed and stiffened.

As tears splashed onto her forearms, she bent her lips to his ear and quietly sang. "Oh Sam-Sammo" came out to the tune of "Oh Susannah."

"One…two…three." Richard marked the seconds and withdrew the syringe. He slipped it back into the case and then into the first aid kit on the floor.

She kept singing.

In seconds, Sam quieted.

Was it her imagination, or had his breath already eased?

Richard wrapped his fingers around the boy's wrist and moved his lips in a silent count.

Only then did she notice how ashen his cheeks were. Minutes passed.

Finally, Sam shuddered and took a deep breath. He gave a hearty sniff and burrowed into her lap. "That was scary."

Withdrawing his fingers from Sam's pulse, Richard met her gaze. "Thank you."

"I think we better call my daddy," Caitlin said.

Tessa cuddled Sam close, her heartbeat slowing with his. Resting a cheek atop his head, she assessed her own condition. Her clothes were adhered with a combination of sugar and sweat, and her stings hurt more than she cared to say.

But Sam would be all right.

She dropped her eyelids with a sigh. When she lifted them again, she discovered Richard still looking at her. Gratitude and respect shone in his eyes. With Richard by her side, maybe…just maybe…she'd find the courage to face Claire again.

****

"They had no idea Sam was allergic?" Tessa asked, just a few hours later.

Richard signaled and turned off Route 45. "Not a clue."

She dropped her head against the headrest. Her right leg throbbed, but she was loath to complain. After all, she hadn't gone into anaphylactic shock in the Softee Freeze parking lot. "They could have been super mad at us."

"Indeed." Richard glanced sidelong. "But Tyler's a doc. He gets it, and Claire is just a really good person."

They'd met Claire and Tyler at the St. Luke's ER. By the time they arrived, Sam was breathing normally, but his parents took him in anyway. Tyler texted an update from the exam room. Sam's reaction was severe, but thanks to her keen eye and Richard's treatment, the boy would be fine.

In minutes, Claire burst into the waiting room and embraced her. "I don't know how to thank you."

A hot lump rose in her throat. "Oh, Claire, I'm so sorry."

Stepping back, Claire had leveled her gaze. "It wasn't your fault. His allergy was bound to show up sooner or later. I'm just glad he was with you two when it did."

Tessa clutched her backpack and watched her

childhood neighborhood roll by. Just hours earlier, she imagined having kids of her own. Clearly, she wasn't ready. Closing her eyes, she took a shaky breath and chased away the image of Sam gasping for air. She exhaled on a slow count of three. Then again, when the moment of crisis arrived, she met it head-on. Sam got stung on her watch, but because of her quick thinking, he was safe. So, was she ready for a family? Maybe yes. Maybe no. Opening her eyes again, she pointed. "Here's my house."

Richard swung into the driveway.

She glanced at the scarlet welt on her thigh. Running a finger over the raised flesh, she flinched.

"What is it?" he asked.

"Nothing." She tugged down her shorts. *Too late*.

Richard nudged her cuff, revealing the flaming lesion. "Hey, you didn't tell me you got stung."

She straightened her knee and winced. "Actually, I forgot about it until now."

"Are you allergic, too?"

Her leg throbbed in deep, achy surges. She tugged down her shorts. "Not that I'm aware of."

He was out the door and at her side in a millisecond. "Let me take a look."

Forgetting about her second sting, she put out a hand in protest and was harshly reminded. She sighed and extended her arm. "Here, too."

"Why didn't you say something? I'll grab my kit." He reached across her.

Against her bare legs, his chest was firm and warm, and for an instant, the pain subsided. She sank into the seat. How could he still smell like a beachside juice bar after all they'd been through? She was pretty sure she smelled like soft serve and Sam's socks.

Tucking the first aid kit onto the dashboard, he stood. "Turn toward me."

She swung her limbs out the door. "Really, I'm fine."

His gaze traveled up and down her legs before fixing on her thigh. "Very nice."

"Excuse me?" She arched a brow.

"Nice reaction. Textbook." Grinning, he placed a hand on her leg.

She started ever so slightly and blushed. He was a doctor, after all. He couldn't examine her without touching her. With steady but gentle pressure, he pressed the flesh around her sting. His hands were clean, with square nails and wide palms. His head hovered just above her knees, and she had a sudden urge to run her fingers through his hair.

"Are you having difficulty breathing?"

She giggled. "No, doctor."

"Any nausea? Tightness in your throat?"

"Nope and nope."

"I have to ask. You're having a significant allergic response. Let me see your arm."

She pushed up her sleeve. With the same firm but tender touch, he rotated her arm, exposing the delicate skin beneath.

Placing two fingers just above her elbow, he traced a small circle around the welt. "This reaction is more severe. Does it hurt?"

A desire to seem too tough to mind a little old bee sting was overwhelmed by an even stronger yearning to experience Richard's bedside manner. Being his patient made her all gooey inside. "They both kind of throb."

"They'll yell at you for a few hours, no doubt." He rifled through the first aid kit and removed a little square packet. "I gave Sam my last ice pack. Do you have one?"

She nodded.

"Apply it for twenty minutes or so, and then smear on a layer of this cream. Do another round before you go to bed." He handed her the packet.

A fresh current of pain pulsed down her arm. "Thanks."

"I recommend an antihistamine pill, too."

The sound of Sam wheezing looped, unbidden, in her mind. She drove a fist into her lap. "I should never have let him out of my sight."

He caught her hand. "Don't blame yourself. He's all right, and you were a champ."

"Thank goodness you were prepared." She collapsed sideways into the seat. "You carry an epi-pen in your car?"

"Pediatric and adult." He gave a small smile. "My dad gave me that kit. He took his old, leather doctor's bag everywhere. Fully stocked. I think he could have done a tracheotomy on the fly. Mine is a little more up-to-date." Pressing his thumb into her palm, he massaged in a slow circle.

With a soundless sigh, she softened her shoulders.

"He told me never to leave home without it. Not a bad piece of advice." Closing his fingers around hers, he leaned closer. "We made a pretty great team. You were better than some of my nurses. We had a rhythm."

She curled into the seat. Supple contours enveloped her like they were molded to fit her body. "I guess we did."

In his eyes, the admiring spark dimmed to a steady smolder. "Let's get together again soon. And this time not by chance."

"Sure. Definitely." Why was her head spinning? Possibly bee venom?

He stepped back and offered a hand. "I really don't spend that much time in the library."

Reluctant to move, she pressed her shoulder into the seat and heaved upward. He helped her down like she was the Queen of England. Landing with a jolt on her stung leg, she yelped and then shook off the pain with a laugh. Just then, she could have had a root canal without novocaine. His touch was a natural anesthetic.

He gave her hand a quick squeeze. "We'll eat inside like grown-ups. No small children or trips to the ER. A real date. What do you say?"

Dating a doctor was every girl's dream, right? At least in 1964. Even today, to meet a stable and accomplished guy who literally swore an oath to care for other people? Dreamy to the max.

As opposed to, say, dating an Amish carpenter. Sure, his fields were full of fireflies and his eyes shone a color blue so iridescent they could only be truly appreciated by hummingbirds. Still, he wasn't likely to return her call.

Slinging her backpack over one shoulder, she curled her lips in a smile. "You got yourself a deal."

****

Early that evening, the landline rang, echoing down the upstairs hallway to the bathroom. Didn't anyone in this town text? Neck deep in a steaming soak, Tessa stretched long and flinched. Those nasty welts hurt like the dickens. Ignoring the phone, she nestled into the fluffy towel draped over the edge of the tub. Vanilla-scented candles lined the windowsill, wafting a delicious aroma. After this roller coaster of a day, she deserved some pampering.

She could still feel Richard's touch on her thigh—still smell his sunscreen. How could the guy possibly be single? He was such a catch. But, according to a five-year-old with reliable sources, he was. Even more astounding was the fact he wanted to see her again. *Wonders never cease*, as her nana used to say.

The answering machine whirred into action.

"Tessa, honey, I'm calling with a question."

She cringed. Hearing Mrs. Diefenderfer's voice when she was in the bath made her skin crawl.

"Claire and I thought you did such a wonderful job with the celebrity auction—"

Uh oh.

"—that we're just dying for you to work on our Midsummer Ball."

Grabbing the sides of the tub, she yanked herself upright. She hadn't thought about the Midsummer Ball in years. The ball was the only formal event her parents attended regularly and possibly the only one of its kind for miles around. As a child, she loved to sit on their bed and watch them get ready. Usually sporting a batter-streaked apron and jeans, her mother became Cinderella in a flowing gown and sparkly earrings that dripped down the sides of her neck like jeweled waterfalls. Her otherwise tweedy father tugged at the collar of his "monkey suit," but he was always willing to go because her mother enjoyed it so much. Tessa had never attended. The Midsummer Ball was a grown-up affair.

"Claire's just crossing her fingers you'll co-chair the event," Mrs. Diefenderfer went on.

Blinking bathwater from her eyes, she looped an elbow over the tub. Co-chair the ball? With Claire? Though terrifying, the proposition almost sounded fun.

"I know it seems like a lot of work, but co-chairing isn't nearly so much trouble as doing it alone. We've hosted balls so many years now they almost plan themselves. The nuts and bolts are already in motion— save the date cards went out ages ago. Just the fun stuff is left to be arranged."

Vaulting from the tub, she wrapped herself in a towel and dashed down the hall, feet spattering on the hardwood floor. What in the world was she doing?

"You kids really seemed to enjoy yourselves at the auction, so we thought it'd be neat, if you had time. Give me a ring!"

Panting, she lunged for the cordless. "Hello, Mrs. Diefenderfer? Co-chairing does sound neat, and I do have time." The words just leapt out. In one impulsive act, she volunteered at the hospital yet again and, in so doing, dumped all her eggs in the Green Ridge basket. For now, anyway. She clutched the towel and shivered. Crazy as the idea was, it felt right.

"My stars, Tessa?"

"I'd be happy to help."

"Wonderful! Claire will be so pleased. She'll call you real soon to iron out the details."

Water streamed down her legs and pooled on the floor. She tapped her toes in the puddle, making tiny ripples. "Thanks for thinking of me."

"Those pies, honey pie—those were some pies."

She ended the call and wiped the wet handset with

a corner of her towel. Sploshing back to the bathroom, she paused in the doorway. The claw-foot tub was the same pearly white as Richard's smile. Dropping the towel, she slipped into the water and sighed.

She could scrounge up a dress and borrow her mother's earrings…but who'd be her date for the ball?

Chapter 6

Was Tessa hallucinating? Morning sun bounced off the hood of a black SUV, temporarily blinding her. Resting one hand on the garden fence post, she tugged down her baseball cap and peeked out from under the brim. Nope. Not a mirage. Richard's swanky ride was parked in her driveway for the second time in less than twenty-four hours. Moreover, the good doctor himself strode across the lawn, carrying a box of plants. She brushed dirt from her hands and waved. "You're up early on a Sunday morning. What's with all the flowers?"

"Isn't it obvious, my darling? They're for your garden."

Turns out Richard was the kind of guy who could call a woman "my darling" after a brief acquaintance and sound completely natural—like someone out of a 1940s film. Dr. Suave, indeed. She stepped through the gate and met him in the grass. The wide, flat tray in his arms overflowed with foliage. She had a silly impulse to jump up and down. Repressing it, she bounced in place. "They're all for me?"

"You and only you. Just tell me where you want them." He shuffled a half step forward and back again. "Believe it or not, I've never really done this. Gardening. But I don't mind getting my hands dirty. For you."

"I'm flattered." She gestured toward the open gate. "Welcome to my garden." For the new cutting bed, she'd chosen a cottage-style plan with whimsical, curved plots and freeform clumps of flowers. Seedlings sprouted seemingly overnight, promising an abundance of color and fragrance by late summer. Eager to add Richard's plants, she poked among the greenery and selected a four-pack of dahlias from amid snapdragons, zinnias, and cosmos.

Following into the loamy soil, he set the tray at his feet. "The woman at the greenhouse said these are all easy to grow."

She grinned. Richard had yet to discover her pea-green thumb. "I think I can handle them." The dahlias would make beautiful bedfellows for a cluster of teddy bear sunflowers she already planted. Kneeling, she plotted a curved stone path and maybe even a trellis for support. "Thank you, Richard. I can't imagine a nicer gift."

He hovered by the fence, kicking clods from immaculate white sneakers.

"Hand me the trowel, will you?" She pointed to the tool. "That little shovel, for you gardening neophytes."

He shot her a look. "It may not be a surgical implement, but I'm familiar." Without moving his feet, he leaned over and tossed it. "Anyway, I thought you deserved a reward for your heroics. How are those nasty stings?"

"Fine, Doctor. Just a tad itchy."

"They should clear up in a couple days. I'll keep an eye on them, if you'd like."

His expression was all innocence, but the subtext was crystal clear. The guy elevated flirty banter to an art form. Happy to play Katharine Hepburn to his Cary Grant, she quirked a brow. "Such personalized care. Do you do this for all your patients?"

He flashed a smile. "Just the redheads."

"Good policy. Statistically, we're rare."

"You certainly are."

She cleared her throat and eased a dahlia into the soil. "Sam's still okay?"

"Ninety-nine percent himself, according to Tyler."

"What a relief."

He brushed together his hands and examined his palms. "I heard you agreed to co-chair the Midsummer Ball."

Patting the soil around her newest garden baby, she laughed. "News travels fast." She sliced into the earth. "Am I completely insane?"

A breeze tousled his hair, and he shrugged. "If you are, I guess we're both bananas."

"What do you mean?"

"I'm doing it too."

Dahlia in hand, she paused. Did Richard just say he was co-chairing the ball? She nestled the plant in the ground and glanced up. "So, there are three co-chairs?"

He thrust his hands in his pockets. "Nope. Just you and me, kid."

"I don't follow. I thought Claire and I were…" *Claire. Of course.* Claire orchestrated the whole arrangement. Tessa didn't know whether to hug her or hate her—the sensation was already familiar.

Sucking his cheeks, he raised his brows. "Is there a problem?"

"No, no." She quickly dug two more holes. "I was just confused. I thought Claire and I…well—great.

That'll be great."

"I think so too."

In awkward silence, she planted the final two dahlias. A cloud of gnats swarmed her face. She swatted them and stood. Squinting from beneath her hat, she took him in. He was dressed like he just walked out of a menswear catalog. Again. She, on the other hand, wore a faded tank top and threadbare cutoffs, and her knees and shins were smudged with dirt. She tugged the frayed hem of her shorts.

"Are you seeing anyone?" he asked.

"I'm sorry?" Embarrassment skittered up her neck on prickly feet—no doubt leaving a trail of tiny, red footprints.

"Seeing anybody? Dating anyone?"

He leveled his gaze like he just asked a clinical question. Do you have a fever? Where does it hurt? Are you snogging another dude? Laughter bubbled out before she could squelch it.

He shifted his weight and jingled the keys in his pocket. "Is something funny?"

Planted at the edge of her garden in previously spotless running shoes, Richard revealed a hairline fracture in his confidence. Dr. Suave was human, after all. She held out a hand. "Goodness, no. It's just—"

"What?" He smiled.

The crack was sealed. She swept a hand down the front of her cutoffs, raining dirt onto her gardening boots. "No. I'm not seeing anyone."

"Well, as Sam made abundantly clear yesterday, I am also single."

So, Richard had excellent hearing and the ability to monitor two conversations at once. *Noted.* She pressed her lips into a smile. "He mentioned something to that effect."

"Clarity. Good." With a tilt of the head, he beckoned. "Hey, enough with the flowers. Plant them later. Why don't you show me around this gorgeous property?"

"You want a garden tour?"

"Indeed."

She chucked her trowel and tossed her cap over a fence post. Dirty knees and all, she instantly became his classic movie co-star. "I'd love to."

Placing a hand on the small of her back, he accompanied her into the sunlit yard.

Like a proud parent, she showed off her perennial beds and then pointed to a flat, grassy area. "...and that's where I developed my unstoppable badminton skills. So nerdy with a capital 'N.' "

He pulled his phone from his pocket. "I'll have to challenge you to a match."

"Challenge accepted. I'm pretty good. Just sayin'." Leaving behind the more manicured gardens, she escorted him into the wilder play spaces of her childhood. "My tire swing hung from that big oak until a huge storm a few years ago." She scooped up an acorn cap and gestured toward the tree. "This massive limb just snapped off in the wind. My mom sent me pictures. Insane."

He didn't respond.

She glanced over and dropped her arm.

Shoulders hunched, he stood typing on his phone.

The rough-edged cap spun in her fingers. "Do you remember that storm?"

He studied the screen. "Hm?"

"The crazy storm, two or three years ago? I think it was technically an F1 tornado." She paused. Nothing. "Or maybe an F5. Hurled livestock all over town…"

Vigorous typing resumed.

"Our shed landed on a witch. I got a cool pair of shoes, though." One more tappity-tap-tap and she might scream. She bounced the acorn cap off his shoulder. "Paging Dr. Bruce. Come in, Dr. Bruce."

He jerked up his head. "Yes, the tornado. Sorry—hospital stuff. I'm listening."

Would a relationship with Richard be a constant battle for his attention? If she took up arms, would she be bested by a device no bigger than a deck of cards? He lowered the phone into his pocket and patted it like he was putting it to bed.

"Tell me more," he said.

Dark smudges shadowed his eyes. Life and death decisions were his daily stock and trade. He lived every moment under pressures she couldn't imagine. She softened her tone. "Are you sure you have time?"

"Definitely."

Spinning in place, she scanned the yard. "Well, that sycamore is pretty special." She pointed to a towering, smooth-barked tree beyond a copse of spindly pines. Increasingly encroached upon by the upstart conifers, the sycamore had nonetheless grown straight and true, with an expansive canopy of leafy branches. Pushing through pine boughs, she stepped into the shade and laid a hand on the trunk. "My dad planted this tree the year I was born. When I turned ten, he carved all our initials in the bark." She peeked over her shoulder.

Richard lingered among the pines, once again staring at his phone.

Phone—one; Meadows—zero. "I thought you were done."

"Urgent text. One sec." After a long minute pummeling the screen, he glanced up. "Sorry."

She pinned him with an accusing glare. "You haven't heard a word I said."

"I was listening. Tell me more about the trees."

With a huff, she dropped against the sycamore, crossing her arms. "Forget it. I might as well talk to myself."

His shoulders sagged. "Look, I'm sorry about—" He waggled the phone and jammed it in his pocket. "Work is insane. Can you forgive me?"

Leaves stirred in the breeze, and wisps of damp hair tickled the back of her neck. "You mean my boring family stories about landscaping aren't doing it for you?"

"Oh no. All this"—he gestured to the expanse of green—"it's all doing it for me just fine." He ambled closer. "I guess I've been distracted."

In spite of herself, she lifted her cheeks. "Saving lives, huh?"

"I'd like to think so. You know what else I'd like?" Fixing his gaze firmly on her face, he placed one hand on the tree just above her shoulder. "I'd like to see you again."

She struggled to keep her tone as light as the summer air. "I guess we'll meet pretty regularly to plan the ball."

Bending his arm, he angled even nearer. "Not just for the ball…I want to see you."

He leaned into that single word, "you," until her knees buckled. After years of crushing on unattainable fantasy men, had she really met an attractive, available guy? And in her hometown of all places?

He settled his free hand on her waist. "I intend to woo you, my darling."

"Oh, do you?" Her voice, while still breezy, fell an octave where it quivered deep in her chest.

"Mm-hm. I've made it my personal mission to sweep you off your feet."

She breathed him in, and notes of citrus mingled with sunscreen in a scent more intoxicating than any cologne. Lightheaded, she pressed her palms into the tree trunk. "I've got a pretty long way to fall."

He inched closer.

His cheek just barely brushed hers. A coarse curl grazed her temple. She allowed her eyes to drift closed.

"Just let yourself be spoiled. Wouldn't you like that?"

The husky whisper warmed the inside of her ear. Her breath caught in her throat. "I think I would."

He let out a low chuckle. "Well, you just go ahead and think about it."

The teasing rasp of his chin made her giggle. But he just nuzzled closer, his lips tracing a soft line down the side of her neck. Her captive breath escaped on a sigh.

Inhaling deeply, he tightened his fingers around her waist. "Do you always smell this good?"

The words tickled sensitive flesh. She took in a breath to respond, but he slid a foot between hers, and his crisp button-down skimmed her tank, depriving her of speech.

"I wanted to kiss you from the second I saw you. You and your lilacs." He met her gaze. "May I?"

Her feelings refused to be wrangled into coherent sentences. She nodded.

In an instant, he pressed into her, covering her mouth with his own.

The force of his kiss chased the breath from her lungs. She stiffened, but he didn't seem to notice. Rough bark dug into her shoulders, and she swiveled her head to the side, scraping her temple.

Just as quickly, he shifted away, gilding her jaw with kisses.

She drank in sweet, summer air and relaxed again, wriggling at the featherlight touch.

Dropping a kiss atop one shoulder, he trailed fingertips down her arm.

Goose bumps emerged in their wake. She shivered and slid her arms over his shoulders, lifting her lids to meet his gaze. His eyes flashed with simmering intensity, but the expression held a hint of humor.

Taking her hips with both hands, he raised his brows.

She lifted her chin in assent. The kiss was deep and full, tasting of mint and coffee and desire. Bark gouged her back again, and she pulled into him to relieve the pressure. His touch moved from strong to soft and back again, making her head spin. Every moment with this man was a surprise.

A sharp inhalation sliced through their kiss, and he jerked away.

She flinched and opened her eyes. Her hair snagged on a jagged patch of bark, and she tugged it with one hand. Several strands tore away with pinprick stings before she finally freed herself.

With a muffled curse, he stumbled backward,

groped in his pocket, and removed his phone.

The insistent, vibrating whine was like the moan of a sick cow. She wanted to curse the thing too. Or just snatch it and hurl it into the woods.

One swift swipe and he silenced it.

She tightened her ponytail. "Is something wrong?"

Stepping into her again, he placed a finger over her mouth and kissed her around it.

His full lips were gentler now. She stilled.

"Look, I'd like nothing better than to stay here all afternoon." Pulling away, he glanced at his phone and expelled a forceful breath. "But I have to go in today after all. My schedule's a nightmare. I hope you can learn to live with it."

"Richard—"

"I'm sorry." He traced one finger along the collar of her tank top.

The ground beneath her seesawed, and she melted into the sycamore.

His finger slid beneath her tank strap, and he gave a light tug. "I am, however, taking you out this week. We'll have to wait until Thursday, but if you can stand it, I guess I can, too."

So many words coming at her when she was still reeling. What did he say about Thursday? "I-I guess."

"Excellent."

His phone buzzed again.

He groaned. "I've got to go."

Finding her footing between tree roots, she pushed away from the trunk. The scratchy imprint of bark tingled on her shoulder blades.

"Thursday night. Seven thirty. Wear something to show off those shoulders." He took up her hand and kissed it, first on her knuckles and then on the inside of her wrist. "I love your freckles."

She let out an airy laugh. "Thank you."

"No, thank you." He backed away in long, slow strides, pivoted, and disappeared into the pines.

With his scent still lingering, she dropped her head against the sycamore. The heat from his body suffused her skin.

What. Just. Happened?

The unseen SUV roared to life and slid into gear. The hum of tires against gravel flared and diminished. Quiet settled over the backyard, save for the laughing call of a woodpecker and wind whistling through the pines.

Trailing one hand over the tree, she circled it until she found the heart. Her father carved it with his red penknife, gouging the initials JEM and MSM in the middle while she watched. Below the point of the heart and under a plus sign, he etched her initials, TRM. She traced the rough letters with an index finger. The sycamore was her special tree, and Jack and Margaret Meadows loved it more than anything else in their yard.

If only the gazebo could be built beneath the tree. An image of Jonas's face flitted through her mind. She quickly swept it aside. The pine trees were too close. The only space was immediately around the sycamore. He'd have to build it around the trunk.

Wait a second...around the trunk?

She stepped back and peered into the branches. Was it possible? Could Jonas construct a gazebo around the sycamore with the tree the middle? Such a design certainly would be unique. And quite a feat of engineering. If only she could convey her idea on paper.

Sensing she'd finally struck inspiration, she twirled in a happy dance. Artistic skills or no, she'd make her best effort and deliver the design to Jonas. Maybe this week at market…maybe next. After all, Jonas Rishel wasn't praising her freckles and telling her she smelled nice and smooching her senseless in the backyard. She gazed again at the tree, where only minutes ago Richard kissed her in a manner that made her knees rubbery even now.

Dinner on Thursday it was.

Until then, she had a gazebo to design.

****

"Wow." Tessa straightened, and her desk chair let out a squeak. The binder was the size of the *Oxford English Dictionary* and covered half her desk in the hospital volunteer office. Recessed fluorescent lights hummed from the dropped ceiling, illuminating inspirational posters of Alpine mountains and kittens hanging from tree branches. A row of brightly colored, dry erase markers lay end to end beneath a spanking clean whiteboard. She cast her gaze over the massive binder. *The ball almost plans itself, huh?*

"The Bible." Claire genuflected with a grin and pointed to a three-drawer filing cabinet on the far wall. "Oh, and a thousand more files are in there. Happy Monday."

She took a fortifying sip of iced coffee. "Are you serious?"

"As a heart attack." Claire shouldered her bag. "Gotta go sell some houses. If I don't hear from you in a week, I'll send the fire department." With a two-finger salute, she spun on her heels and left.

Tessa flipped open the binder and leafed from one colorful tab to the next, a fizzy bubble of excitement growing in her belly. The Midsummer Ball would require organizational skills and creative energy in a much different way from teaching. She spent three long days combing through files, gaining new appreciation for the scope and depth of the robust volunteer corps' work. Their accounting and record-keeping were meticulous. She had to take her hat off to Mrs. Diefenderfer and the gals. Those ladies weren't messing around.

Exiting the hospital coffee shop, she occasionally caught a glimpse of Richard trailed by a gaggle of interns. Still other times, he was deep in conversation with one of the senior attending physicians, following a step or two behind the older doctor and listening intently. But no matter the circumstance, Richard lit up the drab hospital corridors with a trail of passionate sparks. The man loved his job—he fairly glowed with it—whatever his complaints under the sycamore tree.

When Thursday night arrived, she slipped into ballet flats and gazed into the full-length mirror. After trying on and rejecting several options, she opted for a blousy, cornflower-blue dress. Flats or no, she couldn't conceal her height. Richard stood barely an inch taller than she. Did he mind?

She turned in place and retied the sash around her waist. As requested, the dress was sleeveless, and her square shoulders were on full display. She tapped the bony tops with her fingers. Like her knees and the backs of her hands, they were hopelessly freckled. Well, Richard said he loved her freckles, so she'd take him at his word. She styled her hair in a loose bun, but already a few curls escaped the pins and danced around her temples and the nape of her neck. Tucking up one strand, she stuck out her tongue at her reflection.

The doorbell rang.

As she bounded down the stairs, she tried to remember her mother's trick to avoid smearing lipstick on a glass. Why hadn't she listened to Margaret Meadows more often? At least, she might have been able to bake a pie and avoid making a complete mess of herself in polite company. She checked her reflection in the hallway mirror one last time and unlatched the door.

The grandfather clock in the foyer chimed seven forty-five.

"Sorry I'm late." Richard handed her a single crimson rose. "I was actually on my way out a half hour early when one of my patients crashed." Shaking off a sigh, he smiled. "You look like you walked out of a Merchant Ivory Film. Very *Room with a View*."

The guy knew his movies. Cheeks flushed, she tucked another curl into her bun. "Do you always know the right thing to say?"

"Nearly always." He winked. "I took a class."

"Show off." She ran her gaze over his trim figure.

He wore dark gray pants and a lighter gray dress shirt layered beneath a subtly checked, slate-blue sport coat.

The whole look set off his olive skin beautifully. Was this man ever not completely put together?

He extended an arm. "Shall we?"

"Certainly." She looped a hand through his elbow and stepped into the balmy air. "Where are we going?"

"Judy's. Our reservation is for right now, as a matter of fact. Much as I'd like to stand and admire you, we better get a move on."

"Judy's? How fancy. I haven't eaten there yet, but Claire says it's wonderful."

"Only the best, my darling."

One of the surgeons' wives converted a charming Victorian home into downtown Green Ridge's newest eatery, luring a chef all the way from Philadelphia. Climbing the steps to the entrance, she recalled the house was previously a drab insurance agency. When she passed through the arched, wooden doors, all traces of the building's former identity vanished from memory. The home, it seemed, was always destined to be a restaurant.

He paused at the hostess stand and gestured to the candlelit dining room. "You like?"

With lofty ceilings and plush furnishings, the design evoked Victorian luxury with a modern sensibility. "Very much."

"After you."

The hostess led them to a secluded table near an ornate, mahogany fireplace.

"Allow me." Richard pulled out her chair.

"How gallant." She was a modern woman, but she had to admit she appreciated the courtesy. "So, chivalry isn't dead?"

"Not on my watch." He took a seat across from her. "Listen." He cocked his head and pointed at a speaker in the ceiling. "Billie Holiday. They must have known I was coming."

For all his love of modern technology, Richard was surprisingly old school. She rested her chin in her hands. "So, you're a jazz man?"

He unfolded a linen napkin and laid it in his lap.

"Aficionado. I can't carry a tune in a bucket. You?"

"I'm a folk-rock girl. I don't know much about jazz, but this?" She lifted her chin toward the ceiling. "Jazz with singing and a melody? Very nice." Dropping the napkin in her lap, she opened the menu and glanced over the seasonal offerings, all prepared with local, farm-fresh ingredients. Her stomach growled in a most unladylike manner, but, fortunately, the sound was masked by saxophones.

The server approached with a resplendent basket of rolls.

"Good evening, Charles. We'll start with a bottle of Bordeaux." Richard caught her gaze. "Do you like steak?"

"I do."

"Thank goodness—a woman who actually eats." He cleared his throat. "The lovely lady and I will have Judy's Special Filet, medium rare."

Spine stiffening, she lurched against the chair back. Did he just order for her? She barely had time to look at the specials. Widening her eyes, she lifted the menu in unspoken question. He didn't appear to notice.

"Any appetizers, sir?" the server asked.

"Are the mussels fresh tonight?"

"As always, Dr. Bruce."

"That'll be fine."

With a nod, Charles collected the menus and left.

Richard extracted his phone from an inside jacket pocket.

Watching his thumbs fly across the screen, she gaped, utterly struck dumb. He did just order for her. Moreover, he ordered mussels. Apparently, he was too preoccupied to clock her flaming face and wide-open mouth. So, she buttered a roll and took a hearty bite.

Instantly, Charles reappeared with wine and poured Richard a taste.

Swirling the ruby liquid, he sniffed the bouquet and sipped. "Very nice."

On cue, Charles filled both goblets and disappeared.

Richard raised his glass. "To celebrity auctions and Midsummer Balls…" He met her gaze, and his words dissipated. "What's wrong? Is it the phone? I'm sorry, but I'm still dealing with that patient. Here, look, I'm done." He slid the device into his jacket.

She twisted the napkin in her lap. "You ordered for me."

"You said you liked steak."

"Yes, but I didn't say I wanted to *eat* steak. Will you cut my vegetables, too?"

"If you'd like." He laughed. "God, you're gorgeous when you're mad. I'd have ordered a whole cow if I knew it would have this effect."

She yanked the napkin tighter. "I'm serious."

"So am I." Eyes darkening, he took her hand under the table and uncoiled the napkin from around her pinky finger.

At his touch, she tensed.

Trumpets took over the melody of "All of Me," and the lights dipped low.

She exhaled long and slow. Did she really want to make a fuss? Maybe…the scallop risotto looked delicious.

Finger by finger, he unwrapped the napkin until, with a final tug, it fell into her lap. Lifting her hand atop the table, he enclosed it in his. "Please don't be angry. I thought you agreed to let me take care of you."

An abundant mass of fresh flowers cascaded from the mantle, trailing down the side of the fireplace in delicate tendrils. She breathed in the scents of freesia and fresh bread. Without a doubt, this date was the most romantic of her life. She couldn't even remember the last time a guy arranged such a special event. Maybe ordering her meal took chivalry a step too far. But Judy's was clearly his place—he was on a first-name basis with the server, for Heaven's sake. Why ruin the evening over steak?

Shifting in her seat, she crossed and uncrossed her legs. "I'm sorry. You just surprised me, I guess." She let her head dip to one shoulder. "Honestly, I don't even know how to eat mussels." A smile crept into his eyes, but he had the courtesy not to laugh.

"If you like, I'll call back Charles—"

"No, no."

"You use a little fork. For the mussels. I'll show you." He brushed his lips across her knuckles. "New foods can be exciting."

"I know." A bitty shiver danced up her arm, but still, she tugged away in gentle protest and refolded the napkin in her lap. "Can I at least order my own dessert?"

Tenting his fingers, he rested his elbows on the table and gazed over his hands. "You can do whatever you like, Ms. Meadows."

She sipped her wine, savoring the rich, plummy flavor, and her belly warmed. "I'm sorry."

"Stop apologizing. It's forgotten."

After Charles cleared the last of the dinner plates and scraped breadcrumbs onto a half-moon, silver tray,

Richard leaned back and patted his belly.

With the heaviness of a meal in her stomach and the haze of Bordeaux softening the night, she rested her chin in her hands. "You were right. The steak was heavenly."

"What's the verdict on mussels?"

"Slimy, but delicious. I loved the bread dipped in that briny broth." She made a low sound of satisfaction. "You know, your plants are very happy in my garden. Thank you again for delivering them."

"My pleasure."

"You really didn't have to."

He divided the last of the wine between their glasses. "Oh yes, I did. I couldn't count on bumping into you again, and I quite frankly don't have time to stalk you. I decided to take matters into my own hands."

A thrill flittered in her chest like a canary. Of all the gals in good old Green Ridge, Dr. Richard Bruce chose her. Dipping her chin, she gazed from beneath her lashes. "Well, they are capable hands."

He lifted his glass and smiled. "You have no idea."

She walked right into that one. Her witty banter was definitely dulled by drink. She lowered her lashes and ran a finger along the edge of her napkin. The seam tickled, and the tiny bird near her heart fluttered in response.

"Are you sure you want dessert?" he asked.

Placing both palms on the table, she glared. "Absolutely."

"As you wish. But let's order and get out of here. I can't wait to get you back to my place."

She gulped ice water and prayed her ability to walk

would remain intact.

The molten lava cake was decadently rich. She tried to make it last, but she couldn't. Forcing herself to savor the final creamy forkful, she licked her lips with languid pleasure.

Richard didn't notice. He downed his cobbler in two bites and, with a quick word of apology, again extracted his phone.

She dropped her fork onto the plate with a louder-than-necessary clang.

He glanced up and popped the phone into his coat. Mission accomplished.

"Good lord, I thought you'd never finish." He waved to Charles for the check.

"Don't you want to linger over coffee?" She raised a brow. "Maybe cappuccino?"

He narrowed his eyes. "Very funny."

"No? Ready to go?" With a teasing grin, she slid her purse from the back of the chair. "I suppose I don't have a chance of taking the check."

"My invitation. My treat." He slipped a thick, black credit card into the bill pocket. "Chivalry, remember?"

"How could I forget?" The twilit walk to Richard's apartment in another of the stately Victorian homes on Main Street was a few short blocks. As he leaned to unlock the door, he brushed her shoulder with his in a kiss of fabric on bare skin. An electric shiver twitched across her collarbones.

"Ladies first."

She stepped just inside the living room.

He tapped a digital tablet embedded in the wall, and instantly, every floor and table lamp swelled to a golden glow.

The room seemed to beckon her inside. "What is this, witchcraft?"

He laughed. "I just had the place renovated. It may be old, but it's a smart house now."

"It's gorgeous." Sleek, modern lines seamlessly blended with the structure's Victorian bones. The place would have done a design catalog proud—right down to the funky, metal staircase in the corner. "I love the spiral stairs."

"I had it made by a small, family-owned company near Philly. It really opens up the space. The master and home office are upstairs." He hung his keys on a hook by the door. "Arwen, play Swing Mix."

A jazzy tune kicked up from a hidden speaker.

"Arwen?" She swallowed a giggle. "Your nerd is showing." Did a faint blush pinken the tips of his ears?

"I couldn't just call her 'Computer,' could I?"

"Not unless you're captain of *The Enterprise*." She stepped onto the plush carpet.

Down to the smallest detail, his place was as well-curated as her former faculty apartment was not. A mid-century sofa and armchair flanked a Victorian fireplace, painted jet black and filled with chunky pillar candles. Artfully arranged photographs and an assortment of antique cameras adorned the mantle. Old Dr. Bruce smiled broadly from a silver frame, an arm thrown around his cap-and-gown-clad son.

She crossed to towering windows bordered by potted fiddle leaf figs. An antique, cherry rocking chair with a wide, cane seat angled toward her, somehow fitting perfectly into the mélange of old and new decor. Sensing he was as proud of his apartment as she was of her gardens, she gestured toward the rocker. "That's a great chair." He smiled, but his gaze held a hint of sadness.

"It's a nice piece, isn't it? I put most of my parents' things in storage when my father died, but I couldn't part with Dad's chair. He spent hours rocking and listening to jazz on vinyl."

She ran a hand over the curved wood. "The carving is exquisite."

"I'll take you on the grand tour later." He nodded toward a well-stocked bar cart. "Can I get you a drink?"

"I'm good for now, thanks. Is there a little girl's room in this bachelor pad?"

He pointed down the hall.

"Be right back." The narrow passageway led to the rear of the house, ending in a state-of-the-art kitchen. She peeked inside. Even the fridge was equipped with a touch screen. Unsurprising, but impressive.

Safely ensconced in a spotless half bath, she splashed cool water on her cheeks and peered into the mirror. Shimmering droplets clung to her eyelashes.

He ordered her meal. She ate it, and it was delicious. He just assumed she'd come back to his house. She came, and his home was welcoming. Whatever happened next, odds were if she said yes, the night would turn out…agreeably. Right? Blinking, she tucked her bra strap under her collar. If only she knew what she wanted to happen. Honestly, in that moment, she wasn't sure.

Richard, on the other hand, rarely displayed a flicker of uncertainty. The guy was confidence on a stick. So, what did he have in mind for the rest of the evening? She slid the pins from her hair and let it tumble around her shoulders. *For once in your life, why not just go with the flow?* And if the flow led up that spiral staircase to the second floor? She took a deep breath and ran both hands through her curls. One step at a time.

Pausing in the hallway, she took in the gallery wall of artwork and photographs. Adjacent to a watercolor print of Yale University was a column of snapshots, all framed in black. The top one showed Richard rowing crew on a wide river. Thus, his broad shoulders and athletic build. Another shot featured him and a bunch of college guys clowning around with a surfboard on a white sand beach.

She nibbled the inside of her cheek. Peeping into scenes from Richard's past without him present felt a wee bit like prying. She glanced into the living room. He leaned one shoulder on the mantle, typing on his phone. Tacit permission granted. She returned to the photos.

In the bottom picture, he appeared somewhat older. She bent to examine it. A group of young people in skiwear posed beside a chairlift fronting endless, snowcapped mountains. His arms wrapped around the waist of a pretty brunette, Richard grinned from the back row. Tucked under his chin, the girl smiled broadly, her features painting a picture of perfect contentment. Chatting in her garden on Sunday, Richard asserted his single status without even a whiff of hesitation. So, who was this woman? And where was she now? An icy stone landed with a plunk in Tessa's belly.

Trumpets swelled from the living room.

Nah. Richard might be a hair pushy, but he was not the type to two-time a woman. Integrity oozed from every pore of his body.

"You coming?" he called.

She hurried to join him.

Tossing his coat on the couch, he met her with a flawless spin. "Let's dance." He grabbed her hand and twirled her from one arm to the other.

Mid-twirl, she caught her foot on a chair leg and tripped into his arms. "What are you doing?"

"Dancing, darling." He launched her across the floor and pulled her back with one easy gesture.

She giggled like a thirteen-year-old. "I can't dance. I'm all feet."

"Are you kidding?" He placed her left hand on his shoulder and clasped her right in his. His other arm snaked around her waist. "You're a pro."

Horns blared as they stood, eye to eye, in the middle of his living room. His cheeks were as flushed as hers felt. He shifted his weight, and she swayed with him, joining in a gentle side to side rock.

He swiveled, bringing them closer to the spiral staircase. "Listen, I have this great idea for the ball. How about a Fabulous Forties theme? We'll hire a swing band and everything. People can come in vintage clothes—maybe recruit professionals to lead the dancing—and you, my dear, will be the belle of the ball."

Relaxing into the rhythm, she barked a laugh. "I'm way too tall to be swung."

"Never." With his gaze locked on hers, he glided them to the windows. "Some friends and I took swing dancing in med school. It's not hard."

She flashed to the brunette in the picture and tightened her grip on his shoulder. Richard was in her arms now. "Is there anything you don't do?" Her voice dripped honey.

"Darling, there ain't nothin' I don't do." He urged her close.

So close his pager pressed against her hips. At least, she thought it was his pager. Did doctors still use pagers? She flicked her gaze downward. Apparently so. And with the next trumpet swell, she cut a rug.

He twirled her across the floor and back into his arms. "Don't think. And, for God's sake, don't stare at your feet. Just feel the music."

In a wine-hazy whirl, she spiraled, sure-footed and weightless. With a gentle nudge of his thigh—the slightest pressure on her back—he guided her through every step, making her believe, just for a moment, she could dance like Ginger Rogers. Surrendering to the dizzying rush, she threw back her head and closed her eyes, and when the music slowed to a quiet ballad, she knew she would follow this man anywhere. Up that spiral staircase if he asked.

Frank Sinatra crooned "My Sweet Embraceable You," and Richard gathered her in his arms.

Heart pounding, she dropped her head onto his neck, and her cheek slid against the salty sheen of their exertion.

"This is what we call 'slow dancing,' " he said.

"Oh yeah? Is that that what they taught you in med school dance class?"

"Me and Baryshnikov, baby, that's what we insiders call it."

With his lips soft against her cheek and his voice low in her ear, her insides turned as molten as the lava cake.

"Are you glad you came?" he asked.

She raised her head. "Yes."

"Do you think you might like to stay a while?"

She slid her gaze to a metal bookcase so skillfully styled that medical texts and a cactus garden looked like sculpture. "I think so," she said on a breath.

"I'm sorry? I didn't quite hear you."

She looked him in the eyes and nodded.

He lifted his lips in an answering smile. "I'm so glad." Lowering his mouth a fraction of an inch, he kissed her.

He tasted of Bordeaux and blackberries, and she sighed, parting her lips.

With a soft moan, he ran his hand up her back and into her hair, entwining her curls in his fingers. "You let your hair down," he whispered.

His tongue sought hers with a hot urgency that matched the fire in her core. "Mm-hm," she murmured. "I like."

Rock-hard thighs pressing against hers, he coaxed her closer. She closed her eyes and gave in to his embrace—the night and the music as heavy and soft as a velvet blanket…

Until with a scream, an alarm splintered the air like it was made of glass.

Every muscle in her body seized. She covered her ears and staggered backward, slamming a shin against a marble-top end table. Was it a fire alarm? A tornado siren? No, the sound was too painfully close for that.

He growled and fumbled at his belt. "Not again." He silenced the alarm and crammed the beeper back in its holder. "I'm sorry, I have to answer this."

She raised her hands to her face. Her cheeks singed

her fingertips. "Of course."

He located his phone in the inside pocket of his discarded coat. Without looking at her, he pecked her cheek and hurried down the hall toward the kitchen.

Dropping into the armchair, she rolled her head to ease the spasm in her shoulders. Were all beepers that loud? Or did Richard just have the latest high-tech, supersonic model? If the pitch were any higher, it would only be perceptible to dogs. She was amazed the mirrors didn't shatter.

The knob on her shin throbbed. How did anyone get used to that screech waking them in the night? Or killing the spirit on Christmas Eve? More to the point, could she get used to it? Or would the sound and the subsequent disruption of her life eventually drive her bonkers?

The distant mumble of conversation ceased, and he returned.

His face was drawn and his features sharp. She understood without a word their dancing was done for tonight.

"Judge McCracken, the patient I monitored all evening—he just crashed. They had to page me when I didn't pick up my phone. I knew I should have kept it on me." He shoved the end table back into place.

"I didn't even hear it ring."

"That makes two of us." He shrugged into his coat with a grunt. "I know I've been preoccupied tonight. The judge was my father's best friend. When I left, I thought he was stable."

"I didn't know doctors still had pagers."

He let out a laugh. "You better believe we do. Cell service stinks out here in the boonies."

"Of course." She pulled herself from the chair.

"Damn it." He clenched a fist against his forehead.

She laid a hand on his arm. "It'll be all right." Immediately regretting her words, she let her hand fall. He was a doctor. He knew. Sometimes, people were never all right again.

He lifted one shoulder and let it drop. "I'm sorry to cut short our evening."

"Don't be sorry. I understand."

He drew up close and took her by the shoulders. "I can't tell you how much I want to come home to you tonight, but I could be gone for hours."

His hands were gentle, but his voice was rough.

He released her and strode to the wall-mounted tablet.

The lights and music faded—and with them, their date. She hugged herself, running her fingers over her upper arms.

"Come on. I'll drop you off on my way to the hospital."

Late that night, she tucked rainbow sheets under her chin as the walls and ceiling revolved around her. Moonlight streamed through the open window and lit the red, orange, and yellow stripes with a bluish tinge. She closed her eyes against the vertigo, but her bed dipped like a slow-motion funhouse ride.

Duty called before Richard could invite her upstairs—before she had a chance to say yes. Or no. When she was in his arms, woozy with the nearness of him, she felt like that decision had been made. But had it?

She rose to her knees and wrenched wide her window. Resting her forearms on the sill, she gazed over the yard. Night air stirred the curtains, and she lifted her chin to the cool.

Richard was available. Maybe every kiss would be interrupted by a summons from the hospital, but he was there—wanting to kiss her. Boxes of flowers, fine wine, and dancing lessons...the guy could teach a master class in wooing.

She hummed a few bars of "My Sweet Embraceable You" and eased back onto her pillow. He was wooing all right. She simply had to decide to be won.

Chapter 7

A tourist's guide to New York City hurtled across the living room and skidded under an armchair. A second one slammed into the wall and fell to the floor with a thud.

Kicking aside a splayed-out street map, Tessa flattened herself and peered into the dusty no-man's-land under the couch. Where the heck was her phone?

It rang again, drowning out the sound of the television.

Since her date with Richard last week, she kept her phone ringer set to high. She certainly didn't have a pager, and she didn't want to miss him when he reached out next. Still, the deafening ringtone did her no good when she couldn't actually find the darned thing.

She tossed aside the crocheted afghan on the couch. Success! Hitting pause on the remote, she froze the host of the Travel Network's *Mysteries of the Big Apple* just as he bit into a cannoli. "Hello?"

"Are you free?"

"Well, good morning, and how are you too, Dr. Bruce."

"I'll take that as a yes." He cleared his throat. "I have an hour. Can I take you to lunch?"

The brusque greeting rubbed her the wrong way. She hadn't heard from him in three days—hadn't seen him since their date last week—and travel books littered the floor. Nudging them into a pile with one foot, she blew out a breath. "Now?"

"I'll be there in five."

A note of impatience crept into his voice. He was in hospital mode. No time for courtesy, apparently. "Wait, where are we going?"

"It's a surprise."

She glanced at her cutoffs and State University tee. "Do I need to dress up?"

"No. But that's all you're getting." He chuckled, and his tone softened. "I can't wait to see you."

Tapping the screen to end the call, she let him off the hook. Judge McCracken's condition had stabilized but not improved, and Richard was working longer hours than usual. Arriving at the hospital in the morning, she often spotted his car in the same spot as the night before. He went home to sleep, right?

After a week in the volunteer office researching bands, dancers, and more for the newly christened "Swing into Summer Midsummer Ball," she'd hit up the town library in preparation to visit Jenn. Plenty of tourist information was available online, but she loved the feel of a glossy travel book. Unlike Richard, Jennifer texted several times each day, pestering her with a hilarious parade of off-color memes. She couldn't postpone her trip much longer.

She switched off the TV, took the stairs two by two, and pulled a sundress from her closet. Casual or no, she hated appearing anything less than put together around Richard. She had just applied a light sheen of lip balm and grabbed her backpack when the SUV rolled into the driveway. He laid on the horn, and she raced out the door. Breathless and flushed, she bounded into the front seat.

"Hello, gorgeous."

His kiss was cool and minty. Not a bad welcome. "What a nice surprise. I was beginning to wonder if you'd ever escape the hospital."

"Yet here I am, unscathed."

She dropped her backpack at her feet. "Where are we going?"

Draping an arm over the back of her seat, he twined his fingers in the little curls escaping her messy bun. "You'll see."

She pooched her bottom lip. "I changed my mind. I hate surprises."

Chuckling, he massaged a gentle circle into the notch at the base of her skull. "I'll give you one hint. They don't serve mussels."

"Rats." She sighed. "I brought my tiny fork for nothing."

The SUV nosed onto Route 45, heading west toward the roadside stand where she gathered intel just a few weekends before. Speeding by, she strained for a glimpse of Esther King. The woman perched behind the cash register, cooling herself with a paper church fan. The afternoon was a classic "three H" scenario as the Pennsylvania weathermen were fond of saying: hazy, hot, and humid. Despite the air-conditioning, perspiration trickled between her shoulder blades.

Just beyond the stand, Richard veered onto a winding, back road.

She knew these roads so well she could drive them blindfolded. No restaurants of any kind stood in their path. She shot him a glance. "Where are you taking me?"

He bumped the radio and shook his head. "What's that? I can't hear you over this crazy rock-and-roll music!" Beaming, he drummed his hands on the steering wheel and bobbed his chin to the beat.

His entire demeanor radiated smug satisfaction—a welcome sight after the sudden and tense end to their date. She grinned and sank into the seat. *Might as well enjoy the ride.*

He skirted fields and farms, driving deeper into the country until he stopped at a crossroads.

Through the tinted windshield, she spied two of her favorite old buildings. To her left loomed a behemoth, gray barn with a stone foundation and a red tin roof. Though the boards looked old and weathered, the structure stood strong, a faithful companion to the house across the street.

Seeing that house again was like running into an old friend. Out of place among the neighboring shiplap and brick homes, it was shaped like a farmhouse but constructed like a log cabin. The exterior walls were made of massive, squared beams, stacked one atop the next and interspersed with thick, white mortar. Dark red shutters bordered multi-paned windows, topping window boxes bursting with geraniums. The simple front porch lacked the intricate woodwork of her own home, but it was inviting in its rustic simplicity. Smiling, she tapped her knuckle on the window. "I love this house."

"What?" he shouted over the radio.

She clicked off the music. "This house. It's so unusual. I love it."

"Ah, the Lincoln log cabin—that's what I always called it." He leaned over the steering wheel and peered through the windshield. "Do you know it has a covered bridge on the property?"

Covered bridges turned regular old creeks into enchanted, storybook streams. Her favorite house just became cooler. "No way."

"Way. My father used to come out here on house calls, believe it or not. The woman who owned the place was one of my grandfather's patients, and she expected it, I guess. I don't think a single doctor at St. Luke's now has ever made a house call."

She squinted for a peek in the windows, but the glare obscured her view. "Have you been inside?"

Flicking the blinker, he turned back toward town. "Oh, sure. I was just little—six or seven, maybe—but I'd ride along with my father and carry his bag." He drummed his fingers on the wheel again. "Mrs. Raffensburger had Parkinson's, I realize now. She seemed ancient then. I wonder if she's still alive. I wasn't often allowed inside, so usually, I wandered off—that's how I found the bridge. It was just a little, covered footbridge over a stream, but I thought it was pretty neat."

"Very neat. What's the house like inside?"

He scratched his head and combed back his hair with his fingers. "Old. I don't remember much except a huge stone fireplace with a heart-shaped rock right under the mantle. That rock was cool. You like the place, huh?"

"I've loved it for years." She swiveled and watched the house disappear around a bend. Along the road, masses of Queen Anne's lace bowed in their wake. She never told anyone she was drawn to this house. What a funny coincidence Richard had actually been inside.

"I'm looking forward to the day I buy a house like that." He chuckled. "There's a sentence I never thought would come out of my mouth."

His tone was edged with vinegar. She faced him again. "Here in Green Ridge?"

"That's the million-dollar question." He snorted a sigh. "I don't know. The plan was never to end up in the middle of nowhere, you know what I mean?"

Her bittersweet laugh echoed his. "All too well." So, Richard felt trapped in Green Ridge too. Maybe they had more in common than she realized.

"But for better or for worse, I'm still at St. Luke's, and I can't imagine leaving. When my father died, Claire helped me sell the house. I couldn't live there after everyone was gone—too many memories. Someday, I'll buy a place like Mrs. Raffensburger's, but I'll gut it and update the whole interior." He ran a hand over his stubbled chin. "Maybe someday soon."

She waited, but he didn't elaborate.

He just stared at the road ahead.

This road was also familiar. It was extremely familiar. Her breath snagged in her throat. Was today Wednesday?

He swung into the bustling Farmers' Market parking lot.

"The market?" She pulled her backpack into her lap and hugged it tight. "Why the scenic route?"

"I wanted to maintain an element of surprise. From the look on your face, I'd say I succeeded." He grinned. "With my crazy schedule, I haven't been to the market for weeks. It's nothing fancy, but how would you like a hot dog and a bag of world-famous fries?"

Cruising past the line of buggies, she ran her teeth

over her bottom lip. Her stomach rumbled but with burbling nerves, not hunger.

He squeezed her knee and unlocked the doors. "Sound good?"

"Sure." Her voice wobbled. Did he notice? She unzipped her backpack and rooted for her shades, forestalling the inevitable and praying again for anonymity. She snatched her sunglasses from an inside pocket. Could she claim a hot dog allergy? A crippling fear of crowds? *Get yourself together and go eat fries like a normal person.*

He swung open his door and swiveled back. "Now, you like hot dogs, right? You know how to eat them?"

His tone was teasing, but his eyes shone like a puppy's. "See, I knew that tiny fork would come in handy." She slipped on the sunglasses and smooched his cheek. "Thank you for my surprise lunch."

He sprang from the car and opened her door before she zipped her backpack.

Taking his outstretched hand, she followed him through the door closest to the Rotary Club's hot dog stand, the centerpiece of the whole market. Occupying nearly every inch of the lunch counter, the noontime crowd happily munched frankfurters and sausage sandwiches. The combined odors of frying onions and sweaty bodies descended like greasy fog. She scrunched her nose, praying they'd take their dogs on the road.

However, the town's favorite young doctor was ceded a prime spot, and he escorted her to the counter. He leaned on one elbow and crossed his legs. "Ms. Meadows, would you be so kind as to rustle up hotdogs while I fetch fries? That is, if you don't mind ordering on my behalf?"

She shot him a look. "You'll never let me live that down, will you?"

"Not in a million years."

"Fine. How do you want it?"

"Surprise me." With a wink, he knocked twice on the counter and vanished into the crowd.

After ordering two dogs with sautéed onions and a couple of sodas, she settled in to wait.

An old lady grazed her ankles with the wheels of a fully laden cart.

Recoiling, she inched closer to the counter. The jam-packed market was a claustrophobic's nightmare. Thank goodness she towered over eighty percent of the crowd. She could breathe, anyway. Heck, if she were so inclined, she could look over the sea of shoppers to the stalls at the end of the building. Say, just for the sake of argument, to Rishels' Farm Stand.

She'd carried the gazebo drawing in her backpack for close to two weeks. Sure, she was with Richard. So what? This unexpected visit was the perfect opportunity to deliver her design to Jonas. Provided he was there too, of course.

She didn't want to look.

She was dying to look.

Sliding the shades into her hair, she came up on tiptoes…and looked.

As Jonas was also uncommonly tall, she easily eyed him, ducking in through the door with a tray of pies. She spotted Rebecca, too, jumping up and down and flapping her hands like a wee birdie. No sign of Nora, but she knew with stone-cold certainty the woman was on the premises. Was that an icy breeze wafting from the whoopie pies? No way would Nora send Jonas to market alone.

Why did Jonas work at the market anyway? Didn't he have fields to plow and hen houses to build? A few Amish men oversaw stands, but they were typically older men or boys. She gazed around the place. Not another thirty-something Amish guy in sight. Sure, Nora's mobility was limited—she had that mysterious limp. But why wasn't she accompanied by a cousin or a sister? Why Jonas?

Oily smoke rose in plumes from the grill. She felt like one of the sausages sizzling on its surface. Grabbing a wad of napkins, she blotted her forehead.

Jonas swiped his brow with the back of a hand.

He had to be boiling in heavy pants and a long-sleeved shirt. Unpleasant attire for current conditions. Fact: heat made people grumpy. Conclusion: she didn't dare present him her crazy design. A gazebo wrapped around a tree? Ridiculous. He would laugh her out of town. Trees grow. Roots rise. Limbs fall to the ground in storms. Her idea would never work.

She unzipped her backpack and peeped at the drawing. Despite her limited artistic abilities, she put a lot of effort into the sketch, and it conveyed her idea well. The concept was unique. Perhaps even inspired? Maybe Jonas wouldn't laugh. After all, the whimsical gate he built was almost out of place at the entrance to Nora's utilitarian garden.

Except, of course, that it wasn't out of place. It was perfect.

Richard plunked a jumbo container of fries on the counter. "I hope you got onions."

With a smirk, she slid over his loaded hot dog.

"See, I don't get angry when you make decisions for me," he said.

"Not when they're the right ones, anyway." She passed him a soda.

He sampled the hot dog and groaned. "Even better than Fenway Park—and that's saying something."

Courage waning, she scarfed her dog in four bites, downed half the fries in two, and glanced at her watch. "Okey dokey. We should get you back to work, Dr. Saint-Luke's-Would-Grind-To-A-Halt-Without-Me." She'd give Jonas her design another time…without Richard.

He checked his phone. "Just enough time to pick up a pie."

"A pie?" The utterance emerged as more of a squeak than a word.

With a slurp, he polished off his soda. "Tyler's in-laws are coming tonight. Our mission, if we choose to accept it, is to acquire one of those shoofly pies you brought to the auction. Don't know about you, but I never turn down a mission."

"Oh…" She tossed her nearly empty cup toward the trashcan and missed. "That stand is way down at the other end—it'll take forever to fight the crowds. Look, that vendor right there has pies."

Humming the *Mission Impossible* theme song, he scooped up her cup and dunked it along with his own. "Nope. If I don't come back with the right pie—and believe me, Claire will know the difference—she'll be disappointed. Ain't nobody wants to see that happen. They'll get divorced. I'll get fired." He grabbed her hand. "My future's at stake, my dear."

She slung her backpack over one shoulder and

forced a smile. The hot dog and fries heaved in her stomach. Why was she so nervous? Jonas would see her hold hands with Richard. Richard would see her give the design to Jonas. No big deal.

Then why were her palms so sweaty?

Rebecca spotted her first. She tugged her uncle's pants and pointed.

Jonas met her gaze and smiled broadly.

She blushed all the way to her ears. Just what she needed—blazing lobes.

"Tessa!" Rebecca called.

"You're on a first-name basis with them?" Richard said under his breath.

She waved. "As you might recall, I bought a ton of pies."

Checking his phone, Richard picked up the pace.

Rebecca tapped Jonas on the arm. He bent, and she whispered in his ear.

With a glance, he stood, and an invisible veil descended over his face. Dropping Richard's hand, she wiped her palms down the front of her sundress. "Hello, Jonas."

He inclined his head in greeting.

Not a man to waste words. She snugged her backpack tight to her shoulders.

Richard cleared his throat.

She started. "Oh, I'm sorry. Jonas, this is my friend, Richard Bruce. Jonas Rishel." The men clasped hands in what appeared to be a very strong handshake. The little muscle in Jonas's jaw fluttered, and Richard's knuckles went white. She shifted her gaze between them. Two men who still made a living by their hands, yet they couldn't have been more different.

"Tessa tells me this is the place for pies," Richard said.

Rebecca peeked from behind her uncle. "My mother bakes the best pies in the county. Everyone says so."

"Good thing we found you. We want the very best." Richard smiled. "Which do you recommend?"

The girl beamed. "All of them."

Tessa's belly warmed. For a guy so comfortable in the grown-up world, Richard sure had a way with kids.

"Do you think you could show me a few? Maybe a shoofly?" he asked.

Rebecca nodded. "This one is lemon sponge…" She led Richard down the table, naming each flavor as she went.

Releasing her breath, Tessa looked back to Jonas. His gaze was steady on her, his expression absolutely inscrutable. A lump, like a glob of sticky hot dog bun, lodged on her vocal cords. Wishing she hadn't tossed that soda, she coughed and cleared her throat. Why was this encounter so awkward? She was attracted to Jonas, but she was dating Richard.

Boom. She said it. To herself anyway. "Oh, I have something for you."

He crossed his arms. "Have you thought about your gazebo?"

Nodding, she swung off her backpack and extracted the sketch. Two weeks in her bag hadn't done it any favors. She smoothed the wrinkles against her legs and held it out. The paper fluttered between them, and she cursed her quivering fingers. "I'm not much of an artist. It's just an idea." She swatted at nothing. "Probably completely impractical."

He ran a hand over the back of his neck and studied the drawing for a long moment.

The hot dog and soda churned in her stomach. She pressed a palm to her midsection. Finally, he looked up, and his eyes were twin pools of liquid sapphire.

"It's beautiful."

Her heart leapt with such force she feared it might fly out of her mouth. "Really? Thank you."

"I'll need to come see the building site. Take some measurements. You have a particular tree in mind?"

His tone was all business. She nodded.

He shifted his gaze.

Out of the corner of her eye, she spied Richard approaching, shoofly pie in hand. "How soon can you come?"

"Tomorrow if you'd like."

"Great." Her mind raced. How would he get to her house? Would he drive his buggy? Where would he park the horse? "How will you…I mean…how should we make the arrangements?"

"Come by the farm around noon. I'll ride back with you."

Right. She could just give him a ride like a regular human being. "Perfect. I'll see you tomorrow."

Rebecca scooted behind him to the cashbox and laid in Richard's bills.

Jonas stroked his niece's hair. "Tomorrow."

Richard's questioning gaze burned into her cheek like a laser. She eyed the whoopie pies. Maybe she should grab one while she had the chance. Maybe she should grab a dozen.

Pocketing the change in one hand, Richard clasped Tessa's hand in the other and steered her toward the exit. "What was that?"

"What was what?" She was simply driving an Amish guy to her house to measure a tree. Nothing weird about that...

"That encounter."

"I told you that day at the library. I'm having a gazebo built for my parents' anniversary."

"And that man is coming to your house to build it?"

She extracted her hand from what was gradually becoming a vise grip. "I guess that's the process..."

"Why can't you buy a finished one? Don't the Amish sell them out on Route 45?"

With an exasperated grunt, she tightened her bun, narrowly missing his chin with her elbow. "Well, of course they do, but I told you, I want a special one. I came up with my own design—"

"You designed a gazebo after all?" Richard choked a laugh.

A fireball ignited in her chest. She quickened her stride. "Yes, I did, thank you very much, and Jonas said it's beautiful, and he's building it."

"Do you think that's a good idea?"

He stared like she was a little girl about to cartwheel from the roof of her house. "Don't patronize me, Richard Bruce."

Stopping short at the door, he held up both hands. "I'm not patronizing you, I'm just worried. Call me crazy but taking strange men to your house seems rather ill-advised."

She dodged that same old lady with the cart exiting the building. "He's not strange; he's Amish."

"Don't be naïve." He shouldered the door and

stalked into the parking lot.

She stormed past him and yanked on the car door. Finding it locked, she whirled. "Can you please open the car?"

Key in hand, he stood inches behind her, his thumb poised over the button. "You don't know this man. Just be careful."

Maybe she agreed to let him take care of her, but she didn't sign on to be smothered by an overprotective physician with a paranoid streak. Pinned against the car, she caught his gaze and glared. His brow creased with what looked like genuine concern, and his eyes softened. She huffed a breath, and the fireball cooled a couple of degrees. "I can take care of myself."

Sliding the pie onto the hood, he crossed his arms. "I know. But you agreed to let me pitch in. Remember?"

She crossed her arms back. "It's just a gazebo."

"Yeah?" He hooked a thumb over one shoulder. "Tell that to that guy."

With one quick move, she snagged his hand and brought to his side. "I'll look past the whole extremely clingy, borderline-macho display you got going on here, because I take you at your word. But just this once. Got it, Bruce?"

He jerked away and, retrieving the pie, unlocked the car. "Now who's patronizing whom?"

"Touché." She pulled herself upright and swung open the door. But a niggling sense of regret tickled at her conscience. One foot in the car, she paused and glanced over her shoulder. "Look, I don't want to argue in a parking lot—especially not on a surprise lunch date. Besides, you need to get that pie to Claire before it

133

self-destructs. Let's not sabotage your mission." She hummed a few notes of the theme song again, hoping to lighten the mood.

He didn't laugh.

Is it just a gazebo?

During the very direct drive to her house, neither spoke a word.

He pulled into the driveway and dropped his chin. "I'm sorry. I don't want to argue either."

His apology eased her mind, but her stomach still felt unsettled. "It's okay."

"Or be a possessive boor."

"I know." She offered a half smile.

"How are your bee stings?"

"They're better. Thanks." At the return of his bedside manner, her heavy mood lightened.

Resting an elbow on the center console, he turned. "I'd like to finish our dancing lessons this weekend. If it's okay by you?"

She gazed at him sidelong. "Just dancing. No self-defense."

He held up a hand. "Scout's honor."

Leaning across the seat, he brought his face within inches of hers and raised a brow.

She lifted her cheeks and tilted her mouth toward his. Without her noticing, he'd popped a mint, and his kiss was cool and full of promise.

Pulling away, he reached for his wallet. "Do me a favor and take this." He plucked out a card. "My office and pager numbers. You have my cell"—he scribbled on the back—"and here's my landline. Just in case."

"You forgot the carrier pigeon."

"He'll arrive at two."

"Wonderful. He can live in my potting shed." She squeezed his hand. "Thank you." She zipped across the lawn and climbed the steps to the front porch.

The tinted window whooshed down, and his head emerged from the opening. "I don't give that number to just anyone, you know."

With a smile, she shooed him away. "Get back to doctoring." Safely inside, she tossed the card on the kitchen counter. It flipped over, revealing a handwritten phone number next to a single word: home. So few letters for such a big idea. "You can't go home again," Thomas Wolfe wrote. Well, Tessa Meadows was doing her darnedest to prove him wrong. On second thought, she picked up the card and tucked it into the zipper pocket of her backpack.

Her sun-flooded bedroom welcomed her with a warm embrace of antique quilts and rainbow sheets. Slipping out of her sweaty sundress, she tossed it in the hamper. Downstairs, six guides to New York City and a travel show beckoned. Was she ready to answer their call?

She shrugged into an air-dried tank top and drank in the scent no dryer sheet could replicate. Her entire life, Green Ridge had always been home. Could she really move far away—somewhere mountains dwarfed her familiar ridges, or oceans swallowed the lazy river on whose banks her town had grown? Somewhere buildings scraped the clouds?

Faded cutoffs slid over her thighs like they remembered the shape of her body. But to stay in the Ridge? Staying sent a message she couldn't cut it outside her hometown. She'd feel like a failure. Then again, no one would call Richard Bruce a failure. Yet, he was back home and weighing the possibility of putting down roots. She kicked her sandals into the closet and yanked on a pair of long socks. So where were her ruby red slippers? Those magic shoes that, when she clicked her heels, would show her the way home.

The dresser top mirror offered a backward glimpse of her childhood domain. Reversed book titles lined the shelves with through the looking glass versions of *Little Women* and *Misty of Chincoteague*. Were the stories the same in that world of opposites? If she could see out the window, would her van be replaced by a horse-drawn carriage or a piper cub plane? Would Green Ridge be a bustling city? Would Tessa Meadows be a blonde? Leaving behind the imaginary world of reflection, she sank onto her squishy mattress. According to needlepoint pillows and folksy wall hangings, home was a person, not a place. She was enough on board with that sentiment to buy one of those pillows and put it on her bed…if only it could tell her just which person was home.

****

"You know I can't have lunch with you." Late the next morning, Tessa met Richard at the entrance to the volunteer office. Broad shoulders spanning the width of the door, he clung to the doorframe, effectively blocking her exit. She willed a patient smile. "But thank you for asking."

"Tell me why again?"

"You know very well why." She took a final gurgling sip of iced coffee and tossed the cup into the trash.

"Because you have to meet an Amish guy at your

house—"

"Pick him up, yes."

Richard took the stethoscope from around his neck and stuck it in his ears. "Because you have to pick up said Amish guy—"

"Right."

"—and take him to your house."

"Yup. As it turns out, the Amish don't drive." His teasing was an obvious effort to stall her departure. Kind of cute. Kind of annoying. Mostly cute.

He cocked his head. "Tell me again why this is a good idea?"

"Because I have no clue how to build a gazebo. Do you?" Swinging the end of his stethoscope like a cowboy with his lasso, he shook his head.

"I'm still thinking I should be there. I mean, what do you really know about this guy?"

"If he builds like his sister bakes, the thing will be done in three days and delicious a la mode." She plucked her backpack from a hook on the wall. "I thought we settled this yesterday. I'm really not worried."

Still twirling the stethoscope, he propped one shoulder against the doorframe. "Hey, when will you put a picture of us on your desk?"

"When we've had a second date." She balled her fists and plunked them onto her hips. "Move. I'll be late."

He snorted a laugh. "What, like he has a clock?"

"He's Amish, not prehistoric."

Pressing the head of the stethoscope to his chest, he inhaled deeply, puffed his cheeks, and released an explosive breath.

She lifted her brows. "Well?"

"Well, what?"

"Will you live?"

Forehead furrowed and eyes narrowed, he paused. "I believe so." Relaxing his features, he slipped an arm around her waist. "It's you I'm worried about."

"Like I said. I'm not." She leaned into his elbow and flashed a smile she hoped put all fears to rest. All his fears, anyway. While absolutely certain Jonas would never harm her, she did wonder what they'd talk about for twenty minutes in the car. Not to mention for the remainder of the gazebo consultation. She swallowed hard.

Jerking back, he thrust out a stiffened finger. "You gulped."

The guy didn't miss a trick. "I had saliva."

"I'm a doctor. I know a gulp when I see one. I can take off the afternoon."

Though still a tad overbearing, his concern was flattering. She darted a glance at the office wall clock. If she didn't get going, she really would be late. With a peck on the cheek, she slid from his grasp. "You're very sweet, but we both know you can't."

"You're right, I can't." He slumped in the doorway. "But you could reschedule—I'm off Saturday."

"What? Just, like, text him?" With a grin, she elbowed his ribs. "Get out of my way."

He straightened, still obstructing her path. "We certainly don't want to keep Mister Amish Man waiting."

She shoved again and wriggled halfway out the door.

"Mister All-Beard-And-No-Moustache—hey, why don't they have moustaches anyway?"

"Richard." His name came out a laugh.

He grabbed her around the waist and drew her close. "Mister I-Don't-Drive-So-I-Rely-On-Beautiful-Redheads-For-Rides."

"Goodbye," she hissed in his ear.

His body convulsed in a ticklish spasm.

Seizing the opportunity, she broke free and slipped into the hall.

"Maybe I should grow a moustache just to spite him," he called.

"Sure thing, Magnum." She pushed through the double doors and into the noonday sun.

Look out, world. I'm taking an Amish dude for a ride.

Chapter 8

Twenty minutes later, Tessa trundled across the low, metal bridge and swung into the Rishels' lane. Richard's moustache question bounced around her brain. Was their lack of facial hair genetic? No hair follicles under the nose? Or did they whip out straight blades and shave only that upper lip? Now that was a conversation for the ride: "So, you guys just can't grow moustaches or what?"

Nora wasn't present when she gave Jonas her design. Weird, but a stroke of luck. Managing Richard had been stressful enough. Would she be so lucky today?

The motor *putt-putted* as she rounded the bend to the farm. When she spotted Jonas alone on the front porch bench, she unclenched her fingers from the steering wheel. Nora wasn't in sight.

Resting his elbows on his knees, he leaned forward and studied her sketch.

Her cheeks tingled as if he were reading her diary. He was, after all, about to build her dream.

Pulling a pencil from behind one ear, he made a swift mark and unfolded from the bench, stretching as he stood.

She swallowed hard again. *Saliva. Nothing but saliva.* Her mouth tasted of institutional coffee. One of these days, she'd remember to stick a tin of mints in her backpack. She shifted into Neutral and waved.

Lifting his chin in greeting, he grabbed the handle of a wooden box and descended the porch steps, crossing the yard in long, easy strides.

This guy, it seemed, never rushed. She extended a freckled arm, unlocked the passenger's side, and flipped the latch.

The door careened open, and he pulled himself into the seat, knocking his boots against the wheel well before swinging them into the van.

"Your coach has arrived." *Your coach. Really good joke for a guy who rides around all day in a buggy.* She closed her eyes and longed for a cosmic rewind button.

He snugged the toolbox under the dash. "Hello."

A flicker of uncertainty played across his face. Was he nervous too? She gave a toothy grin she hoped was more welcoming than terrifying. "All set?"

"I think so."

"Great." Zipping down the lane, she hit every bump and dip like she aimed for them. For all its vintage character, the van was not a smooth ride. Then again, horse-drawn buggies didn't have shock absorbers at all. Did they? Air-conditioning would have been nice, but the cooling system broke years ago. Shrugging away from the upholstery, she lifted her arms to catch a breeze and peeked at her passenger.

His hat in his hands, he gazed steadily out the window.

"Sorry the air conditioner doesn't work." She giggled, then choked back the laugh. What was so funny about stifling heat? "You can roll down the window if you want."

He looked at the car door.

Did he know how to open the window? Asking would be rude, right?

The glass squeaked into the door.

Of course, he knew how to roll down a car window. He was probably used to automatic ones and only hesitated because he didn't see a button. She made a mental note to search, "why don't the Amish drive," later that evening. From what she'd seen, the Amish accepted car rides regularly. When they needed to travel long distances, they even took the train. So, why was riding as a passenger perfectly acceptable but taking the wheel verboten? She flicked her gaze back to her passenger. Maybe she'd ask him some day.

A pungent smell of freshly fertilized fields rushed through the windows. Whenever Jenn visited Green Ridge in early summer, she held her pert nose and gagged at the pervasive odor of manure. Tessa secretly liked the scent. It smelled like home.

Jonas's eyes were closed, his head tipped against the headrest, damp hair sticky on his forehead. He looked tired. She usually cursed the sluggish forty-five miles-per-hour speed limit on Route 45. Cursed but obeyed it. Route 45 was infamous for speed traps. Today, she relaxed into the leisurely pace, the reassuring chug of the motor like a heartbeat vibrating through the floor.

He lifted his eyelids.

She whipped her gaze to the taillights ahead, catching a glimpse of herself in the rearview mirror. Her hair swirled around her face, lodging in her mouth and lashing her eyes. She swiped at it in vain. "The air feels nice."

He inhaled deeply. "Smells like planting."

As she veered into the driveway and cut the motor, a truck out on the highway downshifted with a groan. Badly in need of oil, the van door squeaked closed. She always thought of her house as so quiet, but it wasn't Amish quiet. She waved in the direction of the sycamore. "The tree's around back."

Retrieving his tools, he followed her, stopping to survey the house. "It's old."

She drew up beside him. "Built in 1893."

"Brick."

"Yup." Afternoon sunlight lit the front façade with a russet glow, and the wide front porch opened its arms to them. A pleasing contrast to the brick, delicate, wooden gingerbread curlicued beneath the eaves. After hours sanding and repainting it butter-yellow last summer, she knew every spiral and spoke of that fancy Victorian trim. The porch swing rocked in the breeze, its metal chains creaking an invitation to sit. Her house never looked more welcoming.

He let out a soft sound of approval.

"When was your home built?" she asked.

"The main structure was built in the early 1900s. My grandfather added the *Dawdy Haus* in the nineteen sixties, and we've altered it several times since."

"*Dawdy Haus*?" The unfamiliar phrase rolled from her tongue with surprising ease.

"The smaller house attached to the big one. For the grandparents."

Nana Shiffer's blue eyes twinkled in her memory. If she squinted, she could almost see her kneeling in the garden, weeding petunias. "I would have loved to have my grandmother live with us."

"When I was a boy, the house was full of family."

His jaw tightened. "It's too empty now."

Sadness darkened his gaze. Where were those relatives now? He shook his head like a horse shaking off a nagging fly and tugged his hat brim.

Mounting the steps, he wrapped a hand around one of the supporting beams and tugged.

The structure barely shuddered.

He peered into the rafters and nodded. "Sound."

And good thing. The dude could probably rip off the porch with his bare hands. As she led him to the sycamore, he seemed to take in her many gardens with interest. Slowing her pace, she tried to see the beds through his eyes. Compared to Nora's orderly plots, hers were jumbled and wild, but they were abundant and colorful, too—kind of like her thoughts these days. "Thanks for coming all the way out here…and for even considering building my gazebo. I know it's a crazy idea. The more I thought about it, the more impractical it seemed—what with bumpy roots and the trunk expanding each year."

"I can build it, I believe."

He spoke with quiet certitude, exuding just as much confidence as Richard, but different somehow. She ducked under the pines.

He came to her side and lifted a bough. "How much land does your father own?"

Nodding her appreciation, she passed beneath it. "Two-and-a-half acres."

"So much land so close to town."

"Unusual, right? The big yard really sold my parents on this house. They're away for work for a year, so I'm taking care of it by myself. Kind of quiet here, too, actually." She glanced sidelong, but whatever he

thought lay hidden beneath his hat. "Well, here it is."
She stepped under the sycamore, and the temperature
dropped what felt like a full ten degrees.

Taking his time, he circled the tree, looking into
the branches and kicking the dirt at the base. He
approached the trunk and examined it, placing a hand
on the mottled bark and pushing, much as he'd done to
the porch beam moments before.

The tree was sound, too. She knew it well. She also
knew the feel of that bark rasping her bare shoulders as
a man devoured her lips with his own. Her face heated
at the memory. Richard's mouth was full-bodied, his
lips as sensual as a woman's. She snuck a peek at
Jonas. This man's mouth was a marble sculpture—a
carved upper lip resting atop a delectably full lower one
the color of a pomegranate seed.

He strained upward and tugged a low bough. The
hem of his emerald-green shirt escaped his pants,
revealing a sliver of skin.

What would his lips taste like? She ran the tip of
her tongue over her own lower lip. If he kissed her here
under the sycamore…Whirling, she shrugged the
sweat-slick shirt from her shoulder blades. Hopefully,
the Amish weren't known for mind-reading as well as
carpentry.

Finished with his inspection, he stopped in front of
her family's carved initials.

She winced. Did the Amish frown on tree
defacement? When he peeked around the trunk, he
looked so like his niece she couldn't help but smile.
One side of that bowed upper lip lifted in return.

"TRM. That's you?" he asked.

"Yes." She took a tentative step in his direction.

He rested one shoulder against the trunk and crossed his arms. "What is your full name?"

She studied patchy grass at her feet. "Tessa Rose." She sighed. "Tessa Rose Meadows. I always thought it was a bit much. Rose Meadows. Botanical overkill."

"It suits you, Tessa Rose. For the roses in your cheeks."

She covered the familiar, flaming bloom with her palms. "So, what do you think? Will my idea work?"

Taking a step back, he regarded the site. "I believe it will. The ground is mostly even, and the pines are a fair distance away. A few of these lower branches will have to come down, but removing them won't harm the tree. It's healthy."

"I'm so glad!" Until he said it, she hadn't fully believed he'd take on the project. Wrapping her arms around her middle, she barely kept from dancing.

He fetched a tape measure from the toolbox and circled the tree again, measuring the thickness of the trunk, the height of the lowest branches from the ground, and the distance to the nearest trees.

"Do you need me to take notes?" she offered.

He shook his head. "I'll do most of my building here. I can cut the lumber ahead of time, but all assembly will be done right around the tree." He slid her original drawing out of the toolbox. "Here's how I imagine it."

She took the paper, and her eyes went wide. Encircling her original design were a dozen or more smaller sketches. His drawings rendered cross sections and details: a view of the ceiling from below, the overlay of cedar shingles on the roof, a railing constructed of twisting branches in their natural state.

The finely worked plans framed her rough sketch like an illuminated manuscript. "Oh, Jonas, it's exquisite."

"The structure will rest on an octagonal platform built around and several inches from the tree. I'll create an opening at the top to allow for growth, but at the slow rate trunks widen, it won't come close to the gazebo any time soon. The leaves will keep out rain in the summer, and in the winter, you might want to consider a plastic covering. I haven't fully figured that out yet—I don't really work in plastic." He ran a hand over his chin. "My guess is a cover won't be necessary."

As he spoke, she pored over the paper. The evidence of many hours' work rested in her hands. Did he sketch in the middle of the house under Nora's watchful eye? Or did he escape to a private spot to draw and think alone? The idea that he passed any time at all pondering her and her project made her collarbones tingle. She shook her head. "You're an artist."

He stepped behind her and tapped the original sketch with one finger. "You had a unique idea—the tree in the middle. I've never seen a gazebo like it." He chuckled. "Not at Lucas King's, anyway."

A renegade curl tumbled loose, and she brushed it aside, turning. "We haven't spoken about a price. How much will all this cost?" Her face heated at the awkward subject of money. Seemingly untroubled, he took in the tree again.

"I can't say quite yet. I can make a good guess on the price of the lumber, but I don't know how long construction will take, since I've never made anything like it." He glanced back, and his eyes crinkled at the corners. "Can we wait on an estimate? Don't worry. I'll give you a fair price."

"Of course." She returned the drawing. Maybe the job would require all summer. Richard would love that.

He dropped the tape measure into the toolbox and followed her around the house. "By market next Wednesday, I should have a rough sense of cost and a preliminary timeline. Do you have a place where I can store tools and lumber?"

Considering, she pursed her lips. The only space large enough was the garage, and it was crammed floor to ceiling with junk. She recalled the pristine shelves in Nora's pantry. *Note to self—clean the garage.* "I'll come up with something." She gestured toward the van. "Shall we?" The steering wheel was even more cantankerous than usual. With a soft grunt, she wrenched it, flattening a narrow strip of lawn. "My car has a stubborn streak."

"I know a mule very like it." He craned his neck and peered into the rear of the camper. "What an unusual vehicle."

She laughed. "That's an understatement. It's a 1979 camper van."

Laying a hand on the dash, he swiveled in his seat. "You sleep in it?"

"Yup. You can climb back and look around if you want."

His brows rose. "May I?"

The request oozed breathless anticipation. He was like a teenager taking his first ride in a sports car. "Go ahead. You'll rarely see another van like it—only a few are still on the road."

Grazing her shoulder with his chest, he squeezed between the bucket seats.

The scents of hay and sawdust lingered. She blinked back a dizzying wave and caught him in the rearview mirror. Planted on the back seat, he spread his feet and surveyed the van with wide-eyed wonder. She adjusted the mirror for a better view. "I like all the cabinets and drawers tucked everywhere."

He tugged the handle of a door nestled beneath the countertop. It didn't budge.

"How do the doors…uh?"

"Open? See the buttons in the handles? They're latches that secure everything when the car is moving. Just press the button and pull. Feel free to open any of them. I don't think much is inside."

With a click, a shallow drawer slid open. "Look at that." He pressed the button repeatedly, examining the latch mechanism. "Wonderful."

His delight in the ingenious engineering was a refreshing breeze on the back of her neck. She refocused on the road, determined to avoid a traffic accident while dying to watch him discover every hidden delight the camper concealed. "See how that countertop fastens with a vinyl strap and a snap? A sink and a propane cooktop are underneath. My mother made three-course meals on that stove. No water's in the sink now, of course, but it runs when the tank's full."

The metal snap popped open beneath his fingers. "Running water."

"Below that panel of electrical switches on your left is a built-in refrigerator." She heard the counter thud closed and the refrigerator open. "The fridge is pretty impractical actually. It has no drainage, so my mom always had to bail it out when stuff leaked or condensed or whatever."

"Where do you sleep?" he asked.

The pot of geraniums in front of the quilt shop waved hello in a flash of pink and green. "That back seat opens into a bed. It's handy, actually, because we can unfold it to haul big loads. Your lumber should fit fine. And—you'll love this—the roof pops open into a tent."

He gaped into the rearview mirror, tawny brows disappearing under his hat brim.

She laughed. "They actually call these vans 'pop-tops.' See that metal bar up top? When you unlatch the roof and push the bar, the ceiling lifts up on a diagonal, and a mattress folds out. Canvas walls are tucked into the sides, and they open like a tent…it's kind of hard to describe. Maybe I'll show you sometime."

He ran a hand along the bar. "Pop-tops." Lifting from the seat, he examined the hinge. "It's really very practical."

The camper rumbled over the metal bridge for the third time that day and down the sun-dappled lane.

"The window curtains all snap closed, so the inside is cozy at night. I had the second floor all to myself."

"You have no brothers or sisters?"

She lifted her shoulders. "Nope. Just me."

Releasing the side curtain from its sash, he pulled it across the window.

His excitement summoned her memory of exploring the van for the first time. Each cubby and cabinet was a wondrous discovery. She could hardly believe they got to take it home. But then she rounded the corner, and the joy drained from her body like water from a bathtub.

Rag in hand, Nora stood on the porch scrubbing a window.

Even at this hottest hour of the day, she worked fully garbed in a calf-length dress, black apron, head covering, stockings, and boots. No wonder the woman was chronically grumpy.

Turning, Nora tented a hand over her eyes and glowered.

Her scowl was a frigid welcome. Tessa gritted her teeth. She darted a quick glance at Jonas, but he didn't appear to see his sister.

He trundled open the side door and ducked beneath the curtain, leaning his elbows into the passenger side window. "Come to market Wednesday, and we'll make the arrangements."

Lips sealed, she nodded and peered over his shoulder.

Nora's frown deepened. She hurled her rag into a metal bucket. "Jonas!"

Her voice rang across the yard like a gunshot.

Jonas jerked and stilled.

Red-faced, Nora marched to the van with quick, labored strides and let forth a tirade.

Though unintelligible, the rapid-fire barrage hit Tessa like a punch to the gut. Her rage just barely contained, Nora spat a final syllable and swiped dripping hands down her apron with such force Tessa half expected her palms to bleed. Sucking in a tight-lipped breath, she checked an impulse to strangle the woman with her own bonnet strings.

Jonas's jaw tightened, and color rushed to his cheeks.

She thought he was unflappable—this strong, silent

man who never hurried. She was wrong.

"Please excuse me." He pivoted to Nora, and just as swiftly as she had, uttered a few hushed words in that same tongue.

Nora's face went white. Eyes blazing, she fisted her apron in tight fingers and whirled.

Her halting retreat seemed to take three hours. Tessa's stomach churned. Being trapped in the middle of a family conflict was bad enough. Being trapped in the middle of a family conflict conducted in another language and apparently triggered by her presence was nauseating.

When the screen door finally banged shut, Jonas turned.

Once again, a veil shrouded his features, as if her afternoon companion had vanished, and a stranger now stood in his place. She felt his loss like a sudden ache.

"Forgive me…and my sister. She has never been easy with outsiders."

"I'm sorry if I'm…if this job is causing problems. If you don't want to do it—"

"My sister does not dictate my actions," he bit out. "I will build your gazebo as we agreed."

The passenger door wrenched open with a jagged squeal.

"I'll see you Wednesday." He pried the toolbox from under the dashboard, elbowed closed the door, and retreated to the barn.

Without saying goodbye.

Heart hammering, she gripped the steering wheel and tore down the lane. What was wrong with that woman? All Tessa ever did was track her down and pay her handsomely for three dozen pies. Wouldn't a nice, fat, gazebo check put a couple more hens in the barn? A fresh coat of paint on the *Dawdy Haus*? The Rishels didn't appear to be suffering, but she couldn't imagine they amassed a fortune in whoopie pies.

A deserted Route 45 beckoned, and she stomped on the gas. Who was she kidding? Nora wasn't the problem. She didn't care what that sad, little woman said about her in any language. Jonas was the problem. She let him get under her skin. For no reason whatsoever—at least none communicated in a language she could understand—he went from climbing around her van like a kid on a jungle gym to scowling like a stone-faced stranger. Just what did Nora say?

As if the glove compartment might come to life and bite her, she trailed cautious fingers over the threadbare fabric where he sat moments ago. Until today, she felt like a trespasser in his domain. This afternoon, for the first time, she offered something in return: her world—with its pop-top vans and crazy gazebos. He seemed open to it and to her. But in an instant, he slammed the door in her face.

Sighing, she pressed a thumb deep into one temple. What was up with this family, anyway? Were all Amish women so creepily attached to their brothers? Where were Nora's husband and Rebecca's siblings, and who ran the farm? Farming was a massive undertaking, and many hands made light work. So, who actually worked the land? Jonas seemed to spend his days doing carpentry and selling Nora's baked goods.

Home again, she flung herself, arms wide, on the front lawn.

A million miles…

A puffy white cloud shaped like a whale scudded

across the sky. Jonas's farm was barely twenty minutes from her house, but a million-mile chasm lay between them. No more fantasizing about his kiss. He was her builder, not her Amish boyfriend.

She rolled her head to the side, and feathery blades of grass tickled her inner ear. Oh, but she had been kissed. And kissed. And kissed again.

Smart, stylish Richard Bruce wooed her with soft-serve ice cream and kissed her silly under the sycamore. Richard, who was in every way the perfect guy. Dazzlingly suave, he made her laugh and showered her with dahlias and, unbelievably, seemed to want her. Maybe he wasn't Prince Charming. But she'd choose *Dr.* Charming any day of the week. Prince Charming always seemed like a bore.

She plucked a dandelion puff, closed her eyes, and blew.

Let the carpenter build and to heck with the consequences. Tessa had a ticket to the ball.

Chapter 9

"It was 'Maneater.' " Nibbling her straw, Tessa flashed a naughty grin over iced coffee in the hospital volunteer office the next morning. Her coffee habit was getting out of hand, but she could imagine worse vices.

Claire swallowed a cappuccino spit take. "You're kidding."

"Nope. They played 'Maneater' twice during the *No Repeat Nine to Five*, and I heard it and called in." She shook her head. She never won anything—not even musical chairs. Even now, weeks later, she could hardly believe her luck.

Claire lifted sable brows. "And won fifteen thousand dollars?"

"Honest to goodness. I was stuck in my crummy faculty apartment grading finals while everyone else sunbathed on the quad. I don't think a single sofa was still indoors. So, when I won, I couldn't find anyone to tell." She plunked her elbows on the desk and rested her chin in her hands. "The whole experience was unreal."

"I never knew which was Hall and which was Oates."

Savoring a frosty sip, she frowned. Thanks to the band, she was fifteen thousand dollars richer. She should at least know which was which. "Wasn't Hall the one with the moustache?"

"I thought that was Oates."

"Well, regardless, because of 'Maneater,' I can volunteer all summer, build my parents a gazebo, and worry about work in the fall." The cup was clouded with condensation, and she traced the shape of a heart on its side. "At this point, I can't function outside of an academic calendar anyway."

Claire tipped her chair against a file cabinet, teetering on two legs. "Does Richard know?"

"About the radio contest?"

Claire nodded.

"No." Wiping away the heart, she snatched the cup and drained the final drops. "I'm pretty sure he thinks I should find a real job." She held up a sample Midsummer Ball invitation. "Too wedding-ish, right?"

"Agreed."

She tossed the card onto the "no" pile. August first was on the horizon, and she and Claire needed to finalize the "Swing into Summer" invitations posthaste. Only two choices remained. One was traditional with sweeping script and elegant, small caps on creamy cardstock. The other was a retro design with a dancing couple inside a whimsical pocket watch and art nouveau lettering reading, "Party Time." She presented the final contenders. "Drumroll, please...which is our lucky winner?"

"Well..." Claire scraped the remnants of foamy milk from inside her cup and licked her spoon. "We usually go classic. Like the letterpress one."

She ran a fingertip over the engraving. "It is beautiful."

"But, maybe for a change..." Claire drummed her fingers on the desktop.

"We choose the pocket watch?"

"Done." Claire high-fived her and swept the rejects into the recycling can.

She trashed her cup and wiped the wet ring from her desk with a napkin. "I suppose I should run the design by Richard—since he's technically planning this thing, too?"

"You can tell him on your next date." Claire swung petite, pedicured feet onto her desk. "How was Judy's anyway?"

She chuckled. "Wow. Can't keep anything on the down low in this town."

"Please. Didn't you grow up here?" Groping in her bag, Claire produced a small, pink envelope. "You and Richard dating? I couldn't be happier if I planned it myself. Which"—she tossed the envelope on Tessa's desk—"I kinda did."

Tessa nodded toward the desktop. "What's this?"

"How about you shower my son with some of those prize winnings this weekend? Sam's birthday is Saturday, and he's dead set on a party in the birthday pavilion at Benton's Grove—you know, the giant, pink cake that says, 'Happy Birthday?' And if that's not enough, he wants his birthday cake to be a miniature replica of the pavilion. Like exactly. Hence, the pink envelopes." She pinched her forehead between her thumb and middle finger. "He's got a color scheme. I swear that kid—he's either a design genius, or he's absolutely bonkers."

Tessa laughed. "Hey, that's somebody's child you're talking about. And he's pretty cute from what I hear."

"He takes after his father." She unwrapped a stick of gum and offered one to Tessa. "He keeps asking if

157

Richard's new friend who saved him from the bees is okay."

With a groan, she accepted the gum. "Seared in your kid's memory as the lady who sent him into anaphylactic shock."

Claire shook her bob. "He says you flew him away like a superhero. According to the kid, you have powers. He specifically requested you to come."

She inhaled a cool breath of relief. "Not sure Benton's parking lot has room for my invisible plane, but I'll figure something out." She smiled. "After all, I have powers."

****

On the Saturday of Sam's party, Tessa hopped into Richard's SUV and swallowed a groan. The dude was glued to his phone. Again. "Don't tell me you have work."

He shook his head. "Just mapping the route."

Chuckling, she clicked her seatbelt and settled into the cushy seat. Through the open moon roof, the sky was a perfect azure rectangle. "It's Benton's Grove, not Cleveland. Just go the regular way."

"I don't know the regular way."

The engine idled with a rhythmic hum.

"I'm sorry, what?"

Tearing himself from the map app, he sucked his cheeks and turned. "I've never been."

She released the belt, tucked one knee under her body, and reeled. "How is that even possible?"

He jabbed the max AC button with his thumb. "By some cruel quirk of fate, I've never been to Benton's Grove. Commence pity party this instant."

Struggling to hold back a smile, she held up both

hands. "Hey, I just didn't think you could grow up in Green Ridge and not go to Benton's at least once." She interlaced her fingers behind his neck and planted a soft kiss on his mouth.

"If I had you around," he murmured into her lips, "I would have gone years ago."

"You have me now," she murmured back and tossed a hot pink, beribboned package into the back seat.

"What did we get him?"

"A book that turns into a robot—"

"Excellent."

"—and comes to life when you put in a battery." She lifted her palms in a raise-the-roof dance.

He gave a fist pump. "Darling, you're a genius."

Several days before the party, she volunteered to buy Sam a joint present—a gesture that dipped a toe into the waters of coupledom. He accepted her texted offer readily, but his delight at her selection was a tremendous relief. Beaming, she refastened her seatbelt. "I'm so glad you approve."

"Oh, I more than approve." With one hand on her headrest, he leaned into her seat and kissed her again, nibbling her upper lip before pulling away. Placing the other hand on her knee, he trailed his fingers partway up her thigh. "I'm so far beyond approving…I'm in full thrall."

While appropriate, his touch danced on the cliff edge of intimacy. Her stomach did an Olympic-quality triple Lutz. "Thrall? Sounds itchy. Do you have a cream for that in your first aid kit?"

Chortling, he flipped down his visor. "I'll check. Now, tell me how to get to this place, or we'll never leave your driveway."

Frigid air poured from the vents, wafting the aroma of leather and sunscreen. She ran her gaze over his profile. He was atypically dressed down in sunglasses, a T-shirt, and a baseball cap, but still, he managed to look totally put together. The fact this guy wanted to go anywhere with her was a miracle.

Come to think of it, when was the last time she visited Benton's? Several years ago, at least. But the beauty of Benton's rested in the fact that, like the Farmers' Market, it never, ever changed. Somehow, time let Benton's off with a pass. An old-fashioned picnic park comprised more of trees than cement, it truly merited the moniker, "grove."

With just a few miles to go, she bounced in her seat like she did as a girl. She loved so much about Benton's—the fried dough, the mini golf, the rides. Benton's hundred-year-old carousel boasted real brass rings to catch. Neck-wrenching bumper cars rattled the bones, and the Cosmotron still blasted Eighties pop. The haunted house used to be scary and might still be now, if it wasn't so funny. At some point, rounding a corner to find a mannequin man with his head stuck in a toilet evoked screams of laughter rather than terror.

However, the Salt and Pepper Shakers ride remained horrifying into the new millennium. She never had the courage or the stomach to be strapped into one of two bullet-shaped cages that rotated end over end on a long, spinning shaft. She half expected the thing to fly apart and catapult the riders into space. Fingers crossed, Richard would not want to risk his medical career or his dental work on the Salt and Pepper Shakers. Knowing she was present for his first trip to Benton's, however, made this visit all the more exciting.

He made his first snide remark the second they drove beneath the Benton's Grove entrance gate, adorned with dancing bear mannequins. Clad in overalls and dresses, the bears spun parasols and played accordions in animatronic spasms, which was somehow even lamer, he explained, than if they had merely been painted dancing bears.

Having yet to meet a soul who wasn't won over by Benton's particular blend of tacky and charming, she brushed off the wisecrack. Just wait until he tasted a genuine Benton's Grove funnel cake.

Rounding the Tilt-a-Whirl on foot, he came face to face with the birthday pavilion and exploded into laughter. "It really is a giant, pink birthday cake."

She put her hands on her hips and grinned. "What did you expect?"

"Not subtlety, but still." He guffawed again. "It's a monstrosity."

"I think it's quaint. I enjoy Benton's Grove, Dr. Bruce, and you will, too." She nudged him with one hip. "Just give it a chance."

"Oh, my poor, sheltered darling. Remind me to take you to a real theme park someday."

With a huff, she thwapped his shoulder. "Don't be a snob."

He hooked an arm around her waist and snugged her close. "God, you're gorgeous when you're irritated. Can I just order you steak and take you to bed?"

"Watch it, Doctor. Children are present." Jabbing his ribs, she squirmed free. "Besides, I wanna eat pink cake and catch brass rings."

He snagged her hand. "I already caught mine."

Hip pressed against his, she stumbled under the birthday pavilion into a scene of loosely organized chaos.

Kneeling on the cement, Claire wiped a sobbing boy's nose with a bright pink, paper napkin. She offered a stiff wave, rolled her eyes, and pointed at her husband.

Tyler wobbled atop a picnic table, straining for a helium balloon among the rafters. The elusive, pink ribbon bobbed just inches above his fingertips.

Richard grinned. "Everything under control, Dr. Macmillan?"

Tyler shot Richard a look. "One hundred percent, Dr. Bruce, why do you ask?"

"No reason." Richard crossed his arms and surveyed their surroundings. "Guess I won't find a salad around here."

"Shut up and indulge." Claire led the red-faced boy to a bench, impaled a box of chocolate milk with a straw, and thrust it into his hands.

"Good thing a couple of doctors are in the house." Richard rocked back on his heels. "This place is a myocardial infarction waiting to happen."

"A what?" Tessa asked.

"An M-I. A heart attack. Claire, you have baby aspirin in your bag, right?"

After balancing their gift atop a mountain of packages, Tessa pointed to the birthday cake and applauded. "Mission accomplished. It's the pavilion's tiny twin."

Claire stuck pink-and-white striped candles into the icing. "We cleverly planned the day so the kids stuff themselves to bursting and then go on rides. Tyler and Richard can escort the little princes. They're used to vomit." She lit the candles with a single match and flashed a smile. "I'm so glad you're here. Now, let's cut this damn cake before we burn down the place."

"Oh, don't worry. Dr. Bruce probably has a fire extinguisher in his back pocket."

Claire stuck two fingers in her mouth and let out a whistle that immediately quelled the insanity. "Okay, boys, time for cake! Caitlin, come sing to your brother."

Tessa hadn't even noticed Caitlin.

Nose deep in a book, she perched on the far edge of the most distant picnic table, out of range of the madness.

"Now, Cait," Claire said.

Her tone would not be denied. When Tessa was a girl, her mother also had a "mom voice." No matter the circumstance, the tone meant, "whatever you're doing, kindly stop this millisecond, and do as I say." The notion of having kids flitted through her brain again. Would the mom voice ever spring from her lips? Looking exactly like her mother just moments ago, Caitlin rolled her eyes and deposited a massive tome on the table. Tessa couldn't see what she was reading, but it was probably light and age-appropriate…like *Anna Karenina*.

"There's my girl." Richard winked and skootched to make space for Caitlin.

The girl's face lit like the Benton's Grove Ferris wheel at night. Tessa had no clue what kind of parent she'd be. Richard Bruce, however, was destined for first-rate fatherhood. She knew that fact for certain.

With another summons from Claire, "Happy

Birthday" was sung, presents were opened, and cake was devoured with just enough time to catch the show in the Enchanted Castle Puppet Theater near the haunted house.

Richard volunteered to accompany Tyler and the kids and, with Caitlin riding on his shoulders, he led away the small party.

Sinking onto a picnic bench, Claire groaned. "Piece of advice? Never have children."

Tessa laughed and collapsed at the opposite side of the table, the cake carcass between them.

Claire licked a dollop of pink icing from a plastic fork. "Not only are they absolute demons, they stole your date. I'm sorry. Did you go on any rides before you found us?"

"Not yet. Do you know Richard's never been to Benton's Grove?"

The fork fell from Claire's fingers, spearing a hunk of cake. "How is that possible?"

"That's what I said." She swung her legs onto the bench and shook gravel from her sandals. "I don't think he likes it very much."

Claire squinched her eyes and frowned. "What's not to like?"

"I know, right? But he's making snotty comments and bragging about the 'real' amusement parks he's been to. Maybe his parents refused to bring him here, and he still holds a grudge."

"You joke, but old Doc Bruce holding out on Benton's?" Claire tapped her nails on the tabletop. "That wouldn't surprise me one bit."

Tessa searched Claire's face for a glint of humor but found none. "Really? Why?"

Claire pulled a metal water bottle from her tote and took a swig. "Has Richard told you anything about his family?"

"Not much. He mostly talks about his dad—going on house calls with him and listening to jazz."

Glancing in the direction the men and kids went, Claire plonked the bottle onto the table. "I didn't know old Dr. Bruce well, but he ran a mighty tight ship. Even Tyler was scared of the guy. Sure, he was 'Beloved Dr. House Call' to everyone in town, but I don't think having him as a dad was a picnic. Rumor is, on the day Richard was born, Dr. Bruce declared to all the OB nurses his son would follow in his footsteps. 'Mark my words, he'll run this hospital someday.' Richard grew up believing his future as a doctor was destined."

No wonder the guy tended toward controlling behavior. He learned it from his dad. She imagined him growing up burdened by his father's expectations, and her heart broke a little. More than once, her own dad squeezed his lanky frame into kiddie rides at Benton's so she wouldn't have to go alone. She couldn't imagine feeling bullied by him. "But Richard loves his job."

"Oh, sure. Hey, maybe Dr. Bruce just recognized his son's natural inclination for medicine. Maybe…" Claire scraped another icing glob from the cake plate. "But has Richard ever mentioned his sister?"

A sister? She gave a strangled chortle. "Not once."

"Guys. Am I right?" Claire washed down the icing with a sip from the bottle. "Samantha was older and a real rebel. Dr. Bruce wanted her to go into medicine, too, but Samantha bailed on college and took off. I hear she's dealing blackjack in Vegas now, but who knows. Anyway, Samantha left, and Mrs. Bruce got sick almost immediately. When she died, Dr. Bruce invested all his hopes in Richard—like Richard was responsible for carrying on some kind of legacy. You know, he got accepted to a residency program in Boston, right?"

Tessa shook her head. Did Richard intend to share any of this information?

"Oh, yeah. The best program in the country. But when Dr. Bruce had a stroke, he really tightened the screws. So, Richard came home." Claire met her gaze. "Please don't tell him I told you. I just—I think you're great for him. You should know this stuff, and who knows when he'll get around to sharing it."

Yeah, no joke. She scooped the last blob of icing from her plate. It was dry on the edges and crunched almost too sweetly between her molars.

Claire leaned over the table and lowered her tone. "In the midst of his residency, Richard became his dad's primary caregiver—not an easy job. Dr. Bruce rode roughshod over his son until the day he died."

"I can't fathom that—knowing Richard now." She twisted her ponytail into a tight bun, as if squeezing her brain would make Claire's story any easier to understand. "So now his father is gone, why doesn't Richard just leave?"

"No idea. Of course, Tyler doesn't want to lose him, but he realizes St. Luke's doesn't offer everything a big hospital in an urban area would. Richard won't even look." Claire dabbed her mouth with a napkin. "You didn't know any of this, did you?"

A second slice of cake was in order. Grabbing the knife, she shook her head. "Not really. He mostly talks about med school, and those memories seem happy. Taking swing dancing classes…"

"Oh yeah, that was all Jane."

Her breath hitched in her throat. "Jane?"

Eyes wide, Claire hurled her napkin onto the table. "Oh, come on."

Tessa shrugged.

"He hasn't told you about Jane?"

From the seismic measure of Claire's exasperation, she guessed Jane was yet another epic chapter in the saga of Richard Bruce. She flashed to the pretty brunette smiling from the photo in Richard's hallway and forked a golf ball-sized hunk of cake. "Uh-uh."

"Jane, his ex-fiancée Jane?"

A glob of icing wrapped around her tonsils, bringing instant tears to her eyes. She spluttered and lunged for her napkin.

Claire offered the water bottle. "Drink."

"I'm good." She gestured toward a box of chocolate milk.

"Drink." Claire nudged the bottle and winked. "Iced tea."

She took a swallow. The tea slid surprisingly warmly down her throat and heated her belly.

"Not gonna lie, but there might be a touch of bourbon in there." Claire lifted a hand in oath. "I swear it's just the tiniest drop, and Tyler is stone-cold sober."

Choking a laugh, she raised the bottle. "Cheers." She sipped again and dragged the back of her hand across her mouth.

"I'll kill him for not telling you." Taking up the bottle, Claire drank deeply. "You didn't hear this story from me, but yes. Jane was his med school girlfriend and, by all reports, practically perfect in every way. They got engaged between their third and fourth years and then matched to the same residency program in Boston. After his father's stroke, Richard asked her to give it all up and come to Green Ridge."

"And she said no?" Tessa whispered.

Claire pressed her palms to her heart and pooched her bottom lip in a frown. "She said no. And broke his heart into a million pieces."

"Poor Richard." Poor Richard who gave his heart to a "practically perfect" physician before Tessa came along. Pity and envy bubbled with birthday cake and bourbon in her stomach.

Claire smiled and squeezed her hand. "You are the best thing that's happened to that man since I've known him. I feel like, with you, he can start to imagine some kind of life outside the hospital, which is more than his father ever did."

"That's...that's really..." She scraped pink frosting from under one fingernail.

"A lot. I know. I'm sorry, honey."

"A lot" was the understatement of the century. An overbearing father and a deceased mother were a lot. Throw in a black sheep sister, a broken engagement, and a delivery room prophecy, and Richard's story was practically Shakespearean drama. Except, of course these events comprised his actual life and were terribly, terribly sad. She ached for him. How could she possibly keep her knowledge secret? She met Claire's gaze and smiled. Thank goodness for girlfriends. "I'm glad you told me. I won't breathe a word, of course. I'm sure he'll open up soon."

"Richard isn't so complicated. Who hasn't been totally screwed up by their family, right?"

A stream of lukewarm water strafed the table,

spattering dirty plates and napkins.

Grimacing, Claire eyeballed her smart watch. "Shortest puppet show in the history of the universe."

A swarm of six-year-old boys descended upon the pavilion, dousing one another with Benton's Grove water cannons.

"That"—Richard paused and wrung his wet shirt— "was the worst puppet show I have ever seen. Absolutely abysmal." He retrieved the phone from his pocket and glared. "Not a single bar."

Claire balled soggy napkins and whizzed them past Richard's face into the trashcan. "More to the point, did Sam and the boys like it?"

"About halfway through, we left and bought the squirt guns." Tyler wiped his glasses down the front of his shirt. "You know, making a convincing puppet of a horse is just really hard."

Claire whirled to the boys. "Okay, fellas, who's up for the bumper cars?"

Caitlin reclaimed her spot at the table and took up her book.

The boys hooted their enthusiasm and squirted the runaway balloon still trapped on the ceiling.

Tyler rounded up the pint-sized combatants and waved off Richard's offer to accompany him.

"Go eat cotton candy." Claire gathered empty drink boxes and crushed them in one hand. "Richard, have you really never been here before?"

Glowering, Richard crammed the phone into his pocket. "Guilty as charged."

"So, scram. Play mini golf. Ride the Cosmotron. Enjoy!"

With a grateful smile, Tessa snatched Richard's

hand and dragged him from the pavilion.

He scuffed beside her, launching clumps of gravel from the path. "I hate mini golf."

She pecked his cheek. "Of course you do."

Perpetually waterlogged and leaf-strewn, the mini golf course lay between the Wild Mouse Coaster and the shady stream bisecting the park. Skirting the course, the path ambled along the creek bank and led directly to the famous Benton's Grove Rainbow Trout Bridge—a huge, colorful covered bridge in the shape of a trout.

Maybe a goofy pic would cheer him up. "Selfie in front of the fish?" His derisive snort rankled, setting her teeth on edge.

"Are you serious?"

She was absolutely serious. The Trout Bridge was legendary, and a pic with the fish was a summer rite of passage. Why was he so determined to trample her childhood memories? On the verge of snapping, she pictured that little boy, cowed by an overbearing father. She dropped back her head and stared into the leafy canopy studded with sky. Time to conjure some Benton's Grove magic. Squeezing his fingers, she brought her lips to his ear. "For me?"

With a chuckle, he shied away.

Richard Bruce was definitely ticklish. Good to know.

He extracted his phone. "For you. But if you post this anywhere, we're officially through."

"Make sure you get the psychedelic lips," she said through a wide smile.

He held his phone high and snapped.

"Text me the pic."

He tapped the screen. "Done."

"That's going on my Christmas card," she hissed and dashed into the belly of the beast. Clutching the graying railing, she leaned over and gazed at real-life rainbow trout hovering above mossy rocks below. A splinter of wood dug into one finger, and she jerked it away. Myriads of hand-carved, love messages traversed the railings and ran up the posts that comprised the fish's ribs. She never had a steady high school beau and thus hadn't watched as someone gouged her initials next to his. Honestly, she wouldn't mind if Richard whipped out a penknife right then and there.

"Just look how kids have ruined this bridge." He thumped the railing with one fist and strode toward the fish's tail.

With a quick jog, she snagged his hand and tugged him close. Maybe the fish didn't win him over, but nothing evoked childlike joy better than a carnival ride. "Let's go on the merry-go-round. Bet you a funnel cake I catch more rings than you."

He glanced at his phone. "It's late, and those kids wiped me out. I knew there was a reason I didn't go into pediatrics."

Swallowing a frustrated sigh, she made a last-ditch effort to spread sunshine in the face of gloom. "How about the Ferris wheel then? Riding that doesn't take any energy. You just sit back and enjoy the view."

He swiped the tiny screen again and again.

Did he really think assaulting his phone would somehow result in service? "Okay, that's mine now." She extricated the device and, thrusting a hip against his, slid it into her front pocket. Slowly. Maybe kind of steamily? "I'll give it back…after we ride the Ferris wheel."

He slid his gaze up her body, from the phone bulging in her shorts pocket to her freckled shoulders, and his face relaxed. "I can't seem to say no to you."

The Benton's Grove Ferris wheel was no London Eye, but it was a decent size for central Pennsylvania.

"You sure this thing can hold us?" He peered into the rusty framework. "I swear, everything in this place looks a hundred years old."

"You're paranoid. It'll be fun." The Ferris wheel line snaked back on itself several times, and she nibbled the inside of her cheek as each car emptied and reloaded. When she finally slid onto the seat beside him, she realized they were the last to join that round of riders. "Lucky us!"

The young operator threw a rickety lever, and with a jolt and the grinding squeal of metal on metal, the Ferris wheel jerked to life.

Richard scowled. "That didn't sound good."

It didn't, but in a moment, she was airborne, and every rational thought flew from her mind. The car soared toward the sky at a belly-turning speed, seemed to slow as it scraped the stratosphere, and plummeted back to earth, only to whoosh upward again. From the top, she could easily see over the flume ride and beyond the sprawling, wooden roller coaster to distant ridges on the horizon. Her wind-tossed ponytail tickled her cheeks, and she giggled, punch-drunk on frosting and adrenaline. All traces of grumpiness gone, Richard threw his arm around her and kissed her senseless at the tippy top of the wheel.

"I told you it would be fun," she purred into his lips. Up the car sailed—high above the pink cake pavilion and the aquamarine swimming pool next to the campground. Down it dropped, so close to the roof of the nearby Peanut Shack that her sandals almost clipped it.

Finally, the Ferris wheel downshifted and slowed. As the last to have boarded, she and Richard were only one level above the ground when the exchange of passengers began. They would be the last to get off. She snuggled into his side and glanced over her shoulder at the other riders. How many of these teenagers would rock their cars while they waited, making the whole wheel shake? She hated that feeling.

The unloading process was as bumpy as the ride had been smooth. Each partial revolution shook the wheel like a mini earthquake, lurching the car and slamming her tailbone into the unforgiving bench. Gripping the bar, she exhaled slowly and stared at her knuckles. Richard's shoulder tensed against hers. All joy was gone, and renewed outrage radiated from him like heat from sun-baked asphalt.

With a grunt, he clamped his jaw, hunching and crossing his arms over his chest.

When the wheel rotated again, taking their car to the tippy top, the motor hacked, and the gears ground with a sickening screech.

Sniffing, Richard sat up and leaned over his side of the car. "Do you smell smoke?"

She shrugged one shoulder and peered down. Her belly lurched at the bird's eye view.

The operator turned around his baseball cap. He jiggled the lever side to side and threw it again.

The wheel rotated just a few feet, shuddered, and ground to a halt.

The boy wrenched the lever again...and again.

The acrid odor of oily smoke was unmistakable, now. It rose from the machinery in a thick, white column.

Richard cupped his hands around his mouth. "Turn off the motor!" He lifted from the seat, and their car heaved.

She gripped the rail so hard her sweaty palms slipped, and she sucked in a tight breath. Dangling one hundred feet above the ground in a tippy, metal gondola, she struggled to put a sunny face on the situation. With every passing second, this amusement park was less and less amusing. Unless Richard had a jet pack in his pocket, they were trapped.

Chapter 10

"I think it's romantic." Tessa ran the toe of her sandal over Richard's sneaker, bumping knees. "We could do anything on this Ferris wheel, and no one would see."

"In about five minutes, this seat won't feel so romantic. Good thing I don't have to make a shift."

A burst of adolescent laughter pealed from below, and the whole structure shimmied.

"Idiot kids." Scowling, he thrust out a hand. "Can I have my phone, please?"

Pressing her shoulder into his, she arched upward and withdrew the device.

He made a disgusted sound in the back of his throat. "Still no service." He shoved the phone into his pocket and leaned over the bar. "What's happening?"

Presumably, someone besides the kid running the ride was aware of their predicament. Hoping to spot a rescue party, she risked a look.

The operator glanced upward. He swept off his cap and scratched his bleached-blond mop.

Richard dropped his head against the seat with a thud. "Moron."

Benton's must have procedures in place for mechanical problems. Surely someone would arrive and help them to safety—she braved the long look down again—somehow.

A balding man in a suit burst from beneath the trees, a retinue of big-haired women behind. He elbowed his way through the growing crowd and planted himself directly below.

One of the women handed the man a bullhorn.

He fumbled for a moment, and the bullhorn screeched. "Is this thing on?" His words echoed across the park.

Richard choked a laugh. "We're doomed."

The man cleared his throat. "Ladies and gentlemen, we're having a minor mechanical difficulty with our Ferris wheel. I guess you could say it's on the fritz! I called a technician and told him to shake a leg—we don't want to keep you all hanging around." The man guffawed. "In the meantime, just sit back, relax, and enjoy the view." He passed the bullhorn to the woman and gave a thumbs-up with both fleshy hands.

Wedging her knees beneath the bar, Tessa crossed her legs. As Richard predicted, the seat already felt hard. "Look on the bright side. I bet we'll get free admission for life."

Two men in gray coveralls appeared, carrying a long stepladder between them. They opened it at the base of the Ferris wheel, and soon, the occupants of the lowest cars evacuated.

"We're gonna need a bigger ladder." Forcing a smile, she gently elbowed him. "You know, like in *Jaws*? 'We're gonna need a bigger boat?'"

Richard sulked in silence.

"Hey, we already survived a ginormous trout. I'm feeling good about our chances."

He tugged the baseball cap over his eyes.

Sliding into her corner, she pressed her lips and

watched tiny heads bob in the swimming pool below. The gondola rocked in the breeze, and her stomach turned. Richard blamed her. His stony silence practically screamed it. Well, she refused to feel guilty. Who could have guessed the wheel would malfunction? In all her visits, she never saw a single ride break down.

Her motives were pure. She wanted to gift him one delightful, dizzying ride with no phones, no work, and no stress. And she almost pulled it off. She dug her fingernails into her palms. Nope—not guilty. Oh, she was plenty annoyed. She did everything short of cartwheels to give him a fun day at the park, and he doggedly refused. Annoyed but not guilty.

Half an hour passed. An hour. Then two. The mechanic didn't arrive.

The setting sun scorched her face, and the skin on the bridge of her nose tightened and burned. His devotion to chivalry notwithstanding, Richard didn't fork over his hat. Why hadn't she brought her own?

In the next car below, a woman huddled with an arm around a skinny boy.

His face was mostly buried in the woman's shoulder, but Tessa made out the hollow curve of one pale cheek.

The woman snuggled him and glanced upward.

Concern hardened her angular features. Smiling, Tessa offered an encouraging wave.

The woman gave a half-hearted wave in return.

She sighed. "Guess I should have had that third piece of cake. Maybe they could throw nuts from the roof of the Peanut Shack."

"What the bloody hell are they doing down there?" Richard ripped off his cap and punched the crown.

"Where are the fire truck and the ambulance?"

A tight nugget of anger rose in her throat like a ball in one of those vacuum-powered lottery machines on TV. Her lips were cracked, her thighs were stuck to the seat, she desperately had to use the bathroom, and, worst of all, her new boyfriend concealed a secret fiancée for weeks. The whole situation was too much to bear. "You know, your attitude really isn't helping."

With a snort, he jammed on his hat. "My deepest apologies."

"What is your problem? I don't like being trapped here either, but at least I'm not being a jerk."

Staring straight ahead, he bounced his right knee, shimmying the entire gondola. "If you hadn't insisted on riding this piece of junk—"

"Oh, sure. The Ferris wheel breaking is clearly my fault—"

"—we wouldn't be stuck up here."

Yup, he blamed her. She knew it. "So, sue me for wanting to have fun." Ignoring the altitude, she whirled. "Look, I get it—for whatever reason, you hate Benton's Grove. You made that perfectly clear from the second we arrived. Well, not that you care, but I love it here, and I was excited to share it with you. This place has charm, which maybe you think is entirely your department, Dr. Bruce, but trust me, you're not showing much today."

He sat up with such force, the gondola lurched again.

A queasy wave washed over her.

"I don't see charm. I see dirt." He pointed a rigid finger at the Peanut Shack. "The trash on that roof down there and the trailer park next to the pool."

She widened her eyes. Was he always so judgmental? "It's not a trailer park; it's a campground. Maybe Benton's is tacky, but that's how it's always been. That's what makes it my place."

"Well, it sure as hell isn't mine."

"So leave!" She shrank away as far as possible and slung her knee onto the seat between them. "If you hate it so much, why don't you just go?"

"Sweetheart, don't make a scene."

An acid-laced laugh squeezed past the flaming, fury nugget and emerged as a strangled cry. "Are you kidding? First of all, nobody can hear us, and second, like, five hundred people are down there. You're smack in the middle of a scene."

He took out his phone.

Again. She wanted to grab the thing and launch it into orbit. "For the love of God, Richard, you don't have service. You want one hundred percent reliable cell service? Then get out of town!" She flung wide her arms. "If you're so much better than all this, why don't you leave?"

He fisted his hands against his thighs. "Because I can't."

"Why not?"

"I have a job for one thing. St. Luke's needs me. My patients need me. I've got a family and friends— and I've got a woman I'm head over heels in love with despite the fact she's damned near impossible. I can't just leave!"

His words tumbled into empty space, and she held her breath. Silence settled over the valley like a sheet snapped upward and left to fall inch by inch onto the bed. The sun slid behind the western ridge, and neon signs flickered on soundlessly all around. "You have family in Green Ridge?" Her voice was barely more than a whisper.

"My father haunts that hospital like some white-coated ghost. I can't sit on a bench without catching my pants on a plaque dedicated to him. And my mother? She died in room 312 so…" He raised his shoulders a few inches and released them slowly. His eyes darkened. "And then there's you. What do I do about you?"

The question landed like a heavy parcel in her lap. She slumped beneath its weight. "I might not be here forever either."

His high forehead creased, and his brows knitted. "If you're so crazy about Green Ridge, why would you leave?"

"I'm not ashamed of where I'm from." She took a breath, and the sky purpled one shade deeper on the color wheel. "But I don't plan to stay for the rest of my life. I'm moving to New York soon."

The wrinkles on his forehead deepened. "I thought you said New York was out of the question."

"The situation changed, but it's not a done deal."

Eyes flashing, he clasped her hand and drew it to his chest. "I know you feel adrift right now, but you won't forever. Before you know it, your parents will come home, and we'll get you a place in town. I'll help you find a job at the hospital—"

"Help!" A terror-stricken voice rang from below.

Dropping her hand, Richard grabbed the bar and lifted off the seat, staring in the direction of the cry.

Tessa looked, too. The gondola beneath them, the one containing the woman and the boy, rocked like a porch swing gone berserk.

Wide-eyed and trembling, the woman looked from car to car. "Help, please! My son!"

In her arms, the boy shook violently.

Tessa gasped.

"Oh, my God." Richard blanched. "He's seizing."

"He has epilepsy!" The mother clutched her boy, but he thrashed beyond control.

The buzzing crowd didn't respond. They couldn't hear or see.

Richard settled back onto the seat. "She can't restrain him. He'll throw himself out of the car or break a limb. I've got to get down there."

His clinical assessment made her blood run cold. She grabbed his arm, sinking her fingers into his bicep. "We're at least a hundred feet high."

"I need to get to that kid." He swung onto the seat and, kneeling, squinted into the twilight.

She followed his gaze to the beam at their rear. Between parallel rows of light bulbs protruded widely spaced metal rungs, creating a ladder of sorts. Their car, the Ferris wheel, the earth below—they all seesawed in a vertiginous heave. "Richard, no."

His phone, keys, and wallet clattered onto the seat.

Her lungs constricted. She struggled to force out a word. "Please. Don't do this."

He thrust his hat in her hands. "I need you to lean forward and don't rock the car. If you shift your weight, you'll counterbalance mine. Then, when I step out, the car will swing forward fast. You'll have to hold on tight."

Explained step-by-step, the plan almost seemed logical. But it wasn't, of course—it was madness.

He swiveled on the bench and, rising, extended one leg. Laying his chest on the seat top, he groped, unseeing, for the first rung on the beam. "Got it." He released his breath on a grunt, rotated, and shifted his weight onto that back foot.

Pale fingers clamped onto the seat. The gondola swung backward, and her stomach heaved like she might be sick. Turning halfway around, she slipped the hat under one thigh and edged forward.

Steadying the car, he slowly lifted his other leg up and over the seat.

She met his gaze. "You don't have to do this." Even as she spoke, she knew her words were futile. Saving people was what Richard Bruce did. He lifted his lips in a smile she knew was entirely for her benefit.

"Hold on, sweetheart. Everything will be okay."

She nodded and spun, skootching as far forward as possible and tightening her fingers around the bar. Bracing herself, she stared at the convulsing boy and his frantic mother—and beyond them to the crowd below.

Spotting Richard, someone on the ground pointed. People shouted and waved their arms. One by one, camera phones illuminated every upturned face in a bluish glow.

The car shuddered and stilled.

"On the count of three, I'll let go, okay?" he called.

Her pulse pounded in her throat. Scrunching her face, she wedged her backside tight against the seat, pressed her toes into the front of the car, and leaned over her hands. "Okay."

"One…two…three."

The gondola jerked and careened forward.

Heart racing, she slammed her body into the seat, closing her eyes as her spine crushed against metal.

The car pitched, rocked, and then quieted.

Her breath high and shallow in her chest and her stomach a roiling, volatile pit, she squeezed her eyes tighter and waited.

"Sir? Go back to your car!" The balding man's voice boomed over the bullhorn.

She dared a glance over one shoulder.

Richard was halfway down the beam.

Her right calf tightened and cramped. Wincing, she flexed her foot and wiggled her toes to ease the ache. One false move and Richard would plummet to the ground. Gripping the bar until her knuckles burned, she searched for the help she had to believe was coming.

In the midst of the throng, the man in the suit gestured to his entourage. "We've got a nutcase on our hands. Somebody, call the cops." With a squawk, the bullhorn went dead.

He's not a nutcase. He's a doctor. Though foolhardy, he was one hundred percent in his right mind. She checked in with the struggling mother. Her efforts were increasingly labored. How much longer could she restrain her boy?

Again, Tessa mustered courage and darted a glance to Richard. He was gone. She gasped and rose a few inches, twisting to search the metal framework. She spotted him at the hub of the wheel, and the torque in her spine eased.

Chest heaving, he paused, head down, clinging to the beam. Slowly, he released one hand, lowered onto the support below, and began the arduous climb back up. Rung by rung, hand over hand, he shimmied toward the swinging car.

Spotting him, the mother sprang to her knees. She crouched over the boy, securing him to the seat with her body. "What are you doing?"

Another rung and Richard was two-thirds of the way up the beam.

"I'm a doctor. Try to stay still!"

With every convulsion of the child, the wheel shook.

The woman's face contorted. "I-I don't understand. What are you doing?"

Tessa clocked his progress up the truss. Three rungs to go. Then two.

He released his right hand and strained for the final rung.

Suddenly, the thousands of colored bulbs ignited in a zillion-watt rainbow.

Recoiling, he flung an arm over his eyes, dislodging his right foot. He slid backward and, grappling for a hold, slipped off the top of the beam.

Tessa shrieked, wide-eyed, her retinas seared by the glare. Heart in her throat, she launched forward and scrabbled at the bar.

He clamped on with his left arm as his right arm flailed. Wrapping both legs tight, he hooked his feet at the ankles, dangling upside down, high above the crowd.

The visible half of his face was a gruesome circus mask, illuminated in shifting colors by maniacally blinking bulbs. Pulse thundering in her ears, she reached toward him. But she was helpless. "Richard!"

Clenching his teeth with a growl, he swung his right arm over the girder and muscled himself back on top.

Every sinew in her body spasmed. She forced enough breath into her lungs to shout. "Are you all right?"

Bracketed by flaming lights, he lay still. His back shuddered with each intake of breath. Lifting his head, he nodded.

Momentary relief unclenched her stomach, and her torso turned to jelly. She had to will herself to keep watching when all she wanted was to curl up and bury her face in her hands. Richard was feet from the boy, and she knew with absolute certainty he would keep climbing until he reached him or fell to his death. And he thought she was impossible.

Bending his knees, he anchored his feet, pressed upward, and clasped the final bar. He heaved his lower body a rung closer and lunged for the back of the car, straining to steady it. Just as he threw a leg over the seat back, two ambulances, a police car, and a fire truck screamed into the park.

"Oh, sure, now you get here!" Eyes stinging, she slumped onto the seat and swallowed gulps of air. In fuzzy fragments, she heard cheers from the crowd, voices on an intercom, and Richard calling in response.

Tears streamed over sunburned cheeks and into her mouth. Thirsty and achy, she closed her eyes, longing to feel solid earth beneath her feet. She wanted to rage at Richard for being a reckless idiot, and she wanted to kiss him senseless for being a superhero. Mostly, she wanted to hold him close and know in her bones he was safe and sound and in one piece. She cracked open an eyelid.

In the car below, Richard struggled to hold down

the boy.

He needed help, and he needed it now.

The fire truck maneuvered under the Ferris wheel and extended a long arm with a basket like a cherry picker at the top.

How could Richard maneuver the convulsing child safely into the firefighter's arms? How could the firefighter prevent him from falling? With barely enough energy to lift her head, she forced herself to sit and witness this rescue come to a close or end in tragedy. For Richard's sake.

Richard knelt on the floor of the gondola and picked up the boy. He swiveled and called to the firefighter.

She swept her gaze to the child and blinked. He was still—his body like a rag doll in Richard's embrace. The torpor was almost more frightening than the seizures. Was he breathing? She squinted through the glare, but she couldn't tell. With almost unbelievable precision, the firefighter maneuvered the cherry picker inches below the gondola. As the boom fully extended, the basket just skimmed the bottom of the car.

Arms trembling, Richard hoisted the boy over the safety bar.

For a brief moment, the lifeless body seemed to dangle above a gaping void. Tessa twisted her T-shirt around one finger and clutched it to her belly.

Grimacing, the firefighter strained upward, caught the boy in a solid embrace, and lowered him into the cherry picker.

Richard dragged an arm across his forehead and sagged onto the bench.

Tessa sagged, too, her limbs as spent as if she just scaled the Ferris wheel herself.

With a whining whir, the ladder descended.

The crowd whooped again.

She lifted her gaze to the horizon and prayed for that boy and his mother. She prayed he would be all right—prayed the rescue wasn't too late. Just above the ridge, Venus shone so constant and reassuring she almost dared to take it as a sign. The bullhorn's squeal cut through her whispered pleas, and she dropped her gaze.

"The boy is stable and on his way to the hospital," announced a uniformed officer. "The mechanic just arrived. You should be on the ground shortly. Just hold on, and please, remain in your seats."

Lights flashing, the ambulance silently slipped between long rows of cars and veered onto the park lane.

The gondola beneath her was empty. Richard and the boy's mother must have descended after him. She shuddered and scanned the crowd. The sky was dark now, but hundreds of people remained. Did Richard go to the hospital with the child and leave her alone, stranded on the Ferris wheel?

Another voice cut through on the bullhorn. "Tessa? Tessa, honey?"

The voice was gravelly and hoarse, but it was unmistakably Richard's. She searched the crowd until she spotted him with a firefighter. Tears sprang again to her eyes.

"I'll be right here when you come down." He handed the bullhorn to the police officer and clapped one hand to his chest, right over his heart.

Finally, the Ferris wheel groaned, and after a few tense minutes, she staggered out of the car and into Richard's arms. He held her so tightly she could hardly breathe, kissing her face again and again and murmuring her name until she almost didn't recognize it. He drove her home, and then he went straight to St. Luke's to check on the boy. His patient came first. His patients, she was learning, always came first.

Late that night, she lay alone in her bed, sunburnt flesh tight against rainbow sheets, her mind spinning like the tilt-a-whirl: Richard and his father...his broken engagement and his career...their fight on the Ferris wheel and the image of his body clinging for dear life.

Still, one thought kept returning. It circled to the forefront of her consciousness again and again like a carousel horse.

In the heat of argument hundreds of feet in the air, Richard said he loved her.

He also talked about her in the third person and called her impossible so...mixed messages to say the least. She stared at a water stain on the ceiling and downshifted her brain to a slow revolve. Maybe she was impossible, but so was he. He was also stubborn and cocky and more than a wee bit controlling.

And he was a certified, grade A, All-American hero. Put together all those qualities, and she had herself a boyfriend straight out of a rom-com. Their happy ending seemed almost inevitable.

When she next saw him, safe and sound on solid ground, would he say it again? She flipped her pillow, longing for cool cotton to soothe her scorched cheeks. And if he did, what would she say in return?

Chapter 11

Early the following Tuesday morning, Tessa opened the front door to a delivery man.

He thrust a top-heavy, plastic-wrapped pot in her hands.

Orchids—fragrant, milky blossoms unlike any she ever saw. They must have cost a fortune. She tipped the guy, thanked the gods she was actually wearing pajama pants, and plopped at her kitchen table. Breathing in the heady aroma of vanilla and spice, she grabbed her phone. According to the itinerary Richard emailed, before sunrise that morning, he left for the airport. He would be on the west coast for over a week. Until yesterday, she didn't even know he was going. She scrolled through their awkward text exchange:

—*Since when do you have a conference in San Francisco?*—

—*Since I registered six months ago.*—

—*I had no idea.*—

—*I told you about it last week.*—

He didn't. She didn't correct him. She pushed away her phone.

What a bizarre couple of days. The boy from the Ferris wheel was recovering. She was stiff and achy but otherwise fine. Aside from a few bruises, Richard miraculously unharmed. Several videos of his heroics surfaced on the Internet. She could tell he was secretly delighted to be a brief viral sensation. Then he flew out this morning without giving her a chance to say, Hey, I might love you, too. Or not to say it.

He was slated to present a paper at some conference on technology in medicine. During their one brief encounter in the hospital hallway, he assured her he wasn't angry. He hoped she wasn't either.

She wasn't remotely angry. Very deep inside welled a hidden pool of relief.

Still bleary-eyed, she sipped lukewarm coffee and uncoiled plastic wrap from her new, floral baby. A creamy envelope protruded from the tines of a plastic holder stuck in the pebbly dirt. She plucked it and hesitated, almost afraid to look. She knew only one guy who could source exotic flowers in the middle of cow country, and that guy had a penchant for grand gestures. The card slid out with a whisper, and she instantly recognized Richard's scrawl.

A rare beauty for a rare beauty. All my love, Richard.

All his love…was she ready for all? Through the window, morning sun slanted from a cloud-streaked sky. He was half a country away in a little tin can winging through limitless blue. She had time to figure out her feelings. When she saw him again, she'd know what to say.

Tossing aside the card, she grabbed a pad and pencil and jotted tasks for the week ahead. Ticking items off a to-do list always gave her clarity. *Clean the garage. Listen to Midsummer Ball band demos. Meet Jonas on Wednesday for estimate and building schedule.* She paused, nibbling the eraser. Did she have nothing else to do? Just a few weeks ago she couldn't catch her breath between the flurry of meetings, classes, and grading. She added: *Don't kill the orchid.*

Half an hour later, garbed in her grungiest clothes, she stood at the threshold to the garage, industrial-grade garbage bags in her right hand and shop vac in her left. A stiff breeze blew through the open door, tossing her hair like a supermodel. Time to get dirty.

She surveyed the cement and cinder block landscape. Behind a dilapidated pair of water skis and an exercise bike resembling a medieval torture device emerged a span of dark wood piled high with dingy paperbacks, broken watering cans, and driveway salt.

Was that a workbench? She wrestled a stack of frayed lawn chairs to the wall, shoved an old cooler against them, and in so doing created a path to the cluttered corner. Sure enough, she discovered a sizeable wooden counter above which her father apparently hung a pegboard many years ago. An honest-to-goodness workshop! Twirling, she clapped her hands, and a cloud of dust billowed around her head. She sneezed. Jonas would be so surprised.

She hung an array of power drills, handsaws and screwdrivers on hooks, and sorted hardware into plastic containers. After scrubbing a thick layer of grime from the bench, she rubbed in conditioning oil until it glowed. She ran a hand over the surface, tracing the grain. The wood was warm to the touch—like a living thing. Decades-old cobwebs and desiccated bugs went to their final repose via the dustpan. With a little elbow grease, the dingy windows let in a bit of natural light which she supplemented with an electric torch, hanging from metal shelves over the bench. She hauled out the stepladder and replaced bulbs in the ceiling until the whole workspace was cheerfully illuminated. Tired and filthy, she sank onto the cooler and reviewed her work. Though it may not rise to Amish standards, the place didn't look half bad.

Satisfied, she made a beeline for the claw-foot tub. Wrapped in a towel, she was steps from the bathroom when she spotted the blinking, red light on the answering machine. Guess she hadn't heard the landline from the garage. Mrs. Diefenderfer maybe? She pressed the button.

"Hello?"

A deep male voice filled the hallway, and her towel slipped a few inches.

"Please tell Miss Tessa Meadows that Mr. Jonas Rishel is ready to build the gazebo for her parents. She—no, Rebecca, not right now—ah, she—Rebecca, go sit by the buggy—she, uh, sorry…she will need the pop-top to carry the wood. I will begin construction Thursday at noon if the time suits. Thank you."

A full body flush, ends of hair to tips of toes, flared like an instant sunburn—but a nice sunburn, making her skin warm and tingly all at the same time. The nubby towel scratched tender flesh below her armpits. She yanked it up a few inches and replayed the message just to hear his voice again. How the heck did Jonas Rishel get her phone number? She hovered a finger over the replay button a second time. Instead, she advanced to the next message.

"How are you, Tessa Bear?"

Her father favored the landline as well.

"Just wondering when you're heading to New York? Mom and I had a few more ideas for house sitters, and I have a lead on a job teaching writing in

New Jersey. Who was it, Margaret? For the house?"

Pots and pans clanged, and her mother's voice rang in the background.

"Oh yes, Marybeth Folkers and Jeremy Rice from up at school. Let us know what you figure out, and I'll email that job listing. Bye now."

Ever reluctant to meddle in his daughter's affairs, her father always seemed to sense the precise moment she needed help. But another teaching job? In New Jersey? She shivered again and pressed the button, saving both messages.

She twisted the individual hot and cold faucets and ran a hand under the combined flow. Just a smidge more hot, and the water was perfect. Dumping in a scoop of orange and bergamot bath salts, she settled into the tub and rolled stiff shoulders. How did Jonas even call? She pictured him plucking a cell phone from beneath his hat and giggled. Well, she'd just have to ask when she saw him Thursday. For a few weeks anyway, Jonas would pass a lot of time at her house, and she vowed to treat him like a normal person. If she had a question, by golly she'd ask.

On Wednesday, she skipped the market, thus avoiding another confrontation with Nora, and worked all day in the volunteer office, arranging linens and furniture rentals. That evening, dressed in her lightest cotton joggers and a threadbare college tee, she watched the credits scroll on the final episode of *Mysteries of the Big Apple*. Just as she turned off the TV, her cell rang. Richard's name popped up on the caller ID, and she hesitated. Would talking to him be weird after the whole Benton's fiasco? With her finger hovering over the decline button, she heard Jenn's voice shouting in her head. *Your boyfriend's calling from San Francisco, Tess, take the darned call.* She took the darned call.

"Darling, I'm dashing for drinks, but I had to check in. This conference is incredible—world-class. I'm exhausted, but Tyler and I are meeting the top researchers in the field."

Whatever that field was exactly. Breathless and ebullient, he described late-night networking over sushi and meet-ups with old friends from school. "This city is even more beautiful than I imagined. And the coffee? Out here, coffee is its own food group. You should have come."

If she knew the conference was happening, she might have. She liked coffee, too.

"I miss you, darling. I'll call again soon."

The line went dead. Abandoning her phone, she slipped into the backyard. Barefoot, she padded through dewy grass and soft pine needles until she rested a shoulder against the tree that would soon transform into a gazebo. Whispering, the wind rushed to distant meadows. "Tomorrow…tomorrow…tomorrow…" She rolled, and the bark of that old tree scraped her back so familiarly. The breeze pulsed until gooseflesh prickled her skin.

She relaxed into a moment of stillness. And with it, the stirring in the pit of her stomach she had squelched with almost constant activity, surged. A liquid warmth rose within, threatening to engulf her completely. She braced against the tide, but with a sigh, she surrendered. Longing, pure and simple, coursed through her body like sap to the sycamore's tiniest twigs. The sensation pulled at her insides, parting her lips until she almost tasted it. She desired…someone, and she desired him deeply. Splinters dug into her shoulder blades, and pain mingled with the breeze's soft kiss on damp skin. The rustling of full summer leaves tickled at her ears. "Tomorrow…tomorrow…tomorrow…"

****

Minutes before noon on Thursday, Tessa turned onto the farm lane too fast, and the heavy gardening gloves she wore to prune roses slid across the dashboard. Lunging, she snagged them and tucked them beneath a denim-clad thigh. Despite stifling heat, she wore jeans.

The seatbelt dug into her neck, and she pulled it slack. She hadn't seen Jonas since the big blowup with Nora and his icy farewell. How would he act today? Moreover, how would she feel? Bolting without saying goodbye was downright rude. But then he left a message. His voice, nervous and sweet, moved over her towel-clad skin like warm mist. Her brittle annoyance softened into a mixture of curiosity and compassion and something else, too. She closed a mental door on what that something else might be. After all, she had an unofficial boyfriend in San Francisco.

She rounded the bend, and the farmhouse came into view, brilliant white clapboards flashing through the trees.

Balancing a piece of rough-hewn lumber atop one shoulder, Jonas strode across the lawn. He lowered it onto a neat pile, and the muscles in his back strained against a sweat-darkened shirt.

A current of last night's longing swirled in her belly. How could she hold a grudge against a man who looked like that? She snatched her gloves and swung out of the van.

Turning, he caught her gaze and broke into a slow smile. "You got my message. I'm glad."

Not a sliver of ice glinted in those blue-lagoon eyes. The guarded stranger was gone, replaced by a man who was simultaneously familiar as a childhood friend and breathtaking as a movie star. Everything about this guy scrambled her insides. "How did you get my phone number?"

A brown boot landed atop the lumber, and he rested his forearms on his knee. "The telephone book."

The phone company still published telephone books? "But where did you…you know…" She gestured weakly toward the house. "Make the call?"

One corner of his mouth twitched. "The community shares a telephone. It's in a shanty about a mile away. In case of emergencies."

She plunked one hand on her hip and raised a brow. "Emergencies?"

His eyes crinkled at the corners. "Or to make appointments or contact family. Most communities have at least one telephone."

Why was he laughing at her? He was the guy who wore funny clothes, rode around in a buggy, yet still used a telephone. His life made no sense. She should be laughing at him. She drove her fist into her hip bone. "Who pays for the phone?"

"Everyone. We're a community."

"I see." The work gloves slid stiffly over her fingers and cracked when she bent her knuckles.

He jerked to a stand. "I almost forgot. I have something for you."

She flicked her hand toward the wood pile. "Looks

like you've got quite a bit of lumber."

"Something else." He bounded up the porch steps and returned with a brown paper bag. "A gift."

Whiffing chocolate, she opened it. "Whoopie pies?"

He looked toward the barn and ran a thick palm over the back of his neck. "Made fresh this morning. I remembered how you like them."

Was this gift a peace offering? If so, it was effective. Softening her shoulders, she smiled. "I love them. Thank you." She popped the present into the glove compartment and opened the rear hatch. With almost zero help, he easily negotiated the lumber into the vehicle. As she predicted, it all fit on the collapsed back seat, and within minutes, she had him on the road, windows down, lush fields of corn rolling by.

"Does this pop-top have music?" he asked.

"I'm sorry?" She must have heard him wrong.

"Does this pop-top have music?" he repeated more loudly.

"Oh, music!" Telephones and the radio. What came next? Online dating? "Sure. My dad had a really nice stereo installed." She reached to switch on the radio and thought better of it. "Do you want me to turn it on?"

"Show me how."

Countless fingers had long since worn off the markings on the tuner controls. "Turn the knob on the left."

Jonas turned it, and "My Hometown" by Bruce Springsteen poured from the speakers.

"Oh, man. Now that's a blast from the past." She hummed a few bars. "The same knob also controls the volume. Feel free to turn it down if you don't like

Springsteen—he's the singer. The other knob changes the station."

He tilted his head and narrowed his eyes. "I've heard this song before."

She gave him a sideways glance. "Really?"

Spreading his lips in a wide grin, he met her gaze. "On the radio."

A mischievous gleam twinkled in his eyes. She pursed her lips in an answering smile. "Intriguing. Go on…"

"As a teenager, my younger brother, Samuel, did odd jobs for an English neighbor. One evening, he came home with a battery-powered radio. He said the man gave it to him as a gift—that was his story anyway—and he stashed it in the hayloft." He shifted in the seat, running his palms over his thighs. "Most nights, my cousins and brothers and I gathered behind the barn and listened to it when our parents were asleep. One of us stood watch, and the rest huddled around like it was some kind of magical box. We played it so quietly we could hardly hear the music, but I remember this song."

A contraband radio. The guy was more interesting with every passing minute. She lowered the volume on the stereo. "Jonas Rishel, you rebel. Did you ever get caught?"

He hooked his thumbs in his waistband and puffed his chest. "I was the oldest and stood watch most often. I was very good at my job."

Imagining him standing sentry behind that big red barn, she let out a giggle. "Do you still have the radio?" He gave a solemn nod, but the rascally glint persisted.

"But we never played it after that summer. One

night during tobacco harvest, my youngest brother, Micah, was on watch. He must have been ten at the time. We were all exhausted from working the fields and far too tired to listen to music, but still, one by one, we sneaked out of the house. We were only outside half an hour or so when we heard our father's voice. 'Wake up, Micah Rishel! Where are your brothers?' "

She gasped and covered her mouth. "Oh, no."

"Samuel picked up that radio so fast I didn't see his hand move and threw it as hard as he could into the woods. Seconds later, my father appeared."

A laugh burbled from her throat. "What did you do?"

Bracing his right hand on the dash and his left on the back of her seat, he turned with a bounce. His hat bumped the headrest and slid cockeyed. "I was terrified. We all were. We just stared at our feet and waited for the switch. But Samuel was fearless. In the sweetest, clearest voice, he said, 'Father, have you come to pray with us?' Standing there in the moonlight, he looked so like an angel come down from Heaven my father believed him." He shook his head, one corner of his mouth lifting into a smile. "For the night, anyway. The next day while my father worked us to the bone hanging tobacco in the barn, Samuel slipped away and scoured the fields for that radio, but he couldn't find it anywhere."

"It was gone?"

"So we thought. Until a couple of nights later, after supper, we took a swim in the creek. I waded upstream a ways and, all of a sudden, I stepped on something hard." He let out a laugh.

The sound cascaded over her like icy spring water.

199

"No way!" That creek was at least fifty yards from the barn. His brother must have the arm of a quarterback.

He thumped the back of her seat. "For days, Samuel tinkered with the radio, trying to make it work. He took it apart and put it back together more times than I can count, but it never played again. I still keep it in the barn where Samuel hid it." With a sound between a sigh and a chuckle, he turned back to the road.

Glancing over, she caught a wistful look in his eyes. Where were Jonas's brothers now? "I think I would like Samuel."

He righted his hat and clasped his hands between his knees. "No one can resist Samuel."

She was fairly certain irresistibility ran in the Rishel family. How many brothers did Jonas have, anyway?

He boosted the volume again.

Cruisin' with the Amish. She giggled. What would Jennifer say? When they arrived at her house, she escorted him into the spanking clean garage and flicked on the lights.

After thoroughly examining the automatic garage door opener, he gave a quick once-over to the workspace. "This'll do."

She wouldn't have minded a tad more enthusiasm...or a trophy. Her hands still smelled like wood polish. *Men.*

"I'll unload the lumber and get to work."

As quickly as he loaded the wood, he had it piled in neat stacks on the garage floor. Clad in long black pants, suspenders, and rolled-up shirtsleeves, he didn't even break a sweat. She, on the other hand, was drenched. Enough modesty. Time to change into shorts.

That first day, he worked in the garage all afternoon. She hovered close enough to clock when his cheeks finally glistened, and he shrugged the suspenders from his shoulders to hang at his sides. She vacuumed the van and weeded the flower garden alongside the garage—peeking through the squeaky-clean window. Though the pegboards offered an array of power tools, he used only his own hand tools with the occasional assistance of a battery-powered drill he brought with his supplies. Like the antique tools her father found in her grandfather's attic after he died, Jonas's had smooth, worn, wooden handles. Her mother donated her grandfather's collection to the local history museum where they were displayed in a glass case. Jonas made his tools sing.

In the afternoon, she brought him lemonade and a box fan. He accepted the drink with a smile but squinted at the fan over the edge of the glass. She plugged it in and, with her fingers on the power knob, lifted one shoulder in question.

He ran a handkerchief down the side of his neck and nodded. "Thank you."

She switched it on and hopped to sit on the wide white, storage freezer her mother kept stocked year-round.

He drained the lemonade in one long breath.

Could he tell she fresh-squeezed it just for him? Was it too sweet? Or not sweet enough? She didn't have the guts to ask. She kicked her legs, and her heels tapped against the freezer. "It's hot today."

Crossing his arms, he settled against the workbench. "Today, I thought best to work in the shade. Tomorrow, I'll prepare the ground."

Some of the wood was sanded and clean, richly lustrous. The larger posts were rough hewn and still stippled with bark, as were many smaller pieces. "The gazebo looks beautiful already."

Circling the lumber, he stopped in front of the fan. "I know much of the wood is rough, but when it's assembled, I hope the structure becomes part of the forest—like it grew from the earth around the tree."

The sky-blue shirt rippled across his shoulders, accentuating his waist. She swallowed. Where was Claire's water bottle when she needed it? "I love that idea."

"The design is inventive. I've never built anything like it."

She recalled his backyard by lantern light. "Except your garden gate." A bittersweet smile teased at the corners of his mouth.

He nodded.

The sun dipped behind a cloud, and the garage dimmed. The lines on his forehead deepened, and he held her gaze. He suddenly looked so sad she wanted to hug him or at least to make him smile. Sliding from the freezer, she waved a hand toward the kitchen. "You know, I have a radio that never once took a swim in a creek…if you'd like music while you work?" She bit her tongue. Did she overstep her bounds?

He slitted his eyes.

After all, he seemed reluctant to use the fan.

A slow smile crept across his face. "I'd like that very much."

When she returned with the radio and the lemonade pitcher, she found him bent over the workbench, drilling a hole in a post with a hand drill. Placing the radio on the windowsill, she plugged it in above the fan. "It's tuned to my dad's oldies station, but you can put it on whatever you want." She refilled his glass and set the pitcher on the freezer.

With each revolution of the handle, curls of fragrant cedar spiraled from the drill bit. Keeping his gaze steady on his work, he nodded. "Thank you."

"Okay." She nibbled the inside of her cheek. "Well, let me know if you need anything else." Kneeling to weed the Shasta daisies just beyond the open garage door, she snuck a look from the corner of her eye.

Lowering the drill, he took up the radio and rotated it slowly in his hands. He flipped the power switch, and the sound of a staticky electric guitar poured from the speaker. Replacing the radio on the sill, he swiveled the antenna but didn't change the station.

The oldies were all new to him, she supposed. Well, most of them anyway. Bruce Springsteen? Who would have guessed? And what other secrets lay hidden beneath his hat?

****

When Tessa arrived at the farm the next afternoon, she spotted Rebecca perched on the front porch rail.

Propped on his elbows, Jonas sprawled on the stairs below.

The girl leapt into a bed of impatiens and dashed across the yard. "Tessa! My cat had five kittens!"

She stuck her head out the window and waved. "How wonderful."

"The kittens were born in a box under my bed, and they are so tiny. Jonas says I can't show them to you until they're bigger. Their eyes are still sealed shut."

She squeezed her eyes and opened them wide again. "He promised to watch them when I go to Ohio, but Pumpkin will be very sad when I go."

"Pumpkin is your cat?"

The girl nodded. "She's an excellent mother." She wrapped her fingers around the open window, stepped onto the wheel, and peered inside. "This is a funny car. It's nothing like the van we take to the train station. Jonas said you have drawers with buttons and a pop-top on top. Our spring wagon is open on top, and I sometimes sleep in blanket nests in the back, but it's not the same."

Jonas opened the passenger side door.

Rebecca flew around and hopped inside in a flash. "Can I go for a ride?"

"Not today." He tugged her sleeve. "Your mother needs help with the baking. Now go, before she gets angry."

"She's always angry." Rebecca furrowed her fair brow. "Even about Ohio she's angry. I said, 'what's to be angry about a train ride,' but she just got more angry. Don't forget to tell Tessa all about Ohio while you build her gazebo."

He lifted the wee fairy from the passenger's seat, kissing her atop the head. "Go make your mother smile. I'll see you for supper."

Rebecca twirled and skipped away.

Jonas took her place in the van, tucking his toolbox under the dash.

She slid him a wry look. "You told her about the pop-top?"

With a shrug, he kicked dirt from his boots. "She asked why your car looks so funny. Now, she's taken to calling the buggy a pop-top. Nora…well, you can imagine how Nora feels about that."

"I think I can." Tromping the clutch, she popped the van into gear. "You know, I'll take Rebecca on a ride anytime she'd like. If she's allowed, of course."

He nodded, switched on the radio, and cranked up the volume.

She passed the early part of the afternoon tending her new cutting garden while he used a post hole digger to make deep holes for the massive support beams. Not coincidentally, the garden offered fairly unobstructed views of the sycamore. With her knees in the dirt, she watched as hour after hour he plunged the digger into the ground, twisted it back and forth, and wrenched out huge amounts of earth. At the scraping thud of iron against rock, he'd take up a crowbar and shovel, digging and prying until he extracted the stone. At some point, he removed his hat, and with every thrust of the digger, every spade of soil, his breath escaped in grunts, and his hair swung in wet clumps around his face.

Sweat-stained and dirty herself after a few hours, she fetched blueberry cake and sun tea. She'd awakened early, feeling adventurous. After foraging through her mother's recipe box and laying out each ingredient with precision, she tackled the cake. The procedure took all morning, but gazing at the caramelized crust on each hunk, she had to admit the finished product didn't look half bad.

Legs extended and feet flopped to the sides, Jonas leaned against the sycamore and rested his plate on his belly. He forked a healthy bite of cake.

She sat cross-legged facing him, balancing a plate on her lap and holding her breath. Would he like it?

Rolling his shoulders, he groaned. "Delicious."

She suppressed a squeal. *Stay cool, Meadows.* "It's my mother's recipe. She's a wonderful cook."

"It's good as Nora's."

Not wanting to encroach on his sister's territory, she shook her fork and crumbs flew from the tines. "Oh no. Nora's a genius in the kitchen. My cake is just beginner's luck." She took a taste. The sugary top crackled between her teeth, and the fluffy inside dissolved on her tongue, leaving behind a tang of sour berry. Not bad, indeed. Maybe she inherited the baking gene after all.

Jonas finished his slice in three bites and, dropping his head against the tree, closed his eyes.

He looked tired. He likely rose before dawn to do farm chores. Gazing at him with his eyes closed, she had a flash of the boy he'd been, sneaking behind the barn to listen to forbidden music. Boys will be boys—Amish or no.

"Tell me about yourself, Tessa Meadows," he said without opening his eyes.

Did he feel her gaze? "I'm sorry? Me?" She constantly doubted her ears when he was around.

"How do you come to be planting flowers and designing gazebos in Green Ridge?" He cracked one lid and raised the attendant brow.

Just what shade of blue were his eyes? Not cornflower. Not quite sapphire. Maybe this man merited a whole, new color—miraculous-blue or impossible-blue...make-me-want-to-marry-you-blue.
She ran her tongue over her bottom lip. The wind whispered, "Tomorrow...tomorrow...tomorrow."

"Honestly, I don't really know. I lost my job in

May, so I came home." She sighed. "For the last couple years, I taught writing to college students, but I'm not sure I'm meant to be a teacher." She took a sip of minty iced tea, rolled onto her stomach, and told him everything. About State's financial troubles and her plans for New York. About Jennifer and Adam and how those plans were derailed. About winning the radio contest and volunteering at the hospital and…well, almost everything. Talking to him was like talking to an old friend, but free from the baggage that comes with a relationship muddied with history. He spoke little, and his quiet attention released her internal floodgates all the more. When the grass tickled her belly and weeds jabbed her legs, she flipped onto her back and glanced at her watch. "Oh my gosh, I've been talking over an hour. I'm so sorry."

He leaned to one side and lifted a piece of dried grass from her hair.

Lurching to sitting, she ran her fingers through tangled locks. Dried weeds and bits of clover rained around her.

"Not at all," he said. "You're a fascinating woman, Tessa Rose."

At the sound of her name rolling off his tongue, she stilled, her cheeks bursting into flame. She tossed her hair and shook it again, hiding behind the coppery mass. "Yeah right. International woman of mystery."

"I like thinking about possibilities. You have so many paths to the future."

She swept her hair over one shoulder and tipped back onto her hands. "Maybe, but I don't see them. All roads seem to lead right back here."

"Your home will always stay with you, I think.

And your family." Resting against the tree, he interlaced his fingers atop his thighs and gazed into the canopy. "But I believe human beings have to move forward. We need change in order to grow."

She considered his thoughts carefully before responding. When she finally dared to speak, she kept her voice soft and deliberate. "I guess I don't know much about your life, but what you just said, doesn't sound very...Amish."

He met her gaze. "I suppose not."

His tone was matter of fact but gentle. She didn't move. Had she really crossed a line now?

Rising, he brushed together his palms, extended one hand, and stroked her hair.

Her pulse quickened at the featherlight brush of his fingertips. Like a poppy drawn to the great, golden orb in the sky, she tilted her head toward his touch.

He dropped his hand and, looping his thumbs through his suspenders, loped back to work.

In a rush, she gathered forks and plates and slipped into the pines. The whistled strains of Bruce Springsteen drifted into the grove, and she paused. Fragrant boughs caught her hair, a teasing imitation of his caress. She was snared in the needly grasp of a hundred thousand questions—the most pressing of which was what, if anything, did that touch mean?

Chapter 12

Several mornings later, Tessa knelt on rumpled sheets and peered out the window. Through the pines, she glimpsed the gazebo support beams standing strong and true. Mottled with bark, they looked almost like tree trunks themselves, as natural as the sunflowers in her garden. Jonas was more than a carpenter. He was a master craftsman.

After a few days, she stopped inventing tasks. When she wasn't honestly weeding her gardens or planning the ball, she simply sat under the sycamore while he worked—to admire his skills and craftsmanship, of course. Definitely not his biceps.

He said he liked the company. "You remind me of Rebecca…and of someone I knew as a boy. Plus, I need your help."

More and more unselfconsciously, she obliged. Sometimes, as she handed him a tool or held a board for him to hammer, their shoulders brushed, or their feet bumped. But inside, she waited, longing for his touch to be deliberate. When she closed her eyes at night, she could still conjure his fingers in her hair.

Days rolled by, delicious and summery. Most mornings, she woke early and combed her mother's cookbooks over morning coffee. Her baking grew more adventurous. She lived for the moment every afternoon when Jonas sank his teeth into her homemade treat, his eyes closing as a sound of utter contentment rose from his throat. The rush was better than any thrill ride at Benton's.

Richard's brief evening calls were otherworldly. She could no more picture the places he described than the landscape of Jupiter. He was invited to stay in San Francisco another week, and she celebrated his good fortune. Somehow, conversation never drifted to how she spent her days. He knew about the gazebo and the Midsummer Ball, and she didn't volunteer extra details. She said she missed him.

She did miss him...right?

What she didn't miss was a single afternoon with Jonas. Like clockwork, she rolled up to the farm when the sun was high in the sky. He vaulted into the front seat, cranked down the window, and blasted the radio, peppering her with questions about auto mechanics and combustion engines until she exhausted her scanty knowledge, and all that remained was to goose the gas and ride. The man loved speed. When the old van kissed forty-five miles an hour, he grinned like a wingman in a jet fighter.

"How fast does this pop-top go?" he asked on the ride back to the farm just over a week into construction.

Dusk had fallen, and the salmon-colored sun dipped behind the western ridge. She checked her blind spot and merged onto Route 45. "The speedometer goes to ninety-five, but I think the car would explode above sixty."

Whipping off his hat, he leaned in front of her and peered at the instrument panel. "How fast have you driven it?"

She inhaled deeply, relishing the scents of spicy

cedar and clean sweat. "I don't like to speed. Plus, the whole car shudders around fifty-five. I'm not kidding about it exploding."

He sat back in his seat, bracing both hands on the dashboard, long, strong fingers splayed wide. "Go fifty-five now."

Tessa Meadows was a rule-follower to her core. Her prime directive for twenty-eight years was to avoid getting yelled at by strangers. She glanced sidelong. He faced her now, right hand on the dash, left hand just below her headrest. She could almost feel the heat from his palm on the back of her neck. "But the speed limit is only forty-five."

He lifted his chin, and his eyes darkened. "Go fifty-five."

She gripped the wheel. "Break the speed limit?"

"Uh huh."

One side of his mouth rose in that delicious, half smile, sending crinkles shooting from his eyes. Her stomach pulled in the tingly flutter of ten thousand, electric hummingbird wings. For this man, anything. With a jolt, she crushed the accelerator, and the needle inched toward fifty-five.

Jonas climbed halfway out the window and let out a whoop. "This is my hometown," he shouted.

His hair tossed wildly, and his shirt billowed like a sail.

Grazing cows lifted their heads and watched them hurtle by.

She let out a peal of laughter and leaned into the gas pedal. Next stop, the interstate! She'd drive to Ohio to keep him shouting for joy. The needle kissed sixty. Just how fast could the van go?

A sudden siren pierced the air.

Too late, she slammed on the brakes. "You've got to be kidding me."

Flashing red lights lit the car from behind.

He slid back inside, darting a look out the rear. "What's happening?"

Blood pounding in her ears, she pulled into the parking lot of a shuttered dairy bar. "The police. I'm going to get a ticket." Her throat went thick. For a sickening moment, she feared she might weep. She yanked open the glove compartment and groped inside, scraping her knuckles over the sharp hinge. Napkins and straws littered Jonas's feet. "Where's the darn registration card?"

"It's all right. Let me help."

His voice soothed the panic bouncing around her lungs like an electrified pinball. She withdrew her hand and blew on her knuckles.

"Is this what you need?" He extended the zippered pouch containing the necessary documents.

With a weak nod, she took them and glanced in the rearview mirror.

A doughy officer lumbered toward her, his blue uniform purple in the taillights' glow. She knew the guy—not well, but she recognized him as a wrestler in high school. She rolled down her window.

He tipped back his hat. "License and registration please?"

Without warning, Jonas threw open the door and leapt out.

"Jonas, no." She scrambled for his arm, but she wasn't quick enough.

The policeman stumbled backward and twitched a

hand toward his belt. But when Jonas, fully garbed in the clothes of his sect, stepped in front of the headlights, the officer froze.

Jonas towered over the man by at least six inches. He put on his hat and extended a hand. "Happy to meet you, sir—I'm Jonas Rishel."

Leaning back, the officer tucked his thumbs into his waistband. "Kindly return to the vehicle."

Jonas lowered his hand. "And your name, sir?"

The man puffed his chest, displaying his badge. "Officer Kunkle. Now, I need you to return to—"

"Officer Kunkle, yes. I believe I've seen you and your wife at market on Wednesdays. My sister, Nora, sells pies and cakes. Your wife is especially fond of strawberry rhubarb, as I recall."

Officer Kunkle floundered for his pad and pen. "Strawberry what?"

Moths spiraled and dove in the headlights.

Jonas swatted them with one hand. "Sir, I'm afraid this incident is my fault. Miss Tessa Meadows—surely you know her father, Professor Meadows, up at the college? Miss Meadows was kind enough to indulge me in an adventure. As you can imagine, I'm not too familiar with motorized vehicles in general, and I asked Miss Meadows to drive a bit faster than she ordinarily would."

Officer Kunkle leaned around Jonas and eyeballed her through the windshield. "I clocked you at sixty-two, Miss Meadows."

"I can assure you she would never have driven so quickly if I hadn't urged her. She is completely without blame and never broke a traffic law in her life." He glanced over his shoulder for confirmation.

She nodded emphatically.

"Now, sir, I take full responsibility for any violation of your laws." He wagged a finger at Officer Kunkle's pad. "Please write whatever you need on that paper for me."

The brazenness. The sheer audacity. She never witnessed anything like it. Officer Kunkle pulled at his collar and shuffled like he was dancing a two-step with an invisible partner.

A pickup truck flew past at what looked like much faster than sixty-two miles per hour, kicking up dust.

"It's Jonas Rishel," he went on, "R-I-S—"

"You don't need to spell out your name." The policeman cleared his throat with a long harrumph. He glared through the windshield and closed his ticket book. "I'll let you off with a warning, Ms. Meadows, but don't let it happen again."

She nodded. Heck, she would have crossed her heart and pinky promised if he asked. Her elbows unlocked, and she released her fingers one by one from the steering wheel. Jonas caught her gaze—the cat that ate the canary—and offered his hand again.

Officer Kunkle stared for a long moment. Finally, his shoulders slumped, and with a pronounced eye roll, he shook and retreated to his car.

"I appreciate your kindness, sir," Jonas called to his back. "And I'll make sure my sister sets aside one of her finest pies for you and your wife." He slid into the passenger seat with a grin.

Slack-jawed, she stared. "So, Samuel isn't the only Rishel boy able to talk himself out of a pickle."

"You might be right." He whipped off his hat and twirled it on an index finger. "But you're also wrong."

Shifting into gear, she nosed onto Route 45. "How so?"

He snagged the hat and tipped it onto his head. "This pop-top can go over sixty without exploding."

Maybe it could, but she was preoccupied with another discovery. It crawled across her brain like a televised news flash. This man, this *Amish* man, compelled her to take risks like no one before. She blew out a breath. That realization was far more unsettling than an exploding pop-top in the heart of the boonies.

****

A seemingly endless string of sunny days snapped when Officer Kunkle let off Tessa with a warning. When she hopped out in front of the farmhouse the next afternoon, the sky churned purple-gray and unsettled.

Barefoot, Rebecca tore across the grass and circled the van, chanting, "Pop-top! Pop-top!"

Spine rigid as a flagpole, Nora sat on the front porch bench, a yellowware bowl balanced on her lap and a bushel basket at her feet. Poised beside the open door, Tessa waved and smiled.

Nora just glowered as fresh, green peas flew from her fingertips.

With grudging awe, Tessa watched her work. Not even Nana Shiffer shelled peas so quickly.

Seconds later, Jonas emerged from the barn, lugging his toolbox.

His pace was slow, and his step was heavier than usual. Maybe she could encourage him not to work such a long day. She glanced at the sky. Maybe the weather would do it for her.

He stopped and spoke to Nora.

Tessa couldn't make out the words.

215

The woman nodded, pressing her lips in a thin, hard line.

Rebecca slipped past her into the driver's seat and clutched the wheel. "Did Jonas tell you about our journey to Ohio?"

Bracing for a shouted reprimand, Tessa shot Nora a look, but the woman was still talking to Jonas. "No, he didn't."

Grabbing the gearshift, Rebecca heaved a sigh. "I knew he would forget. *Mamm* and I are taking the train from Harrisburg to Ohio for cousin Sarah's wedding. Cousin Sarah is getting married in July and not November. Can you imagine? *Mamm* says that's how they do things out there in Ohio." She flicked the windshield wipers and the turn signal.

As the wipers squeaked and the signal lights blinked, Rebecca's eyes flashed. Given the opportunity, the imp would doubtlessly wrench the van into gear and peel out.

"*Mamm* took care of cousin Sarah for weeks and weeks when cousin Sarah was just a baby." Rebecca spun in her seat and peered into the back of the van. "I wish I had a cousin Sarah to take care of."

"My cousins live far away, too." Tessa stepped into the cab and rested a protective hand over the parking brake handle on the dash. "What a fun adventure."

Rebecca peeked from beneath white-blonde lashes. "Would you like to know a secret?"

A cloud, just as foreboding as those overhead, shadowed the child's face. Tessa hesitated. "All right."

Rebecca cupped her hands around Tessa's ear. "One day, I will drive away from this farm and never come back."

The girl's breath was hot and redolent of molasses. Tessa drew back and studied her face. Solemn determination mingled with the glint of mischief her uncle occasionally displayed.

Rebecca placed one finger over her lips. "Shh…"

"Out of the pop-top, Miss Rebecca Beiler!"

Tessa whirled and jounced down, tripping over a tree root.

Jonas extracted his wiggly niece, swinging her in circles until she squealed and giggled. He hugged her tight and plopped her on the ground. "Go help your mother."

The child heaved a sigh from the bottoms of her feet but obeyed. With Jonas in the passenger's seat, Tessa drove away, surveying the porch through the rearview mirror. Rebecca took up her mother's task, her pixie face as placid as a millpond.

Nora limped into the house.

She seemed to move slower than usual as well. As Tessa rounded the bend, the atmosphere inside the van was strangely quiet. For the first time, Jonas didn't click on the radio.

He turned his hat in his hands, running his thumb along the wide brim. "Rebecca…" Dropping his hat, he shook his head and cracked the window.

The metal bridge hummed beneath her tires.

She smiled. "She is a wonder."

"Nora worries about her." He ran the heels of his hands down his thighs. "Sometimes I do, too."

Why were they worried? She never met a healthier, happier child. Perhaps she was a tad strong willed, but based on Jonas's stories, spunkiness ran in the family. "She's just an energetic little girl."

"What did she say? In your ear?"

His gaze was insistent as the damp-earth breeze through the window. Every child threatens to run away. Rebecca's confession was likely the whim of an active imagination. Still, she hesitated to repeat the words. She forced a light laugh. "Now that's a secret between Miss Rebecca Beiler and myself." Feeling an urge for music, she hovered her fingers over the knob, then glanced his way. He looked at her unblinking, the tender flesh beneath his eyes shadowed blue-gray. With a thumb, she swiped dust from the radio display and wiped it on her shorts.

"Tessa. Please."

"Silly talk, nothing more." Despite his open window, the air was stuffy. She cranked down hers an inch. "She told me all about the trip to Ohio, though. She's rather miffed you forgot to give me the details."

For several miles, he was silent.

Green seeped from the trees, and the ridgeline darkened. Like a blast from a water cannon, raindrops spattered the windshield. She flicked the wipers on and off again.

He shifted in his seat and pinched his forehead between thumb and fingers. "Tessa." His voice was thick.

She swung off the highway too fast, and her tires skidded on the gravel berm. Leaning into the wheel, she veered back on course. "Do you really want to know?" Another spatter of rain strafed the windshield. Clumps of wild tiger lilies lining the road to her house undulated as she passed. She lifted one hand from the wheel and let it fall into her lap. "She said one day she'll drive away from the farm and never come back."

With a sigh, he dropped his head against the headrest and closed his eyes.

She wanted so badly to touch him—to reach out and squeeze his hand. "She was just being silly."

He shook his head. "She will break her mother's heart."

"You don't know that." Turning into her driveway, she saw the living room windows were open. White sheers billowed phantomlike in the wind. She should close them before heavy rain came. Craving fresh air, she pulled the latch.

Suddenly, he grasped her arm.

A hot flush raced across her collarbones, and she whirled. His eyes were smoldering blue coals above cheekbones like knife-edged mountain peaks. His fingers pressed with firm insistence.

"Do you know what happens when you leave?"

The words were a jagged whisper, urgent yet costly somehow.

He tightened his hold. "Do you?"

Her mouth was dry. She ran her tongue over her bottom lip and caught the flesh between her teeth. "I—maybe I've heard, or read—"

"Sure, everyone knows about the shunning. Such a queer, quaint ritual." He choked a laugh. "Understand this—nothing about this life is quaint. If you join the church and leave, you are dead. No one speaks to you; no one shares a meal with you. You are no longer a person in this world. You are no one."

He searched her face with a gaze as piercing as his words. The sudden intensity surprised her, and yet didn't, as if she always knew a restless current coursed just beneath his skin. Loosening his grip, he trailed his thumb along the tender skin at the base of her bicep. Goose bumps emerged at his touch.

"That child—that precious child—will be no one."

Shaking her head, she covered his hand with her own. His knuckles were rough. She ran her fingertips between them and down the strong, yet fine, bones of his hand. "Rebecca will always be a person in this world, and someone will always love her. I will."

At her simple admission, he stilled. He lowered his chin to his chest, and his shoulders rose and fell in a single breath torn from somewhere deep inside.

She stared at her hand atop his. Her fingernails were dark from the morning's gardening, and traces of dirt lay in the creases of her skin like contour lines on a map. "Do you ever think about leaving?"

Releasing her, he met her gaze again. "Every single day."

The quiet certainty of his confession caught her off guard, but again, she wasn't wholly surprised. "Why do you stay?" As if the question caused him pain, he shuddered, but his gaze remained steady.

"Why do you?"

Though his tone was even, the question hit her like a roundhouse kick to the solar plexus. Blinking rapidly, she struggled for words.

Before she could utter a syllable, he flung open the door and left.

Once inside, she ran her fingertips over her arm where his touch still tingled and watched him through the kitchen window. The weight of what he dared to speak lay heavy on her heart.

He crossed the lawn in even strides, his toolbox tracing a wide arc at his side, and disappeared under the pines.

Two hours later, the sky opened. With the first flash of lightning, rain poured in buckets. She dropped menu plans for the Midsummer Ball and flew out the back door. Peering through raindrops that pelted her face, she spotted him under the sycamore, yanking a tarp over a stack of lumber. He pushed a pile of tools into her hands, and she fled to the garage. After several more runs, the materials were safely stowed, and she stood by his side, staring at the deluge. "You're soaked." Sneakers squelching, she crossed the cement floor and opened the inner door to the house. "Let me get you some dry clothes."

Staring through the open door, he shook his head. "I'm fine."

She softened her voice. "It's all right. You can come inside."

His shoulders eased. "I'll meet you on the porch." He leaped a puddle and dashed into the rain.

Shivering, she pulled her softest joggers and hoodie and a fresh towel from the dryer. She ducked into the powder room and slipped on the warm clothing, then scurried to the front entryway. The mirror offered a fleeting glimpse of damp curls and ruddy cheeks. With a deep breath, she opened the door.

Hands spread, he leaned on the railing, watching the coming storm. His shirt clung to wide shoulders and tapered in sodden wrinkles to a narrow waist. She hugged the towel to her chest.

The door latched with a heavy thump.

He turned, and a smile flickered across his face.

She extended the towel.

"Thank you." He took it and laid it over the porch

rail. Lowering his suspenders, he unbuttoned his shirt and peeled it from his shoulders.

The cloth was the color of a September sky. Her heart hammered, and she spun. Who told her the Amish didn't use buttons on their clothing, only hooks and eyes? Apparently, that person was misinformed. She flicked back her gaze. Also, turned out Amish men do indeed wear undershirts. Was she disappointed or relieved he didn't stand before her shirtless? Even so, his sopping undershirt clung to his chest, leaving no secrets as to what lay beneath.

He toweled his head with vigor.

The wind gusted, and the leaves on the gnarled crabapple trees flipped upside down.

She pulled the hoodie tight and tugged the strings at her neck. "You must be freezing. Can I get you a jacket or something?"

He returned the wet towel with a nod.

Jogging into the entryway, she tossed the towel over the banister and yanked open the closet. Her grandfather's checked, flannel shirt hung on a hook. On chilly mornings, she wore it to garden, but she hadn't touched it since May. Burying her nose in soft fabric, she inhaled. Fortunately, the shirt smelled more like detergent than shoes. Back outside, she handed it to him and crossed to the porch swing. Even through her sweatpants, the wooden slats were damp and cold.

He pulled on the shirt and lowered himself next to her. "Thanks."

The chains creaked, and the old garment's seams strained tight over his shoulders, but both held. Good construction mattered.

Fiery, forked streaks in shades of blue and gold

crawled from cloud to cloud. When she was a child, she always ran to the swing at the first, distant rumble of thunder and waited, hands clasped and feet dangling, for the storm to arrive. Even now, her breath quickened as the seconds between lightning and thunder dwindled to none. She leaned against his shoulder and shivered.

"Are you cold?" he asked.

"No." She twisted her hair into a bun and let it fall just to feel the tickling caress of her curls. "I like it out here."

Thunder vibrated the chains until they buzzed.

He tilted his face to the sky. "You remind me so much of her."

His voice was so low she barely made out the words. "Rebecca?"

A nearly simultaneous blaze of lightning and crack of thunder shattered the sky.

"My wife."

Her heart launched like a firework into her throat and exploded, raining pinprick sparks in her chest. She formed the word *oh* with her lips, but no sound came out.

"She was beautiful." One corner of his mouth twitched ever so slightly. "She was an angel."

The rain fell harder, overflowing the gutters and pouring from the roof. Yet, their little refuge grew quiet. She ran a nail under a peeling strip of paint on the arm of the swing. "What was her name?"

"Elizabeth. She liked gardening, too. Sunflowers. Sweet peas."

She risked a glance at him. "Sweet peas are hard to grow."

His hands were clasped loosely in his lap. His gaze

was far away.

"But they smell like heaven," she added.

"They do."

In shared silence, she rocked beside him until the rain let up as quickly as it began, and the wind shook drops from the crabapples in spattering spurts.

"Are you in love with that man?"

His voice was gentle and without judgment. In spite of the now-chilly air, she felt her cheeks flame. "I don't know." The cuffs of her sleeves slid over her hands. Shrouded in mist, she could almost believe they floated in one of the low-lying clouds that kissed the ridgetops.

"What is his profession?" he asked.

"He's a doctor. A very fine doctor."

He nodded. "That's good."

How long she sat, his thigh warm against hers, she didn't know. Nor, when she lay on the couch that night, could she recall a single concrete detail from the drive back to the farm. Her eyelids were so heavy. The soft flannel shirt caressed her cheek. Far off thunder rolled over the ridges. Sometime later, her cell rang, jarring her from sleep. The clock on the DVR glowed eleven twenty-two. She ran a hand over the end table, finally snagging her phone. "Hello?"

"Sweetheart, I changed my flight. I'm coming home tomorrow."

"Richard?" She heaved upright, and the shirt puddled on the floor.

"I woke you. I'm sorry. Listen, darling, this Saturday I'm stealing you for the whole day. Just the two of us. I'll pick you up at nine in the morning, all right?"

Panic surged from her toes to her fingertips. Flailing for the end table light, she whacked a stack of coasters, and they clattered to the floor. "What? No!"

"Sweetheart, I haven't seen you for two weeks—"

"I mean—I can't." She groped behind the table for the coasters. They were gone.

"You can't?"

Even half asleep, she couldn't miss the note of annoyance in his tone. She scrambled for an explanation. "I'll…be in New York this Saturday— visiting Jenn. I'm so sorry."

"Seriously? Can't you go next weekend?"

Scooping up the shirt, she cuddled it in her lap. "I already got the bus ticket." She winced. Lying outright left a sour taste in her mouth. "But we'll get together first thing when I'm back. I promise."

"Look, I'll have to work round the clock to make up for the time I've been away. I was counting on seeing you Saturday."

His voice was so very far away. She drew her knees to her chin. "I'm really sorry. I didn't know you were coming home."

His huffed sigh crackled through the speaker. "I guess your surprise has to wait."

"Another surprise?"

Laughter swelled in the background. The sound over the phone muted, and his voice came through muffled and indistinct. Then the line cleared.

"Listen, sweetheart, I have to run to a dinner meeting. One way or another, I can't wait to see you."

She softened her voice. "Me, too." Switching off the end table light, she cringed. Was she lying now, too?

He took a quick breath.

The signal from thousands of miles away bounced off a satellite, streaming into her ear in a nanosecond. She could almost feel the cool vacuum of his inhalation against her sleep-sweaty cheek.

"I love you, Tessa."

The miles between them compressed to a point of infinite density. The phone became a thousand-pound weight in her hand. She bobbled it, caught it again, and brought it back to her lips. "Richard, I…" In the background, insistent voices called his name.

"Gotta go. Bye, sweetheart."

The line went dead.

The phone clunked on the floor, and she collapsed onto her back, tucking the shirt under her chin.

Richard said the "l" word.

She tickled her lips across flannel and inhaled deeply the scent of sawdust.

Again.

Now what? If he said it a third time, she'd have no choice but to respond.

As she surrendered to sleep, a memory shimmered through her final fragment of consciousness—a sensation, really, more felt than thought or seen—the back of Jonas's hand brushing a soft caress over her cheekbone. So quick and so light it might not have happened at all but for the searing recollection of his gently rasping knuckles.

And in that instant, her exhausted brain fired off a thought in response—a miraculous alchemy of chemistry, electricity, and emotion.

I love you, the synapses spoke…once the thunder finally quieted.

Chapter 13

Two days later, Tessa rubbed her eyes and stared through the tinted bus window. The Hudson River sparkled steel-blue, and the massive city rose before her, gray and glassy in the afternoon light. Sepia and silver buildings sprawled as far as she could see. She put a palm to the window. Downtown Green Ridge would likely fit between two fingers with room to spare. From the end of the world to the middle of it all in no time flat, thanks to the magic of sleep.

The butterflies flitting around her empty stomach took up kickboxing. The last time she visited New York, she was fifteen years old. Days before Christmas, her tenth-grade English class came to a matinee of a flashy Broadway musical. After the show, she trooped through the dizzying maze of skyscrapers in a conspicuous herd, finally arriving at Rockefeller Center where ice skaters stumbled and twirled in a scene straight from the movies. Slices of greasy pizza at a fast-food joint near Times Square topped off the experience. Though city grit lingered on her hands until she scrubbed them late that night at home, she couldn't scrub the dazzle from her heart.

Thirteen years later, she pulled into Port Authority not a starry-eyed tourist, but a prospective New Yorker.

Okay, Manhattan, show me what you've got.

With a breath of exhaust-filled air, she exited the

bus into the cavernous depths of the terminal. Hoisting her bags, she peeked through glass doors, and her heart soared.

Inside the station, Jenn charged her, flinging her arms around Tessa's neck.

Laughing, she bent and returned the embrace. Jenn's hair slid coolly over her cheek.

"You look gorgeous!" Jenn gave her the once-over. "You're all skinny and freckly, and your hair is amazing—as always. What's your secret? Are you in love?"

"Guess it's the country air." She had plenty of time for girl talk later. "You look like you walked out of a magazine."

"This little old thing?" Jenn struck a pose in her smart suit, satiny blouse, and trendy heels. "Usually, I'm schlepping around the office in leggings and a tee, but I had a meeting today with the editorial staff. You like?" She made a duck-lipped model face, then burst out laughing and snorted. "Let me help with your bags."

Tessa carried only her backpack, one small duffel, and a tote laden with whoopie pies and Jenn's beloved black jellybeans from the Farmers' Market. She also carefully wrapped a bouquet of flowers from her garden and laid them on top, hoping they wouldn't wilt on the trip.

Jenn slung the treats over one shoulder and danced on the escalator up to the taxi stand singing, "Presents! Presents!"

She sounded exactly like Rebecca when the girl sang "Pop-top! Pop-top!" on a farm that felt ten thousand miles away. In an alternate universe, she could almost believe her goofy friend was the Amish girl's longed-for cousin. They were definitely kindred spirits.

Scurrying, she tracked Jenn's blonde head, weaving through crowds and out the door. Wedging her bag between her knees, she slid into the back of a cab. The car lurched into traffic, and Tessa jolted against the seat. She fastened her seatbelt and clung white-knuckled to the door handle while Jenn, completely at ease, pointed out her favorite haunts. The cab smelled like incense and ham sandwiches, and, slightly queasy, Tessa gladly tumbled out twenty minutes later in front of Jenn's ultra-modern high-rise on the Upper West Side.

Sliding glass doors whooshed aside, revealing a uniformed doorman behind an imposing desk.

He dipped his chin. "Welcome home, Ms. Sweet."

Her roommate flirted shamelessly with the old gentleman until he finally cracked a smile and handed over a bundle of dry cleaning. Jenn always loved a challenge. Tessa gestured to the plastic-wrapped suits. "They deliver dry cleaning to your house?"

Jenn hit the button for the twentieth floor and rested an elbow on the elevator wall. "Nice perk, huh? Adam's working a ridiculous schedule and won't be home for hours. I thought we'd order food and pop some popcorn, and if we feel like it, stream a movie. If you can stand to spend an evening in with little ol' me."

She sighed. "I can't imagine anything better." The elevator gave a cheerful ding, and the door opened soundlessly. In contrast to the dim, interior hallway, Jenn's living room was a lofty expanse, blindingly white in the afternoon sunlight.

Jenn clicked a remote, and translucent blinds lowered halfway down a wall of floor-to-ceiling windows, filtering the glare.

Shielding her eyes, Tessa spotted one or two knick-knacks from their college suite, but the furniture radiated brand-newness. It was sleek and modern with funky, graphic throw pillows and accent pieces right off the design room floor. On the far side of the room, a marble-topped counter separated the dining area from an airy, open kitchen. The space was full of hard surfaces and ninety-degree angles—stunning but cold— a feeling she never before associated with her dear roomie.

"Not bad for an army brat from Virginia, huh?" Jenn hopped onto an industrial-style stool and dug into the bag of treats.

"This place is amazing."

"Don't look at me. Adam's parents have more money than God. I'm just lucky if I make my half of the rent each month." She chuckled deep in her chest. "Ah! You brought jellybeans." Jenn tore open the bag and popped a few onto her tongue. "The bathroom's down the hall. You'll sleep in the office on the pullout couch. Don't worry—it's comfy. I crash there those rare nights Adam's such an ogre I can't stand to be in the same room."

She moved to the windows and gazed over the city. Rooftop gardens, terraces, and hidden backyards unfolded like an urban patchwork quilt.

"And flowers. Did you grow these?"

Tearing herself from the view, she turned and nodded.

"Amazing. I still kill every plant I look at." Jenn

ripped a bunch of fresh tulips from a chunky vase on the counter, crammed them into the garbage, and replaced them with Tessa's bouquet. "So much better."

Tossing thirty dollars worth of tulips and replacing them with Tessa's homegrown gift was Jennifer Sweet in a nutshell. With a smile, Tessa returned to the windows. "I can't believe this view. Quite a step up from our college housing. All that's missing is your *Bull Durham* poster."

"Inside my closet door." Jenn giggled. "I've kissed that thing so many times the CSI. guys could probably get a DNA sample from Kevin Costner's lips. When he was young, he was super hot."

A few hours later, so stuffed with Chinese food she had to unbutton her jeans, Tessa snagged the cellophane-wrapped whoopie pie Jenn tossed from the kitchen. But for the spanking new couches, they might have been back in their dorm room senior year.

"I'm so glad you finally got your skinny butt here to see me." Jenn dove into a pile of pillows on the floor and scooped another handful of jellybeans. "Enough of my boring life. Tell me about you. Mysterious Amish farmers? Dashing young doctors? Spill."

"I think I'm going crazy." She sank into the sofa and licked cream from her fingertips. "Doctors and farmers and me. Oh my."

"What's up with those beards with no mustaches?"

She spluttered a laugh, and a white glob flew onto her lap. She swiped it with a take-out napkin. "I wish I knew. Jonas doesn't have one—a beard—or a mustache for that matter. I don't know why. I can't muster the courage to ask him anything."

"And the good doctor? Richard?" Jenn rolled the

"r" for about five seconds.

"The good doctor is also clean-shaven. Though he's definitely a five o'clock shadow guy."

"Sexy." Swinging around, Jenn dropped her elbows onto the coffee table and smirked. "The question is…is he good?"

Hashing over Jenn's relationships was second nature. Half the time they should have been studying, they obsessed over Jenn's boyfriends instead. Now that the sport sandal was firmly on the other foot, she flushed to her eyeballs. "Quite good from what I can tell. I mean, he's kind of the perfect guy. He's brilliant and witty, and he's so incredibly charming. He swept me off my feet like he had a broom."

"And he adores you?"

The sun slipped behind a nearby building, and the light dimmed like someone slid a switch. With the room in shadow, talking freely came easily. "I think he does. You know how people say in every relationship one person is the flower and the other's the waterer? All my life I've been the waterer—just dousing cacti. Now, I'm the flower. So weird."

Leaning back on her hands, Jenn rested her feet on the table and wiggled her toes. "Um, I think you mean so awesome."

"Maybe…but I might be drowning." She nibbled the whoopie pie, and the rich odor of chocolate immediately summoned a memory of Jonas's peace offering. Her mouth watered. Bordeaux was nice, but what was sweeter than a humble, brown bag of farm-baked treats? "And the thing is—well, to mix my metaphors—"

Jenn pressed a hand to her chest. "Horrors. Go

on…"

"I'm not sure Richard makes my heart sing. I really like being with him. He makes me feel attractive and well taken care of—"

"And drenched…" Jenn waggled her brows.

"So to speak." Her neck flushed hot. Outside, light shone from at least a dozen other apartment windows. So many homes—so many families—so very close. On first impression, the city felt concrete and sterile, but life teemed in staggering density on every block. Likely, more romance thrived in a square mile on the Upper West Side than in all of Green Ridge. She licked squelched cream from between the last bite of cake. "But my heart doesn't skip a beat when I hear his voice."

"And it does when the Amish dude calls his cows?"

She barked a laugh but kept the food inside her mouth. "It does. I know—I sound insane. I doubt Jonas would even consider being with me—dating me is likely flat-out forbidden—but he inquired about Richard the other day. We were sitting on my porch, and he asked point-blank if I was in love with him."

Jenn gaped. "He knows about Richard?"

"He saw us holding hands at the Farmers' Market a few weeks ago." Scrunching her shoulders to her ears, she shivered. "Talk about awkward."

"Holy cow. You're starring in a Smallville soap opera out there. What did you tell him?"

She looked back out the windows. The sunset sky between buildings was the same salmon-tinged violet as back home. "That I don't know. Which is the truth. And I don't know what he thought about that. When I told him Richard is a doctor, he said, 'that's good,' so he probably thinks Richard is the perfect guy, too." She hugged a velvety pillow. "But sometimes…sometimes Jonas looks at me, and I feel like he sees me, you know? Like I'm the only person in the world. And then he touches my face—"

"I'm sorry, what?" Jenn whipped her feet off the table and whirled onto her knees. "The Amish guy touched your face?"

She cringed. "I think." Her voice emerged from pulled-back lips as a squeak. Jenn widened her eyes until they occupied half her face.

"You think?"

"The evening is kind of a blur."

Jenn chased a swig of coffee with a gulp of berry wine cooler. "A blur, huh? You're sure he didn't slip something into your…what do they even drink? Your whole milk?"

Planting her elbows on knees, she clasped her hands under her chin. "The entire afternoon was bizarre and kind of wonderful, honestly. We were all alone on my porch swing during this wild storm—big thunder and nonstop lightning—and then he told me about his wife—"

"Hold up a second."

Jenn thrust out her hands like a traffic cop.

"The Amish dude's married?" Her voice echoed in the marble and stainless-steel kitchen.

Spoken aloud, the entire situation with Jonas sounded ridiculous. She buried her face in her hands. "*Was* married, I guess. She died. I don't know details. He said she was an angel—"

"He's mourning his angelic, dead wife? Oh jeez,

Tess, this story just gets more and more absurd."

"I know, I know." Toppling sideways, she smushed her face into the pillow. How could she convey their connection without sounding trite? As electric as chain lightning? As strong as a riptide? He was Amish. She wasn't. She knew how crazy her crush sounded.

"Want my advice?" Jenn clambered onto the sofa, hauling a heaping bowl of popcorn into her lap. "'Cause I'm giving it to you no matter what."

"Fortunately, I want it." Jenn's expression turned atypically serious. Tessa braced for a dose of reality from her most fun-loving friend.

"Don't dismiss the doctor."

Chucking the pillow, she groaned and snarfed a handful of popcorn.

"Seriously." Jenn took Tessa's arm and pulled her to sitting. "He sounds like real relationship material. Not some hopeless fantasy."

"But Richard doesn't—"

"Make your heart sing opera, I know." She raised her wine cooler in a toast. "Let me tell you, singing hearts aren't all they're cracked up to be. I love Adam, but my heart quit singing when I got a whiff of his running shoes. You need a person you can build something with."

A single faint star twinkled in the space between buildings. She hadn't even told Jenn that Richard said he loved her. With that little detail, Jenn would start shopping for a bridesmaid dress. She sighed. "You're right. You're always right."

"About men, yes. About everything else? Not remotely. Ever since I met you, you've clung to these impossibly high standards only some imaginary dream guy could satisfy. Men are fallible, but you've got to give them a fair shot, fault riddled as they are. And God knows, they are."

That night, as Tessa slipped between crisp sheets on the most luxurious sofa bed imaginable, Adam's voice floated down the hall, followed by Jenn's infectious laugh. She sighed and flipped onto her back. Jenn talked a good game, but Tessa knew. Behind the door of that twentieth-floor, Manhattan bedroom, a pair of hearts sang an operatic duet—smelly running shoes or no. How could she settle for anything less?

****

The next morning, Tessa gazed down a tree-lined path into Central Park.

"New York, New York—it's a heck of a town!" Jenn executed a pirouette in the middle of Columbus Circle, punctuated with jazz hands. "I should have been an actor."

Hazy sunlight glinted off a towering, golden statue that looked like it belonged in a European city.

A guy selling ice cream at its base offered Jenn a fist bump. "You do you."

Jenn flashed a smile. "Here, you got your four-dollar popsicles, your three-dollar bottles of water, and your two-dollar-and-fifty-cent ice cream sandwiches that used to cost thirty-five cents in the school cafeteria. I love New York!"

She eyeballed the sign dangling from the guy's cart and winced. Jenn wasn't exaggerating. "My radio prize winnings will be gone in a week."

"I don't know. Fifteen thousand dollars buys a ton of ice cream sandwiches."

"But doesn't go far in rent." She spent the early

morning browsing a real estate app Jenn recommended, discovering in short order that if she were to even consider moving to New York, she needed either a really good job or to win a bunch of radio contests pronto. This whole moving to the city scheme was way more complex than she imagined.

Honestly, little about city life was as she expected. Central Park, for example, completely astonished her. It was mind-bogglingly large—a vast oasis of green in the midst of the concrete desert. From winding footpaths and whimsical arched bridges to ponds, playgrounds, and even a stone castle on a hill, the park revealed delightful surprises at every turn. And gardens—who knew city parks had gardens? Flowers teemed from manicured beds and cascading planters. Amidst the greenery, parents chatted on benches while children rode scooters, and groups of exotically pierced teenagers strummed guitars. *Sorry, Mrs. Diefenderfer. Not even a little bit scary.*

A subway ride downtown delivered them to Times Square and Forty-Second Street, sporting acres of neon and a family-friendly vibe. Hoofing eight blocks south, she entered Herald Square, where she and Jenn roamed the Macy's cosmetics counters and sprinted by ladies in lab coats spraying perfume. Another subway whisked her to Jenn's favorite neighborhood, Greenwich Village, with its eclectic mix of cafés, pastry shops, and upscale boutiques. She could almost imagine living on one of those shady streets where history oozed from four-story brownstones. Compared to Jenn's neighborhood, the Village felt homey.

Just when Tessa thought she couldn't walk another block, she spotted a funky SoHo café with an unpronounceable French name. She nudged Jenn. "Mocha time?"

Jenn grabbed her elbow and pulled her toward the door. "You read my mind."

At a tiny table beneath a striped awning, she savored iced coffee as decadent as chocolate cream pie while an eclectic assortment of people and dogs paraded for their entertainment.

Jenn licked whipped cream from her straw. "I know you have men falling all over you back home, but Adam invited Dennis, a friend from work, to dinner. We'll meet at eight, and then Dennis's roommate is playing in a band at a midtown bar, so maybe we'll stop by after?"

A piece of ice crunched between her molars. "I do kind of have a boyfriend."

Jenn waggled the straw at Tessa's left hand. "No ring on that finger yet, missy. Seriously, no pressure. Let's just have some fun."

She rolled her shoulders, stretched aching legs, and gave Jenn the thumbs-up. With no idea how she would survive until eight pm without eating, she swiped on her new Macy's lipstick in the cramped café bathroom. All right, universe, bring on the blind dates. And the second iced mocha.

A little after eight, she and Jenn met the guys in front of a pocket-sized Italian restaurant in the East Village. Smelling of stale cologne and whatever he ate for lunch, Dennis smothered her hand in a clammy handshake. Instantly, she knew. This man was not a love connection.

Dennis was undoubtedly smart. He discussed current events with an exhaustive knowledge that excited a modicum of awe, though nothing else. He was also redheaded, with the sallow complexion that sadly plagued some men of their shared coloring. Her order had barely passed her lips when Dennis launched into a lecture predicting the inevitable extinction of red hair from the planet.

He raked his fingers through stringy strands at his temples. "My views are controversial but supported by the Oxford Hair Foundation, who claimed red hair could vanish by 2060."

She ignored him and counted the light fixtures. Jenn and Adam also took no notice of Dennis's lecture. Oblivious to the world, they cuddled in the corner, smooching and giggling. Mildly nauseated, Tessa sipped her seltzer, even while something in her belly pulled, and her mind's eye lingered over Jonas's taut, tanned cheek.

"Most people presume the redhead is of Celtic descent," Dennis droned.

She dipped a piece of crusty bread in olive oil and slipped it into her mouth. Divine. Could she possibly fit a dozen loaves into her tote? She offered Dennis the basket.

He waved her off and kept talking.

You snooze, you lose, dude. This baguette's mine.

Dennis slurped light beer. "They leap to the 'Irish Assumption,' as I call it, when in actuality, many redheads are Germanic, even Italian in heritage. Of course, the Celts spread their seed across the ancient world."

With a shiver, she wiped from her mind the image of Dennis spreading any kind of seed. His subsequent catalog of famous redheads who fought in the Civil

War was interrupted when the food arrived. She thanked the gods of antipasti, ordered a cocktail, and dug in. Her spaghetti carbonara was as flavorful as Dennis was bland. She tuned him out, along with Jenn and Adam and the two men arguing about politics at a table two inches away. The twelve, brass wall sconces emitted a cozy glow, and tea lights illuminated each face, even Dennis's, to its best advantage. Did Jonas eat every evening meal by lamplight, the flickering flame dancing in his deep-sea eyes?

Dennis rapped on the table. "Are you?"

The farm vaporized in a flash. "Am I what?" She sipped her cocktail. Turned out a sprig of rosemary was lovely in a beverage.

"Moving here in the fall?"

Jenn fed Adam a bite of meatball. "Yup. Lizzy needs a roommate in September, and I know Tess will love her. Right, babe?"

"Absolutely." Adam nibbled Jenn's neck.

Jenn swatted him with a napkin.

Tessa cleared her throat. "Well, I'm still working out my plans—"

"You're coming here—that's the plan." Jenn nuzzled Adam's cheek. "Tell Tessa that's the plan."

"That's the plan, Tess," Adam said.

At least, that's what she thought he said. His face was buried behind Jenn's ear. She loved her friend, but where a penchant for PDA was concerned, Jenn apparently hadn't changed a bit. Tessa twirled a forkful of creamy pasta. "I had no idea bacon and eggs were so delicious on spaghetti. And here I thought marinara sauce was the only way to go."

"You know, the origins of spaghetti carbonara are

hotly debated." Dennis gestured with his fork, and tomato sauce spattered the white tablecloth. "But the theories are anecdotal…"

She raised her cocktail to Jenn in silent toast.

"This discussion is not over," Jenn mouthed back.

Shrugging, she nibbled her bread. "Is that right, Dennis?" She flashed a smile. "So, you're a food historian as well as a Civil War reenactor?"

A brief but soaking rain fell as she sped uptown in another white-knuckle cab ride, smushed between Dennis and Jenn. Exiting the car, she stumbled onto the sidewalk, narrowly avoiding a pond-sized puddle along the curb. Once inside, the relentlessly red bar on East Fifty-Fifth Street was a sauna packed with hip New Yorkers in rumpled business attire and man buns who didn't seem to notice that Dennis's roommate's band, Electric Canopener, stunk. Electric Canopener covered nineties grunge tunes so loudly the steamed-up mirrors on the walls rattled along with her fillings. She ordered a white wine spritzer. The bartender looked like she asked for milk and cookies.

Jenn leaned close. "Still can't stand the taste of beer?"

"Makes me want to vomit." As sweat ran between her shoulder blades, she tried to blink the scratchiness from her eyeballs. She groped in her backpack for eye drops. No luck. In her efforts to lighten her bag, they apparently didn't make the cut. Jerking his arms in arhythmic spasms, Dennis sang along with the band, occasionally tromping her foot or elbowing her in the ribs.

Electric Canopener launched into a Nirvana tune, and Dennis hooted and clapped his hands above his head.

Inches from her face, his armpits were dark with sweat. Longing to put a few feet between her nose and his stink, she swiveled, but sweaty bodies packed the room. Warm drops of a liquid she prayed was water plunked on her head from an unknown source. Jenn and Adam smooched against a wall—her petite frame concealed by his Division I soccer player bod. She downed the spritzer in gulps. Just how long would they stay?

Mercifully, Adam was also not a fan of Electric Canopener. After the first set, she trailed him and Jennifer, pushing toward the exit. Fully intoxicated but with zero intention to bail, Dennis scrawled his number on a matchbook and pressed it into her palm with promises to show her his collection of bayonets in the fall. She smiled mirthlessly and stuffed the damp matchbook into her backpack.

After enduring the bar, escaping into the misty night air felt like a dip in a lake—even if she was in Manhattan, and the sidewalks smelled like Chinese food.

The apartment was within walking distance, and Jenn suggested they enjoy a stroll home.

Aching feet or no, she was so relieved not to be sandwiched in the back of another cab, she agreed. Lagging behind the couple, she gazed at skyscrapers shrouded in clouds and couldn't help overhearing snatches of Jenn's and Adam's whispered conversation.

Jenn yanked Adam's hand. "Why did you invite him?"

"You wanted someone harmless, right? Dennis is as harmless as they come."

Harmless? Why harmless? She caught her toe in a sidewalk crack and tripped a step.

"And that band?"

Jenn's voice rose an octave. Ugh. Tessa hated causing a tiff.

Adam extended an arm, steering Jenn around a puddle. "What can I say? Dennis told me they were awesome."

Equally uncomfortable eavesdropping, she quickened her pace.

Jenn threw an arm around her waist. "Dennis was a dud, huh?"

She leaned into her former roomie until their shoulders bumped companionably. "Let's just say he's no Amish dude." As if the very word "Amish" summoned them, she rounded the corner at the base of Central Park to discover a line of horse-drawn carriages.

Outrageously dressed drivers beckoned, promising breathtaking views and a night to remember. The horses swished their tails and clomped the pavement idly.

Not long ago, she fantasized about a moonlit ride through Central Park and an exciting, new life with her best friend at her side. Now, she just didn't know. New York was electric and rife with opportunity. Jenn was living proof. But the city was relentless, too, and years later, she still felt like she couldn't wash the grime from her hands. Plus, the air smelled weird. In fact, it smelled really weird. This place was a medieval gauntlet of odors.

She ambled past an ornate white carriage upholstered in shamrock-green velvet with plastic daffodils protruding from every crevice. The carriage couldn't have been more different from Jonas's plain buggy. She breathed the familiar scent of horse.

Horse and something else—something sharper and more pungent. She sniffed again, and her stomach turned. How strange. She usually liked the smell of horses. It reminded her of home and farms…of Jonas.

"Two lovely ladies." The carriage driver swept off his cap and bowed. "Lucky man. Care for a ride?"

"Yeah. No." Adam said.

Jenn snorted. "We live here."

Well, you do.

Jenn covered her nose with the back of her hand. "What smells?"

Adam scanned the street and pointed. "Maybe that?"

Just beyond the carriages, two police cars and a fire truck idled, lights spinning in ominous silence. A small crowd clustered on the sidewalk, and several officers diverted traffic around the scene. The wind shifted, and a gust of putrid air nearly knocked her flat.

"Seriously, what is that smell?" Jenn said.

Bile rose in Tessa's throat. Rising onto her toes, she squinted into the streetlights.

An indistinct, dark mass lay in the street. A sole festooned carriage stood by.

An equally dark mass of dread coalesced in her stomach. She quickened her step, eager yet afraid to discover exactly what caused such a commotion. Turning her shoulders sideways, she squeezed through the crowd for a better view.

From the amorphous lump on the street, one detail came into focus—hooves sticking out from beneath a wet tarp. Pressing a palm to her mouth, she gasped. *A horse!* An officer stepped onto the sidewalk and shooed the onlookers like they were ducklings.

No one moved. Huddling on the curb in a threadbare top hat, a man lowered his head into his hands. Another officer draped an oversize yellow jacket over the man's shoulders and turned to jot a note on a thick pad. With a series of short sirens, an ambulance glided to a stop nearby.

"Keep walking, people," the officer on the sidewalk said.

The enormous mound in the street loomed, unmoving. Chestnut-colored legs extended, sleek and shiny in the mist. They were inexpressibly fragile and yet so graceful. Silver horseshoes glinted in the streetlight.

What color was Jonas's horse? Gnawing the inside of her cheek, she strained to picture the animal hitched at the back of the Farmers' Market. How could she not remember? The corners of her eyes stung. She wiped her cheeks, surprised to discover her fingers were damp. She approached the officer on the sidewalk. "Excuse me, sir."

"All right, move along."

The officer sounded almost bored.

The wind gusted again, and a piece of newspaper tumbled down the street. It smacked wetly against the tarp and stuck. She wanted to run to the horse and remove it. She wanted to lift the plastic and gaze into the animal's lifeless eyes. She wanted to know what happened.

"Tessa?" Jenn beckoned from several feet beyond.

She held up one finger and stepped closer to the officer. "Excuse me?" she repeated.

He turned. "Yes, ma'am?"

He was younger than she expected, with coffee-colored skin and dark circles under wide brown eyes. The man wasn't bored. He was tired. "I'm sorry, sir. I just…" She gestured to the form in the street. The inside of her mouth was cottony despite the fine mist diffusing the streetlights. "What happened?"

The young man's expression softened. "Looks like he was electrocuted, miss."

Wide-eyed, she gaped at the mountain of flesh. "Electrocuted? How?"

The cop took off his hat and flicked it toward a manhole. "Best we can tell, when the horse stepped on that manhole cover, he got zapped. The electric company is working underground about a block away. Must have been some kind of short, and with the standing water on the street and those metal horseshoes?" He shrugged. "Talk about the wrong place at the wrong time."

"You'd need an astronomical amount of electricity to kill a horse," Adam said.

Pivoting, she discovered Adam right behind her.

With a hand on her elbow, he urged her to leave.

Rooted to the sidewalk, she stared at the animal. Passing headlights reflected in water pooled on the tarp. In her periphery, she saw the man in the top hat escorted, staggering and sobbing, to the ambulance. She shuttered her eyes against the incessant flashing, but the red glare penetrated her lids. A headache she fought since Electric Canopener struck their first chord erupted in full force.

The second officer joined them. "Clear out, people. Nothing to see."

"Let's go home," Jenn called. "I can't stand the smell."

For the rest of the weekend, Tessa was haunted by the lifeless mass in the street. Every wind gust reeked of burnt horseflesh. In every siren, the man in the top hat howled. Even as she laughed with Jenn over cupcakes and coffees, loneliness coiled in the pit of her stomach. Turning her face upward, she searched for more than a sliver of sky. She craved dewy green fields and sweet summer air. She missed home.

Late Sunday evening, Jenn followed her onto the bus platform, even though the posted sign decreed only ticketed passengers were permitted. Those rules were for other people—not her irrepressible roomie.

Adam's roomie now.

She wedged into a front seat and waved, feeling the motor vibrate her thighs through the velveteen cushion.

Jenn jumped up and down and waved back. "I'll miss you!"

"I'll miss you, too," she mouthed.

Jenn whipped out her phone. Her fingers flew across the screen as the bus belched a cloud of exhaust.

—When are you coming to stay?—

With a shrug and a smile, she pocketed her phone and blew Jenn a kiss.

The bus pulled away.

But in her heart, she knew the answer.

Never. For better or worse, Tessa was going home.

Chapter 14

"I couldn't sleep last night. I kept thinking about that horse." Tessa slumped in the seat of Richard's SUV the following evening. He picked her up well after his shift ended, and the huge expanse of sky was speckled with bright stars.

"How much electricity would you need to kill a horse?" Richard popped a mint and shook his head. "A tremendous amount."

She rested an elbow on the door and pressed her cheek into her hand. "That's exactly what Adam said. But it was just so pathetic. Those stiff legs sticking out from under the tarp and that awful smell. I'll never forget it."

"What did it smell like?"

"It was like…execution. And beef jerky."

Richard exploded into laughter.

The tears that inexplicably surfaced whenever she thought about the horse threatened again. "It isn't funny!"

"But it is." He thumped his hands on the wheel. "Freakish and damn funny. Any number of humans probably stepped on that manhole and nothing—their rubber-soled shoes protected them. But it was a horse's worst nightmare. What are the odds?"

She tipped her forehead against the glass. "Standing there with all those people gawking I just thought, what am I doing here? Everything is backward in this city. As great as Central Park is, trees and nature are supposed to surround us, not the other way around." With a sigh, she shifted and stared into the night. Breath came easier, away from so much concrete. "I guess I'm just a Pennsylvania farm girl after all."

He let out a soft chuckle. "I can't tell you how happy that makes me."

Beyond the window, open fields vanished into darkness, dotted only with the occasional light from a farmhouse or barn. She could almost hear cricket song above the quiet purr of the motor. She was home and finally on her way to Richard's delayed surprise. With a flutter in her belly, she glanced sideways. He drove with one hand on the wheel and the other elbow out the window, his carefree grin radiating confidence. What was it with this guy and surprises? "Where are we going anyway?"

He rumbled off the road and cut the engine. "You tell me."

The headlights illuminated a farmhouse, backlit by a cotton candy and violet streaked sky. Clocking log cabin construction and familiar dark-green window boxes, she quirked an eyebrow. "The Lincoln log house?"

"Come on." He exited the car and jogged to open her door.

The chorus of crickets crescendoed.

"Won't Mrs. Raffensburger be, like, asleep by now?" she hissed.

"Just come." Taking her hand, he coaxed her onto the porch.

The house was nearly dark, with just a faint orange

glow in the front windows.

She leaned into him. "My surprise is breaking and entering into an old lady's house?"

"It's not breaking and entering"—he drew a shiny, silver object from his pocket—"when you have a key." The latch snicked, and the front door swung wide. "After you."

She stood gaping on the porch.

He prodded with one shoulder. "Go on."

She stepped over the threshold into a dim foyer, and wide, planked flooring creaked beneath her feet.

Clasping her hand again, he guided her toward a narrow door to her right.

Amber light beckoned, and she entered it. "Oh, Richard." White candles of every size and shape illuminated the room. They flickered from the windowsills, filled the stone fireplace, and clustered on the mantle above an unmistakably heart-shaped rock. The room was otherwise empty, but for a burgundy, chenille blanket in the middle of the floor. Beside the blanket, a bottle of wine, a corkscrew, and two goblets stood at the ready. "What a beautiful room. But, I'm confused. Where's Mrs. Raffensburger?"

He kicked off his shoes and lowered onto the blanket. "Not here." Hazel eyes sparkling, he extended a hand.

His palm was warm and the slightest bit damp. She knelt beside him. "I don't understand…"

He silenced her with a kiss. "God, I missed you."

Sitting back on her heels, she lowered her chin, and her hair tumbled across one eye. "I…missed you, too." The cork popped, and crimson liquid swirled into crystal glasses. Her brain eddied with it. Why didn't the room have any furniture? And where was Mrs. Raffensburger?

He handed her a goblet. "To coming home."

Her raised glass glinted in the candlelight, and she joined him in a drink. The aroma was earthy as fresh-plowed fields after a spring rain. With the tip of her tongue, she caught a drop at the corner of her mouth. "Delicious."

Rising onto both knees, he reached into his pants pocket and removed a small, rectangular box tied with a red ribbon. He handed it to her.

As if the slightest tremor would cause the pretty, little thing to detonate, she stiffened. Throat clenched, she stared at the box and struggled to breathe. A tiny box. The tiny box she longed to be given one day by a man who looked at her the way Richard looked this very second.

His full lips spread in a wide smile. "Just open it."

Did she really want that day to be today? True, the box was an odd shape for a ring, but it was doubtlessly a jewelry-sized box. The backs of her hands prickled. They hardly knew one another. She wasn't ready. "Richard, I—"

"Trust me." He placed a hand on her knee. "Open it."

The satiny bow slipped free, and with fumbling fingers, she lifted the lid to reveal…a silver house key nestled in a bed of crimson tissue. Breath returned to her body in a rush, even as she struggled to make sense of the gift.

"It's a match." He held up the front door key. "It's yours if you'll have it and the house that goes with it. Yours and mine."

She froze. Honestly, she would have been less stunned by a diamond solitaire.

"Told you I had a surprise." He chuckled. "Welcome home."

The box suddenly felt like a thousand-pound weight. Hands shaking, she lowered it onto the blanket directly between them. "I don't know what to say—"

"Mrs. Raffensburger passed away last year, and thanks to a brilliant realtor, one Claire MacMillan, her daughter sold me the house at an amazing price. It's rustic, but I'll have the whole place gutted, just like my apartment. The renovation will take some time—time I think we need to finish what we've started. But don't worry, when we're both ready, I'll get down on one knee and do it all by the book."

Shadows pranced over hand-hewn logs and licked the low ceiling. To her, the house was aged to perfection.

He bent his knees and draped his arms over them, spinning the glass between his fingers. "San Francisco changed my life. Did I tell you the conference centered on a field called medical informatics?"

Afraid of snapping the stem, she loosened the grip on her own glass and shook her head. Naked enthusiasm flared in his gaze.

"Informatics is the integration of technology and medicine to improve patient care and outcomes. It incorporates computer science, biotechnology, and clinical work all in one. I haven't been this fired up since I started hospital rotations the third year of med school." He downed half a glass of wine in a single breath.

She only had one sip, but still her head spun. No

man had ever given her a key, let alone an entire house. Just when did he expect to move in?

"We had to scramble, but Tyler and I left that conference with enough funding to create a Medical Informatics Department at St. Luke's. Over the next couple years, I'll be away a lot for conferences and to get another degree, believe it or not." He swirled the glass, and wine whirlpooled up the sides, just short of sloshing out. "But just think, through digital transformation, I'll take my father's hospital out of the dark ages and into the twenty-first century. I'll make advances he never could have dreamed of."

A note of excitement hummed beneath his words. But she was confused. Richard was a gifted doctor. Why give up clinical practice for technology? She ran a finger over plush, chenille threads by her knee. "Will you still take care of patients?"

Finishing the drink in a final swallow, he set down the glass and rolled up his sleeves. "Not as much, but I won't be stuck in a lab. I'll maintain a modest private practice."

She gave a small smile. "No house calls."

With a laugh, he cupped her cheek in one palm. "My darling."

The glass was warm against her bottom lip. Wine slid down her throat like molten gold.

"Everything's clicking into place. This transformation is a massive undertaking, and I'm terrified. I really am." He cradled her hand in his. "For a shot at success, I need someone at my side who gets me—who knows this community and supports my work. You said yourself that you belong in Green Ridge—thank you, NYC! You already joined the team at the hospital. I want you to be a part of my home life, too." Tightening his hold, he leaned toward her. "What do you say?"

The air was thick with the scent of wax and heavy with expectation. She moistened her lips and swallowed.

What do I say?

She flicked her gaze to the key and heard her own heartbeat thump in her head. The tops of her feet tingled beneath her weight. A candle popped, and with a hiss, a bright orange spark flew onto the hearth and died. She cleared her throat. "Wow. That's just…wow, I—"

"Look, you were the last thing I expected this summer. Our relationship knocked me off my feet, and I'm reeling, too." He lifted the nearly full glass from her fingers. "I don't mean to rush you. We'll have plenty of time to talk." He set the glass on the floor by her side.

His jacket slid from his shoulders with a rustle of fine linen.

He folded it with precision and placed it at one end of the blanket. With a single tug, he loosened his tie. "Anyway, I'm tired of talking." He caught her gaze. "How about you?"

More than happy to postpone answering, she lifted her chin. "Talk is overrated."

Sweeping her into his arms, he laid her back, her head on the cushion of his coat. In an instant, he was beside her and above her, one arm beneath her neck, the other hand tucked under her hip. He drove his fingertips into the muscles of her lower back and massaged in deep circles. "I want you in my life."

The touch bordered on too firm, but it felt good, too. Tension seeped from her muscles. "I thought you were done talking."

"I changed my mind."

With a gentle nibble, he tickled behind one ear. His stubbly chin chafed tender skin and drew gooseflesh down her arms. She let her eyelids fall.

He tugged at her earlobe and made a sound low in his throat. "Just say yes." He traced his lips down the valley of her neck to her collarbone.

She shivered. The role of Mrs. Dr. Bruce was hers for the taking. She had only to step onto the stage. Slipping her arms over his shoulders, she urged him closer.

"I love you," he whispered and claimed her with his kiss.

The strength of his passion took away her breath. Trapped under his chest, she winced as the knobs of her spine rolled over the plank floor. She jerked her head to one side and arched onto her shoulders.

His grasp on her hip eased. "Please, let me make you mine."

His breath tickled like a downy feather inside her ear, and she broke out in goose bumps on top of goose bumps. Richard Bruce was the man she waited for. He wasn't some unattainable fantasy. He was real and solid, and he wanted her. Why not say yes?

He lifted away.

Missing his kiss, she reached with pouted lips. "Richard…?" Her voice was deep and throaty. She opened her eyes to find him looking at her. His face was in shadow, but she made out the lines of his features—the strong curve of his cheekbones, dark hair curling over a high forehead, kissable lips arcing into a smile of…what? Of triumph? As if in response to her plea, he lowered himself fully, deepening the kiss.

Above her, wide boards crisscrossed heavy beams. She could just discern a network of spiderwebs disappearing into dusky corners.

This moment can't be real.

She was surrounded by him—almost absorbed into him. His citrusy scent mingled with red wine and a hundred different candles, perfuming the air like incense. Lifting her a hairsbreadth from the blanket, he threaded an arm around her waist. Her mind clouded.

This person can't be me.

In a split second, it wasn't. Unzipping from herself, she floated upward, leaving her body like a stranger's below. As if she were dying, she hovered among the cobwebs, gazing at the shimmering room. She saw her own freckled hands caress his shoulders and his body move against hers, cajoling, enticing.

Again, he pulled away, and she saw rather than felt her flushed cheeks and swollen lips. Her mass of curls splayed across the blanket.

"My God," he whispered. "You're a Renaissance painting come to life."

Who were those people, tangled in the enchanted glow of candlelight? Could one of them possibly be herself?

"My beautiful Tessa."

Then, like a hurricane, she plummeted from the ceiling, inhabiting again the full length of herself. Every hair prickled. Every inch of skin throbbed. Her burning lungs strained for breath, and she tore from his lips with a muffled grunt. She shot her left arm over her head, knocking her wine glass and launching it across the floor. The glass clattered over uneven planks, and she groped with one hand, trailing her fingers through warm liquid.

He grabbed her wrist and lowered her arm to her side, planting kisses along her jaw. "I don't care about the stupid glass."

His voice was teasing but rough. She tensed, her thigh muscles hardening against his grip. "The wine is everywhere—please, Richard." She planted a hand on his shoulder and pushed. As if her palm was suddenly hot coals, he reared and shrank away. She clambered to sitting, twisting her rumpled dress into place.

Breathing hard, he rolled to one side. "What's wrong?"

"I don't know, I…" She swiped wet hands down the front of her dress.

His cheeks blanched. "Sweetheart, did I hurt you?"

Her spine was still tender. She rolled her shoulders and retrieved the glass from inside the fireplace. The night took on an air of unreality—the room so fuzzy she couldn't make out the edges of windows and walls. She supposed out-of-body experiences could muddle a person. Ultimately, though, she was unharmed. She met his gaze. "I'm fine."

The lines on his forehead released, and he puffed out a breath. "Thank goodness. I forget my vow of chivalry sometimes. I'm sorry." Flopping onto his back, he waved a hand. "Don't worry. I'll refinish these floors." His fingers found hers on the soggy blanket, and he lowered his voice. "Do you want me to stop?" He tilted his head an inch and caught her gaze.

She took him in—his handsome face, every facet

etched with intelligence—his trim, toned body tempting her. He wanted her right now. Right now, and forever. The future he offered pulled at her heart. It was strong as the undertow and easy as surrender to sleep.

With a full-bodied shake, she swept her gaze around the room. "So, this is your house now? You bought it, and you're going to live here forever?" He lifted her palm to his lips and kissed it so tenderly she almost forgot the single-minded passion of moments before.

"The house, the land, the covered bridge—I bought it, and it's all for us."

She looked into his eyes. This man took a giant risk. Giving her a key was a massive gesture with an equally massive potential for heartbreak. For all his swagger, Richard lay before her now exposed and vulnerable. Did the thought ever cross his mind she might say no? Did he even consider she might not want the role he offered? She pushed him away once already tonight, and he responded appropriately. But the final outcome rested in her hands. She alone held the power to accept his gift and in so doing, accept him.

He rolled and swiveled to sitting, curling her fingers and wrapping both hands around hers. "Tessa Meadows, I want to lay you by the hearth and love you until the sun comes up on the first day of our new life together. Please let me."

Sudden tears burned in her eyes. Never in her life had a man made such an offer. If she refused, she risked never hearing those words again. But she couldn't silence the voice within. The still, quiet voice that spoke just one syllable.

No.

Without a word, she pulled away her hand and shook her head.

His brows drew together, gouging a deep crease between them. "Darling?"

The atmosphere was suddenly stifling. The walls spun, and the heady odor of wine flooded her sinuses. She dug her fingers into her temples. "I have to go." Legs wobbling, she stood. "I need—"

"What?" He jerked to his knees. "Tell me, and I'll give it to you."

The box was soggy and blood-red with wine. She stooped and picked it up. "I've never received such a generous gift, and I'm so grateful. But it's all just too soon. Richard…" She took a deep breath. "I know your heart was broken not long ago. I know about Jane and the pressure from your father to stay in Green Ridge. I know everything."

His face flamed. "What do you know about Jane?"

Fearing just such defensiveness, she'd hesitated to discuss his past. He was a proud man. Arguably, bringing up an ex-girlfriend right as she broke up with him was insensitive. She did it not to hurt him but to commiserate—to let him know she understood why he might have jumped into a commitment too soon. But he couldn't hear that right now. She shook her head gently. "You could have told me."

He balled his fists against his thighs. "The past doesn't mean anything. Our future is all I care about."

"But I can't commit to that future—not yet. I need time to figure out who I am and what I want…and maybe you do, too."

Eyes flashing, he leapt to his feet. "You don't know what I need."

He was in pain—the kind even the finest doctor couldn't cure. She cursed herself for causing that pain. Wanting to touch him but not daring, she held out a hand. "I don't. Any more than you know what's right for me."

"Give me some credit here." He stabbed a finger at the box. "I didn't give you a ring—though God knows I've never wanted anything more in my life. I gave you a key. I know we need time. I gave us time. Now, you need to give us a chance."

"I think maybe what I need is out in the world—" she flung a hand toward the window "—beyond Green Ridge."

Rocking back, he pressed the heels of his hands to his forehead. "But you just said—"

"I know!" Not wanting to argue, she forced a calming breath. "I know what I said about being a country girl, and maybe I am. My feelings are all over the map here. I'm just figuring this out as I go…" Her voice broke, and she dropped her chin.

He clasped her shoulders. "Oh, sweetheart, I know I moved fast. This night was crazy and impulsive and honestly completely out of character." He stepped closer and smoothed his hands up and down her arms. "Look, I'm sorry I didn't tell you about—about everything. But from the moment I met you, nothing from my past—not Jane or my father—none of it mattered. When I know what I want, I go for it. And I want you."

She met his gaze. His jaw was set. His eyes sparked with the single-minded determination that served him so well his whole life.

"I want you," he repeated.

Closing her eyes, she inhaled to the soles of her feet. She counted her heartbeats. *One…two…three…* Her breath released with a sound like a ghost sighing. She lifted her lids, and the room stopped spinning. "I can't." With two backward steps, she slipped from his grasp.

His hands dropped to his sides, and his face drained of color.

"I'm so sorry." Brushing away tears, she spun and escaped into the dark hallway. Her hair fell in tangles before her eyes. She shoved it aside and grappled for the front door latch.

"Wait!"

His footsteps rang in quick succession at her back. Yanking open the door, she flew onto the porch, down the steps, and into the moonlight. She drank the night air like ice water and refused to look back.

"Tessa!" His voice echoed from ridge to ridge in the windless night. "You took the box."

"What?" She whirled. "No, I didn't." He stood in the doorway—the doorway of their house—and pointed a trembling finger.

"You took it. Why?"

She dropped her gaze and blinked, unwilling to believe her eyes. "I…I don't know." Tripping over her sandals, she lurched toward him, thrusting out the box. "Here! Take it back."

"Keep it." He shoved his hands into his pockets. "Keep it, and we'll talk later."

"But it's yours."

He shook his head. "It was a gift."

At a complete loss for words, she stared through the moonglow.

A single cricket chirped.

Richard's jaw was soft and slack. His trademark confidence abandoned him.

He met her gaze. "I love you."

His voice was so ragged she almost didn't recognize it. Tears pooled, and her vision blurred. With a quick nod, she clasped the box to her breast, wheeled, and fled. After several long minutes, the front door slammed, and her belly clenched in a sob.

Unseeing, she quickened her pace, the box turning to pulp in her hand. Why did she take the darned thing? She could have dropped it in the driveway or left it on the hood of his car. But she didn't. For whatever reason, she couldn't.

She imagined him alone, mopping up wine and blowing out candles one by one. Another sob wracked her chest like a blow. She was running now, up and down the rolling hills toward home. Trees loomed black against the indigo sky. Spiky weeds sliced her calves. Her sandals pounded across a low, metal bridge, drowning out the rushing brook below. She dragged a forearm across her eyes and pressed on.

She wept for Richard—because she broke his heart when he offered it, and he didn't deserve that. She wept for herself—because in saying no, she broke her own heart just a little bit, too.

But never once did she question her actions. She knew exactly what choice she made. She recalled the moment—the singular instant when his fingers found hers, and she could have given in. Breathless and running, she felt him again like a warm tug in her belly. Intoxicated by the night and his words, she could have lain back on that blanket and surrendered to his vision for their life. Saying yes would have been so easy.

But if she did, she never would have left—never found her own path. Never made her way into the night—where another man slept in a candlelit room of his own.

Chapter 15

Tessa dropped the cold washcloth in the sink and blinked into the mirror. Beneath puffy lids, two bloodshot eyes met her gaze. Since leaving Richard last night, she barely slept. Late morning sun streamed in the bathroom window, almost mocking in its cheerfulness. Head pounding, she popped two aspirin and let the water soothe her throat. A tube of concealer sat on the shelf next to her new Macy's lipstick. Why bother? She couldn't hide the fact she cried half the night. The situation was what it was.

Her phone buzzed, and Richard's name popped up. Again. All morning, she ignored his calls and texts. Answering now would just be weird. She powered off the phone and jammed it in her pocket. She wouldn't need it anyway. Not with Jonas. Half an hour later, still blotchy and raw, she pulled up beside the barn.

When he saw her face, Jonas started almost imperceptibly.

She braced for questions, but in an instant his expression cleared.

Nodding his greeting, he climbed into the van and shifted his gaze out the window.

He was a private man. Her business was her business. Unclenching her jaw, she relaxed. Simple silence was his gift to her that noontime.

How many more car rides did she have? The

gazebo was almost complete. When they last discussed a timeframe, he reckoned he would finish by the end of the week. Come Friday, she'd hand him a check, say, "thank you very much," and never speak to him again. Back to hours alone in the garden with no company but her own thoughts and an empty calendar.

Empty except…

She cranked the gearshift, lurching onto Route 45. Empty except for one very important event—an event briefly forgotten between the trip to New York and the utter shock of Richard's offer. An event that was now a quagmire of complication.

The Midsummer Ball.

She blinked achy eyes and refocused on the road. The ball was her baby. She made a commitment to Mrs. Diefenderfer, not to mention to Claire and Richard. The hors d'oeuvres, the decorations, and a hundred other details remained to be finalized. With little time left, she still had so much to plan. She couldn't just abandon it now.

Once in the driveway, Jonas took his toolbox and headed for the backyard.

Her mother's kitchen offered refuge. Slumped at the table, she scrolled through floral designs, the images dancing a conga line before her eyes. She closed her laptop and stared out the window. Shadows shifted, indicating the passage of hours in a way she could reckon had she been born a druid in a time before time as she knew it.

A *tap-tap-tap* came from behind.

She jumped and swung around.

Hat in hands, Jonas stood at the back door. His face was crimson, and his hair matted with perspiration.

She glanced at the wall clock and sprang to her feet. How had three hours passed while she did nothing? She opened the door and beckoned. "I'm so sorry!" Dashing to the counter, she rummaged through cabinets, not quite sure what she hoped to find.

He stepped inside. "I'm just here for water."

A glass—she needed a glass. "I can't believe I forgot your drink." The afternoon was beastly, and she was drenched just from sitting. She yanked out a glass and a plate and plunked them onto the counter.

The door closed quietly behind him. "Don't trouble yourself."

She fumbled through the silverware drawer. Where were all the dessert forks? "But I saved the rest of the peach cobbler—it's in the fridge—and I meant to make a pitcher of lemonade…" She flung wide the refrigerator door and grabbed the dish with the remains of the cobbler. As she closed the door with a hip and reached for a wooden spoon, the dish slipped from her sweat-slick fingers. End over end, it tumbled through the air and crashed to the floor in a spectacular explosion. Sticky pastry and chunks of broken glass careened outward, spattering the cabinets, the fridge, and her own feet. She dropped her arms at her sides.

Everything. Absolutely everything. Was ruined.

As tears streamed down her cheeks, she tucked her chin and closed her eyes. The refrigerator hummed the same endless note. The syrupy scent of cooked peaches flooded the room. Her chest heaved in silent sobs.

Footsteps came her way—worn leather soles on a hardwood floor. One step followed another. Gentle hands clasped her shoulders from behind. His breath tickled warm on the back of her neck.

"Mei wildi ros…"

The unfamiliar words needed no translation. They whispered straight to her battered heart like a lullaby. With a gentle tug, he spun her and wrapped his arms around her, enfolding her in the scents of cedar and sunshine. Her cheek sought cool cotton, and she surrendered, her breath gradually slowing to match the steady rise and fall of his chest. When she slid her arms around his waist, she fit into his body like a missing puzzle piece—snug, unforced, and so very right.

Had she really not seen him since they sat on her porch in the storm? So much had happened since then, but at that moment, none of it mattered. In his arms, she felt the world turn more slowly. She made peace with Time.

Her tears subsided. She sniffed and turned her head, pressing her forehead into the soft firmness of his chest. The last thing she wanted was to let him go, but she did, taking half a step backward, crunching glass and squishing peaches.

He pulled a spotless, white handkerchief from his pocket.

Unwilling to soil it, she dabbed her eyes with one corner.

"Ach," he scoffed. "Go on and use it for what God intended."

She let out a laugh and blew her nose. "I'll wash it and get it right back to you."

"No hurry." Pulling out a chair for her and one for himself, he sat.

Shoes sticking with every step, she joined him. He was so patient, this gentle giant of a man. Sitting beside him, she felt like the only human being on the planet. "I broke Richard's heart yesterday," she said finally. "He offered me a tremendously generous gift, and I didn't take it. I walked away."

He knitted his brows. "You're crying for Richard?"

"For Richard…and for me." Tears clouded her vision again. She lifted her hands and dropped them in her lap. "And for the horse."

The crease between his brows deepened. "What horse?"

She shifted, her toes bumping his boots. Her knee brushed his thigh, and she stared at her kneecaps—her freckled skin so fair against his black pants. "Over the weekend, I visited a dear friend in New York City, and we came upon a carriage horse that was killed in an accident. It just lay there on the asphalt, and I don't know…something about that horse got to me. I can still smell it. It was awful." She wiped her nose with the handkerchief and buried it in her pocket. "Richard didn't understand about the horse at all. I tried to explain, but he just laughed."

The little muscle in his jaw fluttered. "Is that why you refused his gift?"

"Partly. And partly I don't know." She shrugged. "I don't know much of anything anymore." Her neck gave out beneath the weight of her head. She tucked her chin and let tears flow.

He rose and returned with a glass of cold milk, placing it in front of her.

She hiccupped a sob. "Why are you so nice? It just makes me cry."

With a chuckle, he sat, interlacing his fingers atop the table.

Condensation frosted the glass. She clasped it with

tight fingers and drank deeply. "I guess what I meant to say was thank you."

"You're welcome."

Like a deer in the woods, he was so still and so alive. His calloused hands were relaxed, but she knew the power they possessed. She ached to feel the strength contained just beneath his skin. Holding her breath, she extended one hand and ran a fingertip over his knuckles. Ever so lightly, she traced the veins on the back of his hand and down the valley between his thumb and forefinger.

He inhaled deeply and stiffened.

She pulled away. "I'm sorry," she breathed.

He met her gaze.

His jaw was tight, but his eyes were soft—an expression guarded but kind. What was he thinking?

His lips hinted at a smile. He shook his head. "You have nothing to be sorry for."

She slid her gaze from his. The constellation of freckles on her right knee looked like the Little Dipper—a nearly vertical scoop dumping star stuff across the sky. She raised one shoulder in a half shrug. "I don't mean to burden you with my problems."

"A friend's problems are a joyful burden. Sharing them is an honor."

Tears burned again. "You're very generous." Exhaustion descended in a fog. She was too tired even to cry. "I should probably lie down for a while."

He pulled back her chair and followed her into the living room.

Kicking off her shoes, she collapsed onto the sofa and gathered the afghan in a bundle. Her body yearned for him, but her mind was numb.

"I'll be outside," he said.

In a daze, she felt his fingers cup her face and his thumb trace the line of her cheekbone. She opened her eyes though she didn't remember closing them. He stood over her like a guardian angel. A sensation of absolute security settled upon her. Nestling into throw pillows that smelled of home, she fell asleep in an instant.

She awoke to dusky darkness, rolled onto her back, and stretched. Bleary-eyed, she rose and padded barefoot into the kitchen. With sudden memory of the broken dish, she came up on tiptoes. No need. The floor was spotless. All traces of broken glass and ruined cobbler were gone, and her empty milk glass rested upside down in the dish drainer.

The porch swing creaked.

Following the sound, she discovered him outside, eyes closed, rocking in a slow, steady rhythm. "There you are." Her voice was barely audible even to herself.

He opened his eyes and turned.

Something in his gaze shifted. The knowledge she refused Richard shimmered silvery between them. An overwhelming desire to slide onto the swing and snuggle close rose within, and she licked dry lips. Was hugging now on the table? The memory of being in his arms liquefied her bones, and she leaned against the doorframe. "Thank you for cleaning the kitchen. What time is it? You should have woken me."

"You seemed to need sleep." He tilted his head to one side and studied her face.

His gaze lingered over every freckled feature like his earlier caress. Where did they stand now? She didn't know, and not knowing was murder. She flushed and stared at her feet. The tops were lightly tanned in tiger stripes from gaps in her sport sandals. Even as her cheeks flamed, she dared to test the boundaries of the new status quo. "Nora and Rebecca will expect you, won't they?" The question, though light, betrayed the slightest hint of a challenge.

Squinting, he swung his gaze to the cloud-streaked sky. "I imagine so." He unfolded and stood.

For Richard, patients always came first. For Jonas, his family did. Her heart sank. "I'll take you home." In the van, she switched on the radio, but the music was little more than noise. When she pulled up at the farm, she spotted Nora on the porch bench, reading by lamplight.

Rebecca streaked across the yard in a blur.

Without even a glance, Jonas said a quick goodnight, took up his toolbox, and left.

As if he hadn't just held her in the kitchen. Or touched her face. Or poured her a simple glass of milk. He was home again, and he was gone. But what happened between them was palpable. She could still feel the warm solidity of his chest beneath her cheek. The scent of cedar lingered.

"You're back so late Jonas missed supper, and the lightning bugs are out." Rebecca jumped up and down outside the open window, her flaxen head appearing and disappearing with each bounce. "Tonight might be one of their last. Come see them."

Just one more moment in that field of fireflies…

Jonas disappeared into the barn.

One more touch of his hand…

"Not tonight, Rebecca."

Rebecca wrapped her fingers around the open

window and stepped into the wheel well. "Would you like one of my kittens? My mother said they are almost old enough to live on their own."

In the distance, Nora sat like a stone statue. She tightened her fingers on the gearshift. "I'd like one very much, but I have to go home now. I'll see you tomorrow."

Rebecca danced into the twilight.

Nora glanced up from her reading. She closed her book and, rising slowly to her feet, locked her gaze on Tessa's.

Though the light was dim and the distance between them great, she felt Nora's glare like a shot across the bow.

Rebecca skittered up the porch stairs. Beckoning to her mother, she slipped inside.

Holding her gaze, Nora shuffled to the railing.

Tessa didn't blink. *If you have something to say, why don't you say it?*

With a snap of her apron, Nora turned and followed her daughter inside.

A reckoning was coming. Maybe not tonight, but soon.

****

When Tessa pulled up at the farm the next afternoon, she spotted Nora in the doorway. Had the woman been waiting since the night before?

Scowling, Nora lurched from the porch and stalked toward the van.

Tessa flicked her gaze to the barn. No sign of Jonas. Despite a sense of impending doom, she observed Nora's halting gait with new fascination. What happened to the woman? Was she injured, or was she born with the limp? And why was she always so angry? Tessa broadened her collarbones and lifted her chin. For weeks, she sensed this moment was coming. She pulled the parking brake and hoped she was ready.

Nora approached the open passenger side window, crossing her arms over her chest like a shield.

For the first time, Tessa truly took in the woman's face—the sharp angle of her high cheekbones and the graceful line of her neck. Her tidy hairline betrayed a thick, tawny mane disappearing in a widow's peak under a gauzy prayer cap. Her dove-gray eyes were stormier twins of Jonas's miraculous blue ones. They were the exact same shade as her plain gray dress and glittered diamond hard. In her outrage, Nora was strangely beautiful. Tessa clutched the wheel and met her gaze.

"Hear my words," Nora said without preamble. She shot a quick look toward the barn. "I will not allow you to steal my brother from his family and the community where he belongs. Once he completes his work, you are not to set foot on this property. Do you understand? You will not speak to him or to my daughter ever again."

Her cheeks flamed as if she'd been slapped. She never faced such naked hatred in her life. "I'm not stealing anyone—"

"Our family has suffered enough." Nora thrust out a tense and quivering finger. "You're reckless. Leave before you cause any more pain." She whirled and strode into the house.

Tessa dropped her head against the headrest and gulped a shaky breath. Suffered enough? What in the world happened to this family?

Just as the front door closed, Jonas emerged from the barn. Smiling, he jogged to the van. "I thought I heard someone." He hopped into the seat. "Did you see Nora?"

"No." She threw the van into Reverse and peeled out in a cloud of dust. Her hair thrashed in the wind. With a trembling hand, she scraped it from her eyes. She hadn't been ready. Not for that assault. She crushed the clutch, slammed into fourth, and barreled down the road.

Jonas drummed his fingers on his thighs. "Easy now. We don't want another meeting with Officer Kunkle."

She gnawed her bottom lip.

"Are you all right?" he asked.

How could he possibly think she was all right? Didn't he remember what she'd been through? The roller coaster ride to which he himself added a few heart-stopping curves? "I'm fine." His insistent gaze tugged like a child on her sleeve. She refused to look at him.

"Mind if I turn on the radio?"

"Whatever." Once at her house, she trailed Jonas into the yard where he set immediately to work. Whistling, no less. She ignored him. She'd just about had it with the entire Amish population of central Pennsylvania. Besides, she had her own chores. Not a drop of rain fell since the storm the week before, and the garden was parched. All summer, she lugged her mother's cumbersome watering cans back and forth from the spigot on the side of the house to her flower beds. Not today. Her back hurt just thinking about it.

Having escaped her cleaning spree, the top storage

shelf in the garage was caked with dust and dead bugs. Balancing on a milk crate, she groped until her fingers lit on the curved metal tube that sprayed a moving curtain of water. Or at least it did ten years ago. What were the odds the ancient contraption still worked?

Sprinkler in hand, she dragged a dirty, green hose from under a hedge, attached one end to the spigot, and struggled to right the many kinks and knots riddling the unwieldy thing. When at last she had it untangled, the hose spread like a snake way across the lawn and around the corner of the house. Finally, she coupled the hose to the sprinkler, trudged back to the spigot, and wrenched it open.

An unmistakable string of Pennsylvania Dutch curse words echoed from one green ridge to the next.

With a gasp, she dashed around the house.

Mere inches from the sprinkler, Jonas stood completely drenched. "Next time, warn me before you do that!"

She stopped cold, just beyond reach of the spray. Yup. The sprinkler worked fine. "I'm so sorry."

His eyes blazed. "What is the matter with you, woman?"

Just then, the water rose, spraying up his legs, across his chest, and directly over his face. Rivers streamed from his hat brim.

With a grimace, he spat and whipped off his hat.

A renegade laugh, silly and stupid, bubbled from deep in her belly. She slapped a hand over her mouth, but she couldn't squelch it. She giggled. Then she snorted.

Sodden and seething, he gaped as sheets of water doused him.

She gritted her teeth and mustered sobriety. "I'm sorry." Then she exploded in laughter.

His eyes widened.

As if about to respond, he opened his mouth and took a shot right to the kisser. She held her breath, bracing for her second Amish scolding of the day. Instead, his scowl cracked open, and he, too, began to laugh—deep and resonant—a laugh she knew she could listen to the rest of her life.

"Might as well come in. The water's fine." He flung his hat, threw back his head, and opened his mouth to the cascade.

The spray ignited in arching rainbows. She unleashed a whoop and scampered through the water, dancing and twirling. When was the last time she ran through a sprinkler on a hot summer day?

With a leap, he dashed to the opposite side and shook his head. "Why can't I spend a single afternoon with you without getting soaked?"

The streams almost stung as they peppered bare skin on her legs and arms. Dizzy and breathless, she shrugged. "Just lucky I guess." She raised her arms in a vee and bent one knee. "I'm an Olympic athlete! I'm a gold-medal gymnast! Perfect ten!" With a running start, she cartwheeled over the sprinkler to his side of the yard. When her sandals hit the wet grass, they slid out from under her, sending her reeling. The horizon lurched, grass and sky seesawing before her eyes.

Lightning fast, he shot out a hand and caught her, pulling her into his arms.

Her body pressed slickly to his, and she scrambled for balance, fingers driving into rock-hard biceps.

He tightened his grip, lifting her just a whisper off

the ground and setting her back on her feet.

Breathing hard, she turned her gaze upward. Water trickled down his neck and disappeared in the notch of his throat. Sun-kindled droplets haloed his face.

His chest rose and fell in a quick, deep surge. "Are you all right?"

She nodded.

He twitched to release her.

Skin tingling, she locked her arms around his neck. She felt everything—from the single drop of water sliding down her left cheek to her belly moving against his with every panting breath. Blades of wet grass poked between her sandal straps.

"So much is changing in your life." He dropped his hands. "I can't…"

Another sheet descended, and she tightened her hold. Icy streams coursed down the backs of her legs. "Yes, you can. If you want to, I mean."

One corner of his mouth lifted into a smile. "*Mei wildi ros*."

She caught his gaze and tilted her head in question.

He settled his arms around her waist. "My wild rose."

His embrace asked nothing. He held her close, but he didn't smother her. He enfolded her yet gave her room to breathe. Her pulse slowed. She rested her head in the hollow beneath his chin and felt again how their bodies fit together like they were carved from the same stone. For one delicious moment, she stood, warm where she touched him and cool where jets massaged her limbs.

In an instant, he released her, stepping away but not leaving the arc of the sprinkler.

Free from his sheltering arms, she flinched as the water turn colder. An "oh" of surprise escaped her lips. She wrapped her arms around herself and shivered.

"Tessa Rose?" He kicked wet grass and looked up from beneath his brow. "Would you like to go on a picnic with me?"

Her T-shirt clinging to her body and her hair spiraling in soggy ringlets around her face, she bounced on her toes and grinned. "I'd love to."

Chapter 16

Tessa brushed a thorny vine laden with wild blackberries, and a pricker caught her sleeve. The morning sun was toasty, and she missed the cool shock of the previous afternoon's frolic in the sprinkler.

Pinching the stem between thumb and forefinger, Jonas lifted the vine an inch.

The briar tore free with a tiny pop. She flashed a grateful smile. Behind the firefly field, blackberries thicketed the edge of the woods. Tart and seedy, the fruit burst in her mouth and lodged between her teeth. Still, she couldn't get enough. Her fingertips were tinged violet, and she guessed her lips were too. Such was the price of ambrosia.

When she'd pulled up to the farm that morning, she half expected to find Nora guarding the house with a menacing Amish dog. Thankfully, Jonas sat alone on the front porch steps, a picnic basket and blanket at his side. With caution, she exited the van and scanned the upstairs windows.

"What's wrong?" he asked.

"I don't believe your sister would like me to be here. Going on a picnic." She tugged her ponytail and twisted her lips into a smile. "With you."

"Nora is on a train to Ohio." He grabbed the basket and threw the blanket over one shoulder. "And I don't care what she thinks."

Giddy with the knowledge they were completely alone on the farm, she wanted to dance. She pressed her lips to hide a massive smile and rose up on her toes.

"You coming?" he tossed over one shoulder.

She scampered to catch up. July was in full bloom, and the breeze carried its sweet, grassy perfume. Once again, she passed the elaborate garden gate and crossed the wooden bridge spanning the creek. The firefly field remained fallow, and she quickened her pace, trailing him over uneven ground until they'd reached the blackberry bramble on the far side. Free from the pricker now, she left behind her foraged feast.

Unexpectedly, their path met the creek again, and she trailed Jonas along its bank into the woods. Sluicing between mossy rocks, the water burbled clear and inviting. Ignoring its call, she plunged deeper into the forest, skirting the stream on one side and the gently sloped ridge on the other.

Sunlight filtered through the leaves and painted kaleidoscopic patterns on the forest floor. Ambling with his face to the sky, Jonas whistled a simple tune. The occasional answering scurry of an unseen critter reminded her they weren't truly alone. The path widened, and she came to his side, his easy stride comfortably matching her own. With every step, he spirited her farther from the modern world. She lifted her cheeks and relished the journey.

The path forked, and he cut into a hidden, grassy meadow fringed with wildflowers. On the far side of the clearing, the stream widened into a pool. A crumbling dam of piled-up creek stones thwarted the current, and the water appeared a few feet deep. She knelt on the edge and plunged in a hand. "Wow, that's cold!"

He laughed. "It's spring fed. Wait until you feel it on your belly." He squatted and immersed two metal containers, securing them with rocks. At the edge of the dam, he cocked his head, surveying the structure. "Doesn't look bad, all things considered."

Sensation returned to her hand with a zing. She shook it, clenching and unclenching her fist. "Who made it?"

"I did. With my brothers. Some summers we had up to six feet of water." He sat on the bank and pulled off his boots.

Was he serious about swimming? She, for one, did not have a bathing suit.

He tucked his socks into neat balls, shoved one in each boot, and stood. "You going to help me?"

"With what?"

He shot a thumb over one shoulder. "The dam. It needs repair."

Did he bring her all the way out here for creek maintenance? She only signed up for the picnic. "Uh…okay." She toed off her sneakers and socks and tiptoed through prickly, dry grass to the edge.

Jonas tossed aside his hat and sloshed in, long pants and all. "Careful. The stones are slick."

"Not my first rodeo," she muttered. She waded in two steps, and icy fingers shot up her legs, gripping her lungs. All around, tiny bubbles surfaced from underground springs. Her entire body seized. As a girl, she swam in lakes from Maine to Montana. This creek was, without a doubt, the coldest water she ever felt.

He rolled up his sleeves and pulled a big, round stone from the creek bottom, turning it in his hands.

The stone wedged into the wall with a resonant crack of rock on rock.

Or was that sound her teeth chattering?

"Wonderful, isn't it?" He prized another stone from the bed and glanced over his shoulder, grinning.

"Just great." She clenched her jaw and promptly stumbled, one foot sliding between rocks. Her ankle twisted, and she yelped. Long limbs flailing, she fought to stay upright. She was used to creeks, but her bare feet long since lost the summer toughness of youth. Scraping her heel along a rough edge, she extracted it and planted it in spongy mud. Annoyance buzzed in her ears like angry bees. "Why do you always look at me like that?"

He shifted the stone from hand to hand. "Like what?"

Struggling for balance, she shot out an arm. "Like you're laughing at me." What was she even doing in this stupid creek? The whole event was like some cruel joke—pranked by the Amish. Any second, Jonas's brother Samuel would leap from a bush with a contraband video camera.

An angular stone jutted like a tooth and jabbed the arch of her foot. She pitched in the opposite direction, fully soaking the hem of her shorts. Her other ankle wrenched, and she bit back a curse. She was like a moose on roller skates—her awkwardness on full display for his enjoyment. "You've been laughing at me since June."

His smile only widened. "You noticed?"

Her cheeks flamed. "I could hardly miss it. What's so funny?"

He heaved the rock into a crevasse and turned.

"You."

With his hands on his hips and his legs spread wide, he towered like a mountain creek deity. She spluttered. "Me?"

His eyes crinkled at the corners. "You."

Hugging her middle, she stared at her feet. They were pitiably fragile beneath the rippling surface—so pale as to be almost blue against brownish-gray stones. Shame burned in her lungs, banishing the chill. And she actually thought he liked her.

A gentle laugh rumbled from his chest. "Now, don't stand there like somebody spilled your milk. Tessa Rose, you surprised and delighted me the first day we met, and you have surprised and delighted me every single day since."

So, he hadn't laughed *at* her? He'd been laughing *because* of her? She jerked up her head. "I surprise you?" Her voice rose to a squeak. "Like in a good way?"

"Just look at you." His face softened. "You're a gift."

The air between them undulated like an invisible curtain caught in a strong gust. His image wavered before her eyes. For just a heartbeat, time itself possibly broke. Oceans dried and filled and dried again. Stars were born. Then, in the meadow, a red-winged blackbird warbled *okalee-okalee* and started the earth spinning again.

She was lightheaded and trembly…or faint from hypothermia. Possibly both. Silencing every voice that urged caution, she dove headfirst into the arctic waters of Jonas's swimming hole. Her heart stopped, and angels chorused in her head as she slid like a mermaid under the surface. The pond was nearly four feet deep, and she opened her eyes to striped minnows skittering beneath stones.

With a gasp, she emerged, her hair tumbling in wet spirals around her face. Jonas gazed from the dam, his expression as intent as hers was doubtlessly euphoric.

Without a sound, he dove.

She tracked his long, lean body cutting through the water.

He surfaced inches away, breathing fast. "You're shivering."

His voice was rough. Her own breath came in shuddering starts. "The water's cold."

"I warned you." Beneath the surface, he pressed his palms forward.

An underwater wave pulsed over her thighs. "You did." His mouth curved upward, and his cheek creased the way it did every single time he smiled.

He stepped nearer and hooked an arm around her waist. "We're drenched again."

He was so close now and so tall she had to arch her back to look into his eyes. "This time we chose to jump."

"You jumped. I followed." With his free hand, he traced a finger along her temple to her cheek, over her chin, and down her neck. "Do you have any notion how beautiful you are?" He lowered his lips to the tender spot where her pulse pounded beneath her chin.

Heat radiated from every point where her body touched his. She shivered. "I have big feet."

He wrapped his other arm around her.

She could feel the whole of him, solid and firm. Then his face was before hers again, his breath warm on her cheek.

"You're a butterfly in a swimming hole."

His lips met hers, and she stopped shaking. Beautifully simple, his kiss was a gift in itself. His touch was equal parts strength and generosity.

He ran his hands up her spine, over her shoulders, and through her hair until he cupped her cheeks and drank from her lips. With a deep, throaty sound, he took her around the waist again, lifting her feet from the bottom.

Curling her toes, she buried her fingers in his hair, her fingertips massaging his scalp until he groaned and lowered her. Time bent again until she had no idea how long she stood, her bare feet now massaged by smooth stones, her legs numb, and her lips lost to his kiss. Water dribbled down his cheeks, mingling with his tongue in tantalizing sweetness. She nibbled the delicious crinkles to the sides of his mouth, as she longed to do from the first moment she laid eyes on him. She basked in the sun on her shoulders.

He slid his hands to her hips, drawing her closer. His lips curved into a smile against hers, and he laughed. Threading his arms around her waist, he spun into the water with a gigantic splash. He sank deep—lips still sealed against hers, legs tangled. He pulled away underwater and surfaced with her, laughing and spluttering. "Are you hungry?"

For nothing but your kiss. "Starving."

He swooped her out of the water and plopped her on the faded, patchwork quilt, then collapsed beside her.

Out of the water and away from his body, she shivered again. But a warm breeze caressed her through wet clothes, and she knew in moments she would dry.

Sliced ham and cheese, homemade bread and butter, pound cake, and ripe plums appeared from the hamper. Jonas jogged to the creek and returned with iced tea and whipped cream for the cake. He drank straight from the canister and passed it.

The can was cool and tasted of metal and the slightest hint of soap. Plum juice dribbled down her fingers, leaving a sticky coating on the inside of her wrist. She made a silent pledge never to buy grocery store whipped cream again. When he returned the canisters to the creek, she curled up on the blanket, sated and content. Sunshine weighted her eyelids. Not certain she wasn't already dreaming, she dozed.

When she lifted her lids again, the blanket was in shade. The crack of stone against stone echoed from the creek. Sun-baked and slack, she reveled in a long stretch and rolled onto her belly.

Thigh-deep in water, Jonas again worked on the dam.

She propped on her elbows and spied through tall grass with seed tufts like squirrel tails. Apparently, while she napped, he doffed his shirt and undershirt. She spotted them spread out to dry on a bush. He bent low, pants stretched tight over his backside, and wrestled with a submerged rock. Corded muscles in his back and arms rippling, he wrenched a stone the size of a compact car from the creek bed. Water poured from it like a mini waterfall, and he stumbled beneath its weight. Revolving, he maneuvered the rock atop the dam. Sunlight caught his torso. His collarbones were pink with fresh sunburn, and his arms were bronzed in a deep farmer's tan.

She dragged her upper teeth lightly over her bottom lip. She could just imagine him as a child, straining to carry rocks with his younger brothers, hour after hour until the creek slowed and the pond formed. If she admired anything about the Amish, it was their single-minded dedication to work—even when that work was as frivolous as building a secret swimming hole in the middle of the woods.

Turning from the dam, he scanned the creek and then drew up short. He sloshed to the far bank, tilted his head, and reached into the brush.

She squinted and pressed to her knees, but she couldn't see what he sought until he pulled it out. One wild tiger lily—still holding out in late July.

Fingering the petals, he waded along the rock wall. When he reached the center, he stopped and rotated the blossom, taking it in from all angles. Then he tossed it over the rocks and watched it bob in the current until it rounded the bend and vanished. He hoisted himself atop the dam and hung his head.

She picked her way across the creek and climbed up next to him. The remnants of a rope swing dangled from a branch, the ends frayed and graying. Did Jonas climb that tree and tie the rope? Every inch of this farm must hold memories.

"Do you believe in God?" he asked after a moment.

"Yes." She wiggled her toes in the mushy mud. "Do you?"

With a ruffle of wings and leaves, the blackbird alit in a bush a few feet away.

"I seek Him every day of my life." Wedging his heels between rocks, he bent his knees and laced his fingers loosely atop his thighs. "You know, I didn't want to join the church."

He had a choice? She lifted her brows.

He nodded. "The decision was mine. When Amish children turn sixteen, they are given the choice to join the church. With the community's permission, many youths begin a time of experimentation. I suppose you've heard about that. Most come back, but a few don't. I wanted so badly to be one of those few."

The blackbird called again, but the cheerful song rang hollow. "Why did you return?"

"Elizabeth could never leave her mother. And I couldn't leave her."

She ran her finger over a smooth gray pebble lodged in the dam. "I see."

"Nora married Elizabeth's brother, Levi. Rebecca was their first child. I never saw her so happy as when Rebecca was born. She was always singing—so in love with that baby girl." He dropped his gaze and traced his right thumb back and forth along his left, following the line of a raised, white scar. "Elizabeth was expecting our first child, and Rebecca was almost three. We had an off Sunday—no church in our local district—but Elizabeth planned to worship in her home district, north of here. Eli and Nora wanted to go along, but Rebecca was feverish and miserable, the sickest I've ever seen her. The girl begged me to stay, and I was only too glad." He let out a bitter laugh. "I was baptized for my wife, not for off Sunday services." He lifted his gaze downstream. "It was too late—too dark when one of your police cars arrived at the house. My Elizabeth was dead. Levi was dead. Nora was in the hospital with a badly broken hip."

The blackbird sang again. Water trickled through the dam like the tinkling of bamboo chimes. "Oh, Jonas," she breathed. If he heard, he gave no indication. His gaze remained soft and distant.

"The driver of a logging truck carrying a full load of timber didn't see the buggy in his path. By the time he realized Levi was stopped to make a turn, he couldn't slow down." He nodded slowly and clenched his fingers until the knuckles cracked. "The driver survived with mild injuries. Of course, the horse was dead, too. Levi's best mare. Without Levi, I couldn't handle the farm. Maybe I lost the heart to try. I leased the fields. I can earn more money doing carpentry."

She shuddered. Whenever a logging truck barreled by on the highway, she gripped the wheel and hugged the berm. The idea of such a massive piece of machinery hitting a horse-drawn buggy from behind? A memory flashed of the mound on the Manhattan street. She blinked and rubbed her eyes. The scene was too brutal to imagine.

Through the lens of tragedy, the Rishel family portrait sharpened. She understood Nora's bitterness and why a cloud sometimes shrouded Jonas's features in sorrow. But what of everyone else? "Where was Samuel? And your other brothers? Couldn't they...?"

He shook his head. "My father died suddenly, not long after Elizabeth and I were married. The farm should have gone to Micah as the youngest, but my mother took the boys and went to her sister in Ohio. They never came back. Neither is farming any more. Not enough land to be had. Micah makes hats, and Samuel does carpentry and woodworking." He gave a sideways smile. "Gazebos. Now Nora stands market Wednesdays, and I build."

She shifted closer, not quite daring to touch him. "You build beautifully."

"The garden gate was a birthday gift for my wife." He shrugged and sighed. "Nora disapproved of it even then. Too showy. Now, I think she hates it. These days she seems only to hate. She has withdrawn. The community is concerned but tolerant...for now. Sometimes, I think her life would be better if she left—if we all left."

Would he really leave Green Ridge? Imagining never seeing him again sapped green from the grass and dulled the sky. She took the little, gray stone from the dam. On one side was a smooth, oval indentation that fit her thumb like she rubbed it there. "Where would you go?"

He forced a sigh and stood. "I don't know." In a rush, he clambered out of the water and threw himself onto the quilt.

She drove a car. She was part of the society that murdered his family. Stomach knotted, she followed and sat beside him. "I'm so sorry."

"The apology isn't yours to make."

His tone was kind but firm. She worried the stone between her fingers. He was right. Guilt was easy. She pushed aside hers and tried to put herself in Nora's shoes. Forgiveness was the real challenge.

"Like me, you cannot be asked to bear the burden of your community," he went on.

"Is that how you feel?"

"Sometimes." Propped on an elbow, he smoothed the quilt until the regular squares lined up in unrumpled rows. "Anyone who holds himself apart is suspect. The community is patient because of the accident, but the mandate is clear—forgive and let God's will be done. Now several years have passed. They believe we will return with full hearts, but we are not the people we were. My sister won't admit she's changed—that's not our way. She is at war with herself, and she takes it out on those like you...and, at times, on Rebecca." He rolled onto his back.

The hairs on his arms and chest caught the sun, gilding him in golden softness. He lay before her so open and vulnerable—the skin on his belly as delicate as a newborn babe's.

He ran a hand through his hair and tucked it beneath his head. "I know I am not the same. I cannot adhere to the rules of the *Ordnung* as did my father and his father. For now, I stay. But I will shave my face, and I will build for the English, no matter what the deacons say. I will seek God my own way. I will live, to some degree, by my own rules."

"Will they allow you your own rules?"

"Grudgingly. For Nora. And for Rebecca. But their patience runs thin."

The blackbird hopped from branch to branch. She squinted into the leafy tangle, searching for its crimson-splotched wings. "Your sister forbade me to return to the farm after the gazebo is finished."

He closed his eyes. "Forgive her."

Silence fell over the clearing. She extended cautious fingers and stroked the soft curls at his temples. They were almost a baby's curls, like the curls he never caressed on his own sweet baby's head. The tragedy was unimaginable. Yet, this man lived it.

"Sometimes, when I'm out here, I feel God." He opened his eyes and gazed into the treetops. "When the fog lies thick on the ridge and the world is quiet, I can begin to believe He is here."

After so many weeks of restraint, to have him confide in her, even about such painful subjects, warmed her heart. She hugged her knees and opened to him in return. "I see God in the ocean."

He rolled onto his side, facing her. "What's it like? The ocean?"

Closing her eyes, she conjured the endless, undulating expanse and tasted salt on the sweet water breeze. "Vast. And moody. It's never the same from one day to the next." *Rather like the color of your eyes.*

"I would like to see the ocean."

"I would like to take you." His expression lit like fireflies flickered in his irises.

"In the pop-top?"

She smiled. "In the pop-top."

"Where else have you been in the pop-top?"

She tucked her chin between her knees and rocked onto her tailbone, pointing her toes. "Gosh, all over. When I finished tenth grade, my family took a six-week camping trip out West."

"Out West."

He echoed the words as if tasting them.

"What did you see?" he asked

"Oh, huge canyons and the Great Plains and the desert. I loved the Rocky Mountains most. Colorado was my favorite state. Even in summer, snow tips the highest peaks, and the fields are blanketed with flowers." Her lungs quivered with the remembered exhilaration of hiking to a Rocky Mountain summit.

"The mountains there are nothing like ours. They're rough and craggy and so, so tall. They make a person feel small." Those kissable creases cleft his cheek. She caught a flash of white teeth.

"You liked that?"

She shivered. "I did. I don't know why. They're so big they scare me, but the energy out there is magnetic. Sometimes I feel these rolling ridges lull me to sleep. The Rockies throw you out of bed every morning and say, come and get me."

"Colorado," he repeated.

"Colorado." She stretched out on her back, tossing the stone from hand to hand. "The storms out there are massive. You see them come across the plains from miles away, and then they just descend on you."

His brows rose. "Bigger than the storm we watched on your porch?"

"Way bigger." Deep longing darkened his gaze.

"I've never been outside of Pennsylvania."

She shoved the stone into her pocket. She understood now why he'd never traveled. His life was woven into the fabric of this countryside. "Do you really think Rebecca will leave?"

"I know it."

She winced. The world was punishing. Rebecca had spunk to spare, but without her community and Jonas, she would be lost. "How?"

"She knows she will. That certainty is enough at any age." He took her shoulder and coaxed her onto her side.

Nose to nose, she reveled in the joy of simply looking at him. Up close, his face was rougher than she realized. Fine lines traversed his forehead, and another small scar, pale against brown skin, ran just beneath his chin. She touched the rounded rise of his shoulder, running her fingers over the muscle and down his bare arm. Gooseflesh prickled the hairs, and he quivered like an aspen leaf. Her skin flushed. She longed to lay her head on his chest and fall asleep, safe in the circle of his arms.

"A gift," he said again and lifted one cheek in a crooked grin.

She pursed her lips then relaxed them into a languid smile.

His eyes darkened.

Her belly tripped, and she caught the tiniest bit of lower lip between her teeth. How delicious to know she moved him.

Lifting his chin, he kissed her with slow tenderness.

She closed her eyes and felt the light flick of his tongue. His hand rested softly on her shoulder, urging her closer as he deepened the kiss. The longing that whispered in the leaves returned in a rush, but it did not compel. It flowed through her in waves, but it didn't drag her under.

Reluctant to leave this hidden meadow in the heart of the forest, she idled on the blanket for an afternoon that seemed to span three days. Quiet conversation ebbed and flowed. She dozed and woke to his kiss.

When twilight fell, he took her hand, and he didn't let go until they returned to the farm. In total darkness, he emerged from the barn with a lantern and guided her to the van.

Even the rumble of the motor couldn't break the spell. "What happens now?" she asked.

"We finish the gazebo."

Through the open car window, his lips met hers in a kiss full of promise. The day was too beautiful to ruin with thoughts of the future. She gave herself the gift of one perfect picnic with no care for what came next.

Chapter 17

With the sprinkler teetering on her fingertips, Tessa strained to reach the top shelf in the garage. She could easily grab a stepstool, but less than twenty-four hours after hiking and swimming and dam building, stretching felt good. Her muscles lengthened, and her T-shirt pulled from her waistband, allowing soft, summer air to stroke her skin. Today, she wanted to touch the sky.

A trickle of water leaked from the pipe and dripped onto her cheek. It was warm and slimy, the polar opposite of the crisp creek water that stopped her heart the day before. She brushed it with her shoulder and hopped, attempting to shove enough of the sprinkler onto the shelf that it would balance and stay. It teetered on the edge and tipped back into her hand. She was tall, but not quite tall enough.

"Close your eyes."

The unexpected voice hissed in her ear, cutting through the whir of the fan and the hum of the freezer. She gasped, and the sprinkler rolled off her fingertips and clattered to the floor. Whirling, she came face to face with Jonas. Or rather, face to chest. He was very close. Dropping her hands to her hips, she steeled herself against the wooziness that turned her kneecaps to oatmeal every time he came near. "Why are you sneaking around my garage?

"I wasn't sneaking." He fished the sprinkler from

under a lawn chair, reached over her shoulder, and slid it onto the shelf. "Now, close your eyes."

The smile tugging at the corners of his mouth belied his firm tone. "Yes, you were, and why are you smiling?"

"Close them." He thrust his hat in front of her face.

The straw scratched her forehead, and she jerked, bumping her bottom against the shelves. "Fine." She huffed and squeezed shut her eyes. "Happy?"

"Very. Now take my hand and come with me."

"Jonas—"

"Do as I say."

Even with her eyes closed, she could hear his smile widen. She felt calloused fingers wrap around hers.

"Come with me."

As insistent as a child on Christmas morning, he tugged her hand. She followed, and as the surface beneath her feet changed from concrete to gravel and then to grass, she let out a squeal. "Is it finished?"

"Just keep your eyes closed."

She stumbled over bumpy lawn until the ground softened, and pine boughs ruffled her hair with fragrant fingers. "It's finished, isn't it? I know it is."

"Easy now. Step up."

He was ahead of her now, holding both hands and leading her up three wide steps. Her sandals clomped on hard wood. She breathed in the smell of fresh-cut timber. Sawdust tickled her nose.

"Sit here," he said in her ear.

Sit where? The gazebo she designed didn't come with seating. Still, she allowed him to guide her down next to him and leaned into the warmth of his body, knees bouncing in anticipation.

"Now. Open your eyes."

She did…and drew in a quick breath at the sight. Before her were her initials and her parents' initials, lovingly etched into the sycamore so many years ago. All around, surrounding and embracing her, was the completed gazebo. Though she watched it grow over the span of several weeks, today, with Jonas beside her not just as her builder but as someone far dearer, she took in the structure afresh.

Nothing like the curlicued follies of the Victorian era, this rustic structure was of the earth. It was built upon an octagon and supported by rough-hewn posts. An intricate and beautiful support system allowed for an octagonal opening, through which her family's beloved tree reached to the sky. A smooth railing encircling the outer edge spanned artfully placed branches in an Adirondack style. The wood glowed with the richly golden hue of fresh-milled lumber. Yet, she could almost believe the gazebo had been there for years, growing inch by inch with the tree it encircled and the red-haired girl in the house down the hill.

Giggling with glee, she dashed across the floor and down the steps. Cedar shingled and sturdy, yet at the same time airy and wind-filled, with the towering sycamore canopying the entire structure…the gazebo was magic. She clasped her hands beneath her chin. "I can't imagine a more perfect gift."

Crossing his arms, he regarded his work. "I sealed the wood to protect it. Your parents can paint it if they want, or they can just let rain and snow weather it. I'd probably do the latter. By the end of this winter, it should blend into the surrounding trees."

She scampered back up the steps and opened her

arms. "This is so far beyond the gazebo I imagined. Jonas, you're an artist."

The apples of his cheeks pinkened. "You like it?"

"Like it?" She spluttered, still agog. "I adore everything about it. You even made me a bench."

He leaned and pointed around the trunk. "I built a second bench on the other side."

"Two benches." With a contented sigh, she collapsed next to him. His work pants were scratchy against her bare knee, but she didn't mind. "Thank you, thank you, thank you."

"It was my pleasure." He brushed his lips against hers and smiled.

She slipped an arm through his and dropped her head onto his shoulder. Resting atop his thigh, their forearms pressed together, and she interlaced her fingers with his, one by one.

A catbird cried in a dogwood tree. Clouds gathered in the southwest, but they were still far away. Quiet minutes passed, and her excitement at seeing the completed gazebo ebbed, leaving behind a growing sense of unease. She lifted her head and with one finger, turned his face to hers.

He raised an eyebrow.

Questions and promises danced on the tip of her tongue. Forbidden thoughts and dreams she had no right to dream tapped her skull from inside. She lifted one shoulder and let it fall. "The gazebo is finished."

"It is." He dropped a kiss on the tip of her nose.

Once she returned from Ohio, Nora would ensure Tessa never set foot on the farm again. She and Rebecca needed Jonas. Given their history, she would fight tooth and nail to protect her family. Who could blame her? Tessa and Jonas would return to their separate worlds, and somehow life would go on. How could she let him go?

She caught his gaze. "What happens now?" Her voice wobbled. The catbird mewed again. Or was it a mockingbird?

He tightened his grip. "I don't know."

Those three syllables tore from his body on a breath forced from somewhere deep. He was always so steady, but in a heartbeat all composure vanished. He sounded like a man who was trapped.

Sudden as a sea squall, he wrapped his arms around her and gathered her close.

Her eyes flew wide, and her breath hitched in her chest. She lifted her chin, and he kissed her like she was his only hope for escape. This kiss was different, full of urgency and searing with need. Almost, she thought somewhere in the dazed recesses of her brain, like a last kiss.

She clung until they finally parted, breathless and rumpled. She nuzzled his neck and closed her eyes. His skin was slick and salty and smelled of sawdust. "Please don't go away."

He ran his knuckles down her cheek. "To everything there is a season, Tessa Rose."

His voice was tinged with regret. Her throat tightened. Was this the season for good-byes? She took a breath to ask but didn't have the chance.

"Well, isn't this a cozy sight."

The icy voice froze her insides. She jumped and whirled for the second time that afternoon, landing her gaze on a pair of immaculate running shoes.

"Surprised to see me?" Richard mounted the top

step and stared. "From the look on your face, I'd say very surprised indeed." He shifted his gaze to Jonas. "I believe we've met. Dr. Richard Bruce."

"I believe we have." Jonas stood. "Jonas Rishel."

"This is a fine piece of work, Jonas Rishel." Richard yanked one of the hefty support posts.

The gazebo barely shuddered.

Jonas retrieved his hat from the bench. "Excuse me."

Richard kept hold of the post, blocking the entrance. "No need to leave. We're all friends."

He flashed a wolflike smile, and Tessa winced.

Jonas stepped toward Richard. Face to face, he towered over the young doctor.

Richard cleared his throat and stiffened.

The hair on the back of her neck prickled as if at any second lightning would strike. For a sickening moment, she feared one of them might do something stupid.

"Excuse me," Jonas said again.

His tone was firm but without malice.

"But of course." Richard stepped aside.

Jonas loped down the steps and disappeared into the pines.

Richard barreled into the gazebo.

He paced the octagon like a caged animal. Stomach tightening, she shrank against the railing.

"I texted. I called. Why the hell didn't you tell me?"

A twiggy spindle gouged her spine. "I had nothing to tell."

He let out a snort. "Apparently, you did."

How dare he cast her as the cheating girlfriend

when she was unequivocal that night at the Lincoln log house? Cheeks ablaze, she leapt to her feet. "Not until yesterday." She scanned the pines. Where was Jonas? She hoped he couldn't hear Richard, but at the same time, she longed for his return.

"Right. So, two things are happening now. Number one: in all the excitement, you might have forgotten we have a major hospital event on August first—one you and I have been planning for nearly six weeks. I'd like all the relevant files."

So, now he claimed ownership of the ball? As if he made one phone call or sent a single email. "I'm not finished with the arrangements. I need to confirm the band—"

"You've clearly got a lot on your plate. Claire and I will handle it."

The sarcasm was mean-spirited but effective. Tears stung in her eyes. "I've put my whole heart into this ball—"

"Your heart, huh?" He barked a laugh. "Spare me." He took the phone from his pocket and tapped the screen. "And there's the small matter of a house key."

She caught her breath and pressed her palms to her cheeks. The ball was hers but the key? The key belonged to him.

"I'll take that back, too," he said without looking up.

His actions were punishing, but hard as he tried to hide it, the pain creasing his forehead was unmistakable. Bludgeoned by malice and weighted with guilt, she sagged. "Of course. The key is upstairs."

"I'll be in the car."

Half blind, she gathered the materials for the

Midsummer Ball and climbed the stairs to her room. The little, warped box sat on her dresser top where she placed it just nights—and a lifetime—before. The cardboard was brittle and the color of dried blood. She lifted it as if it might disintegrate in her fingers and, balancing it atop the files, went outside.

With a low hum, the tinted glass slid into the door. An air-conditioned breeze wafted through the open window.

She handed over first the file folders and binders and then, finally, the box. "I'm so sorry."

Stone-faced, he chucked everything into the passenger seat, shoved on his sunglasses, and started the engine.

"Richard, we should talk."

With one press of a button, the window closed.

She knocked on the glass. "Richard."

The engine revved, and he drove away without a backward glance.

Breaking up with Richard after he gave her a whole house was perhaps the meanest thing she'd ever done. Yet, somehow, returning the key felt even worse. With a taste of curdled milk on her tongue, she retreated to the garage in a daze.

Jonas dropped a hammer into his toolbox and slung it onto the workbench. He unplugged the fan and whipped the cord around its base. The sun vanished behind thickening clouds, and the garage grew dim.

She sank onto the cooler and tugged her ponytail. "I've never seen Richard so angry."

A handful of nails rattled into a metal coffee can. He snapped on the lid and jammed it in the toolbox.

"Are you mad at me, too?"

Wood scraps tumbled into the garbage, spewing a dusty cloud. He fanned it away and wheeled to the bench.

She waited, the ball of her right foot driving into the floor, her right knee bouncing. "Say something, please."

He hung the dustpan and brush on the pegboard and switched off the work light. "Perhaps he is entitled to be angry."

Her stomach churned. "Why?"

He fixed her in his gaze. "Because you never spoke to him."

First Richard accused her of impropriety and now Jonas? Disbelief flared in her chest, singeing her lungs. "What was I supposed to say? That I had a crush on you? That we sat on my front porch during a thunderstorm? I had nothing to tell."

He dragged the back of his hand across his mouth. "Nothing to tell."

"Not until yesterday." She searched his face. His expression was a mask of inscrutable, infuriating composure.

Nodding slowly, he settled his hands on his hips. "Maybe now I understand the difference between us. To you, nothing mattered until our lips touched and our bodies met. To me, weeks of shared work—hours passed in silence and in conversation—that time meant something. But perhaps such moments are nothing to people like you."

His words stoked her outrage until it blazed. "How could I have known what you were thinking? I can't read your mind."

His jaw tightened. "I hoped you could read my

heart."

She reeled, and the cooler tottered. Wedging her hands beneath her thighs, she gripped it. "That's not fair."

"Everything needs to be spoken aloud for you people," he snarled. "You print your feelings on billboards and shout them over the radio. Can nothing be understood without words?"

She jerked to standing, toppling the cooler. "My world is an easy target, isn't it? Well, maybe I am hopelessly corrupt, but I haven't lied to myself for years. I don't live a life I don't believe in, just because I don't have the courage to leave." His studied composure cracked, exposing a hurricane of raw emotion. She braced for the backlash.

"This discussion isn't about me, and you know it. It's about the freedom you took to toy with two men—and your inability to make a choice, any choice, about how you want to live your life."

"I had a choice to be with you?" Swiping curls from her eyes, she held his gaze. "How could I possibly have known? Did I think you cared about me? Yes. Did I believe our relationship could ever be anything more? How could I?"

He spun and leaned into the workbench, back heaving. His shirt strained at the seams.

She watched him struggle to contain the passion she knew his upbringing taught him to suppress. After weeks of restraint, she was not so fettered. "You live in this closed-off community I can never enter. When I'm around, your sister speaks in another language. She told me flat out to leave and never come back! How could I hope to be part of your life?"

His fist crashed onto the workbench, jarring the toolbox and all its contents.

With a cry, she stumbled backward, tripping over the cooler.

He pivoted slowly. "You speak of things about which you know nothing."

His face was granite. Steeling her spine, she refused to back down. "Exactly." With her gaze locked on his, she stood tight-lipped, daring him to speak. His silence double dared her in return.

Thunder rumbled in the west, echoing the sound of bone hitting wood and the hum of vibrating metal.

Grabbing the toolbox, he closed the distance between them in three paces and yanked a piece of paper from the tools, tearing one corner.

Catching sight of her gazebo, she felt her heart balloon until it strained against her ribs. Her original drawing was now fully encircled. To his earlier sketches, he'd added the bench, the railing, and the octagonal window to the sky. The paper quivered between them. "Jonas…" Funny, she didn't remember swallowing sandpaper, but her throat seemed freshly coated with grit. "Just calm down a second and talk to me. Look, I'm sorry—"

"No, I'm sorry," he snapped, "for believing you had more imagination than you do." He thrust the paper into her hands. "Enjoy your gazebo."

Then he stormed from the garage and out of her life forever. Like a snowman in July, she melted until she was no more sentient than two buttons and a mushy carrot in a lukewarm puddle—which was good because water felt no pain.

Lightning flickered, and rain fell in buckets. A

chilly wind gusted through the open garage door, spraying her curled-up form with stinging drops she only half registered. The deluge overwhelmed the gutters and splattered the gravel around the spout with a sound like grapeshot.

A black-and-yellow spider made a perfect web between two legs of the workbench. In the middle of the web, it spun a line of zig-zagged silk that to Tessa's shell-shocked brain almost seemed to form a word. A fly occasionally alit on her legs. After a while, it didn't return. Maybe the spider completed her web in time.

The steady downpour echoed until her ears ached. She couldn't recall such a rainy summer. How did the clouds have water left to give? If she waited long enough, maybe the sky would collapse like a rain-puddled tent pulled down by its own weight. If she could just stay perfectly still, she might not have to feel or think anything ever again

Afternoon surrendered to evening, and evening fell to night. Her body stiffened against the concrete, and her left arm prickled with pins and needles. Maybe she dozed. Maybe she imagined the spider. At a certain point, she couldn't see the web at all.

The automatic outdoor lights tripped. She sat and rubbed her eyes. Delirious with hunger and misery, she was seized with a sudden obsession: did the gazebo leak? Jonas prided himself on the quality of his work. When she saw him next, he would want to know.

She streaked out of the garage and across the sodden grass, but when she finally clomped into the gazebo, the world was too dark to see. She rested her cheek against her own initials and let the trickle of rain wet her face. When she began to cry, she couldn't feel her tears.

Now everything really is ruined.

Was Jonas right? Had she been playing with them? Leading on both men? Impossible. Jonas wasn't exactly forthcoming. Until yesterday's picnic, she had no idea how much he cared.

But what if she did date Richard because he was safe and convenient? A future with him was so concrete. Afraid of her feelings for Jonas and cowed by the challenges his family presented, she didn't dare imagine a world in which they could be together. Because if that world turned out to be a fantasy, her heart might shatter beyond repair. Just like it was shattered now.

She collapsed onto the bench he built, under shelter of a roof he shingled by hand, and surrendered. Her heart had no room for denial, and she was too exhausted to fight.

She loved Jonas. She loved him completely. And she lost him.

The sky flashed nuclear white, and a splintering crack fractured the air. This wave of the never-ending storm was dangerously close.

Sinuses filled with the odor of burning electrical wires, she stumbled back to the kitchen and picked up her phone. Instinctively, she keyed in her mother's cell number. She hung up before the first ring. If she called Tucson in the middle of the night, her voice ragged from sobbing, her mother would book the first flight to Harrisburg.

Jenn? Jenn had seen this train wreck coming a mile away. She couldn't bear to admit how miserably she'd failed both relationships. She broke Richard's heart, and she destroyed Jonas's trust. At two for two, she was batting a thousand. She scrolled her contacts for Claire's number and dialed.

"Hello?" a male voice answered.

Tyler. He sounded sleepy. What was the time anyway? She cleared her throat. "It's Tessa. Is Claire there?"

"Oh, hey. One second." Tyler covered the phone.

She could just make out muffled voices in the background.

"Tessa?" Tyler went on. "Sorry, Claire can't come to the phone right now. She…uh, she'll call you back."

Her head was a bowling ball perched atop a bendy straw. The straw accordioned, and her chin nested into her chest. Claire was first and foremost Richard's friend. No way would she call back. "I'm sorry for calling so late." Her voice broke. Was she supposed to hang up? Would Tyler end the call? She sniffled through awkward silence.

"Tessa, are you all right?"

Tyler's voice was kind—more kind than her arguably lousy treatment of his friend and colleague merited. That drop of humanity soothed her parched throat. "I'm fine. Thanks for asking." She ended the call and slid her phone across the naked kitchen table. No longer buried beneath Midsummer Ball files, it held only her backpack and its contents, strewn in her rush to collect everything for Richard.

She ran her thumb over the edge of her checkbook, fanning the pages in a smooth swish. Even after everyone switched to online banking, she still managed her accounts the old-fashioned way, relishing the sense of accomplishment when the numbers all worked out. If only her life could be reckoned so easily.

She flipped open the cover. Only one blank check remained.

One check.

Jonas's check.

She clutched the checkbook in rigid fingers. How much did she owe for the gazebo? He never quoted a price. Hours upon hours went into its construction and stacks upon stacks of beautiful wood. He deserved to be paid.

Unzipping a pocket in her backpack, she found a pen and scribbled the check for the balance of her radio winnings. She stuffed it in an envelope and shoved it into her backpack with her wallet and the pen. Grabbing her keys, she tore outside into the rain.

The motor whined and sputtered and finally turned over. Blindly, she reversed down the driveway—she had zero vision through the tiny back window—but she trusted her memory to get her safely on the road. Once on the street and pointed in the right direction, she could still only see a few yards ahead. She nudged the gas pedal and eased the clutch.

Even at a crawl, the van hydroplaned every mile of the way. She glided through the intersection of Route 45, narrowly missing an oncoming car shrouded in torrents. The unyielding steering wheel refused to cooperate. Battling to stay in her lane, she gritted her teeth and peered into the opaque night.

Her memory flashed to her first drive to the farm that golden June afternoon. How giddy and frightened she'd been. A lump of fear lodged in her chest now but for entirely different reasons too numerous to consider.

Rounding the bend by Esther King's farm stand,

she suddenly lost all vision in the high beams of an oncoming truck. Pulse racing, she clamped her bottom lip and tasted blood. The truck screamed by, dousing the windshield and jarring the world in its wake.

Seconds later, another driver laid on his horn and shot around from behind, taillights instantly snuffed by the storm.

She stepped on the brakes and leaned hard into the steering wheel, just barely managing the turn off the highway.

With every curve in the road, the trees leaned farther, and the rain pelted harder as the van wrested away her control. The headlights were pinpricks in a monstrous void. Where was the lane? Was she beyond the new Mennonite church and Stoltzfus's quilt shop? Was she even on Old Cowan Road?

She was on the verge of giving up when her headlights caught the railing of the bridge over Buffalo Creek. Stomping on the brake pedal, she wrenched the wheel. The tires shrieked, and she swerved onto the shoulder. Branches lashed the windshield and gouged the sides of the van. She gasped and pulled the wheel in the other direction with all her might.

Where was the opening to the bridge? The defogger was no match for the cloudy windshield. The broken fan clicked like a playing card wedged in a bicycle wheel. She swiped a palm across the glass. If she could just cross the creek, she'd find Jonas's lane on the other side. She veered again, and the bridge came fully into view. She blinked.

Correction: the portion of the bridge that was above water came into view.

Paralyzed, she stared into menacing darkness,

sweaty fingers clamping the wheel. The creek was flooded. It overtopped its banks in a raging torrent, completely submerging the span in a race to the river. Gasping, she slammed the brakes like her leg was a pile driver.

The tires screeched again, and the pop-top skidded off the road. Out of control, it crashed through brush and into the roiling depths. Chunks of debris hammered the doors and the windows.

Lifted by the current, she spun ninety degrees and hurtled downstream. "Jonas!" she screamed.

The van listed and rammed headlong into the bridge with a thunderous crunch.

She vaulted onto the steering wheel, driving the shaft into her ribs and knocking the wind from her body. Fighting for breath, she opened her lips fishlike, just as the camper lurched again. Like it had a score to settle, the angry current caught the rear of the bus, swinging it around and slamming it sidelong into the span. Her forehead smashed into the driver's side window, and a million, zillion fireflies zoomed before her eyes. Then the night faded to inky black.

****

Rain lashed the windows and seeped under the door, soaking the rag rug and puddling on the kitchen floor. Jonas thought he'd fixed that leak. Not that he cared tonight. He slid the lantern closer and squinted, barely able to see in this light.

Almost in a trance, he sketched, smudging a soft shadow under her chin and arcing long lashes.

"Don't forget the freckles on my nose," the bowed lips whispered. "Let me look at you."

Even as he gave it life, the familiar expression

skewered his heart.

Gnawing the eraser, he stretched his legs under the kitchen table, arching against the hard-backed chair. His calves cramped. The walk home was torture in the rain, and he jogged at least half of it. Maybe a bath would help him relax...and finally sleep. How many hours had he been awake anyway? Twenty? Twenty-one? Yes, a bath.

He stared at the paper. He didn't want to draw her. He didn't want to think about her. But he had no other choice.

Alone in his bed, sleep had mocked him. He closed his eyes, and her face appeared on his eyelids. He stared at the ceiling, and she was there, too—that full lower lip smiling...laughing. Not just her face, her limbs splayed across the picnic quilt while she dozed in the sun. He felt again those long legs wrapped around him as he tasted her kiss. How satisfying it was not to have to bend down to kiss a woman.

Maybe drawing her face—capturing it on paper— would chase it from his mind.

The drawer of his night table was full of such drawings. Drawings he hadn't shown a soul. Not since Elizabeth died. Elizabeth, always in his heart but now in his past.

He'd found a new love—a love born of freedom. Tessa's love opened a whole new world.

He cursed and threw the pencil. It bounced off a cabinet and rolled under the counter. Freedom? He choked a laugh. His existence was nothing but bounds and borders, rules and walls. He was chained to this farm, and he was never going anywhere.

Lightning turned the night to day. A cannon blast

rattled the windowpanes and blew open the back door. As thunder ricocheted down the valley, he heard something else.

His name.

His name as he heard it called for years in his nightmares.

"Jonas!"

He stilled. Night after night, the cry tormented him until he woke in a sweat to the sound of Elizabeth's dying voice. Night after night, she pleaded in vain. Snared in his sheets, he shook, a useless mass of muscle and bone.

But her voice faded years ago. Elizabeth slept in peace. His heart had healed.

"Jonas!"

Who summoned him now?

He closed his eyes, and wind parted his hair like a September breeze through a cornfield. He felt a faint thrum of wings across his face.

"Jonas!"

He opened his eyes, and the sketch seemed to glow from within. It shimmered for a heartbeat and shot across the table in a gust from the open door. This was no dream.

He sprang up, launching his chair into the cabinets. Throwing on a coat, he caught the drawing and stuffed it in his pocket. Then he grabbed the lantern and sprinted into the storm, praying he'd find her in time.

Chapter 18

Soft pillows. The trilling coo of a mourning dove. Crisp, sun-scented sheets. Darkness.

Tessa wiggled and registered somewhere in her body that movement was bad. She lay completely still, boneless on the edge of oblivion, until consciousness hummed like a mosquito she couldn't quite shake, tugging her back to a world of hard edges.

She rolled her head to one side, and her temples pounded. Her mouth tasted like cotton. Through slitted lids, she saw Jonas slumped in a chair, asleep. Her lips formed the shape of a word intended to be his name. A barely voiced whimper came out.

The bed sagged under his weight, and his face appeared, indistinct in the pre-dawn glow. She licked cracked lips. "Hi." Even her voice was bruised.

"Hi."

Where was she? She swung her gaze over plain, white walls. On a wooden peg rail by the door, a pair of pants dangled from suspenders beside a black suit and white shirt neatly arranged on hangers. She blinked, and her lashes stuck like they were coated in half dry glue. "Am I in your bed?"

"Yes."

Her head hurt way too much to unpack the implications of that discovery. She arched her lower back. "It's kind of lumpy."

"How do you feel?" He pressed a hand to her cheek.

Swallowing took monumental effort. "My head hurts."

He crossed to a spindled washstand by the door and picked up a pitcher.

Water flowed into a basin with a sound that echoed the creek. *The creek that tried to kill me.* She took in a breath, and searing pain in her ribs temporarily overpowered her headache.

He dipped a washcloth in the basin, wrung it, and draped the cloth over her forehead.

Cool streams trickled down her temples, and her vision cleared. Though Spartan, the room was cozy. Simple, green shades covered the windows, dim light glowing through the spaces around them. A masculine, oak bureau stood alone to the left of the bed. Above the washstand at her feet, the peg rail extended the length of the wall. A beeswax candle in a tin candleholder and a worn Bible lay on the bedside table.

He poured a glass of water and joined her again on the bed. Sliding a hand behind her head, he touched the glass to her lips. "Drink a little."

She obeyed. The water was sweet and cold. Sated, she settled back and traced her fingertips over her forehead to the burning locus of pain above her left eyebrow. A knobby lump throbbed beneath her touch.

He took her hand and cradled it. "You have a serious welt. I'm relieved you woke on your own."

"What time is it?"

He rose and lifted a pocket watch from the dresser. "Six thirty."

In the a.m. she assumed. Then again, could the dim

light be dusk the following day? How much time had she lost? She bunched the sheet in one hand. "So, I've been here…?"

"About six hours."

With a sigh, she eased her grip on the bedclothes. "How did I end up in your bed?"

"Not now. We'll talk when I come back."

A wave of panic tightened her chest, stinging her lungs like saltwater. She groped for him with one hand, and pain surged from her ribs, nearly knocking her into the headboard. "Wait. Don't go," she choked.

He caught her hand again and pressed it to his cheek. "Easy, now."

The stubble of a tawny beard chafed her palm.

"Only for a short time," he went on. "To do the milking. You rest now."

She nodded and closed her eyes. When she lifted her lids again, the room was suffused with the mouthwatering scents of biscuits and bacon.

Jonas placed a steaming plate on the night table and raised the shades. Stark, morning light streamed into the room. He thumped one side of the window frame and forced open the window.

A chatty robin took over for the mourning dove.

She squinted and winced. Squinting hurt, too.

His wet hair dripped dark spots onto a deep purple shirt. His face was clean-shaven and ruddy. "I'm sorry to wake you. But with that bump, I felt I had to."

Her head was clearer, though no less painful, and her sinuses ached, too. Forgetting her bruised ribs, she heaved to sitting. A groan fought through her clenched throat.

He eased onto the bed and placed the plate, laden

with scrambled eggs, bacon, and buttered biscuits, into his lap. "Are you hungry?"

Her belly soured. "Not really."

"You should eat." He forked a bite of eggs, aimed it at her mouth, and raised a brow.

Even incapacitated, she wasn't going to be fed like a toddler. She shot him a look and grabbed the fork. Cloudlike eggs dissolved in her mouth—almost a different substance from the gummy things she hitherto knew as scrambled eggs. She let out a moan and scooped a second bite. "Did you make this?"

His lips curled. "Not hungry, huh?"

When the plate was scraped clean, she lowered onto a pile of pillows and sipped honey-sweet tea. "I remember being in the van… I searched for your lane, but the bridge was washed out. How did you find me?"

He yanked off his boots, pulled his feet onto the bed, and stretched out beside her. The toe of his right sock pooched where someone darned it with thick yarn. "I heard you."

Impossible. That wind was loud as a freight train. "How?"

"When the van lodged against the bridge, you hit your head, and the horn stuck."

"And you heard it over the storm?"

He nodded.

A strange expression passed over his face and vanished in an instant. Guess she needed to get the horn fixed. She took in a breath. "My van!" The van was her baby. With no regard for pain, she strained upward. "Where is it?"

He took her hand. "I called a truck. Some men came and towed it to a repair shop."

Jonas would no sooner abandon her van in the creek than he would a baby bird fallen from its nest. Not only did she trust him with her van, she trusted him with her life. Very possibly, she owed it to him. "Thank you." She met his gaze. It was solid as bedrock.

"My pleasure."

She stared at her freckled hands sticking out from white cotton sleeves. Sleeves that ended well above her wrists…sleeves she did not recognize. Yet another realization skittered up the back of her neck. She licked her lips and swallowed. "What am I wearing? Is this Nora's?"

His gaze was unfaltering. "Yes."

The cotton shift turned to poison ivy, toxic and itchy, crawling like spiders over her skin. Squirming, she yanked one cuff and tried to wrench her arm from the narrow sleeve. Her ribs throbbed, and her breath quickened. "Where are my clothes? I should go home."

Big hands settled on her shoulders. "You will not leave this bed until I say so. If you hadn't wakened easily, I would have taken you to the hospital. You're injured, Tessa. Quiet down now and rest."

Ignoring the pop of stitches, she twisted in his grasp. "But Nora—"

"Nora and Rebecca are away, remember? Be still."

With a jerk, she broke free, bumping her head against the wooden headboard. A hot poker of pain blurred her vision, and she let out a cry. Hugging herself around the middle, she took a deep breath and held it.

"Forget the nightgown. It doesn't matter." He opened his arms. "Please stay."

She couldn't have taken off the garment if she

wanted to. Her head hurt too much. She untwined her fingers from the fabric, and her muscles unknotted. With a sigh, she relaxed into his embrace, blocking out everything but the reassuring beat of his heart. Exhaustion dulled her thoughts and pulled at her eyelids. Surrender seemed inevitable. First, though—first, she had something to say. She forced a quick inhalation. "Jonas?"

"Hmm."

His murmured response fluttered the curls at her ear. "I'm sorry for everything I said…and for what I did. I never meant to hurt anyone."

"I know." He tightened his arms around her. "I'm sorry for walking away in anger."

She nuzzled into his shirt. It smelled faintly of biscuits. "Then it rained and rained."

"I've never seen the bridge wash out so quickly."

"Thank you for finding me." Ever so gently, he rested his chin atop her head. His chest rose and fell in a rhythm as comforting as a lullaby. A volley of chipmunk chatter came from the yard, but inside, the house was silent. "Are we really, truly alone?"

"Yes."

The single word vibrated deep in his chest, tickling her cheek. "Can I stay a while?"

"As long as you like."

The farm was theirs. She snuggled closer. "I can help with chores. I'm very good at weeding."

"I know."

"Once I get out of this nightgown, I'll…" Hold on. How she get *into* this nightgown? She stiffened and inched away. "You changed my clothes," she said on an exhale.

Beneath tanned skin, his neck pinkened. "Not all of them."

"Most of them!" Scootching onto her backside, she clutched at the collar of Nora's nightdress. "How?"

He stared at the ceiling as color crept over his jawline to his cheeks. "Not easily. You helped some."

"I don't remember."

"You hit your head."

Would the mortification ever cease? She dropped her gaze. Her wrist bones were peaky knobs, inelegantly splotched with freckles. Sometimes she felt like nothing but gawky, pointy bits. And he got an eyeful of them all. "I'm sorry."

"Your skin is like finely woven silk." With the back of his index finger, he traced the contours of her cheek. "Cool to the touch."

She peeped from beneath her lashes. "Have you ever felt silk?"

A smile crept across his lips. "I've imagined it."

She buried her face in his work shirt, more precious than the finest brocade. "Have you ever spent all day in bed?"

He let out a low chuckle. "Not once."

"You should try it sometime."

"All right."

The floodgates of inquiry burst wide, and she was curious as a five-year-old. "Can I explore all over your house?"

His laughter made the bed squeak. "If you want. Not much to see."

More mirth at her expense? She tensed and shot him a glance. The tenderness in his gaze melted her brittle pride. In the creek, he said she gifted him with laughter—a lifeline after years of grief. Nonetheless, she felt a need to defend the request. "I've never been inside an Amish house. Except your pantry."

"It's plain."

She followed his gaze to the unadorned walls. "I have lots of questions."

He dipped his chin. "Time for answers."

"When may I start?"

"Whenever you like."

Sunlight toasted the room, and she kicked out from under the sheet. With care for her injuries, she shifted to face him. "Why do Amish men have beards and no moustaches?"

His laughter rattled the headboard. "Of all things!"

Resisting the urge to punch him, she balled her fist and plunked it on her hip. "I'm serious. Why?"

"An earnest request for Anabaptist history. As you wish." He raked his fingers through his hair. "The soldiers in Europe where our ancestors lived wore moustaches. As Christian pacifists, we do not wish to emulate them."

"But you do have beards." Sunlight caught his chin, and the little scar beneath his jaw flashed white. "Most of you."

"When a man is married, he allows his facial hair to grow. Our images of Jesus show him bearded. We strive to be like him, but we know we fall short."

"Huh." She nodded. "That's a really satisfying explanation."

His lips pressed into a firm line. "Not everyone agrees with my decision to shave my face."

His jaw was so square and strong she wanted to bite it. "You are very handsome."

He rolled his eyes and groaned.

"You are!"

"I'm getting old."

How old was he? She studied his features. Thirty? Thirty-two? She nuzzled beneath his chin and brushed a kiss over that tiny scar. Sleep settled over her body, unclenching stiffening muscles and easing bruised limbs until another chuckle roused her. "What?" she murmured.

"Do you know what we're doing?"

She pointed and flexed her toes, and her ankle cracked. "Going back to sleep?"

"We're bundling."

"Fascinating. Tell me more after I nap."

He snuggled her closer. "In the past, when an Amish boy and girl courted, they would get into bed together and crawl under the blankets—"

"Wait—what?" Sleepiness evaporated in an instant. Bruised ribs or no, she raised onto one elbow.

"Fully clothed—"

"Did their parents know about this?"

"Their parents encouraged it."

His expression was serious, but a flash of mischief pinballed in his gaze. She whapped one rock-hard pec. "No way."

"Actually, yes. Bundling is a traditional custom among Amish youth—quite common in this area until recently."

As insane as the notion was, he spoke with such decisiveness she almost believed him. "Okay, so they're lying together in bed…and then what?

"Well, then they would…" He cleared his throat.

"They would what?"

He shrugged. "Talk."

She tucked her chin and gave the hairiest of eyeballs. "Talk?"

"Yes, talk."

A guffaw burst from her lips. "I don't think so!" He raised his hand in apparent oath, and for a second, she thought he would grab his Bible and swear. "You're saying teenagers—boyfriends and girlfriends—lie in bed together, under a blanket"—she lofted the quilt—"and talk?"

"With their parents' blessing."

She leveled him with a gaze worthy of an ace prosecutor. "Did you and your wife just talk?"

His jaw dropped for long enough a daredevil fly could have buzzed in and out again. He snapped it shut. "Bundling has fallen out of fashion."

"Yeah, 'cause parents are catching on to the fact their kids aren't just talking under that blanket." With a good yank, she freed the quilt and kicked it onto the floor.

"I don't think so."

She snugged beneath his chin. "You have some strange customs, my friend."

He was quiet a moment. "So, tell me more about this…Easter hare…"

Despite bruised ribs, she laughed until her belly ached.

In truth, talk was all she and Jonas did that afternoon. Eventually, she dozed, and when he left to do the evening chores, she barely stirred. When she woke again, the room was silent save for cicada song and the gentle puff of his breathing. She groped on the nightstand for matches and, finding them, lit the candle.

Taking careful hold of the candleholder, she slipped out of bed. One hand atop the bedpost, she steadied herself. After a full day off her feet, her legs were wobbly as a baby deer's. Overwhelmingly, however, she needed to find the bathroom. Or the outhouse. Or whatever.

In the doorway, she hesitated and peered into the upstairs landing. With no hum of electric fans or air-conditioning, the house was eerily quiet. One step into the hall and the floorboards yelped in protest. She poked her head into the adjacent bedroom and made out a curved, wooden rack draped with a quilt and a plain, cedar chest at the end of the bed. Dark-hued aprons and dresses hung from pegs in a tidy row. The windows were stark, covered only by the same dark-green shades as in Jonas's room. Nora's bedroom?

Spying through the next doorway, she spotted two faceless, cloth dolls on a hastily made bed, reminders of the Old Testament warning against "graven images." Rebecca's room, no doubt. She stepped inside. Acorns, pebbles, dried leaves, and bird nests lined the windowsills and dresser tops, and a jelly jar of colored pencils sat atop a messy pile of paper on the desk. The absence of photographs came over her with melancholy stealth. No wedding photos or snapshots of a grinning baby Rebecca lined the walls. The family had no reminders of loved ones lost. Someday, Rebecca would no longer remember her father's face.

As she descended to the front hall, every step creaked. She paused at the bottom of the stairs, unsure which way to go. A spacious living room opened to her right. To her left, a dark paneled wall appeared to slide in and out of a groove with another sitting room beyond.

Earlier that day, Jonas described how the Amish held church services in their homes.

This pocket door must allow them to create a space large enough for community worship. She ran her palm over the polished wood, admiring the fine craftsmanship in the traveling wall.

Whereas the upstairs rooms were straight out of a nineteenth-century farmhouse, the living room was fairly modern, even by candlelight. A sofa ran along the front wall of the house, bracketed by end tables. In the far corner, an upholstered armchair and a rocking chair clustered cozily before a wood-burning stove. She padded across the hardwood floor, scattered with a few braided area rugs. Imagining those icy boards beneath bare feet on a winter morning, she shivered. Hopefully, Rebecca had slippers.

The windowsills were lined with houseplants, and next to the chairs squatted a chunky magazine rack, full to brimming with periodicals. Her curiosity piqued, she passed through a wide opening into a spacious kitchen, at first glance remarkably like her own.

The stairs groaned, and she whirled to discover Jonas in the living room carrying a chimneyed oil lamp. She cringed. "I didn't mean to wake you."

He tilted his head toward the staircase. "You need to know just where to step if you want to sneak out. Do you need something?"

Prickly fingers of embarrassment crept across her chest and tickled her neck. She set the candle on the table. "Honestly, I'm looking for the bathroom or…the outhouse?"

He pointed toward a door at the far side of the kitchen.

"Oh. Just right there?"

The corners of his mouth crept upward. He nodded.

"Thanks." Bumping into a chair, she crossed to the door.

"You'll need the candle."

"Right!" Her voice rang too loudly in the empty kitchen. She snatched it from the table. "Thanks," she added in a hushed tone. Taking hold of the doorknob, she hesitated. To say she had no idea what to expect from the bathroom was an understatement. She darted a glance over one shoulder. "Is there anything I need to know…about the facilities?"

"Don't think so." The shadows creasing his cheeks deepened.

"I am a gift. I am a gift," she murmured and spun the knob. To her surprise, the small half bath was entirely twenty-first century. The toilet flushed. Hot and cold water poured from the faucets. She burst into the kitchen, now brightly lit by an overhead lamp, and tented her hand over her eyes. "Your toilet flushes!"

"Want some ham?" He extended a forkful.

She smiled. "Kinda middle-of-the-nightish for ham. Thanks, though."

"How about a whoopie pie?"

Whether intentional or not, the offer was full-on sexy. Her mouth watered. "Now you're talking." She sat at the table beneath a big brass lamp suspended from the ceiling. Hissing cheerfully, the lamp easily illuminated the whole kitchen. The house was a mixture of the familiar and the just different enough to create the impression Jonas lived in a parallel universe. Perhaps that was the point.

He retrieved one of the chocolaty delicacies from

the pantry and poured a glass of milk.

Slinging the snack like a bartender, he sat beside her. She smiled. "You have a refrigerator and hot and cold water." His smile mingled pride and satisfaction.

"A diesel-powered pump brings well water for drinking, and we pipe wash water from the creek." He stabbed his fork toward the ceiling. "The light runs on propane, and gas powers the hot water heater, refrigerator, and stove. When we began standing market, we bought the new stove and refrigerator. Before that, Nora did all her cooking on the Monarch."

Following his gaze, she swiveled to the great grandmother of all kitchen stoves. It was massive and black with shiny, metal trim. Like the rest of the kitchen, it was utterly spotless.

"She still uses it to fill big orders on short notice—lots of pies, for example." He winked.

"Don't be cute." Next to the stove, a hutch displayed antique, patterned china. Jelly jars, bursting with plant cuttings rooting in water, lined the immaculate countertop. Rich, russet cabinets covered the walls. Other than the dishes, the only decoration was a calendar by the sink, printed with an illustration of Jesus. She bit into the whoopie pie and moaned. "Your sister is a genius."

Tipping back on two chair legs, he patted his belly. "Do you like it?"

"It's even better than the ones at market," she said through cream.

He grinned. "I made it."

She dropped her jaw, revealing a mouth full of half-chewed, chocolate cake. "Then you are a genius, too. How do you mix the ingredients?"

Half a whoopie pie vanished in one bite. He licked his lips. "Air-powered mixer."

She knew he was ingenious, but could the guy actually harness the wind? "Air-powered?"

"Compressed air. We get it by the tank."

"Really?" She couldn't suppress a skeptical tone. She planted her elbows on the table and rested her chin in her hands. He nodded like he knew what was coming. "So compressed air, diesel engines, and gas lamps are all permitted, but regular old electricity isn't?"

"Yes." With another bite, his whoopie pie disappeared.

"Forgive me, but I just don't understand."

"With respect, the rules of the *Ordnung* were not designed to make sense to you." He dipped his head. "They vary widely by community, and to tell the truth, I don't even understand all of them. Nor do I always obey them." He jutted his smooth-shaven chin. "I do know that electric power lines are a literal connection to the world as well as a symbolic one. We refuse to accept such ties. If we want to preserve our separateness, we cannot accept them. Our mandate is Biblical—to be 'in the world but not of it.' "

Unable to recall the last time she drank whole milk, she drained her glass. It was almost too creamy. "So, I am both in and of the world."

"You are."

"Because my refrigerator runs on electricity, and yours runs on gas."

"You have milk around your mouth." Hooking her chair leg with one foot, he dragged her closer. He dabbed her milk moustache with his thumb and cupped her cheek and kissed her.

His lips were salty from the ham. She interlaced her fingers around his neck and urged him nearer.

Deepening the kiss, he grazed the lump on her forehead.

With a start, she flinched.

"I'm sorry." He released her chair. "Do you feel sleepy?"

A yawn unhinged her jaw, and her throat creaked. The distant rush of the still-swollen creek floated through an open window. With a shiver, she nodded.

"Why don't I take you upstairs?"

She silkened her voice. "Kiss me first."

He did—so tenderly she was amazed she didn't dissolve into a puddle on the floor. When he shifted away, she restrained him with a teasing nibble on his bottom lip.

Exhaling a soft sound, he slid an arm around her waist, drawing her tightly to his chest.

He was so solid and strong. Tired and bruised as she was, she wanted nothing more than to feel her body match his strength. "Stay with me," she whispered.

"You need rest." With a smile, he swept her into his arms and carried her upstairs.

She wriggled under the sheet and, taking his hand, urged him closer. Feeling something inside him respond, she nudged his thigh with a knee. Was desire a particle or a wave? Whatever it was, palpable energy coursed through his fingertips at the speed of light.

Still, he resisted. "Not tonight, Tessa Rose."

"But we don't have to—"

"Trust me." He brushed his lips over hers and squeezed her hand. "Goodnight."

The stairs whined, and the glow from the upstairs landing dimmed as he extinguished the lights.

She twisted her lips in a naughty smile and tucked the sheet under her chin. Jenn would never believe it. She, Tessa Meadows, was just caught seducing an Amish guy. Given the chance, she'd do it again.

Chapter 19

Sitting on the back steps the next morning, Tessa shoved her sneakers over stiff, line-dried socks and tugged down her tee. Broadfall trousers, rolled at the ankles, hung loosely from suspenders buttoned over her shoulders. She grabbed the rail and pulled herself to standing, amazed just how much better she felt after one day of total rest.

"I don't have much to offer." Jonas tossed a peach pit into the grass. "But how about a day on the farm?"

"I'd like nothing better." With a peck on the cheek, she followed him into the sun-dappled morning. Needless to say, she hadn't been awake for the early milking. Nor for any number of pre-dawn chores Jonas completed. A roof repair was next on the docket. The same winds that blew her van into the creek also rocketed a tree limb through the pantry roof, scattering a mess of debris. Several jars of preserves shattered, spewing their contents all over Nora's pristine counter and floor—an open invitation to hungry critters.

Jonas put off the job a day, but it couldn't be postponed any longer. He leaned a ladder against the roof and mounted the bottom step.

She hooked her thumbs through the suspenders and rocked back on her heels. "I'm really so much better. I can climb up and help."

Chuckling, he cocked a brow. "Absolutely not. I

didn't pull you from the creek just to tumble off my roof."

So, she held the ladder, handed him tools, and cleaned broken glass and pickled asparagus from the pantry floor. The sound of hammer on wood was familiar and comforting. He completed the gazebo just two days earlier, impossible as that trick of time was to comprehend, and she already missed the sounds of carpentry.

He sang hymns in German and whistled Bruce Springsteen.

She cleaned until the wood and linoleum sparkled, then she nudged the remaining jars into the spaces left by the ones that fell. When she came home, Nora would never know what happened.

When Nora came home.

Tessa shoved the thought from her mind and ran outside to catch tools as he lowered them. With his family away, this man's life was no vacation. Staying on the farm meant earning her keep. Her shoulders and knees ached from scrubbing, but she was ready to tackle the next task. She never relished sweating so much as when they worked together.

Dodging the ladder he slung over one shoulder, she toted the toolbox to the barn. The earth was banked up to the second floor on the back side, allowing a ground-level entrance on both floors. "Where do you keep the buggy?"

He nodded toward an outbuilding. "The old chicken house. Turned it into a buggy shed after Levi and I built a new one."

The shed was open on one side, and she spied the buggy with its orange, triangular reflector parked next to an open-topped wagon.

He tucked the ladder just inside the barn door and led the way into another outbuilding.

Two different power saws and several machine tools she couldn't identify flanked a red, metal chest. A workbench twice the length of her father's spanned the entire back wall. The space was as neatly organized as Nora's pantry and almost as clean. It smelled of sawdust and just a hint of oil, and given the opportunity, she would absolutely make out on that workbench.

He slid the toolbox onto a shelf. "I built your gazebo right here." He ran a hand over the wood surface and brushed a few shavings to the floor. "Used to be the wash house, but when we installed the washing machine, I expanded it into a shop. Most everything on this farm was once something else, I suppose. All these tools run on compressed air like the mixer."

His life was a far more curious mix of old and new than she ever imagined. "A washing machine?"

He flashed a smile. "The best gift I ever gave my mother. It's in the basement. I've got it running on the same diesel engine that powers the pump."

Not only a carpenter, he was a mechanic and an engineer as well. Dreamy. If she jumped onto the workbench, would he get the hint? "But no clothes dryer?"

He shook his head. "Rain or shine, clothes dry on the line."

She buried her nose in his shoulder. "They smell better that way."

"Come. I want to show you something."

Taking his hand, she followed him from the shop into the second-floor entrance to the barn. Darkness suffused with the scents of animals and damp earth enveloped her.

"The horse and livestock are on the ground floor." He unlatched a tall door on the far wall. "But back here…" He beckoned.

She followed him into an immense room where bales of sweet-smelling hay were stacked floor to ceiling, two stories high. "The hayloft!" She inhaled deeply and sneezed.

"We're lucky. Ours is really tall." He scampered up several bales and glanced back. "Care for a roll in the hay?"

Unsure if the double entendre was intended, she laughed and scrambled behind him, picking her way toward the peak of the roof. Sharp-edged straw jabbed her hands and arms. No wonder cows chewed each bite for an eternity. Still a few levels below him at the top, she clung to a bale and gazed upward.

From behind a heavy rafter, he removed a bundle of canvas work gloves. Then something small and black emerged from the shadows. He held it out, and it caught a sunbeam streaming through a crack in the wall.

She gasped. "Samuel's radio."

"Don't tell my mother."

With a finger, she traced an x on her chest. "Cross my heart."

Grinning, he returned the device to its hiding place.

Seconds later, a brownish blob descended. The gloves stayed together and landed as a pair in her hands. She studied them for a moment and glanced up. "What are these for?"

He unleashed a thick brown rope from a hook on the wall. The top of the rope vanished into soaring eaves. In seconds, he donned the gloves and planted a foot on a bulky knot. "Amish skydiving."

She stared way down to the hay-covered floor. No skydiving of any variety was on her bucket list. Stomach clenched, she clambered upward. "You wouldn't!"

With a whoop, he vaulted from the ledge. His straw hat took flight, and his face lit like a sun-sparkled, spring-fed swimming hole.

She flattened against a bale, scrabbling at straw. He swooshed past her perch almost close enough to touch, soaring in ever-widening circles. A laugh of pure joy rang from the rafters, and for half a second, she forgot she teetered in the stratosphere.

Then, he let go.

Clawing the rafter, she watched him plummet what looked like a mile, landing in a mountain of hay. Dropping to her knees, she peered over the edge. "Are you all right?"

He flipped onto his back. "Better than all right! Spectacular!" With a quick thrust, he pointed upward. "Grab the rope before it stops swinging."

She scampered to the top bale. Tucking the gloves under one arm, she waited for the knotted end to circle within reach and lunged. She caught it and held on. "Now what?"

His face cracked into a smile. "Put on the gloves."

A deepening certainty he wanted her to take up skydiving, too, blossomed in her belly. She tucked the rope between her knees and shoved her fingers into the heavy canvas. It was rough and brittle from years of dried sweat. "This seems like a genuinely bad idea."

"Just try it!"

Still safely on the bale, she untucked the rope, placed a cautious toe atop the knot, and yanked. The rope pulled taut and shimmied in her grip. It seemed secure. After all, it just held Jonas.

He cupped his hands around his mouth. "I'll be right here!"

This man... For him, she designed a gazebo and dove headfirst into frigid waters. She baked cobbler and broke the speed limit, and eventually, she drove her van into a creek. Now, he wanted her to fly. She dug her fingers into the braided cord, wrapped her other leg around the rope, and hooked her feet at the ankles. *For this man...anything.* Closing her eyes, she jumped.

The earth dropped out from under her, and she let loose a sound she didn't know her body could make. Baled hay spun in dizzying loops as she pirouetted in space like a circus performer. She arced up high, and her belly leapt into her chest with a zinging whirl.

"Wait until you're over the middle and then let go," he shouted.

She froze. What if a pitchfork was hidden in the hay? What if she landed on his head? She gripped the rope and squeezed her legs tighter. "Let go?"

"Trust me!"

She closed her eyes. *With my life.* Then she lifted her lids and let go.

Her stomach dropped, and her arms helicoptered in frantic circles. In seconds, she landed with a jarring thud just a few feet from Jonas. Chest heaving, she lay in a daze as the rope gyrated overhead.

He rolled to her side. "How was it?"

"Glorious!" She grabbed a handful of hay. "And terrifying!" Like a ninja, she sprang and stuffed it down his shirt.

His eyes flew wide, and he laughed, spluttering straw.

On hands and knees, she knelt over him. "Dude, for someone who had, like, six brothers, you're so easy."

"Not that easy." In an instant, he flung her over one shoulder and dumped her on her backside. "And I had three brothers. Samuel..."—he shoveled an armload of hay onto her belly—"Micah..." Another handful rained down. "And Hannes." The final pile cascaded over her face.

Ignoring her bruises, she tensed, ready to strike. "And I was an only child." With a leap, she bowled into him, knocking him flat. "I'm skinny, but I'm wiry." As if she weighed no more than a sack of flour, he tossed her onto her back again and held both arms over her head with one hand.

"You're beautiful."

Hay the color of his hair stuck out from his head in ten different directions. His cheeks were flushed, and his eyes blazed. He had her in a vulnerable position—supine and breathless, soft underbelly exposed, but she wasn't afraid. The feeling was a warm weight in her gut. Like that mound of hay, Jonas was a safe place to land.

Something hard and scratchy jabbed her lower back. She squirmed. "I think I flattened your hat."

He freed her hands. Sliding one arm under her waist, he lifted her and retrieved the mangled chapeau. He shrugged one shoulder. "I'll get a new one."

Every inch of skin prickled. "I have straw in places I don't even want to think about."

He hovered above her on elbows and knees. "How about a bath later?"

"I'll need it." His chest grazed her with a tantalizing sensation of hard and soft, and she let her eyes drift closed, surrendering to that familiar, liquid stirring deep inside. She glided her arms over his back and pulled him to her, stroking her fingers up the back of his neck and into his hair.

He let out a throaty moan and nudged his head into her hands. "I think I've done enough work today." Barely making contact, he skimmed his mouth over hers.

Once. Twice. Three times. She arched her back and strained to meet his lips. "For the love of Mike, just kiss me."

He pressed up and away. "Who's Mike?"

"Jonas!" The word was a simultaneous laugh and plea.

Finally, he lowered his mouth, his lips curving into a smile against hers.

Imagining an entire afternoon in the hayloft, she sighed deeply.

Then something fuzzy tickled her arm.

Only partly aware of anything beyond the deliciousness of his kiss and desperate to keep it that way, she shifted. When the unidentified critter returned, she shrieked and scrambled onto her elbows.

He recoiled into a crouch. "What's wrong?"

For a pacifist, the guy looked ready to grab the nearest farm implement and defend her life. "I felt something furry."

Relaxing onto his knees, he scanned the hay. "A mouse?"

Mice she could handle. This critter was no mouse. Could it have been a rat? "Bigger."

From behind came a plaintive meow.

She whipped around. "Oh, look!"

At the base of a bale, a scruffy orange kitten placidly washed its face, mindless of the hubbub it created.

With one hand, he picked up the creature and plopped it into her lap. "Rebecca's cat had kittens. Good thing we didn't hurt it."

"Hello, little one." She scratched the kitten's neck.

It smashed its face against her hand and purred.

"He's the cutest, scrawniest-looking thing I've ever seen."

"He is a she, and I know for a fact Rebecca wanted you to have a kitten. She couldn't believe you don't have 'one, single animal, not even a turtle' at your house."

His wide-eyed imitation of his niece was spot on. She giggled. "I've never had a pet. My father is allergic to everything."

"You do now. She's an adventurer." He gestured through the door. "Let's take her back to her *mamm*."

She carried the kitty, clinging to her tee with pinprick claws, to a cardboard box lined with flannel scraps. Four more kittens snuggled inside, eyes closed in blissful slumber. The adventurer's siblings were orange calicoes spotted with patches of white and black. "Her" kitten was entirely orange except for snow-white toes and a white splotch under her chin. "I think I'm in love." She buried her face in the kitten's back. It smelled like a wool sweater. Reluctantly, she lowered the animal into the mass of sleeping furballs.

She turned to Jonas, and her breath hitched in her chest. His look held her as strongly as his arms had moments before. His gaze was intimate as a kiss. Could she lure him back into the hay and pick up where they left off?

With a quick move, he smushed the pancaked hat onto his head. "Hey, are you hungry?"

He looked so goofy she giggled. "You know"—she hooked her thumbs through the suspenders—"that's the second time you've postponed kissing me for food."

"Is that right?" He slipped his arms around her waist and leaned in, his lips a hairsbreadth from hers.

Despite the lack of power lines, the air was electric. "I believe so." A shiver danced up her spine. Would she ever get used to the rush of being so close?

"Just think how much more we'll enjoy it after we eat." With a resounding smooch on her cheek, he dashed out of the barn.

He rustled up a late lunch of cold ham and cheese. Minty, iced tea soothed the tickle of hay dust in her throat, and she glanced out the window at lengthening shadows cast by Nora's fruit trees. Already the days seemed shorter. What was the date, anyway? July twenty-something? She extracted a piece of hay from her sock and tossed it at him. "What's for dessert?"

Their dishes rattled into the sink, and he spun, eyes bright. "Blueberry pie."

"I don't see any pie."

"Correct."

Was a trip to Esther King's farm stand in the offing? Would she experience her first-ever buggy ride?

"So…?"

He tugged an apron from a hook and tossed it in her lap. "So, we'll make one."

Shoulders aching, she slumped on the kitchen table. Already today, she fixed a roof, cleaned a pantry, and bungee jumped from a hayloft. Forget baking, she wanted a nap. "Do you even know how to make a pie?"

"Of course. Don't you?"

Apparently, every Amish child emerged from the womb knowing the secret to a flaky crust. "I don't want to bake a pie. I'm tired, and I have a head injury. Can't we just go buy pie? Is my van fixed yet?"

A smile twitched at the corners of his mouth. "The men will deliver the van once it's running. It's high time you learned to bake a pie, Tessa Rose." He produced a container of blueberries from the refrigerator. "I picked these this morning. Open up."

She obeyed.

He popped a berry into her mouth.

It exploded in a tangy burst of summertime. "I'm not the only person who can't bake a pie, you know."

He simply grinned and removed unrecognizable kitchen gadgets from the drawers.

She skated her hands across the tabletop and lowered her cheek to the surface. "None of my friends can bake pies either."

"Well, you can teach them. Now pay close attention. The importance of measuring precisely cannot be overstated."

Under his gently teasing tutelage, she managed to heat the oven and measure the flour, salt, and shortening. Pastry cutter in hand, she attacked.

He laid a hand on her arm. "Gentle. Don't overwork the dough."

Choking a laugh, she dropped the cutter. "My mother's going to love you." Cold water and a tablespoon of vinegar joined the pastry, and the dough came together in a crumbly ball.

He extracted a rolling pin from a drawer and dusted it in flour.

She bounced a blueberry off his forehead. "Hey, you know what they say about the size of a guy's rolling pin."

Brow furrowed, he blinked. "Don't they just come in a standard length?"

Nearly convulsed with hysterics, she made a sudden dash for the flush toilet. After ten minutes struggling to roll out a piecrust, however, she was no longer laughing. The irascible dough stuck to the pin and tore apart the second she made any progress. Annoyance snowballed into red-cheeked vexation. She dropped the fully gunked pin and collapsed into a chair. "This dough is impossible."

Planting his hands on the table, he faced her. "Do you want pie or not?"

As if baking the pie was her idea in the first place. "Let's have ice cream instead."

"I don't have a freezer."

"Then we'll go shopping. Does Esther King sell ice cream? You can take me for a ride in the buggy." She dangled the offer like a particularly delicious carrot on a stick.

He narrowed his eyes. "Am I to conclude my sister can make a piecrust, and you can't?"

Thrusting out a hand, she glared. "Gimme that stupid rolling pin." With a grunt, she faced off against the recalcitrant pastry and plunged the pin in flour.

He came behind her and slid both arms around her waist, covering her hands with his. "You're pushing too hard. Let the rolling pin do the work." He nudged the pin into the floury mass.

Stroke by stroke, the dough blossomed. She relaxed and let her eyelids drift shut. His chest was warm against her shoulder blades, and his breath stirred the hairs at her temples. With any luck, rolling out this crust would take hours.

"See, that wasn't so hard."

"Is it done?" She fluttered open her lashes. Before her was a perfect circle of dough.

"Flawless."

Trapped between the table and his body, she swiveled. "You're flawless." She kissed him, and just when she was certain they'd abandon the pie altogether, he moved away.

"Ready to make the filling?"

She swallowed a curse. "Just so you know, I'm totally stealing your recipe and entering the county fair."

As the sun vanished behind the ridge, she sat by his side on the front porch bench and ate hot blueberry pie with fresh whipped cream. While the pie was in the oven, he'd done the evening milking, and she peeked at the catalogs and periodicals in the living room rack. "I didn't know you had your own newspapers," she said between bites.

"Several. I prefer the *New York Times*."

Lowering her fork, she gave him a sideways look. "You get the *Times*?"

He shook his head. "The library does. Nora likes

Die Botschaft."

"*Die Botschaft*," she repeated, trying out the unfamiliar sounds.

"The Message." He licked his plate, catching her gaze over the rim. "My sister hates when I do that."

"Does she?" With a smack of the lips, she licked hers, too.

The sky glowed a shade of blueberry filling. The air was perfectly still.

He shifted, and the bench creaked. "You have flour on your cheeks."

On television, men always found flour-dusted women irresistible. She just felt grungy. "I'm a mess. I'm still pulling straw from my underwear."

His brows shot to his hairline.

She had to admit she loved shocking him.

"Wait here and come inside when I call." Taking her plate, he withdrew into the house.

Crickets chirruped in unending chorus, and in the distance, she heard the clop of hoofbeats on asphalt. She pressed her lips and inhaled the lingering scent of baking. Sitting on Jonas's porch with her belly full of pie and her limbs heavy from work, she basked in peace. She was unemployed, and Jenn chose Adam, and Richard would likely never speak to her again, and none of those things mattered. Today was a productive day spent in the company of a genuinely good man. If she could say the same about the rest of her days, she would die a happy person indeed.

Her name floated through the window, and she shivered as much from the sound of his voice as the evening chill. She slipped inside. He hadn't lit the propane lamps, and as she crossed the living room, her eyes adjusted to the dim.

"I'm in here."

Entering the kitchen, she nearly bumped into the table. He had apparently pushed it aside to make room for the large, metal washtub, standing nearly full in the middle of the floor.

He emptied a steaming kettle into the tub and plunged in a hand. "Nice and hot."

The cabinets glowed in the light from a single kerosene lamp. A bar of soap and a washrag lay on a stool next to the tub. Two towels draped over a chair.

Back at the stove, he tilted his head toward the tub. "You first."

Her heart skipped a beat. "A hot bath?"

"Only hot if you hurry."

Trailing a finger through the water, she caught an herbal scent. "Lemon balm? Fancy."

He shrugged. "Just smells nice. Is the water warm enough?"

"Heavenly."

He poured in a final saucepan and headed for the living room. "I'll be outside."

"Will you have a bath, too?"

In the doorway, he paused, glancing over one shoulder. "After you."

She grimaced. "But the water will be dirty."

Lamplight shadowed the creases bracketing his smile. "I've bathed after three boys. Your bathwater will be clean enough to drink. Now go."

Towel in hand, she scurried into the bathroom, stripped off her soiled work clothes, and wrapped herself before returning to the kitchen. Tossing aside her covering, she slipped into the tub and rested her neck against the rim. A whistled tune drifted in from the porch.

Floating her palms on the surface, she relaxed into a moment of lemon-infused bliss. She could forsake showering for baths like this. Hauling herself upright, she snatched the soap and set about a thorough cleaning. Driving her fingers into her scalp, she lathered her hair, untangling stray bits of straw. Totally soaped, she closed her eyes and slid beneath the water. She hovered, luxuriating in weightlessness, and surfaced again, fresh and new.

She could have soaked for hours, until the water cooled, and she had no choice but to dash, dripping and chilly, into Jonas's arms. But he deserved a hot bath, too. When she stood and stepped onto the rag rug, her skin puckered with goose bumps. She shivered with the delicious, clean feeling and dried herself quickly. Glancing about, she discovered he left one of his shirts—so much more palatable than Nora's nightgown. Falling just above her knees, the shirt was huge, but the fabric slid over her skin in a cottony caress. "Okay, Jonas. I'm done."

The screen door slammed, and quick steps came across the living room floor. In the entry to the kitchen, he stopped short.

Her hair hung in heavy coils, and the shirt clung wetly across her shoulders. "Your turn." Her voice caught. She smiled and tugged at the hem. "Thanks for the shirt."

The oil lamp flickered, and shadows glided across the walls like ghosts.

He cleared his throat. "It suits you."

Blood rushed to her cheeks, and she dropped her

gaze. She clutched the towel to her chest.

Coming into the kitchen, he met her in an awkward two-step in the narrow space between tub and table.

Bare feet bumped leather work boots. "Here let me—"

"I'll just—" he said at the same time.

She laughed lightly.

He laughed, too, sidling past very close and ducking into the bathroom.

In seconds, he would return in some degree of undress. Much as she wanted to spy from behind a chair, modesty required she retreat to the porch. A breeze rushed through the screen door, and she hesitated, wrapping the towel around her shoulders. Where to go? Upstairs felt weird—like she expected him to join her in the bedroom. Was the living room too intimate? She scanned her surroundings. An armchair tucked in the corner by the woodstove faced away from the kitchen, seeming a safe choice.

She settled into it and took up *Die Botschaft*. Two fat drops fell from her hair and splatted onto the front page. When she wiped them, the newsprint smudged gray beneath her fingertips. The bathroom latch clicked, and the paper slid unopened into her lap. Tiny hairs on the back of her neck stood on end. But for her index finger tickling back and forth over the hem of his shirt, she sat unmoving. Every inch of skin tingled with awareness he was steps away and about to get into the bath. Bare feet padded across linoleum. She heard the gentle sloosh as he lowered first one leg and then the other, followed by a bigger splash when he eased into the tub.

He let out a breathy groan.

She licked her lips and let her lids fall. Eyes closed, she pictured him with golden lamplight playing over his back while lazy rivers trickled down his forehead and into the hollows of his cheeks. Big shoulders crushed against either side of the tub he'd long outgrown. Rugged knees broke the water's surface.

As he began to wash, barely voiced exhalations escaped his lips. The soap slid between his palms with wet smacks and plopped into the tub. His fingers rasped against his skull, quick and strong. She ached to pull up the stool and massage his soapy scalp until every ounce of exhaustion ebbed into her fingertips.

With a sound like buckets of water poured from above, he stood. In her mind's eye, she followed every droplet down his chest, over his belly, and into the tub. She swallowed and stiffened. Then came a spattering splash as he shook his head like a dog and stepped from the bath. A towel scritched over bare skin, and the tender flesh beneath her arms twitched sympathetically. She caught a gentle grunt as he reached for his clothing and the tread of each foot as it pushed through cotton and landed on the floor.

Stillness settled over both rooms until she heard only her own breath, fast and light. The silence teemed. The space between him unseen in the kitchen and her alone in the chair was alight with what felt like a million fireflies—a humming, living thing. She rose, letting the newspaper slide, and stepped under the archway.

Wearing only a simple pair of long johns, he stood with both hands splayed on the counter, staring out the window above the sink.

"Jonas?" she whispered.

He turned.

The ruddy hairs covering his body shone amber in the lamplight. His limbs were corded with work-hardened muscle. A single drop snaked over his collarbone, just as she imagined. Despite his near nakedness, he showed no embarrassment. No shame.

"We need to talk," he said.

His tone was level, his expression inscrutable as the day they met. Her heart sank. She swallowed and steeled herself for the inevitable letdown: *Look, it's been fun, but we both know…* "About what?" Her voice wobbled, and she winced.

With two quick strides, he came to her and cupped her face in his hands.

Startled, she grabbed his forearms, as much to keep from stumbling into the tub as to pull him closer. His chest heaved like his ribcage might splinter. His gaze could have melted Antarctica. He softened his hands on her cheeks, and his lips sought hers, but unlike their desperate kiss in the gazebo, this one didn't feel like an ending. It felt like just the beginning. He deepened the kiss with delicious firmness, and she glided her arms over his shoulders, relishing the warmth of his skin.

"About how much I love you." He met her gaze. "*Mei wildi ros.*"

Forget the hayloft. Hearing those words was a base jump from a skyscraper. Her heart soared. "I love you, too." What glorious relief simply to say the words. She seized his lips, smiling into his kiss even as she tasted desire. Every inch of her—from her toes on the lumpy rag rug to the still-tender bump on her forehead—crackled like a Fourth of July sparkler catching a ride on a rocket ship. He was a walking pyrotechnic, and she was nothing but a bundle of fuses.

He kissed her again and again before finally pulling away. Locking his gaze on hers, he caressed down her arms and took her hands.

For the first time, his expression was utterly transparent. Not a wisp of a cloud shadowed his thoughts. They shone from his eyes with crystalline clarity. The room itself seemed to catch its breath, like it knew something important was coming.

He tightened his fingers around hers. "I am not a man of means, but I am a man of my word. I will never ask of you more than I am willing to give. Tessa Rose, I'm yours, if you'll have me."

She summoned a sigh, pulled from mountain peaks on the opposite side of the earth, and accepted his gift. "I don't need anything—nothing in this crazy, messy, beautiful, old world—but you. Oh, I'll have you, Jonas Rishel. I'll have you, and I'll never let you go." A rainbow of joy shimmered across his face, then dissipated quick as morning fog.

With a leaden breath, he inclined his head and touched his brow to hers. "My life is not simple. Ironically. And you know how I am bound."

For a life with him, she'd weather any complication—outlast any bond. Steadying trembling knees, she brushed her lips over his forehead. "I know."

He gathered together her hands and lifted them to his heart. "I swear to you—I will leave this place. I will walk away and never look back, if you'll go with me."

She met his gaze. It was unflinching and true as the North Star.

"I've had a fire inside since I was a child, but I could never leave. Never until now—until you. I love you." He drew her into his arms again.

The borrowed shirt parted at her throat, allowing a tantalizing taste of skin on skin. His flesh burned like an ember, igniting an answering spark in her core. "I love you." Running her lips along his collarbone, she breathed the words into his skin. "I love you, I love you, I love you."

"Come away with me."

The words welled with longing deep and wide. Her shoulders tightened. "I want to…but…" She caught her bottom lip between her teeth. To summon them into the sacred space she and Jonas created felt wrong somehow, but she had no choice. She forced herself to back away a half step. "What about Rebecca? Nora?" His eyes deepened to ocean blue. His jaw hardened like a boulder on a shoreline he'd never seen.

"I will not abandon that child."

His voice was as level as hers had been trembly. Swallowing against the lump in her throat, she nodded.

"I will hold her in my heart and do everything in my power to care for her and her mother. Rebecca will understand my leaving far better than you know. I'm confident she'll join us someday. But I do us all a disservice by staying. I have to go. I have to believe all will be well."

"You have to have faith," she whispered.

"Faith." Tears shimmered on his lower lids.

She embraced him with all the strength she had. "Jonas Rishel, you are a good man." Holding his hand, she followed him up the stairs to his bedroom.

One by one, he pulled each shade.

With her breath fluttering high in her throat, she settled on the edge of the bed. One side of his face obscured in shadow and the other luminous by candlelight, he kissed her as gently as a sigh. Drawing him to sit beside her, she embraced him, there in the room where he'd passed so many solitary nights. His skin smelled of citrusy mint and soap. She nuzzled his neck and eased her fingers into his scalp, as she now knew he loved. With a muffled groan, he surrendered to her touch. All she wanted was to lay down by his side.

He shifted away. "Tessa, I…"

His voice was thick with longing and with something else, too. She met his gaze. His eyes shone a silent request tinged at the edges with bittersweet regret. He offered the trace of a shrug. Understanding coalesced in her belly. "Oh, my sweet love." She interlaced her fingers with his and lifted her cheeks, flushed with the thought of what his gaze implied. "I'll wait for you a thousand years." Gratitude softened his brow.

Closing his eyes, he reached for her again. "I love you."

She snuggled into his chest, knowing in her heart she spoke truth. That evening he'd dared to voice thoughts that for years had been unspeakable. He allowed himself to imagine a life hitherto unimaginable. In that humble farmhouse kitchen, he handed her his dreams and trusted her with their safekeeping. Her gift to him was the possibility they could become reality. In her heart of hearts, she pledged him all the time he needed to create that reality together.

Soon his muscles slackened, and he jerked in her arms. Half asleep, he didn't fuss as she released him onto the mattress and slid into the chair where he kept his vigil. His breath eased into a rhythm regular as clockwork. The wrinkles on his forehead vanished, and she smoothed the creases next to his eyes with gossamer kisses. By moonlight, she studied him. His face relaxed into the image of the careless boy he once was—some portion of the burden he carried no longer etched in the lines of age.

With that shared weight lodged close to her heart, she slipped from the room, praying she was strong enough to carry it.

Chapter 20

Some hours later—maybe two, maybe three—barefoot and barelegged, Tessa stood on tiptoes and peered through candlelight. Not a single bag of chips in Nora's kitchen cabinets. She pushed aside a jar of molasses. Surely, she could rustle up a midnight snack.

As she woke and rolled over on the lumpy living room couch, a thick, soft blackness had engulfed her—the kind of true dark that never fell upon her parents' house in town. She'd no idea of the time or how long she'd been asleep. Her stomach let out a seismic growl. After a long day of carpentry, pie baking, and rolling in the hay, she never ate a proper supper. Now, she needed a snack.

She had lit a candle, tiptoed to the kitchen, and scoured the cupboards for junk food. What she found in the fridge was far better. Their partially eaten pie glowed heavenly blue in the refrigerator light. Pie again at—she opened the door wider, illuminating the wall clock—almost midnight? How scandalous! How decadent! She'd whip up some fresh cream, and her treat would be complete.

Certain she'd seen Jonas retrieve an eggbeater from a top drawer, she yanked it and pawed through the contents. No dice. She slid it shut and grabbed the handle below.

With a click and a squeak, the front door opened.

"Hey," she hissed. "No milking cows in the middle of the night. Go back to bed, you goof. I'll bring you a treat."

No answer came.

In the brief hush, she thought she heard an engine rev and a car pull away. Clearly suffering hunger-induced hallucinations, she plunged a hand into the second drawer. "Where did you put the eggbeater?"

Quick, uneven footsteps tapped across the living room floor.

A chill wind raced up her legs and under her borrowed shirt. She froze. "Jonas?" Met with silence so loud it practically screamed, she turned.

Fully shrouded in a black bonnet and layers of traveling clothes, Nora stood, bag in hand, scowling.

Tessa clutched the collar of Jonas's shirt around her neck. Blood pounded in her ears. "Nora...you're back."

The bag thudded to the floor. Nora marched into the kitchen and ignited the overhead lamp.

The light felt like an assault. Tessa shielded her eyes.

Keeping the table between them, Nora gripped a chair back and glared. "Get out of my kitchen."

Stunned and immobile, a trespasser in Nora's most private sanctuary, Tessa felt more naked than if she wore nothing at all. Shame blazed across her cheeks. "Of course," she whispered, groping for the gadget drawer. Now thoroughly jumbled, the drawer jammed. She leaned into it with one hip, and a metal cherry pitter popped free and crashed to the floor. She scrambled to retrieve it just as Jonas's heavy steps echoed down the stairs.

"Did you hear a car?" he said through a yawn. "I thought I heard a car."

He'd tossed a shirt over his shoulders, but his hair was tousled and his eyes heavy with sleep. When his gaze landed on his sister's back, he pulled up short. The soft, drowsy lines on his face turned to stone.

Tessa shrugged in wordless agony. With the speed of continental drift, Nora revolved to face her brother.

For one excruciating moment, all three stood in a shocked standoff.

Jonas shifted on the stairs, and the board beneath him creaked.

Nora uttered something quick and quiet in their language.

Though Tessa didn't understand a single syllable, she felt the malice in Nora's tone like a gut punch.

Jonas's eyes flashed, and he clenched the newel post with white fingers. "Tessa is a guest in my home. You will do us both the respect of speaking English."

Nora stormed into the living room, screeching in Pennsylvania Dutch. With a gasping breath, she broke off and seized the armchair. At her feet, *Die Botschaft* lay open where Tessa dropped it just hours—and a lifetime—before.

Jonas stepped into the room, shook his head just once, and crossed his arms over his chest.

Compared to his sister, he was a mountain of a man. If anything, Nora looked smaller than the last time Tessa saw her, as if bitterness was literally eating away at her body.

Nora shoved aside the chair and advanced on her brother. Weeks of repressed rage spewed in guttural German. In a flash, she raised her arm as if to strike him.

Tessa drew in a sharp breath.

Lightning quick, Jonas caught his sister's hand. "Think of your daughter," he said through a rigid jaw. "If you raise your hand to me again, it is you I will ban from this house."

Nora yanked away her arm and turned on Tessa. "She has shamed you and shamed the memory of your wife."

Something hard glanced off Tessa's ankle bone and bounced under the table. She cringed and jerked up her foot. The cherry pitter. She must have dropped it. She sank to her knees and groped for it beneath the kitchen table.

Nora resumed shrieking.

Whether in English or German, Tessa couldn't tell. From below, the woman's twisted face loomed horribly, raining spittle and hatred onto the floor. Tessa's eyes burned. She'd done nothing wrong, yet Nora made her feel dirty. Would anyone notice if she just curled up under the table? Better yet, could she sneak out the door and flee into the woods?

She swung her gaze toward the front entrance, but her escape was blocked by Rebecca's small form.

Like her mother, the girl was wrapped head to foot in traveling clothes. Standing just inside the doorway, she clutched a small suitcase in one hand.

But something was very wrong. Always bright and alert, Rebecca stared, dead-eyed and pinch-faced, unmoving but for a gentle sway side to side. The bag slipped from her grasp, and she raised limp arms to her head. Her body listed, as if at any moment she might topple under the weight of her garb.

She struggled to form a word. "*Mamm…*"

Cold as a dead man's handshake, fear scuttled up Tessa's spine and clutched at her throat. Not again. Paralyzed in the face of a child in danger, she felt utterly helpless. She stared at the girl's mother, but Nora couldn't hear her daughter through the thunder of her wrath.

Rebecca pressed the heels of her hands to her eyes, and her rosebud mouth contorted in a grimace. She teetered and staggered forward, clinging to her mother's skirt. "*Mamm…*my head…"

Spurting venom, Nora shooed away the girl, tore the shawl from her shoulders, and tossed it over a chair.

Rebecca stumbled into the kitchen, squinting in the bright light. "I want my kitty."

What was Nora doing? Her daughter needed help. Now! Tessa swiveled to Jonas, cracking her head soundly on the edge of the table. Her vision blurred, and she closed her eyes, collapsing onto her heels. The last thing she wanted was to insert herself in the middle of a family crisis. But Nora and Jonas were locked in a battle that had been simmering for years and finally erupted like a geyser. They were blind to Rebecca. Once again, Tessa was on her own.

She choked down her fear and rubbed the new lump on her skull. Pain cleared her foggy brain in an instant. In a moment of crisis, she helped Sam, and she could help Rebecca now. *Just stay calm and keep your wits, Meadows.* She sucked in a breath and extended a hand. "Rebecca?"

Slumped against the counter, the child swung her gaze to Tessa.

Not even a glimmer of recognition sparked in her

eyes. Tessa beckoned. "What's wrong?"

Rebecca's eyes went wide, and she clamped a hand over her mouth. With a moan, she doubled over and vomited on the kitchen floor.

Tessa bolted and caught Rebecca in her arms. She held a palm to the child's forehead and recoiled. Rebecca's skin was on fire. She stripped the girl's sweat-soaked bonnet and shawl and fumbled with the buttons of her coat.

Between sobs, Rebecca writhed, clutching her head in her hands.

Nora whirled. "Don't touch my child!"

Ignoring her, Tessa removed the soiled coat at last and carried Rebecca to the sofa. Just as it did that day at the Softee Freeze, her focus sharpened. The child's elfin chin, the delicate curve of her ear, and the purple veins pulsing just beneath translucent skin at her temples all came into sharp relief. Tessa had no clue what Rebecca was suffering from, but she knew with absolute certainty it was no common cold. She turned to Jonas. "Rebecca needs a doctor."

Nora limped to the sofa and shoved between Tessa and her daughter. "She needs her mother."

Fighting panic, Tessa beckoned Jonas. "I've never in my life felt anyone with such a high fever."

He placed a hand on Rebecca's forehead, and his shoulders tensed. "How long has she been feverish?"

Nora pushed away his hand. "Two days. She worsened on the ride from the train station. She's tired. I'll make tea."

Though she acted the role of an attentive mother, Nora's gestures were increasingly empty. Rage succumbing to fear, she fluttered her hands above her child like a frightened bird. Maybe, just maybe, Tessa could persuade her.

Rebecca's head lolled to one side. "*Mamm*?"

The girl was a pale outline of herself—a black-and-white rendering of a child who laughed rainbows. With every passing second, she faded. "Jonas, we need to take her to the hospital."

"My child will not leave this house." Wheeling, Nora snatched a blanket from the back of the couch and tucked it round her daughter with shaky hands.

Tessa spent enough time at the hospital to know what a sick child looked like. Rebecca belonged at St. Luke's. Period. She gentled her tone. "Nora, please."

Jonas placed a hand on his sister's shoulder. "The child needs English medicine. Let me fetch the elders."

The woman's laugh could have corroded granite. Tessa wrapped her arms around her belly, coiling into herself.

"Summon the elders here? To a house blackened with sin?" Nora shrugged off Jonas. "How dare you."

Tessa wanted to scream. She wanted to defend her honor and Jonas's too. But he looked to be hanging on by a thread. He pressed a fist to his mouth as if to bottle his rage.

"Think of the child," he growled.

"Rebecca is my daughter, not yours. She's fine." Nora yanked off the blanket. "Get up!" She hauled Rebecca to her feet.

Tessa gasped, driving her fingers into her palms.

Rebecca stumbled and swayed to one side. "My head hurts."

If only she had her van—she'd grab the child and race to the hospital, whether Nora was willing or not.

Nora took her daughter by the shoulders. "Go to bed, and I'll bring you a cold rag."

"*Mamm*…" Rebecca tried to curl into her mother's body.

Nora pushed her toward the stairs and followed on her heels.

Her own head throbbed with pain and disbelief. How could Nora be so cruel? She lunged for the woman's arm. "Please, let me call an ambulance."

Recoiling like Tessa was the one diseased, Nora wrenched her arm, slamming her elbow into the banister. Bone met wood with a sickening crack. Her cheeks went pale. "Put on some clothing and leave my house."

"Look, *Mamm*, *Daed*'s home. *Daed*'s home with Chestnut." Rebecca wandered to the open front door and stared outside. Bouncing on wobbly ankles, she raised a hand in a feeble wave and fell through the doorway, vomiting again.

Nora rushed outside so fast her limp vanished. With the child in her arms, she returned and lurched up the stairs.

Rebecca thrashed weakly. "Let me go. I want my *daed*."

Just as Nora disappeared onto the landing, she spoke one brief sentence in German.

Tessa looked to Jonas. "What did she say?"

His eyes were dull. His shoulders slumped. "She told me to summon the elders."

She'd never seen him look defeated. Fighting achy despair that knotted her stomach, she closed the front door and sagged against it. "Rebecca needs a doctor. She needs real medicine."

"My sister will never allow it." He shuffled to the base of the stairs and lifted his gaze to the darkness. "She won't leave this house."

"But she has to!" As tears stung the backs of her eyes, she slammed her shoulders against the door. "If only doctors still made house calls. If only…" Her breath caught in her chest. *If only.* She hung her head. The realization of what exactly she had to do soured her stomach until she thought she might be sick. *If only…* If only she had another choice. She wracked her brain but could think of none. The elders might be well-intentioned, but Rebecca needed modern medicine. *If only…* If only she wasn't trapped.

She peeled herself off the door and drew up behind Jonas. She wanted so badly to wrap her arms around his waist and lay her cheek between his shoulders. But given what she was about to propose, she couldn't. Not now. Now, only one option remained: the last thing she wanted to do and the only thing she could do.

"Jonas. Rebecca needs"—she inhaled deeply—"a doctor." And with that final word, she made clear what she intended. Jonas tightened his hold on the banister until she thought it would splinter. Would he demand she leave, too?

He gave a long exhale and dropped his chin to his chest. "Call him."

He couldn't even look at her—might never do so again. "Where's the community phone?"

****

"No, I need to talk to Dr. Bruce." With every stinging breath, Tessa's chest heaved. She gripped the handset and clamped her bottom lip. Running full out, she'd still taken fifteen minutes to reach the phone.

"Dr. Miller is the attending on call," the page operator repeated in a clipped tone.

"I don't want Dr. Miller!" She squeezed shut her eyes and saw flickering, white streaks like her own private aurora borealis. Snapping would get her nowhere. She rubbed a palm down her thigh and leveled her tone. "I don't mean to be rude. I'm in the middle of an emergency."

"Did you call 9-1-1?"

"I can't call 9-1-1. Please—I don't have time to explain, but I need Dr. Bruce. Please page him."

The operator huffed a sigh. "I'll try. What's the callback number?"

She read the numbers off the big, black phone and hung up. How long before Richard called? If he called. She collapsed onto the stool, retying the sneakers she slipped on with her shorts before running out the door. Looping the bottom of Jonas's shirt into a knot at her waist, she tightened it with clumsy fingers and stared at the wrinkled business card on the table—the card Richard gave her all those weeks ago with his pager number neatly printed below his name and title. Thank goodness she'd kept it in her backpack.

She stood again and rotated her ankles, stretching tight calves. Her body hadn't been ready for a sprint. Staring at the phone, she willed it to ring. Why hadn't she memorized Richard's cell number? Where was her phone anyway? At the bottom of the creek?

A moth circled in the beam from her flashlight. The shed housed only the phone, the stool, and a narrow telephone table upon which rested a spiral-bound notebook. She shoved the card into her pocket and opened the book. Every call was meticulously logged: Stoltzfus. King. Yoder. Lapp. Rishel. She traced a finger over Jonas's tidy lettering. He had an architect's hand, square and regular.

An ear-splitting *ding-a-ling* rang like a phantom phone calling from 1975.

She jumped and grabbed the receiver. It thudded her jaw hard enough to leave a mark.

He finished a muffled conversation with a laugh. "Dr. Bruce."

Resolve weakening, she clutched the stool with rigid fingers. "Richard?"

The line went silent.

"Richard, are you there?"

"What do you want?"

What she wanted was escape—to go back in time to lemon-scented bathwater and blueberry pie in the hours before Nora came home. What did she want? Where to begin? "I…I know I have no right to call—"

"I'm rather in the middle of something."

His voice was steel. She'd need a blowtorch to melt him. Still, she had to try. "Please. I need your help."

"Why didn't you call my cell? Are you all right?" He fired questions without waiting for a reply.

"I'm fine. It's a little girl." Rebecca's face, sunken and sallow, flashed in her mind. Her throat tightened. "She's sick—something's very wrong, and I don't know how to help. Could you possibly come see her?"

"Are you serious, Tessa?"

His tone was so weighted with disgust she almost dropped the phone. She grabbed the spiral cord and pulled it against her belly.

"I'm not a pediatrician. Have the kid's mom take

her to the ER if she's concerned."

How do you rebuild a bridge and cross it at the same time? She coiled the cord around one finger until the tip went white. *One board at a time and without looking down.* "The girl's Amish. Her mother won't leave the house." Richard's breath rasped in her ear, quick and tight. She licked dry lips and pressed on. "She refuses to take her daughter to the hospital."

The line went silent. She could almost feel the battle Richard waged in his heart—his pride versus his responsibility. *Please let the physician win.*

He gave a sharp sniff. "What are her symptoms?"

He spoke in his clinical voice, not his angry voice. She had a chance. "She has an incredibly high fever—"

"How high?"

"I don't know. I don't have a thermometer—"

"Anything else? Give her ibuprofen."

Her pulse throbbed in her fingertip, and she loosened the cord. "Richard, her skin is on fire. I've never felt anything like it."

"Any other symptoms?"

Dr. Bruce didn't respond to hyperbole. He needed facts. She shut off the valve of emotion and concentrated, ticking off Rebecca's symptoms. "She vomited—twice. Her head hurts, and she's confused. It's weird—she keeps covering her eyes with her hands, and she thought she saw her father but he—"

"Is anyone in the house sick?"

"No, but she's been with family in Ohio. She just got home."

"Look, it sounds like the flu. Call an ambulance if you're concerned."

Forget clinical distance. She had to reach the man

she knew was a healer at his core—the man who risked his life climbing a Ferris wheel to save a stranger's son. "You don't understand. Her mother won't let anyone in the house. Please. I'm not sure how, but I just know in my gut something is very wrong. The girl's name is Rebecca. You met her that day at the market. She sold you a pie, remember? She has blonde hair, and she's only seven years old, and she needs you." Her voice broke, just a smidge. "I need you, Richard. Please."

She spotted a calendar tacked on the wall. In the picture, Jesus sat on a bench, embracing a blond boy with one hand and blessing a dark-skinned girl with the other. The caption read, "Jesus loves the little children. All the children of the world." The calendar was turned to August, but the July page had been torn out and tucked into the call log.

Richard cleared his throat. "Give her fluids and try to lower her temperature. I'll be there as soon as I can."

After giving hasty directions, she hung up and raced back to the farm. Heart pounding, she burst into the kitchen, barely able to speak. "He's coming. We need to give Rebecca fluids—water or tea."

Slumped over the table, Jonas nodded but didn't stir.

This man who raised buildings with his bare hands sat before her now, completely powerless. A thousand impulses tugged in different directions. Should she kiss him or give him space? Run upstairs or hide in the bathroom? Boil water for tea or fetch cold from the tap? At a loss, she grabbed a cup and filled it at the sink.

When she turned, she found him looking at her. Instantly, the swirling uncertainty stilled. He held her gaze, and an unspoken understanding settled upon her heart. Their time on the farm was over. Something delicate and sacred was shattered, and a gulf lay between them now neither knew how to bridge.

A vehicle skidded to a stop outside the window.

"I love you," she said.

"Wait for me."

His words were swallowed by a forceful knock. She took in a breath and was cut off by pounding she thought might wrench the door from its hinges. She broke away and ran to open it.

Richard was dressed in a tuxedo with a stethoscope slung round his neck and his father's old, leather doctor's bag in one hand.

He kept that bag on a shelf like a museum piece. She had no time to consider the significance of calling it into active duty. And why a tuxedo? She flashed to the calendar in the shanty, and her heart plummeted. August first—the night of the Midsummer Ball.

He hooked a thumb over his shoulder. "Your van looks like it's been through a war. Where's the girl?"

Her van? She darted a glance out the door and spotted it, battered but intact in the shadow of the barn. Blinded by panic, she hadn't even clocked its return.

Jonas approached and extended a hand. "Thank you for coming, Doctor."

Richard shook it. "You're welcome."

She sensed no repressed animosity or thinly veiled demand for thanks. Richard came simply because he couldn't *not* come. Her throat went thick, and tears pooled on her lower lids. He was a good man, too.

"My niece, Rebecca, is upstairs. Follow me." Jonas led them to the second floor.

Tessa hovered in the doorway. Rebecca's thin face

emerged pale and wan from a pile of quilts.

Nora sat on the bed, holding a glass of water to her daughter's lips. Seeing Richard, she jerked to her feet. "Who are you?"

"I'm Dr. Bruce." With authority, he crossed to the opposite side of the bed and placed a steady hand on Rebecca's forehead. He shifted his gaze to Tessa.

Though his expression remained neutral, his gaze confirmed what her gut told her. Rebecca was very ill. Though she'd have felt like a fool, she couldn't help wishing she'd been wrong.

"I don't know you." Nora balled her skirt in tight fists. "Please leave."

"I'm here to help." Richard sat on the edge of the bed and lowered the quilt.

His voice was so even, his demeanor so reassuring that Tessa's lungs opened, and her heartbeat slowed. Even Nora seemed to release her shoulders just a bit.

"How long has she been feverish?" Richard held the diaphragm of the stethoscope to the palm of his hand.

Tessa had seen him do this many times but only now realized why. He was warming the instrument before placing it on his patient's skin. The gesture was a small act of tenderness—one of a thousand he made every day. Sudden affection bloomed in her chest.

"Two days," Jonas answered.

"Have you seen my *daed*?" Rebecca's voice was little more than a whisper. "He went into the barn with Chestnut, but I didn't get to hug him."

"You can hug him very soon. Right now, I need to listen to your heart and lungs, okay?" Richard gently lifted her and held the stethoscope to her chest and back. "Very good, Rebecca. Just lie back now." He flicked his gaze toward Nora. "Are you her mother?"

"Yes." Nora released the apron and fluttered her hands to her sides. "And her father is dead."

"I see." He slid up Rebecca's sleeve and wrapped two fingers around her wrist. "Rebecca should come to the hospital for a complete examination and some tests, but in the short term, we need to lower her temperature." He retrieved his bag and pulled out a plastic bottle filled with pink liquid. "I'd like to give her medicine for the fever. Do you consent?"

Nora shot Jonas a look.

Jonas nodded.

"Yes," she said.

Richard poured a small amount into a little cup and held it to Rebecca's lips. "I have some medicine for you. It will help you feel better, and it tastes like cherries. Do you like cherries?"

Rebecca drank and, glassy-eyed, lolled her head to one side. A trickle of pink oozed from the corner of her mouth.

"Very good." Dabbing the liquid with a tissue, he turned his gaze to Nora. "The medicine will take effect shortly. Right now, I need you to bring me all the ice you have."

"Ice…?" Nora whirled and reached for Jonas with an open hand.

He came beside her and squeezed her shoulder. "We don't have much ice."

"Find some." Richard tucked Rebecca's hand under the quilt. "Immediately."

Jonas took off down the stairs.

"I need to cool her stat," Richard said, almost to

himself. "Do we have a water source up here?"

In an instant, Tessa was at his side with the pitcher and rag from Jonas's bedroom.

He plunged in the rag and dripped water on Rebecca's face and neck.

Rebecca wiped her cheeks and writhed. "Where's Pumpkin?"

She stilled and fixed Tessa in a gaze as clear as the day they met. Could Richard's medicine have worked so quickly?

"Pumpkin had five kittens. You can take one home since you don't have even a single pet at your house."

She stroked the girl's damp forehead. "Thank you, sweetheart."

"I need to examine her fully," Richard said. "Help me remove her clothes."

She sat across from him and, just as with Sam, worked in tandem to undress the wiggly child.

The moment the pinafore slid from her shoulders, Rebecca stilled. "*Mamm*? I feel…" In a flash, her eyes rolled back in her head, her spine arched, and her arms stiffened at her sides.

Tessa jerked back, panic squeezing her lungs. "What's happening?"

"She's seizing." Richard vaulted to his feet.

"What do we do?"

He shoved the blankets to the end of the bed. "Roll her on her side, facing me. We don't want her to aspirate if she vomits again."

Inert and frozen, Rebecca seemed unmovable. With a grunt, Tessa heaved the girl just at the moment she began to thrash. Her rigid arms bent and straightened like a robot gone wild—up and down, up and down. Her back arched again and again.

"Hold her tight," Richard said. "Keep her on her side and don't let her fall."

With strength she didn't know she had, she locked the child in a snug embrace. Heat radiated into Tessa's skin.

Richard glowered at the empty doorway. "We need to cool her now!"

Jonas ran into the bedroom with a mixing bowl of ice just in time to see Rebecca collapse onto the bed, limp and lifeless. His face went white.

Richard snorted. "I need ten times this much."

Jonas started to place the bowl on the dresser, then paused and shuffled toward the bed. "I'll ask for help."

"We don't have time to wait." Richard shot Tessa a glance and jutted his chin toward the ice. He pulled his phone from the pocket of his coat and tossed the coat over the desk chair.

His gaze fixed on Rebecca, Jonas stood immobile.

Easing the bowl from his grasp, Tessa nudged her shoulder into his. "Go for ice."

Coming to, he blinked and nodded, then dashed out the door.

She spotted Nora quivering against the dresser and offered a smile. "Richard is a good doctor. She'll be all right."

Nora let out a whimper.

Richard beckoned. "Help me get her out of this dress so I can cool her and figure out what the hell is going on." He tapped the screen and put the phone to his ear.

His tone was brusque, but she knew his agitation sprang from Rebecca's suffering and not from anger with her. Her muscles were leaden, but she thrust the bowl into Nora's hands and unbuttoned the back of Rebecca's dress.

"This is Dr. Bruce from St. Luke's. I have a 911. Female, seven years old. Febrile. Seizing. Her vitals are stable, but she needs to come to the ER. I don't have anti-seizure meds on-site, so get a team here now." He handed the phone to Tessa. "Give them directions."

She wedged it under her chin and relayed the information as calmly as she could while still opening buttons. When she finished, she ended the call and tugged the garment with her free hand. "I can't get the dress over her head." She passed the phone to Richard and tried again with both hands. "Her neck is stiff."

Leaning over, he carefully manipulated Rebecca's head. "You're right."

The girl's eyes half opened. "*Mamm*, I want my kitty," she slurred. "Where am I? Where's my *daed* and Chestnut?"

"She's disoriented." With his hands on his hips, he stared at Rebecca, lips moving in silent litany as he reviewed her symptoms, honing in on a diagnosis. He beckoned to Nora. "The bowl."

With trembling hands, Nora handed it to him.

Melting fast, the ice rattled and sloshed.

He looked to Tessa. "Pack it under her arms and around her groin."

She folded back the sheet, exposing Rebecca's torso and legs, and barely suppressed a cry. The girl's slender, white limbs were completely covered with reddish-purple spots the size of pinheads, as if she had been bruised or bitten from hip to ankle. "Richard, look."

Nora let out a cry and shrank into the corner.

Shoving the ice into her hands, Richard lunged for his bag. "I think this child has meningitis. We need to suppress her fever and start her on antibiotics immediately."

Her throat closed. Even Tessa knew meningitis was often deadly. Still, her breath was calm and her mind clear. Her faith in Richard was absolute. "Tell me what to do."

"Apply the ice." He produced an IV and a syringe from the bag. "Has she been around other children?"

Nora righted herself and limped toward the bed. She held a hand just above Rebecca's legs but didn't touch them. "Her cousins in Ohio."

Richard drew some fluid from a small bottle and injected it into a larger one. He shook it rapidly. "Were any of them sick?" He drew fluid from the second bottle and injected it into an IV bag.

"Maybe. I don't know." She twitched her hands to her breast. "What are you doing?"

Nora's voice was thin and reedy. Tessa didn't blame her for being terrified. This woman had lost so much. To lose her daughter, too? She plunged her hand into the bowl and winced. No matter. She'd freeze to death before she'd let Rebecca die.

Richard held the IV poised over Rebecca's body. "I can't do a CAT scan. I can't do a lumbar puncture." He cursed under his breath and shifted his gaze to Nora. "I'm sure your daughter has meningitis. I'd like to start IV antibiotics."

Voices from the front yard drew Tessa to the window. In the moonlight, she spied a group of Amish men hurrying down the lane toting buckets.

Then Rebecca seized again, even more severely than the first time.

Richard lunged for his patient. "Where the hell is the ambulance?"

Sweeping aside a bird's nest, Tessa flung the bowl onto the dresser and knelt on the bed. Rebecca flailed her arms so forcefully Tessa was sure she'd injure herself. With combined strength, she and Richard rolled the girl onto her side and pointed down her head just as she vomited again. And again. And again.

When she finally stopped convulsing, Rebecca lapsed into a completely lifeless stupor.

Richard put his ear to her mouth, confirmed she was still breathing, and sprang into action.

Jonas appeared at the door with two pails of ice—the first in a bucket brigade already in motion.

Not waiting for Richard's order, Tessa grabbed a fistful and tucked it under Rebecca's arm.

Richard readied the intravenous antibiotics. "Is she allergic to any medications? Penicillin or amoxicillin?"

With an aching heart and hands like icicles, Tessa shot Nora a glance. Clinging to the bedpost, the woman wavered, seemingly helpless to do anything but watch her daughter suffer.

"I don't know. She's never had English medicine." Nora's voice cracked again. "She's always been such a healthy child."

Richard came to Nora's side. "Ma'am, I need you to listen carefully. I believe your daughter has meningitis, which is a very serious disease. If I don't give her intravenous medicine, she might have permanent brain damage, or she might die. Now, a small but real chance exists she'll have an allergic reaction to the medicine. In the majority of cases, allergies can be managed. To me, the benefits of treatment significantly outweigh the dangers, but to begin, I need your consent."

As tears spilled down her cheeks, Nora turned to Jonas.

Leaning against the wall, bucket in hand, Jonas nodded.

With an answering nod, Richard started the IV drip.

Handful upon handful, Tessa packed ice around Rebecca's body. Bucket after bucket plopped at her feet. She scooped until her fingers burned and she had to shove them under her arms for a moment's relief. Peering out the window again, she searched for the ambulance. Several buggies stood silhouetted in the moonlight. How much time had passed since Richard called? How long before help arrived? She plunged her hands back in the bucket, and finally, the cry of a siren cut through the night.

"About time." Richard held aloft the IV and placed a palm on Rebecca's forehead.

Jonas dropped yet another bucket by the bed and ran out the door. "I'll show them up."

Tessa heard a commotion as he cleared the stairs. Moments later, a stringy man barely old enough to drive and an older technician with streaks of gray in his dark moustache burst through the doorway carrying a backboard.

"Dr. Bruce. We had a heck of a time finding the place," said the elder one.

"Yeah. Went right by on the first pass," the other said with a laugh.

The older one silenced his partner with a look. He cleared his throat. "What've we got?"

Richard moved to the head of the bed and placed a hand on Rebecca's shoulder. "Febrile seizure. Stiff neck. Headache. Altered mental status. Petechial rash. Probable meningitis. Started IV penicillin."

The young EMT swung one end of the backboard to Richard, narrowly missing Nora's head. "Good call, Doc."

Tessa smashed herself against the wall and massaged her lower back with numb fingers.

With an energy that struck her as both a little rough and almost casual, the technicians slung Rebecca onto the backboard. In seconds, they secured her and maneuvered through the narrow door onto the landing.

Trailing them closely, Jonas held the IV bag. He threw a glance over one shoulder and beckoned to Nora.

She bustled out the door on his heels.

Left behind, Tessa stared into the landing. Hollow thuds and shuffling filled the hallway. That staircase was steep. She hoped the EMTs knew what they were doing.

The front door opened and closed. A hush settled over the house.

Rustling came from behind. Richard. She almost forgot he was there. Richard, who came from a ball just when she needed him most. Richard. Whose heart she never intended to break. "Hey." Pushing through a wave of shyness, she faced him. Regardless of how she felt…and really, how did she feel? Too muddled to name the emotion. Regardless, he deserved her gratitude. "You were amazing. Thank you."

"You were right to call." He coiled his stethoscope atop the other instruments and buckled the bag. "The girl should be fine."

"You and kids." She raised her brows. "You sure you weren't meant for pediatrics?" He ran a hand over the bag, caressing the leather, and his expression softened. Her joke suddenly didn't feel like a joke.

Outside and below, car doors open and closed. Voices rose.

He darted a glance to the window. "I guess neither of us is too old to become…something else."

"Maybe so." She retrieved the tuxedo jacket and extended it. "You left the ball."

With a shrug, he slipped into the coat. "I can go back."

All business again, he took up his bag and strode to the door. She held out a hand. "Richard." Every ounce of fondness she once felt and probably would always feel shimmered in the saying of his name.

Pausing in the doorway, he turned.

"Your father would be so proud."

Through flickering lamplight, he met her gaze. "We made a great team."

The corners of his mouth rose in a smile that didn't quite reach his eyes. She nodded, offering a bittersweet smile in return. His words were true, but they weren't enough to build a life on. Not for her.

He rapped the doorframe twice, spun, and vanished.

She crossed to the window and raised the shade fully. The scene below knotted her stomach.

Nora and Jonas stood locked in an embrace as the EMTs loaded Rebecca into the ambulance.

A crowd of Amish men clustered nearby, hats in hand. Buckets of ice littered the lawn. Buggies stood in the shadow of the barn.

Striding from the porch, Richard beckoned Jonas into the front seat of the ambulance. Jonas nodded, and Richard crossed to his SUV, parked akimbo to her van.

Nora limped to the back of the ambulance.

Jonas lifted her to join Rebecca and the older EMT.

The young EMT closed the rear doors and hopped into the driver's seat.

Slipping into the cab, Jonas paused and glanced up at the house. Richard's headlights sliced through the dark, catching him in sudden brightness. He lifted a hand.

Wait for me.

She touched a palm to the wavy glass. At that moment, the driver must have said something, because Jonas snapped around his head and disappeared into the ambulance. It sped down the lane, rounded the corner, and was gone.

Ice is a valuable commodity in a community with no electricity. She remained at the window until the men retrieved their buckets and vanished into the night. Likely, the precious resource would be halfway melted by the time they returned home.

Her pulse rushed in her ears. From all sides, darkness encroached, cold as the vacuum of outer space. Her lungs seized, and she clutched her belly with raw fingers. From deep within, a single sob rose and tore from her throat in a strangled cry. She dropped her forehead against the glass, and pain split her skull. Her body was one giant bruise. As her cry echoed to nothing in the empty house, she too was left feeling hollow. A shell of a person who just hours ago had been a warm being, suffused to the tips of her eyelashes with love.

She pried open the window, and fresh air stirred the rank odors of sweat and sickness. She blinked and stared at the scene. The room—the entire house—was in shambles. How could she let him come home to a mess?

Tapping reserves she didn't know she possessed, she hefted Rebecca's sodden mattress down the stairs and onto the porch. Then she gathered the soiled throw rugs from around the child's bed and hung them over the porch railing. She doused them with steaming water boiled in the same pots Jonas used for her bath and left them with the mattress to dry. The cherry pitter snugged into the kitchen drawer which now closed without a hitch. Discarded travel clothes and bags were returned to their proper rooms where they lined the walls with military precision. Finally, she mopped the floors and opened almost every window in the house. She didn't weep. She didn't think. She just cleaned.

Only after she spread her arms wide and leaned into the kitchen counter did she realize she'd assumed Jonas's position from earlier that night—yesterday, really. If she closed her eyes, could she summon the warmth of his body, as if he still stood here and she just slipped beneath his arms to nestle into the Tessa-sized space against his chest?

Gazing at the dawn, all she felt was loneliness. The sky shifted from charcoal to heathered gray. A bar of soap twirled in her fingers, giving off the faintest scent of oatmeal. She held it to her nose. The smell was subtle but undeniably him. She replaced the soap by the sink.

With every step, her feet rooted into the floor, and she had to rip them free. No matter what her body wanted, her brain knew better. She had no reason to stay. Nothing remained to be cleaned.

In the doorway to Jonas's room, she paused, allowing her eyes to adjust. He left his bed in the middle of the night, and the shade was still drawn. She gazed over rumpled linens to the Bible on the nightstand. The cover was cracked at the binding, and the gilt pages were faded and warped. She entered the room, running a hand along the top of the dresser where her backpack now lay, lingering until she imprinted every object onto her heart. She melded the cool solidity of the porcelain bowl into her skin…memorized the simple floral pattern punched into the tin candleholder…captured the cottony, woody scent of the air deep in her lungs.

Only then did she finish the work she'd begun. She raised the shade and opened wide the window. Stiff shoulders cracking, she made his bed, tucking quilt beneath mattress and smoothing the wrinkles. She fluffed the downy pillows but didn't let herself sink into them. If she did, she would never have the strength to leave. Instead, she sat on the straight-backed chair and picked up her backpack.

From it, she drew the envelope containing the check and a pen. On the outside, she wrote simply, "*For Jonas. With my thanks.*" She propped it against the candleholder, folded her trembling hands, and let her head fall. Even the rosy glow warming the planks at her feet couldn't thaw the icy void inside. She raised her gaze to the envelope, wrinkled and rough around the edges, and swallowed a lump like jagged glass in her throat.

She wanted to snatch back that envelope—to stuff it in her bag and high tail to the hospital. She pictured Jonas alone in the waiting room, hunched in a too-small, plastic chair. This night wounded him deeply. He would need her.

Even more, she wanted to rage—to weep and shout and shred this room to pieces. This room, this chamber of secret dreams, that sheltered their love and allowed them both to heal. But no tears stung her eyes. Her spent body remained motionless. She knew in her heart she couldn't do those things—shouldn't do those things. Breath after breath filled her tender soul with quiet resolution. She had to leave.

But where were the keys to her van? She scanned the dresser and the nightstand. Nothing. She opened the single nightstand drawer. No keys, but something else. With a whisper-soft inhalation, she released the knob. Then she grabbed it again and tugged the drawer wide. Inside laid a collection of the most exquisite pencil drawings she had ever seen.

She brushed together her palms and grasped the pile lightly between thumb and fingers, easing it out. Hardly daring to breathe, she paged through the sketches. Most looked to have been made quickly in stolen moments amid hours of work: Rebecca and Pumpkin asleep under a tree, Nora rolling a piecrust in the kitchen, buggies in a line beside a snow-covered barn, and Elizabeth's garden gate. At the very bottom of the pile, she found several detailed drawings of a woman with a round, generous face, dimpled cheeks, and kind eyes. *Elizabeth.* Her breath hitched in her throat, and her broken heart softened. *I'm so very glad to meet you.*

In one drawing, Jonas caught her pinning sheets to the wash line. Elizabeth glanced over a shoulder, fine hair escaping her cap at her temples and her lips parted in an expression mingling surprise and tenderness. Jonas's wife had loved him. Tessa ran a finger over the delicate lines and sent up a prayer of thanks. She clearly brought Jonas joy, if only for a time.

Please let it be enough.

As she returned the papers to the drawer, a drawing of Nora snagged her attention. She pulled it from the pile and studied it. Never once had she seen a smile cross that woman's face, but Jonas drew her laughing, her head thrown back in joy. Tessa pictured Nora clutching a bowl of ice in helpless agony, and pity welled in her heart. Nora had known profound loss. The kind of bitterness she displayed could only come from deep hurt. Every day, Nora fought to preserve the only family she had left. How could Tessa even think about taking them away?

She found the van key dangling from a hook by the kitchen door, and indeed, when she turned it, the motor spluttered to life. Idling in Neutral, she slipped from the cab, dashed into the barn, and returned with the kitten, mewing and wriggling in her hands. She deposited it on the floor behind her, swung around, and drove down the lane.

When she rounded the bend, she stopped, rolled down the window, and took a long look back. The sun just cleared the eastern ridge, and a cascading veil of purple morning glories covered Elizabeth's garden gate. The well-appointed farm awaited its family of three.

Not a traditional Amish family, but a family, nonetheless.

With a sigh, she shifted the van into gear and drove away forever. Jonas would be home for the evening milking that night and every night after. She knew it with as much certainty as she'd ever known anything.

What she didn't know, as she rounded the bend and the Rishel farm slipped into the landscape of memory, was where she was headed. Or what she'd do when she arrived. But for the first time, Tessa Meadows didn't fear the open road. With her hometown in the rearview mirror, she was finally ready to step on the gas and drive.

Epilogue
Aspen, Colorado. One year later.

Time for a walk on the wild side, baby.
Snugging a hip against the counter of her cozy cabin kitchen, Tessa plunged a finger into uncooked, blueberry muffin batter. Risking salmonella poisoning wasn't exactly Russian roulette, but it tasted a smidge daring. She licked with gusto. Comfort food with a dash of adventure. Her mood lightened.

Butternut rubbed against her ankles, angling for a treat. She messily spooned batter into muffin cups and sprinkled them with coarse sugar. Her mother's recipe from the *Margaret Meadows Does Desserts* cookbook was hands down the best. She knew, because she'd tried others. Gently crushing half a cup of fresh blueberries into the batter before adding two cups of whole ones infused blueberry flavor and gave the muffins such a beautiful color. Over the past year, her taste refined with her baking skills. Maybe she should start creating her own recipes.

Grasping the back of a kitchen chair, she twisted and stretched out her back. Her spine released tiny *pop-pop-pops* reminding her she was out of popcorn. She stuck a hand in her pocket and drew out a little, gray creek stone. It slid between her fingertips with soothing coolness. She stared out the kitchen window.

The view was spectacular as ever. In mid-July the

ragged peaks still sported snow, and the mountain meadows were laced with lupine. Aspen leaves shimmied beneath a clear, blue sky, and her restless spirit stirred. She spun back to the kitchen. Even the view couldn't satisfy her today. Had the time come to move on?

A breeze rustled the torn piece of paper stuck to her fridge with a llama magnet. If she stared long enough, could she enter that picture? Could she skip up those steps and sit on a bench near a sycamore tree?

The timer dinged with aggressive cheer. Shaking herself, she slid out a tray of golden muffins and popped in the next one.

Butternut leapt onto the kitchen table and sat on the keyboard of her laptop. The cursor blinked accusingly from a blank screen.

She should have listened to Marcia at last week's editorial meeting, but she didn't. So often these days, she let her thoughts wander far from the Rockies, skipping down paths along spring-fed creeks. Jarred from her daydream, she proposed composting for the theme of this week's column. Why hadn't she offered "The Lovely Lupine" or "Your Vegetable Garden at Midsummer" or even "Rocky Mountain Pests?" Nope. Composting it was.

The voicemail alert on her phone demanded attention, too.

Composting could wait. Spotting Jenn's number in the call log, she tapped the speaker button and boosted the volume.

"I found the perfect Maid-of-Honor dress! I just texted, like, seventeen pics. The color is stunning, and you'll look so elegant, men will fall all over you, and no one will even notice me. So. Call me! It's on sale at Sak's, and I want to get it today, but I'm holding back until I get your okay. If you don't call soon, though, I'm buying the darned thing, and you can take it or leave it. Preferably take it. Call me, okay? Bye."

The message was time-stamped two hours ago. She navigated to Jenn's texts. The dress was, indeed, perfect and doubtlessly already hanging in Jennifer's apartment. She really should call her friend. They texted regularly, but they hadn't spoken for weeks, and she missed her. Crazy, fun-loving Jenn, who was the only person she could talk to that day last summer when the planet stopped spinning.

Dazed and achy, she had curled up on the porch swing, called Jennifer, and told her everything: how she and Jonas lived together those magical few days on the farm, how Jonas promised to leave with her, how Nora came home and twisted everything until she didn't recognize her own face, and how the Rishel family rode off in the ambulance, leaving her alone.

"Do you love him?" Jenn asked.

"Yes."

"Why?"

The reasons unspooled from her heart like a silken thread. "He's gentle and kind. He listens to me, and he cares about what I think. He's interested in everything—he reads the *Times*, believe it or not. And I admire him. I love how hard he works. I love that he spent hours designing and building me a gazebo. I love his boots and the stupid straw hat…and that he taught me how to make a blueberry pie from scratch and thinks I'm pretty with hay in my hair. I just love how simple life is with him."

"Simple, huh?"

The chains squeaked. Distant haze shrouded the ridgeline. "When I'm with him, I see clearly. On the farm you don't have time for anything besides the work and being together—"

"And the hayloft, apparently." Jenn capped a giggle with a snort.

A flush spread across her collarbones. "And the hayloft. And the milking and the baking...and the lamplight." Just for a moment, she allowed herself to drift into that shadowy kitchen. To luxuriate in warm, fragrant bathwater, knowing he was just outside.

"I'm going out on a limb here, sweetie. Sounds like a whole lot of what you love about this guy is that he's Amish."

She lowered a foot, slowing her rocking. Was Jenn right? Did she love the trappings and not the man? "I mean, he's Amish, but he lives by his own rules, too."

A siren wailed through the background of Jenn's call. Tessa's own surroundings were perfectly still. She loved Green Ridge. Would she really leave?

"Even so," Jenn went on, "could you live with yourself if you took him away from his family and his community? I almost hate to ask, but would you still love him if he weren't Amish?"

She gripped the chain, pinching her index finger between links. She winced and pulled herself upright. "Well, he'll always be Amish—"

"No. If he leaves with you, he'll just be Jonas...in suspenders and a funny hat."

She dropped her head against the swing. Jenn was right. Tessa couldn't steal Jonas from his family, his heritage, and his Amish life. She'd never forgive herself, and no matter what he said about wanting to leave, Jonas might not forgive her either. She had hung up the call, more certain than ever she needed to go far, far away from Green Ridge.

Would I still love him if he weren't Amish?

Comforted by the smell of fresh muffins, she stared through the patio doors and hopped her gaze from peak to peak. Last August, she couldn't even begin to wrap her mind around that question. She needed time…and distance. So, she said goodbye to Green Ridge and set a course for Tucson. Some days she felt like she left home ten years ago. Today, her hurried departure felt like yesterday.

Aspen was not remotely on the route from Pennsylvania to Arizona. But at a rest stop in Indiana, she uncovered a stash of her father's John Denver cassette tapes. In a soaring tenor, he sang about Starwood and Aspen, conjuring a sweet Rocky Mountain paradise.

Colorado called. Tessa had to see the mountains.

When the camper's motor died on I-82 just outside Aspen, she wasn't surprised. The Rockies took a toll on the transmission of a 1970s pop-top van, and she'd been smelling smoke since Denver.

The mechanic who ran the nearest vintage camper repair shop determined only a complete reconstruction of the motor would render the van mobile. Learning Tessa was stranded, he made a few calls.

Though a much bigger small town than Green Ridge, Aspen proved itself even more welcoming. Within hours, she was invited to stay in the log cabin guesthouse of a friend of a friend of the man's wife.

Marcia, the cabin's owner, not only possessed

every one of Margaret Meadows's cookbooks but also was the features editor of the local newspaper.

So, "Tessa's Corner," a weekly gardening column, was born. Even after the van was repaired, she stayed, paying a modest rent for the digs. The tiny, rustic cabin suited her fine. Mountain air eased her battered heart.

Could almost a year have gone by since she quite literally drove into the sunset? The notion seemed impossible, but the calendar didn't lie.

She peeled the paper from a steaming muffin and replayed Jennifer's message just to hear her laugh and snort. Then she read a juicy email from Claire, with all the local scuttlebutt.

According to Claire, construction was underway on a state-of-the-art medical clinic Richard designed to serve the rural communities surrounding Green Ridge. An article in a well-regarded medical journal profiling his handling of Rebecca's meningitis, the efforts to stop the spread of disease among her Ohio family, and his campaign to bring high-tech medicine to rural populations would publish this fall. He'd been spotted making house calls with a curvy ER nurse named Cindy, and rumor had it they were dating. Claire long since forgave Tessa for breaking Richard's heart, and Tessa spent a wonderful week with the MacMillans when the whole family traveled to Aspen for a spring break ski trip.

She took a bite of muffin. The top offered a satisfying crunch, and the fluffy inside dissolved on her tongue, leaving behind a tang of berry. Delicious. Happy almost-one-year-Colorado-versary.

She had a good year…a peaceful year. Who would have thought such a profound life change could be so simple? But, under all that snow, the world was quiet. Marcia graciously introduced her to a wide circle of friends. They were largely city-folks who forsook the rat race for a life at eight thousand feet. Bankers and businesspeople turned ski instructors and chefs, they were thoughtful folks who kept her smiling through Marcia's weekly potlucks. She'd been content…mostly. Until the snow melted…

What was dinging?

She caught the smell of caramelizing sugar. The second batch of muffins! She completely forgot them already. Out of the oven and onto the trivet they went. Jeez. She just couldn't focus on anything.

Up to her elbows in soapy water, she cringed when a knock on the door tapped into her consciousness. Marcia's latest email remained unanswered. Her column was two days late.

The knock came again, more firmly.

She dried her hands on her apron and grabbed a muffin. "Marcia, I'm coming. I haven't written a word, but you've got to try a blueberry muffin. It's my mother's recipe." She flung open the front door.

And she very nearly passed out.

He wore faded blue jeans and a white T-shirt, his old boots, and a pinched cowboy hat. His hair was shorter, and his skin even more tanned.

In his face was a freedom she'd never seen. In his eyes breathed the open road. In his hands was a bouquet of wildflowers.

His lips lifted in a crooked grin. "I'd love a muffin. Thanks."

Jonas.

She opened her mouth, but no sound came out. She

blinked once…twice. He didn't disappear.

He held out the flowers. "I've been looking all over for you."

Releasing a breath she held almost a year, she fell into his arms, knocking the hat clear off his head. A rainbow of flowers scattered at her feet. She buried her face in cottony softness and nestled her head in the hollow beneath his chin. After a long, lonely winter dreaming about him, she could feel him, warm and solid in her arms. She closed her eyes and breathed his scent—recognizable but changed, infused now with fresh mountain air and pinesap.

He was just Jonas—just one man alone in the world, and she knew with absolute certainty, suspenders or no, she loved him. "How did you find me?"

"I came to Colorado and looked."

His voice rumbled in his chest, vibrating her cheek. *He looked?* A breathy laugh whooshed from her lungs, ricocheting off her ribs as she snuggled closer. "But how? Where?"

He tucked a finger under her chin and tilted up her face.

She'd almost forgotten how tall he was, and she'd never seen him with the perfect dusting of scruff. Her stomach pulled. She wanted to kiss every inch of it.

"Tessa Rose, I knew you'd be in the Rockies. Did you think I'd forget?"

So, he just came to Colorado, asked around, and somehow found her? Presumably without the assistance of a cellular phone? Impossible. Her pulse thudded faster than the timer ticking on the kitchen counter. "But Colorado is a really big state."

"I didn't want to cash your check, but I had to if I wanted to find you. Since September, I've worked my way from county to county. Mostly carpentry and odd jobs. I was even a cowboy for a week or two." He inclined his head toward the fallen hat and grinned. "At a newsstand in Aspen yesterday, I finally got lucky." He slung a duffel from his shoulder, unzipped it, and pulled out a copy of the local paper.

She laughed. "It's not the *Times*."

"No. It's much better."

When he smiled, and his eyes crinkled at the corners, and his cheek creased the way it always did, it was so heartbreakingly familiar she thought she might weep. But she didn't. She flushed a deep, hot flush stored up over a year in his absence, a year without the kind of blush he summoned straight from her hammering heart to every inch of supersensitive skin. She grinned like grinning was going out of style. "You left Green Ridge."

He nodded. "So did you."

"And Rebecca? Nora?" She spoke their names with ease. Any animosity she felt for his sister couldn't survive the high-altitude. That kind of fire needed oxygen. And Rebecca? Her love for the girl was old as the mountains and twice as big. Jonas's expression didn't falter. He seemed at peace, too.

"In Ohio. They're well cared for. I'll tell you everything later."

She bounced on her toes, and her bare knees grazed denim. "Tell me now. Tell me everything."

He shook his head. "Later. I promise. I'm not going anywhere."

"You're really staying?" She couldn't repress a

tremor in her voice.

"As long as you'll have me."

Forever.

Stories and promises could all come later—that night by the fire pit or curled up on her couch. Jonas found her. He left on his own accord, searched, and, somehow, miraculously found her. Nothing else mattered. "Thanks for the flowers."

"Thanks for the muffin."

"Oh gosh!" She glanced at the mangled pastry and let muffin crumbs rain among petals. "I have two dozen more in the kitchen."

He embraced her again. "I've missed you."

Her lips found his, and like an alpine primrose, she opened. She was rooted in confidence earned through a Rocky Mountain winter. She bloomed with desire that lay dormant since the spring.

With his hands still firm on the small of her back, he pulled away.

Crisply outlined against a cloudless sky, he met her gaze with unfettered passion—nothing held back.

"I love you, *mei wildi ros.*"

"I love you, too." Ten thousand times since August, she whispered those words to a memory. To say them now kindled equal parts relief and joy. Closing her eyes, she basked in the warmth of that love. When she opened them again, she was blinded by a revelation as incandescent as fire from the sky.

That indefinable color of his eyes?

Colorado, summer-sky-blue.

Peeking beneath her lashes, she caught his hand and interlaced her fingers between his. "Do you want to come inside?"

His gaze darkened. "I do. But first, I want you to show me something."

She honeyed her voice. "Anything."

He grabbed her around the waist and pulled her close. Lowering his lips to her ear, he took in a whispered breath. "Show me how that pop-top opens into a tent."

Just like that, she was back in the front seat, cruising Route 45 with a drop-dead gorgeous Amish dude with insatiable curiosity and a lust for speed. Laughter bubbled inside. She rose onto tiptoes and planted a kiss on his cheek. "Oh, I'll pop the top, all right." She dashed toward the van, pausing only to toss a wink over one freckled shoulder. "But first? I'm teaching you to drive."

A word about the author…

Wendy Rich Stetson is a New York City girl who still considers the green ridges of Central Pennsylvania her home. She grew up watching the country roll by from the back of a 1979 VW camper van, and she keeps a running list of favorite roadside attractions from coast to coast. Now an author of clean and wholesome romance, Wendy is no stranger to storytelling. She's a Broadway and television actress, an audiobook narrator, and a mom who enjoys little more than reading bedtime stories to her daughter. And cake. Wendy lives in Upper Manhattan with her family of three and Maine Coon kitty, Tessa.

Find out more at www.wendyrichstetson.com

Thank you for purchasing
this publication of The Wild Rose Press, Inc.

For questions or more information
contact us at
info@thewildrosepress.com.

The Wild Rose Press, Inc.
www.thewildrosepress.com

CPSIA information can be obtained
at www.ICGtesting.com
Printed in the USA
BVHW030511161122
651987BV00012B/334

9 781509 235643